Drowning in Deception

SUSANNA SULLIVAN

Azuero Publishing

ISBN 979-8-9936127-1-3

Cover Art by Daniela Colleo of StunningBookCovers.com

One

My retirement — you know, the time when I could finally rest and relax after years of backbreaking and heartbreaking work as a nurse — began with the furor over Lottie's stairlift. Well, the stairlift and a murder.

Okay, if you want to be technical, it officially began after my final shift at the hospital the previous Friday. There was a brief recognition of my forty-plus years as an RN, and a so-sad-to-see-you go speech. The cake was beautiful, and whoever ordered it knew I love chocolate, so that was okay.

Saturday my husband Michael put together a party for me at the clubhouse at Happy Oaks. That's the small, over-fifty-five condo complex where we live, in Winter Park, near Orlando. Sunday was a much-needed lazy day, so I was thinking of Monday as my first day as a retiree, my first working day when I had no work scheduled.

My plan for that day was to celebrate my retirement by sleeping in, reading some books, and not much else. Too bad it didn't work out that way.

***

That early June day began innocently enough.

Sunlight streamed in through the bedroom's sliding glass doors, forcing me awake. Getting out of bed felt like a lot of work, but I struggled to my feet. I might have groaned a little. The aroma of freshly brewed coffee drew me into the kitchen. When I stumbled in, Michael raised a mug in my direction. "Here's to you and retirement."

He handed me a filled mug and I raised it back at him and forced a smile. "And here's to sleeping late!" I flopped down at the table, took a sip, and savored the rich taste of dark coffee with real cream. "What should I do on my first day as a lady of leisure? I have no idea how to spend a day that's not already planned out for me."

I took another sip of coffee. "This is fun." Maybe if I said it aloud enough times, I'd convince myself.

"You looking for suggestions? How about relaxing by the pool?" He slid a plate of bacon and eggs in front of me. Have I mentioned that he spoils me? I wouldn't have it any other way.

"I'm not sure I know how to do that." I considered for a moment. "I've never liked the idea of sitting in the sun and baking, but maybe I'll go for a swim, that would be nice. And goodness knows I could stand to lose a few pounds."

I glanced at him out of the corner of my eye and saw his lips twitch, but he just sipped his coffee and wisely didn't respond to my provocation. Being married for forty years can do that to a man.

"Or maybe I should sit on the porch with a book. It's a beautiful day, and I've got that whole stack of new ones I bought for just this occasion."

He smiled. "That sounds more like you."

"What do you have planned?"

He set his cup down. "I need to meet Jeff at ten at the clubhouse to go over a few things."

"Condo board business?"

He nodded.

"Okay. You go ahead and meet Jeff. Since you were nice enough to make breakfast, I'll tidy the kitchen."

"You've got it." He stood and planted a kiss on my forehead. "I'll grab some stuff and get out of here."

Even eating felt like a lot of effort, and I took a while to finish. Eventually I took my plate to the dishwasher. Humming *When I'm 64,* I tidied the kitchen, the one room in our condo that always made me smile.

A pair of sliding glass doors opened onto our porch, bathing the room in natural light. When we first moved in, the sunlight only highlighted the ugliness of the hideous fluorescent light fixture and the nasty spit-colored paint on the walls, but after we replaced the fluorescent with two banks of recessed lights on a dimmer switch and swapped out the spit-color for a full-bodied red — Michael complained it was like painting blood on the walls — it was gorgeous if I do say so myself. The red picked up the rich undertones of the oak cabinets and made the room warm and welcoming. Just what a kitchen should be, and it got tons of compliments.

Once I'd loaded the dishwasher and tidied up, I showered and dressed right away so I'd be less tempted to crawl back into bed. I considered my slightly saggy, heart-shaped face in the mirror and added the bare minimum of makeup. A light dusting of powder, eyeliner, and lipstick, then I put my glasses back on and I was done.

Well, not quite. I reached into my jewelry box and took out my new earrings. I love earrings. Not the fancy, dangly ones, necessarily, but colorful or quirky appeals to me, and of course, I couldn't wear those when I was working. Today I put on a pair

I'd been saving for this occasion — little silver charms in the shape of flip flops. I'd bought them specially to wear on my first day of freedom because seeing those little sandals dancing on my ears made me smile.

Carefully I removed Michael's toothbrush and shaving cream from my side of the double sink and put them where they belonged. I swiped a comb through my short, gray hair, and I was ready for the day.

I nodded to myself in the mirror. "Congratulations on your retirement, Lily Gallagher!"

A few minutes later I was ensconced on my favorite chair on the front porch with a brand-new book. Ah, this was the life . . . for somebody. I wasn't sure it was *my* life, though. At least not yet.

I admired the view from the porch, one of the reasons we'd picked this particular condo seven years ago. Out of the six buildings in the Happy Oaks complex, only the D and E buildings faced the pool. Michael and I lived in E, and my best friend, Pru McLeod, was in Building D directly across the pool. Behind her building were three others, and one more building behind ours.

Like I said, a small community, and it was all straight lines and right angles. The pool was a giant rectangle, the paths leading to it were all straight. Nothing meandered or curved. Bushes were ruthlessly trimmed to contain them in their assigned locations, with not a leaf allowed to spill over into an area where it didn't belong.

Except for the bougainvillea. Off to the right, at the end of the pool, stood the community clubhouse. An eye-catching mass of lush purple bougainvillea blossoms covered the pergola over the (straight) walkway between the pool and the clubhouse. It was the only plant in the place that was allowed to grow unchecked and I admired the graceful arch of its fronds which broke up all that rigid symmetry around it. The view sure was pretty, and I hadn't taken nearly enough time to enjoy it since we moved in seven years ago.

The buildings around me were all equally rectangular, of gray stucco and white trim, and each one contained two downstairs and two upstairs apartments. Michael and I lived upstairs, in E4 and our immediate neighbors were Jennifer Nelson, in the other upstairs apartment, E2. The unit below us, E3, was owned by a pair of snowbirds who'd already flown back to Milwaukee or Minneapolis or one of those place, and under Jennifer was a quiet guy named Keith Johnson in E1.

My eyes started feeling heavy, so before they closed entirely I opened my book, *Her Royal Spyness* by Rhys Bowen, first in a new-to-me series. The story began back in 1932, and the main character, thirty-fourth in line to the British throne, was a young woman camping out in the family home in London, with no money and no servants.*

I was chuckling out loud over the description of Georgiana (Georgie to her friends), the heroine, learning how to get coal out the coal 'ole and start a fire to warm the freezing house, when I spotted Michael coming out of the clubhouse. I watched as he walked under the arch of bougainvillea and turned toward our building.

At sixty-seven, he was nearly as handsome as when I first met him. He still had a thick head of hair, though today it was mostly white where it used to be black. He smiled when he saw me, but I knew from his walk and the stiff way he held his shoulders that he was upset.

As he headed up the stairs, I called out, "What's the matter? Jeff say something to upset you?"

"Oh, just board business. You don't want to hear it."

"If it's got you worked up I do!"

"Let's go inside. I need something to drink." He wasn't normally so abrupt. What could Jeff have done to upset him this much?

I followed him into the kitchen.

He grabbed a glass and took the iced tea out of the fridge. "Want some?"

"Sure." I took out a glass and he poured for both of us. "Now, what's got you all stirred up?"

He leaned against the counter and drank some tea before he spoke. "You're not going to believe this, Lily. Jeff and I were in the office going over some landscaping bids when Betty stopped by, and it's a good thing I was there."

He took another big gulp of tea, then carefully placed the glass on the counter. I recognized it as the controlled action of someone who would rather have thrown it across the room. "It's Charlotte's architectural waiver."

"Oh, no, is there a problem with it?"

"It sure looks that way." He frowned. "Okay, so you remember that I brought all the forms to Charlotte when we visited her last time?"

"Of course." Charlotte Delaney, a close friend, had lost her left foot a few months before and now she was stuck in rehab. They wouldn't release her until she could manage on her own, and that was a big problem because she had an upstairs apartment in Building C, behind us. Since Michael was on the condo board's architectural committee, he'd been helping her with her plans to put in a stairlift, a chair-like device on a track that carries someone up the stairs.

"When I was with Jeff just now at the clubhouse, Betty came in with a stack of mail. It included Charlotte's waiver request. Betty looked it over, then handed it to Jeff. She said — honestly, honey, you're not going to believe this — she said, 'toss this in the trash where it belongs, would you sugar?' And he actually did!"

I stared at him, then realized my jaw was hanging open and he was still talking.

"I was stunned. I knew exactly what it was — after all, I'd gone over those forms with Lottie myself — and I snatched it out of the wastebasket."

I closed my jaw with an effort. "I can't believe it. What did you do?"

Michael put his hands on his hips. "I made sure they didn't get away with it, that's what I did. First I logged it into the system right away, then I made a copy for the architectural committee, which I kept. I put the original in the file. And because it's in the system now, the property management company automatically gets it as well."

"Good for you. Are you going to tell Lottie?"

"Certainly not."

"Good," I said. "There's no point in getting her upset. Betty and Jeff are only two votes out of seven, when it comes down to it, right?" I was appalled. Talk about your basic high-handed — and probably illegal — action. Should I be worried about it? They only had two votes out of seven, I reminded myself. Still. . . Michael was talking again.

"I'm calling Dave right now to make sure he reviews her application right away, since he chairs the committee. That way one more person will be aware she's officially made the request. I don't trust Betty any farther than I can throw a grand piano."

"Really? There's more?"

"I don't know, I can't put my finger on anything specific, but it's just this feeling that's been growing for a while. Sometimes she seems, I don't know." He thought for a moment and his frown deepened. "It's just a feeling."

He took another gulp of tea. "I'm ready for some lunch, how about you?"

"Sure, but is there something I can do to help Lottie get her waiver?"

"That's sweet of you, but I can't think what it would be. And besides, you've always avoided board business like the plague."

"This isn't 'board business,'" I said, making air quotes. "This is helping a friend!"

"I can't think of anything."

"So Lottie has to rot in rehab because we can't do anything? There's got to be something. What if I start a petition? March up and down with a sign that says *Free Charlotte?*"

Michael laughed and the tension left his shoulders. "I'd love to see that!"

"I'm not trying to be funny." And I wasn't, I was irritated if you want the truth. "This is my first day of retirement, the day I'm supposed to be just enjoying and relaxing. How can I relax when Betty's trying to keep my friend from moving back home?"

Michael blew me an air kiss. "Maybe get a bullhorn and march up and down in front of Betty's apartment. I know how much you love direct, loud confrontations."

My chest tightened at the very thought, and I guess I shivered because he stopped fooling around and said, "Aw, honey, I'm sorry. I'm sure you'll figure something out."

While I fixed lunch, I seethed quietly. Well, maybe not so quietly. There may have been some banging of plates and silverware. I'd looked forward to this day for so long. One lousy, stinking day to relax, was that too much to ask? I'd been so bone tired, all the time, for years. But instead, here I was worrying about Betty's odd behavior, and what was going to happen with Lottie.

We were halfway through lunch when Michael got that faraway look in his eyes that told me he was thinking hard about something. "Actually, there might be something."

"Something that will help Lottie?"

"Maybe."

I waited for him to continue.

"Well, people are always telling you things, you seem to attract confidences. Maybe you can get out and about a little more, steer the conversation toward Lottie, and listen to what folks have to say. Especially if you run into any of the other board members."

"What good will that do?"

"I don't know. Maybe none. But you could drop a few words, plant a few seeds reminding people what a valuable member of this community she's always been. And maybe you can find out why Betty tried to make her waiver request go away."

"Sure, I get it. You want me to be a spy. Lily Gallagher, Secret Agent for the Happy Oaks Condo Association."

"No, not for the condo association. For Charlotte."

"Very funny."

"Well, let me know if you think of something better."

I couldn't imagine it would do any good, but I didn't have any other ideas and getting out and talking to my neighbors couldn't hurt. Today was Monday, and the meeting wasn't until Thursday, so I decided to stick with my relaxing agenda for today by finishing the book I'd started this morning. It was exactly the kind of reading I enjoyed — light hearted, fun, a few adventures. Maybe it would be enough to distract me.

After lunch, I went back out to the porch with my book, but thoughts of Lottie, the stairlift, and Betty kept getting between me and Georgie's adventures.

At some point I realized I'd read the same page three times without taking in a word, so I set the book down, frustrated. Looking over the porch railing, I noticed a couple of men leaving the clubhouse and walking under the purple bougainvillea toward the pool area. The tall one was obviously Greg Harris, Betty's husband.

Maybe Greg could shed some light on what Betty was thinking. This would be the perfect time to go for that swim, and if I just happened to chat with Greg at the pool, well, maybe I'd learn something useful. Although I didn't have the faintest idea what I'd say to him and even thinking about it made me nervous.

Oh, well, if nothing else the physical activity would be good for me. I ran inside and wriggled into my bathing suit as quickly as I could, grabbed a towel, and headed for the pool.

With his height, Greg was easy to spot. He was sitting at a table in the corner with three other people. It was the table where the Mah Jong players usually hung out, so he'd likely stay for a while. Did I have time for a quick swim? Sure, I wanted to talk to him, but I also wanted to make it seem casual. And, to be honest, I was procrastinating because I had no idea what to say.

I bypassed a couple of sun worshippers stretched out on loungers and laid out my towel and glasses on a chair some distance away from them, then walked to the edge of the pool and eased into the water.

While I swam, I tried to figure out how to approach Greg. I couldn't just march up to him and ask, "What the heck is wrong with your wife?" At least, not without seriously offending him. As someone who hates confrontations, I was hoping to find an opening, a way to change Betty's mind about Lottie's stairlift before I approached her. The last thing I wanted was to get into a conversation with her and then freeze up.

After a couple of laps, I was out of breath, my arms were burning, and my right knee wasn't exactly hurting, but it wasn't happy. Was I so out of shape that I couldn't swim more than two laps? Sadly, I was.

In fact, I couldn't remember when I'd been in the pool last. I'd used it a few times right after we bought the condo, but was it possible I hadn't taken advantage of it since?

Alright, enough delay, I told myself as I toweled off and tried to catch my breath. I put my glasses back on, but before I could make my move, someone stood up at that corner table. If the group was breaking up, I'd better hustle over if I wanted to catch Greg. No more stalling, something I'm unfortunately quite good at.

I was wrapping my towel around myself when Pru came through the gate. "Lily!" She raced over, "I thought that was you! I can't remember the last time I saw you here."

I shrugged. "I can't remember the last time I was here at all. I only swam two laps and had to stop, I'm horribly out of shape. What are you up to?"

"I just came from visiting Lottie at the rehab center. I was going to ask if you wanted to come, but I figured you might want to spend your first official day of retirement doing nothing."

"Oh, I did, but I've already had a monkey wrench thrown into those plans."

"Want to tell me about it?"

"I do, actually, but first I need to catch Greg before he leaves and it looks like the Mah Jong group is breaking up. Why don't you go ahead with your swim? You can come up for some tea when you're done and I'll fill you in."

"Sure, sounds like a plan." Pru removed her cover-up and walked to the side of the pool. In her bathing suit, she reminded me of a greyhound, sleek and trim and bursting with nervous energy.

As I headed over toward the corner table, Greg stood and pushed his chair back. I took a deep breath and called out, "Hi neighbors!"

Greg waved to me and resettled himself in his chair, and now that I was close I recognized his companions, Dave and Deb Wheelock. Even sitting down, Greg towered over the other two. Where he had to be at least six-foot-four, or maybe even six-five, Dave was short, about five-nine, and stocky. The two of them had been best friends for as long as I'd known them.

"Hey, Lily, how are you? I don't see you here at the pool very often," Deb said, a wide smile on her pixie-like face.

I smiled back. "I know. Like, never, in fact."

"How's retirement treating you?" Greg asked. He and Betty, along with Dave and Deb and many of our other neighbors, had been at my retirement party at the clubhouse on Saturday.

"So far so good. I've done pretty much nothing all day although it hasn't been quite as relaxing as I'd hoped. What are you all up to?" Be casual, I reminded myself.

"We were playing Mah Jong, but Michelle got a call and had to go, so that broke up the game," Deb said. "Here, sit down." She gestured at the vacant chair next to her.

When I sat, the heady smell of jasmine filled my nostrils. I glanced around and saw masses of it growing on the fence in back of me. Pru was swimming, streaking through the water much more efficiently that I had, the sound of her strokes creating a steady rhythm.

"Do you play?" Deb asked. "You should join us sometime."

"I've never played in my life, if you don't count Mah Jong solitaire on the computer. Never really had the time, but I'd love to learn."

"I'll tell Michelle, she's always looking for victims... uh, players." Deb grinned again.

"You can take my place any time," Dave said. "I'd rather be playing golf anyway."

"That's right," I said, "you're one of the golfing maniacs around here, aren't you? I guess I'll have to start paying more attention to everyone's hobbies now that I have time to develop some of my own."

"Right you are. Greg and I usually play at least three times a week. Sometimes more if we can sneak away from our wives." He winked at Deb.

"Which they do pretty often," she said. "Sometimes they're on the golf course so much Betty and I feel like they've abandoned us. She spends her time on the condo association stuff, but I'm at loose ends a lot."

"I'm actually hoping to learn what that feels like." I turned to Greg.

"How about you, Greg? Besides golf, what do you do?" I wasn't sure how to bring up Lottie, but this seemed like a good opening.

"Mostly hang around and wait for Betty to finish whatever she's up to. She gets worked up over the darnedest things." He sounded amused.

"Oh? Like what?"

"Well, right now she's in a tizzy because Charlotte Delaney has asked for permission to put in a stairlift."

"Stairlift?" I asked, trying not to sound too interested.

"It's like a chair on a rail that goes up the stairs. For some reason Betty's dead set against it."

"I think it's a reasonable request," Dave said in his slow, deliberate way. "She should be allowed to get in and out of her apartment, even with her disability. In fact, if this were a different type of place, like an apartment complex, they'd legally have to make accommodation for her." He looked directly at Greg. "What's Betty's beef with it?"

Greg shrugged. "Oh, I think she just doesn't like Charlotte much."

"That shouldn't have anything to do with it." I noticed my voice was a little louder than usual. Trying to ignore the tightening in my chest and forcing myself to speak more quietly, I asked, "She wouldn't let her personal feelings influence a decision she's involved with as president of the condo board, would she?" Greg shrugged again and didn't respond, instead turning to Dave and changing the subject to their most recent round of golf.

Deb scooted her chair closer to me, glanced at the men, then leaned in and spoke quietly. "Trust me, Lily, you don't want to get on Betty's bad side. She's a lot more ruthless than she looks." The pixie grin was gone, and a small frown line appeared between her eyebrows.

I was surprised. "Seriously? A little bossy, sure, but ruthless?"

Deb glanced at her husband and Greg to make sure they weren't listening, then she leaned in farther and now her voice was so soft I could barely hear her.

"I don't want anyone else to hear this. Somehow Betty found out about a thing from my teaching days that I'm not very proud of. It's not a big deal, and it was a long time ago. But she tried to use it against me."

I must have looked surprised, because she elaborated, "When she first ran for the board she made it clear that she expected my vote or she'd embarrass me in front of all my friends and neighbors by telling them about it. In the sweetest possible way, of course."

My eyes widened. "Seriously?"

"Yes, I'm afraid so. I've seen and heard about other things as well. There's not much I would put past her when it comes to getting her own way."

"But I thought the four of you were friends?" I was having a hard time keeping my voice down.

"I thought so too, for a while. But really, Greg and Dave are friends and I just go along." Deb scowled. "I don't like being in the same room with that woman any more, and I honestly don't know how Greg stands her."

"So she threatened to spread malicious gossip about you if you didn't do what she wanted?" It didn't make any more sense when I said it the second time.

"Yup."

"Wow, I'm having a hard time taking it in," I said, "but this is the second time I'm hearing this today. I only found out an hour ago that Michael doesn't trust her, either."

Deb nodded. "I don't think anyone does, who's had much to do with her. That southern belle thing is an Oscar-worthy act."

After a second, I asked, "Just out of curiosity, what do you think about Charlotte's waiver request?"

Deb didn't hesitate. "I think she should have it, of course. I think she's a real asset to this community."

"Thanks, that's good to hear. Does Dave agree?"

"Of course!"

"Well, hello y'all."

Startled, I turned toward the voice.

"Oh, hello Betty," I stammered. Betty was tall, only about six inches shorter than her husband so I had to crane my neck pretty far up to see her face. Note to self: pay more attention to my surroundings. I never saw or heard her coming.

Fortunately at that moment Pru loped over to us, wrapping a towel around herself. "Hey, how's everyone doing?" It was a welcome interruption.

After exchanging a few pleasantries with the others, she said to me, "Just let me go home and throw some clothes on and I'll be over in ten minutes."

"Sounds good."

As I stood to go, I tipped my head toward Betty and said quietly to Deb, "Thanks for that insight."

Walking home, though, my shoulders sagged. If Betty's objection was truly because she didn't like Lottie much, nothing I could say would change her mind. It was a good thing I'd spoken with Greg or I might never have found out this tidbit of information.

Lottie was one of the most likable people I'd ever known, so I didn't understand Betty's dislike. She was pleasant, smart, always interested in other people, and over her years as a family therapist she'd developed outstanding interpersonal skills. I'd have to find out from Lottie if she and Betty had some sort of falling out, because with Deb's strange warning ringing in my ears, I didn't even want to talk with Betty.

Two

Before I left to visit Lottie the next morning, Michael said, "Say hi to her for me. And you can tell her that her stairlift will definitely be on the agenda at the meeting on Thursday."

Outside, I headed straight for my carport. As I opened the door, I patted my Prius affectionately. It was minty green, another color choice I'd gotten some pushback on from Michael. But it was my car, so I got to choose.

Before the Prius, my cars had merely provided transportation, but I truly loved this little vehicle. It was fun to drive and even though it was small, I felt like I sat up higher and had better visibility than with other compact and midsize cars I'd owned in the past. The fact that it was kinder to the environment and cheaper to drive was just icing on the cake.

As I eased into the velour-covered seat, I was glad I'd chosen that instead of the leather the dealer had tried to talk me into. It didn't get so hot in the summer, which was important to me since I liked wearing shorts and didn't like burning my legs. I glanced around to make sure nothing was out of place, then pushed the start button.

At the rehab center, I found Lottie waiting for me in the lounge, which was slightly more inviting than in most nursing homes. Of course, that's not saying much. I sat down next to her.

"You're looking well, how are you feeling?"

"Good! I'm feeling really good." She beamed at me. "They tell me they'll probably clear me to go home in a couple of weeks, as long as I can get in and out of my apartment. I can't wait!" Then her face clouded. "I will get the stairlift, won't I?"

While she spoke, I took a good look at her. Her chin-length bob was neatly combed and complemented her round face, and she had adapted the tailored style she favored to her new circumstances, pairing a colorful floral button-down shirt with beige slacks, one leg neatly pinned at the bottom.

She was one of those people who made me feel calmer just being in the same room with her, at least on a normal day. That sense of calm probably helped her to be an effective family therapist. Today, though, her hazel eyes looked worried.

"The good news is, it will be on the agenda at Thursday's meeting," I said, and watched her face light up. Then I added, "The bad news is, Betty seems to be against the idea, so I'm hoping you have an idea about how to change her mind before the meeting."

Her smile disappeared and she sighed. "Probably not. I was afraid of something like that."

"Why's that?"

"I haven't spoken with her in months, but the last time we talked, Betty was annoyed with me for butting into something that was none of my business. In fact, 'annoyed' doesn't begin to describe it."

"Oh?"

She shifted uncomfortably in her wheelchair. "It was a family thing, with her sister, and I *was* butting in, but I was only trying to help. I overheard a phone call between Betty and her sister, and all I did was suggest it would be a good idea to mend her fences because family is important."

"That doesn't sound so outrageous."

"She got really quiet, and, Lily, the look on her face was scary. She told me it wasn't any of my business, and I agreed that it wasn't. After that we exchanged a few more words, and that is literally the last time I ever spoke with her. I can't describe it, but there was something ugly about her."

"That's crazy," I said after a minute. "If that's what she's holding a grudge about, she's either just plain nuts, or else that family has an awful lot going on behind the scenes."

"I agree, but that doesn't change anything."

Intentionally I tried to relax my forehead. "And if she's fighting your stairlift as some kind of revenge, that doesn't leave much of an opening to try to change her opinion."

"No, it doesn't." Lottie's eyes started to mist up. "I've gone over and over every conversation I ever had with her, and that's truly the only thing I can come up with. But maybe you can talk with her. After all, everybody always tells you everything."

"That's funny, Michael said the same thing yesterday." Were they right? I'd never thought about it until now. "I guess I'm a good listener, but you know what happens to me when there's an argument. I just freeze up and can't say a word."

"I know," Lottie said. Her voice oozed sympathy. "Have you ever thought of doing some therapy for that?"

"Oh, sure, in all my copious spare time." Actually, I did have some free time now. I was going to have to get used to that. "I'll try to talk to her. And the good news is, she only has one vote." As cheerfully as I could I added, "And I'm going to do my best to lock in the others on your behalf."

"Thanks, Lily, you're a good friend."

"Well, I do have an ulterior motive."

Lottie's eyes widened. "What?"

"Once your waiver is approved I can figure out this relaxing retirement thing. So far it's been a total bust." I winked.

She actually laughed. "I honestly can't imagine you filling up your days with sunning by the pool."

"Neither can I, but at least I ought to be able to stop feeling so tired all the time."

Driving home after the visit, though, I was bummed. Yes, Jeff and Betty were only two votes out of seven, but as board president and vice president they had a lot of influence.

And what was the deal with Betty and her sister? I remembered plenty of teenage squabbles with my own sister over things like borrowing clothes or makeup without permission, but it never got more serious than that. Either Betty's sister had done something terrible, or else the woman truly was nuts. Either way, I felt uncomfortable at the thought of talking to her about Lottie, especially after Deb's warning. How do you talk with a blackmailer anyway?

Well, whether or not I talked with Betty, I could certainly talk with the other board members. Michael was sure Dave was already on board, so that left Tim, Linda and Liz. For the first time in my life, I was beginning to feel a little sympathy for politicians.

As I pulled the Prius into my carport, I decided to go back to the pool this afternoon, try to bump into my neighbors casually and get them talking — it was a very small community after all. I still had a couple days before the meeting, and after that, I'd finally be able to relax. I hoped.

Three

First thing Wednesday morning I headed out to talk with Linda Barry. As board secretary, her support for Lottie at tomorrow's meeting would carry a lot of weight.

After lunch yesterday I'd gone to the pool again where I overheard the Mah Jong players talking about Charlotte, and I didn't enjoy it one bit. One of them, I think it was Michelle, called the stairlift an ugly thing, and Tim was going on and on about how it would have a negative affect on our property values. I ended up storming home without speaking to anyone, but it made me even more determined to make sure Lottie got her waiver even though I got a knot in my stomach every time I thought about talking to people who might not agree with me.

That's why I was starting with Linda today. We'd always had a friendly relationship and she was easy to talk to.

Keith was on his porch and greeted me as I came down my steps, so I changed direction and spoke with him for a few minutes. Then Jennifer Nelson called down, and I visited with her briefly. Keith said he was "not opposed" to Charlotte's stairlift, and Jennifer was very supportive, which was nice.

When I knocked on the door of apartment A1, Linda came to the door, wiping her hands on a dish towel. "Lily, hello," she said, smiling. "This is a surprise. What brings you here? Come in, come in."

She waved toward the kitchen, shoving an errant lock of dark hair behind her ear. "You don't mind sitting in the kitchen, do you? I was just putting dinner in the crockpot."

Patrick and Linda Barry were among the younger residents. I knew he'd just turned sixty, because Linda had thrown a birthday party for him in the clubhouse a couple months previously. I figured she was a few years younger, and I envied her energy.

"Sure, that's fine," I managed to say before Linda was talking again.

"Patrick's out right now, he'll be sorry he missed you. Now, what can I do for you? Oh, would you like something to drink? Coffee? Sweet tea?"

"No thanks, I'm good." Bustling around her kitchen, Linda looked like a stereotype Italian mamma with her olive skin, a smile lighting up her face, dark hair pulled back, and brown eyes dancing.

"How are you liking retirement so far?" she asked. "We enjoyed your party on Saturday, it was a lot of fun."

"It was, wasn't it?" I smiled. "But sadly, I haven't been able to enjoy the rest and relaxation I planned on."

"No?" She looked at me quizzically but didn't say anything more.

"It's Charlotte," I began.

"Oh, that poor thing." As usual, once she started talking, she went a mile a minute. "I feel so bad for her. I keep meaning to go visit her at that rehab place, but I haven't managed it so far. Maybe we could go together."

"Maybe, but you know there's a good chance she can move back home soon."

"Really?" Linda stopped adding onions and carrots to her slow cooker. Her brown eyes widened. "How's that?"

"You haven't heard? I thought, being on the board, you'd know all about it."

My surprise must have shown, because Linda rinsed her hands at the sink and sat down at the table across from me. "No. Tell me about it." She started drying her hands on the dish towel that hung over her shoulder.

Just then the front door opened and Patrick called out, "Hey, hon." He stopped when he rounded the corner into the kitchen. "Oh, hello, Lily, what brings you here?"

"Patrick, how are you?" I smiled. "I was just telling Linda about Charlotte."

"Charlotte?" He arched an eyebrow at me as he joined us at the table. He still had a full head of hair, the dull brown color that used to be red, tinged with silver around the ears, and his brows were redder than his hair. He carried his years well, with only a hint of a belly.

Once again I described the stairlift and Lottie's request for an architectural waiver as Linda frowned.

"This is the first I'm hearing about it," she said. "It wasn't listed on the agenda for Thursday's meeting."

I gulped. "Michael told me it would be discussed on Thursday. And you don't know anything about it?"

"Sorry, no." She drummed her fingers on the table. "It wasn't on the agenda I prepared, and usually when something like that is on the agenda, board members also get a package of information about it ahead of time."

"Betty," I muttered to myself.

Linda's hearing must have been pretty good, because she immediately asked, "What do you mean, Betty?" Her frown deepened. Patrick opened his mouth, then closed it again.

"I'm not sure if this is something I should be sharing," I hesitated for a moment, "but Michael was in the office the other day when Betty came in with Charlotte's waiver request in her hand. She and Jeff were going to toss it in the trash and pretend they never got it, but Michael stopped them."

Linda stared at me, her mouth open slightly. There was a moment of silence as she twisted the chunky gold bracelet she always wore around and around.

Patrick looked at his wife and said in a low voice, "You know I don't trust her."

Linda stared back at him, and I had the impression this was not the first time they'd discussed Betty. After a moment she turned to me. "When did the waiver request arrive?"

"Yesterday morning."

"And Betty went over the agenda with me yesterday afternoon and I sent it out last night," Linda said, twisting the bracelet around. "Looks like there's more than one way to do something underhanded, at least if you're Betty-freaking-Harris."

The bitterness in her voice surprised me. "What do you mean?"

"I won't bore you with all the sorry details, but let's just say that Betty has ways of getting people to do things the way *she* wants." She was practically spitting out the words, and Patrick was nodding.

"How do we get it on the agenda?" I asked.

"You leave that to me, Lily. I'm the secretary of the condo board, I'll take care of it. Do Michael and Dave have any information about the stairlift they want sent to the board members?"

"I have no idea. How about if I have Michael call you?"

"Sure," Linda said. "As soon as possible. There's no good reason why Charlotte shouldn't be able to move home as soon as the rehab people say she's ready. She's always been a terrific member of this community. Unlike some, who only like to throw their weight around."

I had a feeling I knew just who she was talking about, but all I said was, "Thanks, Linda. I'm glad we talked."

"I am too," she said as I pushed back my chair and stood, "and I hope to see more of you now that you're retired."

"Me too. I'll have more free time once Charlotte's got permission for her stairlift."

"She'll have my vote," Linda promised.

Patrick stood. "I'll walk you out." He accompanied me to the porch, and said quietly, "Watch out for that Betty Harris."

I didn't hide my surprise very well. "Why's that?"

"She's devious and malicious. Trust me, I know." His mouth was set in a tight line.

"You're not the first person who's said that in the past couple days. Can you tell me more?"

I couldn't see his face because he was looking down at his feet. He spoke so quietly I barely heard him. "I can't really talk about it, but watch out for her."

"Patrick, you're scaring me a little. What can she do?"

"I have no idea what she'll try to do to *you*, but, well, let's just say she's been making my life difficult for a little while." He looked up and added, "Linda's had her own issues with her on the board, but she doesn't know about this and I'd like to keep it that way." Then, in a more normal tone of voice, he said, "Thanks for stopping by," turned, and went back into the apartment.

Strange. Out on the sidewalk, I pulled out my phone and hit Michael's speed dial. When it went to voicemail I left a quick message asking him to call Linda right away about Lottie's waiver.

Patrick had sounded so bitter when he talked about Betty. He must be another one Betty had tried to manipulate. Until yesterday morning, I would have sworn Betty was just a slightly pushy but pleasant woman. Was I that bad a judge of character? Despite the warmth of the day, I found myself shivering.

Well, I still had a mission to accomplish. I was just consulting my clipboard when Minnie Nguyen, racing down the steps of her apartment upstairs, almost collided with me. Minnie was a diminutive Vietnamese woman who had come to the US with her husband, Kim, back in the eighties, two of the many so-called boat people.

"Hey, Minnie," I said.

"Hello, Lily. How are you?"

"Good. You seem to be in a big hurry, do you have just a minute?"

"I have to get back to the salon, but if you can walk to my car with me, I wanted to talk with you."

"Sure."

As we walked toward the parking area, I felt like a giant next to her. Minnie plunged right in. "You're friends with Miss Charlotte, right?"

I nodded.

"I think it's terrible, what's happened to her. What can I do to help her?"

"You want to help?"

"Yes. She was big help to Kim and me when we had troubles before, and I want to help her now. I hear rumors she wants a lift thing to help her go up and down the stairs? So that she can come home?"

"That's right, she wants to install a stairlift, but the condo association has to approve it."

"Can I do something?"

"You can." I smiled at her. "Talk to your neighbors, especially the members of the board, and tell them you support the architectural waiver for the stairlift."

"Architectural waiver." Minnie enunciated the words carefully. "What does this mean?"

"It's a fancy name for getting permission to build the stairlift."

"I see."

Minnie repeated the phrase a couple more times, fixing it in her mind.

"And come to the meeting on Thursday!"

"No problem. We usually come to meetings. Please tell me if I can do anything else."

"I will. And thanks, Minnie, you have a wonderful day."

"You too, Lily," she said, unlocking her car.

After Minnie pulled out of her parking space, I stood for a minute, clipboard in hand. It was nice that Lottie had some support at least. My next stop ought to be the Ericsons, who lived in the upstairs unit next to Minnie and Kim Nguyen.

I trudged back to Building A, thinking as I went. Minnie's enthusiasm was encouraging, but I wasn't happy about the little bombshell Linda had dropped. Betty must have left Lottie's waiver request off the agenda on purpose. This was a side of Betty I never imagined before. Were she and Jeff in cahoots on this? There was only one way to find out.

I made my way upstairs to the Ericsons' apartment. I was a little nervous about talking to Jeff, but he was on the board so I felt like I had to. Or, if he wasn't home, maybe his wife Martha would have some insight into his thoughts. I should have known better.

Dinner that evening was delicious. Michael had volunteered to cook, and since I was tuckered out, I was happy to let him. While he worked in the kitchen, I spent some quality time reading about Georgie, her old grandad, and their friends. When she described her attempts at cleaning the loo, I was in stitches.

I needed the break after being out and about, talking with all of our friends and neighbors. Well, except for Betty. I was still avoiding her. But I sure hadn't gotten the rest and relaxation I was entitled to as a brand-new retiree. Still, I'd done everything I could and felt like I could breathe a sigh of relief. Lottie would have the votes she needed tomorrow night, so I would curl up with my book again and forget about it until the meeting.

So when Michael wanted to talk about the stairlift over dinner, I was a little miffed because I didn't want to rehash it. I heaved an overly dramatic sigh. Still, he had put together a delicious meal — baked chicken, asparagus and mushroom risotto, and a salad of mixed greens, pecans, strawberries, blueberries, and a tangy cheese — so I guess answering his questions was the least I could do.

He started innocently enough. "Have fun today?"

I stared at him. "Fun? You call busting my butt having uncomfortable conversations with people fun?"

"Oh, Lil, I'm sorry, I know you've been working hard, and it's not how you envisioned spending your time. But I need to prepare for the meeting tomorrow night, and it would help if I had a sense of the way the board was leaning."

"Okay, you have a point." I thought for a minute. "Let me grab my clipboard with my notes and I'll just run through the main conversations, alright?"

He nodded.

Clipboard in hand, I reseated myself, forked some salad into my mouth and chewed, then started talking.

"It's easier if I just tell you everything in chronological order, okay?"

"Okay."

"So, starting with yesterday morning. I was heading out to talk with Linda, but Keith was on his porch when I went downstairs, so it made sense to talk with him. He was pretty neutral. Said he didn't have a problem with the stairlift, and he wouldn't oppose it, but he doesn't plan to attend the meeting." I took a bite of risotto. "It may be the longest conversation I've ever had with him. How long has he been here, about six months?"

"Sounds about right."

I tapped the clipboard and took another bite of risotto — it was truly yummy — before I continued. "Jennifer heard us talking and called down so I went up to her apartment. She has these interesting hanging basket chairs on her porch, and she's like me when it comes to color." I glanced around my red kitchen and smiled. "I really loved it. Best of all, she's completely in favor of the stairlift and she'll be at the meeting. She also said she'd share her opinion with the board members beforehand."

"Then I visited Linda. You already know about that, because you and she had to untangle the mess Betty made when she tried to keep Lottie's waiver off the agenda."

Michael nodded, but didn't say anything.

"She's totally supportive of Lottie and plans to vote in favor, and she was pretty upset by Betty's machinations."

He nodded again.

I took a bite of chicken. "Ooh, is this rosemary? It's really good."

Michael smiled. "Yup. Bought it fresh from the store this morning."

"Mmm. Okay, let's see." I ran through a few more conversations with him, including the interesting one with Minnie Nguyen. "Minnie was fiercely supportive of Lottie. Apparently she and Kim were having some problems a couple years ago, and Lottie helped them a lot."

"That doesn't surprise me, she's helped a lot of people."

"That she has." I went back to my list. "Talking with Jeff was a complete bust. He just waggled those intimidating eyebrows at me and glowered."

Michael chuckled. "Yup, that sounds like Jeff."

I ignored him and continued. "It's pretty obvious he and Betty are in agreement on this, though I don't know if he has a beef with Lottie or if he's just being a jerk. His wife, on the other hand, well, calling her a doormat would be an insult to all the doormats of this world. I don't think Martha has a thought in her head that he hasn't put there."

Michael nodded.

Quickly I reviewed the remaining conversations. "Sam Hoffman was quite supportive, which surprised me since Michelle was one of the people out by the pool trash talking about the stairlift. Then Liz, well, she was pretty appalled at what she called 'Betty's shenanigans' with the agenda, and told me she's had to remind Betty of her legal obligations as board president more than once. Good thing she was a paralegal." I paused to take another bite of risotto. "She also said something interesting. I asked if she had any idea why Betty disliked Lottie, and she said that Betty doesn't seem to need reasons for what she does, that she's a 'difficult' person." I put air quotes around 'difficult.'

"Oh, and she promised to vote in favor of the waiver, so with you, Dave, and Linda, that makes four votes out of seven."

"I hope you're right," Michael said.

"Something wrong with my math?"

"No, just that I don't trust Betty."

"What can she do? She only has one vote."

Michael answered quickly, "She can talk to people. She can do what you're doing. And," he paused for a moment, "she doesn't play fair."

With a groan I lifted my right foot onto the chair next to me. "My knee is really throbbing. I should probably put some ice on it. It's all those stairs over the past couple days."

"Let me grab you an ice pack." Michael pulled one out of the freezer and deftly wrapped it in a clean towel from the drawer. "See if this helps."

"Thanks, honey, you're an angel."

"Liz told me something else interesting, about the history of this place." I settled the ice pack on my knee and took another bite of risotto. "Apparently it wasn't always an over-fifty-five community."

"Jeff said something about that once, but I wasn't paying a lot of attention."

"Well, according to Liz, it started out as just a regular condo complex. It was built in the eighties, but because all the units are two bedrooms, it never attracted families with kids and more and more older people moved in. Around 2000, everyone here was over fifty-five, someone suggested making it official, so they changed the bylaws."

Michael thought for a moment. "That actually explains a lot."

"What do you mean?"

"Well, think about this for a minute." He smiled at me and said, "If this had been a planned over-fifty-five community, your knee wouldn't be throbbing so much."

"What? I don't get it."

"That split staircase is the reason our entrance and porch area are private. We have one set of stairs going up to our front porch, and Jennifer has a separate set going up to hers, even though our unit and hers share common walls, and our porches are only separated by a wall. So if you want to visit your next-door neighbor, you have to go down a set of stairs, and then up again. If this community had been planned for fifty-five and over, we'd have a single set of stairs and our porches would be connected."

"Oh, you're right. Or we wouldn't have a second floor at all, or it would be more institutional with fewer, bigger buildings and elevators."

"Exactly."

"Here's another thing," I said. "Liz also told me that if this had been planned from the start as an over-fifty-five community, Lottie wouldn't even need the waiver. But because of the way the bylaws were written, the condo association doesn't have to abide by the Americans with Disabilities Act."

Michael nodded. "A good example of unintended consequences."

I was pondering what the ADA would have meant for Lottie if it applied here when my phone rang. It was Pru, and she was very upset.

Four

Late Thursday morning I was sitting on my porch, enjoying another beautiful day. From somewhere nearby, the heady fragrance of blooming jasmine filled the air. I held a book in my hands, but I'd given up trying to read. Instead I was staring off into the distance, worried now about both my friends. I'd done everything I could to help Lottie, but what about Pru?

Poor Pru. The worst kind of pain is when your kids are going through something and you can't do anything about it. She'd called last night to share the unexpected news that her daughter and her husband were separating, and it was tearing her up. And to pile on her misery, she had a dentist appointment this morning. I'd have to come up with a way to take her mind off it later.

Even though the call with Pru had kept me up late last night, a good sleep had restored my optimism. I was reasonably happy with the way my politicking had gone, and I didn't think I could have done any more. I'd helped Linda, Michael, and Liz make sure Betty didn't get away with keeping Lottie's waiver off the agenda, and best of all, I'd avoided talking to Betty.

Lottie would probably be back home in a few weeks, depending on how long it took to install the stairlift. I'd find out soon enough, and for now I'd done everything I could. Time to relax and rest up before tonight's meeting.

I sucked in a big breath, exhaled slowly, and started reading. I was just beginning to chuckle over Georgie's latest escapade when I heard footsteps coming up the stairs.

I looked up and met Betty Harris' pale blue eyes. My stomach lurched. I guess I wasn't going to avoid talking to Betty after all.

She reached the top of the steps and stood towering over me, her waist at my eye level. I took in her stylish capri pants and a patterned blouse that looked like silk, all *greenery yallery* in discordant tones. Definitely not a sight I wanted to see this morning.

"Betty!" I struggled to my feet, not wanting to be at a disadvantage sitting down. "What brings you by this morning?"

"I just wanted to have a little word with you, sugar." Her gaze never left my face and I felt my cheeks flush. I hated it when I blushed, but I couldn't control the telltale color that rose in moments of stress.

"Have a seat." I gestured to a chair, but Betty remained standing.

"Oh, this won't take long. I just stopped by to tell you I know what you're trying to do to help your little friend, but it will never work."

"Why is that?"

"Simple." Betty's mouth smiled, but her eyes didn't. "You don't have the votes. You'll find out. That woman will move back into Happy Oaks over my dead body."

"You may be the board president, but you still only have one vote." My voice sounded strident, and I started to feel the anxiety pressing on my lungs.

"You really don't know how this works, do you?" Betty said languidly. "Well, it doesn't matter. You'd do well to leave it alone.

Don't say I didn't warn you." She stared at me for a moment, then tossed her long black hair and chuckled. "Bye now, sugar. See you at the meeting tonight."

She turned and made her way down the steps, grabbed the stroller with her little dog, Flossie, and continued on her way.

As she walked away, Keith stood on the sidewalk by his porch, watching Betty's retreating back.

I sank into my chair and realized I'd been holding my breath. My heart was beating faster than normal, and I felt as though I'd just come face to face with a rattlesnake. Despite the warm day, I shivered. Lottie told me she'd seen something ugly in Betty, and now I knew exactly what she meant.

Watching Betty walk away, sunlight sparking off her dangling earrings, I couldn't help comparing this encounter with our first meeting. She'd been friendly and charming that time, and she'd been wearing capri pants and a silk blouse then, too. I had even liked her at first, even though I found the whole dog in the stroller thing a little weird, but now? Like Michael, I didn't trust her farther than I could throw a grand piano.

How did Lottie not have the votes? Out of the seven-member board, Michael, Dave, Linda, and Liz were in favor, leaving Betty, Jeff, and Tim to vote against. That was four to three in favor. It didn't make any sense to me. Well, I'd find out soon enough.

Should I be doing something more? If so, I didn't have a clue what it would be, and I needed to calm down.

Thinking of calming down, I realized there was no way I'd be able to relax here, not after that conversation. I needed a change of scene, and Pru could probably use one, too. She should be back from the dentist by now. Maybe we should go into town and grab a coffee. Later we could all eat dinner out so we'd be fresh and alert when we picked Lottie up for the meeting that would decide whether she'd be able to move back home. I reached for my phone.

FIVE

It was pandemonium. Residents were shouting, Betty was banging her gavel, and nobody could hear a word anyone else was saying. Or, more accurately, shouting.

Hanging on the opposite wall was the banner featuring our community slogan, "Welcome to Happy Oaks, the Happiest Over-55 Condo Community in Central Florida." It always felt smarmy to me and now, with all the uproar, it made me want to gag. The sound of all those yelling voices, and the sight of open mouths and pointing fingers wasn't pretty. Even less pretty was the anger behind it all.

Lottie, the innocent cause of the furor, was visibly drooping in her wheelchair next to me at the side of the room. Despite the anger and the uproar, I felt confident that Lottie would have the votes she needed to move back home. Of course Betty and Jeff would oppose the waiver, and Tim would vote no because that was his way. But Dave, Michael, Linda, and Liz were in favor, making up the majority.

I squeezed Lottie's hand. "It'll be okay," I whispered.

The meeting room at the clubhouse was packed. The board members had lined up twice as many folding chairs as they usually did for the monthly meeting — forty instead of twenty — because they expected Charlotte's waiver request to be a hot-button issue. They were right. Every seat was occupied, as well as all the stools by the kitchen pass-through at the back of the room.

Betty, as board president, sat in the power position at the center of the long table at the front of the room. Tonight she was wearing her black hair long and loose, like a teenager. She had on one of her signature outfits, similar to what she'd been wearing this morning. This one consisted of beige capri pants with a navy blue shirt made of shiny, silky material and matching navy sandals. A pair of sparkly, dangly earrings danced around her face and distracted attention from her cold eyes.

Funny, I had never thought of Betty's eyes as being cold before. Until this week I would have described her as friendly. And what was happening with my neighbors? Over these past few days I'd talked to almost everyone in the community, but this outpouring of anger from them was new and I wasn't sure where it was all coming from.

While I waited for the tumult to die down, I scanned the other board members. Michael was at the end of the table closest to me. He and Dave, who sat next to him, had put a lot of work into helping Lottie learn about stairlifts and all the different options available. Linda was next, and then Betty. That left Jeff, Liz, and Tim, who served as treasurer, at the far end.

Jeff's head was bald, but he made up for it with his bushy white brows that seemed to have a life of their own. In fact, he'd used those eyebrows to intimidate me when I'd spoken with him about Lottie's waiver.

Liz' short, silver hair resembled a close-fitting cap, and her brown eyes looked troubled as she scanned the room. In a tee shirt and jeans, she was dressed more casually than any of the other board members.

Tim projected a military bearing with stiff, erect posture, an effect heightened by his buzz-cut gray hair. I suspected it was compensation for his height, which was only about an incher taller than my five foot four.

I had plenty of time to survey the board members since it took a good three minutes before the room was quiet again. Betty banged the gavel one final time. "Obviously there's a lot of strong feeling about this issue. Everyone will have a chance to speak their piece, and then the board will discuss it and make a decision."

"Now, just to recap. We have a proposal from Charlotte Delaney, who owns unit F4. It's an upstairs condo, and she wants to install one of these stairlift things so she can have easier access to her apartment. As you're all aware, Charlotte was recently disabled."

Betty's voice took on a sickly sweet quality as she talked about Charlotte, and I hunched my shoulders involuntarily, the same reaction I have to fingernails on a chalkboard or someone rubbing a balloon.

"According to her," Betty looked at Charlotte, and she had that not-really-a-smile thing going on again, "she has only two options. She can move somewhere else, or she can make some changes here so she can deal with the stairs. She's requesting a waiver of the architectural guidelines to install a stairlift. If you want details of the lift, our Architectural Committee Chair David Wheelock can share that information with you."

"Let's start with the board." She looked up and down the long table. She pointed to the far end and asked, "Tim, do you have any questions?" I felt pretty sure Betty had intentionally chosen the one person she could count on to start them off in a negative direction. Tim didn't disappoint.

He stood up. "I have a few." For such a small man his voice was deep and gruff. "First, where is she living now and how did she get here tonight?"

From his spot at the other end of the table Michael volunteered, "I can answer that." Betty gestured to him to continue. "Lily and I drove over and picked Charlotte up from the rehab center where she's been living since she was released from the hospital, and we brought her here for the meeting. When it's over, we'll be taking her back."

Tim harrumphed. "Okay, next question. How much will this dad-blamed thing cost, and who the hell's going to pay for it?"

Betty nodded at Dave. "I have several different proposals here," he began.

"Bottom line!" Tim growled.

Dave continued calmly, ignoring the interruption, "One option is for a small one that starts at just under $8,000, but they've already told Charlotte that price won't include the extra installation materials needed to attach it to the type of stairwells we have in our buildings. So around about $10,000 all told. There are other options that would cost more, but might look better."

"Charlotte has indicated she's willing to pay the basic cost, but if we request any upgrades, she would like us to take care of those."

Residents started muttering and Betty banged her gavel again. "Dave, do you have pictures or drawings we can look at?"

"Sure do." He pulled several brochures from a stack of papers and passed them to Betty.

The board members handed the brochures back and forth. After a few minutes, a voice from the back of the room called out, "Can we see those brochures?"

"We'll pass them around in a few minutes," Betty said without looking up.

When the board members were done studying the brochures, Betty held them out toward the front row. Deb Wheelock jumped up and took them. She leafed through them quickly, then handed them down the row.

Looking up and down the long table, Betty asked the board members, "Do any of you have any other questions or comments at this time?"

Liz nodded. "What about liability? If Charlotte has some sort of mishap with it and gets injured, or if somebody's visiting grandkid starts playing with it and gets hurt, what's our exposure?"

Dave looked blank. "Charlotte? Is that something you've discussed with any of these vendors?"

She shook her head.

"Then I suggest we consult our attorney and insurance company about that," Dave said.

"Once it's approved, what sort of time frame are we expecting for installation?" Liz asked. "And how disruptive will it be to the community? Noise, mess, all that."

Dave said, "I don't think the community as a whole will be impacted, although it won't likely be an uplifting experience for the other residents of Building F." Nobody smiled at his pun. "It would depend on which type of lift we decide on, but probably two to three days."

"What kind of precedent will this set?" Jeff's bushy eyebrows were drawn together in a ferocious scowl. "I mean, this place will look pretty ugly if we have one of these stairlifts in front of every upstairs unit. I've lived here eighteen years, and I remember several people who've moved out when they couldn't manage the stairs any more. Why should Charlotte be any different? Why can't she just live somewhere else? I don't want this trashing our property values."

Michael stared at Jeff in disbelief. "Our friend and neighbor has just suffered a terrible disability, and you're worried about your property values? Don't you think she deserves to be able to access her own home? Or did she somehow lose that right when she became ill?"

"That's *her* problem," Jeff said, bushy eyebrows working. "I don't want it to be mine."

"Well," Michael said, "since you live in an upstairs unit, I sincerely hope you never have to worry about managing the stairs due to age or infirmity."

Lottie reached for my hand. "I've really started something, haven't I?" she asked quietly. "I knew some people wouldn't like the idea but I never thought it would be so hateful." She looked near tears.

"Do you want to leave?"

"No, I'll stay."

"Can I get you anything? Some coffee? Water?"

Lottie shook her head.

Betty turned her attention to the board members on her other side. "Linda, any questions?" Betty was eyeing Linda in a way that made me want to squirm, another forced smile on her face, and she was using that sickly sweet voice again.

"Not at this time," Linda stammered, twisting her chunky gold bracelet.

Betty turned her attention to the end of the table. "Michael, Dave, being as how you're on the Architectural Committee I'm sure you don't have any questions."

"That's right," Dave said as Michael nodded.

"If the board members don't have any more questions or comments at this time, we'll open it up to questions and comments from residents."

Michael interrupted. "Maybe we should hear from Charlotte first. Is that okay, Lottie? Can you tell us why you're asking for an architectural waiver?"

Betty glared at Michael, then turned to the figure in the wheelchair. Her lip curled slightly, unseen by the residents in the folding chairs in front of her but visible to me off to the side.

"Charlotte, do you want to say something?"

"Yes, please."

She maneuvered the wheelchair to the front of the room and spoke.

"I'd stand up if I could, but I didn't bring my crutches so you'll just have to bear with me." Betty banged her gavel to quiet the muttering that was starting again at the back of the room.

When the room was quiet again, Lottie continued. "I moved here eleven years ago. I had just turned fifty-five, I had lost my husband to cancer the year before, and I was looking for a home I'd be able to manage on my own both before and after retirement. I wanted it to be someplace I'd love so much that I'd only leave when they carried me out feet first." She paused and tried to smile. "Or foot first, as the case may be."

Nobody laughed.

"This seemed like the perfect place to put down roots. Because it's a condo, I didn't have to worry about mowing the yard or fixing the roof or any of that. And it seemed like such a friendly community, with great neighbors, and in a town I really like."

Pointedly she looked around at her neighbors, many of whom appeared anything but friendly at that moment.

"A few months ago, complications from diabetes led to the removal of my left foot. I was in the hospital for a couple weeks, and in rehab ever since. They won't release me until I'm able to manage on my own, and that includes getting into and out of my apartment. After I leave here tonight, I'll be going back to the rehab center. I'm well enough now to be able to move home if access wasn't a problem."

She took a deep breath. "Please let me come home."

The room exploded into noise as everyone tried to comment at once. Betty gave the gavel another brisk workout before the residents subsided.

"Any more questions or comments?" she asked, looking up and down the board table. Betty whispered something to Linda. "Linda Barry has something to say." Betty pointed at her.

Linda stood slowly, still twisting her chunky gold bracelet. "Well, this is nothing personal, but we have architectural rules for a reason. It's to protect our property values. I'm sorry that Charlotte is going through some troubles, but we're an over-fifty-five condo community, not a nursing home. If we let Charlotte put in this ugly thing, then we'll end up with them all over the community. I don't think we should do it." Her voice shook slightly.

To say I was shocked was a meaningless understatement. I had to force myself to breathe.

"Anyone else? No? Well I guess we're ready to hear from residents, then. One at a time. If you have something to say, please raise your hand and I'll call on you."

Hands shot up all over the room. "Rick Brophy, there in the back, do you have a question?"

"Not a question," Rick said, "just a comment. I live next to Lottie, and I'm also in an upstairs unit. She's been a great neighbor, and she's done a lot for our community over the years. If a stairlift will let her stay, then I say the quicker it's installed the better."

Rick was one person I hadn't been able to talk to before the meeting, so I was pleased that he'd spoken up in favor of the waiver.

From her seat in the second row Michelle Hoffman stood, not waiting for Betty to call on her. "I live in Charlotte's building, and I agree with Linda!" Michelle's husband Sam looked at her in surprise.

"Michelle," he hissed in an audible whisper, "I can't believe you."

"That's not what we signed up for when we bought the condo," she said loudly. "If living here the way it is doesn't work for her, she should move out."

"Mrs. Nguyen," Betty called out.

Minnie Nguyen stood up in the middle of the third row. She was so tiny that even when she stood, residents were craning their necks to see her. Her husband, Kim, rose next to her and took her hand. She spoke softly, with a slight accent. "When we came to this country as refugees more than thirty years ago, we had nothing. Over the years we made a good life for ourselves and for our children. We had to face many obstacles, and we know what it feels like to be left out, to be treated like second class. When we were thinking about buying the condo here, we felt welcomed and included, and we thought this was a good community. If we make this change so Miss Charlotte can still live among us, it shows we are first class. If we don't, then this community is no longer first class and I don't want to be part of it."

She sat down with a thump. A few of the residents smiled and nodded. Some looked a little shamefaced, but quite a few still seemed angry. Half a dozen people still had their hands in the air. This was not going well.

Betty surveyed the room. "Does anyone have something new or different to add?" One by one the remaining hands went down, although I could still hear muttering.

"I'll entertain a motion at this time."

Dave stood up. Reading from a piece of paper in front of him, he spoke slowly and clearly, "I move that we authorize an architectural waiver for Charlotte Delaney to install a stairlift, in order to allow her access to her second floor unit F4, and that we allocate funds not to exceed $2,000 to pay for the customization required with Charlotte picking up the bulk of the cost. Before any work commences, she must submit drawings and photos to the Architectural Committee to sign off on."

"Second," Michael said quickly.

"Any debate?" One of the residents started to speak, but Betty glared at him and he closed his mouth. She glanced at each of the board members in turn.

"No, then all those in favor?"

Dave and Michael raised their hands.

"Opposed?"

Tim and Jeff shot their hands into the air. Linda raised hers more slowly. Firmly, Liz said, "abstain."

"The motion fails." Betty banged her gavel as the room erupted noisily again.

While the gavel banged, Liz slipped out of her chair, walked over to Dave, and spoke quietly into his ear. He nodded his head and stood. "What is it?" Betty asked. She sounded impatient.

Dave spoke in his usual deliberate fashion. "I'd like to make a new motion. I move we submit Charlotte's request to our legal and insurance advisors, and schedule a special meeting to discuss the question of her architectural waiver again when we have their responses. We can't let her rot in rehab forever."

Michael seconded it quickly.

"Those in favor?"

Dave, Michael, and Liz shot their hands into the air. Linda's followed a second later. "The motion carries. After we have a response from the lawyer and the insurance company, we'll set a time for the special meeting to discuss their recommendations and decide if Charlotte's request goes any farther."

As the noise level grew in the room, Betty banged her gavel again and glared at Liz. "No further business. Do I have a motion to adjourn?" A moment later the gavel came down again, closing the meeting.

Hunching my shoulders didn't help block out the sound of my neighbors squabbling as Michael came over. "Let's get out of here," I said, pushing Lottie's wheelchair toward the door. Pru joined us from where she'd been sitting in the back of the room.

"If you don't mind, Lottie, I'm going straight home. I've got a bit of a headache." She certainly didn't look like her usual bouncy self. She'd been fine just before the meeting, so it must have come on suddenly.

"Sure, Pru, whatever you need. Take care of yourself. Thanks for coming tonight," Lottie said, and Pru turned and made her way out the door.

Nobody spoke during the short drive to the rehab center. When we pulled in, I said quietly to my husband, "Do you mind hanging out for a little bit while I try to settle her?"

"I'll wait in the lounge, so take as long as you need." He helped me maneuver Lottie's chair into the building, then, after we all signed in, he headed down the short hallway to the residents' lounge while I took Lottie to her room.

Lottie managed to keep her composure until she was safely inside her room, where she promptly burst into tears. "Oh, Lily, what am I going to do? I don't want to have to move."

I crouched down and hugged her, even though it made my pesky knee twinge like the dickens. "We'll figure something out, it'll be okay."

"I can't believe Linda and Liz voted against me, I thought they were supportive."

"Well, two days ago they were. I can't get over how both of them changed like that. It's very strange."

Lottie reached for a tissue and dabbed away some tears. A thought occurred to me. "Did Linda seem nervous to you?"

"I don't know, maybe? She was fussing with that bracelet a lot," Lottie said, sniffing.

After talking around in circles for a few more minutes, Lottie's tears subsided. "Want some help getting ready for bed?"

"No," she said, speaking slowly. "I can manage. I think I need to be on my own for a while."

"I'll tell you one thing." At that moment I felt quite fierce. "Dave bought us some time with that new motion, and I'm going to figure out a way to take advantage of it to make sure the next vote is in your favor, starting with finding out why Linda and Liz voted the way they did. You're coming home if it's the last thing I do."

"You're a good friend, Lily Gallagher," Lottie said slowly, "and I appreciate the thought. But I'm not going to hold you to a promise you can't keep."

"Well, if I don't, it won't be for want of trying." I gave her another big hug. "You're sure you can manage?"

"Of course. If I have a problem I'll ring for the aide."

"Okay, well, try and get some sleep if you can. We'll talk more tomorrow." Lottie nodded.

***

After that travesty of a vote, Patrick interrupted Linda mid-conversation and hustled her out of the meeting room with a curt, "We need to go. Now."

Leaving the clubhouse, he walked so fast Linda almost had to run to keep up with him, but he was too upset to slow down. He rarely felt angry with his wife, but he was angry now, and confused. He needed to find out why she made that ridiculous statement, and cast that shocking vote. But he wasn't going to discuss it in the clubhouse or outside, so he said nothing the entire walk.

Once they were home he marched into the kitchen and sat. She followed. He finally spoke, and it was an effort not to yell.

"Linda, what in the name of all that's holy what was that about?"

"What are you talking about?"

"You, with that ridiculous statement about stairlifts, and then voting against Charlotte. When we talked earlier you were planning to vote for it. You promised Lily you were voting for it."

Linda started fiddling with the dumb bracelet. She loved the thing, but he was almost sorry he'd given it to her. Oh, great, now she was going to cry.

He steeled himself to withstand her tears. "Why?"

"Betty came by earlier. I didn't have a chance to tell you."

"So?"

Now the tears were coming for real, thick and fast. "She threatened to tell everyone about the fire if I didn't vote against it. I was trying to do the right thing for you. For us."

He jumped out of his chair and stood, hands clenched, trying to control his Irish temper. "You should have told me."

"I'm sorry." She sniffled and reached for a tissue. "But you've been carrying guilt for that fire for so long, and I know there's something you haven't told me about it."

"What do you mean?" He braced himself.

"It was Frankie, wasn't it? My no-good cousin, he did it. Please, Patrick, I deserve the truth after all this time."

He sank back down into the chair and put his hands over his face. He couldn't look at her. "Yes," he said dully. "It was Frankie."

"Oh, Patrick." She was almost wailing.

He took his hands away from his face and rested them in his lap. "And I knew about it before he did it. I okayed it." For a moment he thought she didn't hear him. But he saw the instant the message penetrated, because her head shot up and she stared at him.

"Why do you think I felt so guilty for that man's death all these years?" His voice sounded harsh. "If it had been an actual accident I would have been sorry as hell, but it wouldn't have eaten away at me like this did. Do you know what I did?" His voice was getting louder.

She shook her head.

"I actually went through the entire building an hour before it was supposed to happen, checking that nobody was in there."

"It was Thanksgiving, you didn't go downtown!"

"Yes, I did. I told you I was going for a walk, and I let you think I was just driving to the park."

She gulped, and reached for another tissue. "Patrick, I'm so sorry. If I hadn't insisted you do that deal with my no-good cousin, none of it would have ever happened. From something I heard Frankie say once, I was pretty sure he was behind it, but I don't understand why you went along with him. Or why you never told me."

"I don't know either." He looked down at his lap. "I think I must have been a little bit out of my mind with worry. Of course I knew it was wrong, but I was desperate and it seemed like the only way out. I was out of my depth with a commercial building. I should have just stuck to the apartment buildings. And then the economy crashed right after we started renovating the thing, it was going to completely wipe us out. We would have lost everything." He looked at Linda again.

Her tears were coming faster. "Why didn't you talk to me about it back then? I would rather have had no money and a whole husband than a half a husband and money for the last ten years."

Instead of answering, he snapped back, "So why didn't you tell me when Betty started making those threats?"

Linda's face scrunched into her "I'm thinking about it" expression, mouth screwed up and eyebrows furrowed. Finally, in a small voice, "I didn't want to worry you."

"Well, at that meeting tonight, watching you go against what you know is right, that worries me."

He began pacing. The witch had been hinting for weeks that she knew something that would be damaging to him, but he never imagined she'd find out about the fire. How could she? His chest felt like someone was sitting on it, and his throat tightened. His fingers began to tingle. No! He was *not* going to have a panic attack. Not here. Not again. He continued walking up and down the kitchen, trying to calm down, while Linda sobbed quietly at the table.

"Look," he said circling the kitchen a couple more times. It was an effort to speak in a normal tone, because he wanted to yell. "I'm supposed to meet Betty in the morning early, at six. She set it up so we'd have some privacy to discuss her 'findings,' as she called them. I thought she was full of nonsense. It never occurred to me she knew anything important."

Linda looked up, eyes wide and mouth slightly open. Even now, after more than thirty years of marriage, those big, beautiful brown eyes still made him feel weak in the knees, but at this moment they looked fearful and the weight started pressing down on him again.

"What are we going to do?" Her voice trembled.

"I don't know, sweetheart, I don't know." Once he started shaking his head he couldn't seem to stop.

His mind was whirling. He couldn't go through that again, all the stares and pointing fingers, but he couldn't let his wife suffer for his past mistakes either. Or Charlotte. He swallowed hard.

"I don't think I can go through all that again, but I won't let her use you because of it. I want you to promise me that you won't let her push you around any more. When you have another opportunity to vote on Charlotte's thing, promise me you'll vote for what you think is right."

"But what if. . ." He held up a hand.

"No what ifs. I'll deal with Betty in the morning." His tone was grim. Then, more gently, "You just do your job on this condo board without worrying about me, alright?"

Without another word he turned and left the kitchen.

***

I retrieved Michael from the lounge, and we went back out to the car. I couldn't wait to get home and try to forget what happened.

Once we were on the road, he asked, "How's Lottie doing?"

"Not so good, but she wanted to be alone."

He didn't respond, so after a minute I asked, "Any idea why Linda seemed nervous?"

"No, but I'm afraid I might know why Liz abstained from voting." He sighed audibly.

"Afraid?"

"I'll tell you about it once we're back home. If I talk about it now I'll get too worked up to be safe to drive."

I stared at him. His lips were set in a grim line. "Michael, you're scaring me. Does it have something to do with Betty?"

"Just wait a few minutes. Please."

The next five minutes passed in slow silence while my thoughts raced. I was still shocked about Liz and Linda's votes, and now I was also impatient to hear what Michael had to say about Liz. What could have changed her mind and her vote? And even if Michael shed some light on it, how would that help Lottie?

Despite my impatience, when we arrived back at the apartment, I headed for the kitchen. "Tea?" I could see that my husband was wound pretty tight right now and tea would relax him.

"Sure." Michael sat down heavily at the table while I started the kettle. I chose chamomile since we both needed soothing.

Once the tea was ready, Michael wrapped his hands around his mug as if he needed the warmth.

"Okay, what's bugging you?"

"Something happened this morning. I didn't know what to make of it at the time, but it seems obvious now, after what just happened at the meeting."

"This sounds serious."

"It might be. Probably." He shifted uneasily in his chair.

I reached for his hand. "Tell me about it."

He stared at nothing, eyes unfocused, as he replayed the scene in his mind while I sipped my tea and waited as patiently as I could.

"You know what's really sad?"

"What's that?"

"I was actually happy, having a rare chance to do something practical. Anyway, here's what happened. I was under the kitchen sink in the clubhouse working on that clogged pipe Helen asked me to fix before the meeting. I heard the door open, and a couple of women talking, but I didn't pay any attention. Then they must have gotten close to the kitchen, because then I heard them clearly. One of them sounded upset, and she said something like, 'You're willing to put it on the agenda, but only if I agree to vote against it? Why on earth would I do that?'

"Well, that got my attention, so I eased out from under the sink. By this time they must have been standing right by the kitchen pass through, and then I heard Betty saying, 'It wouldn't be the first time you forced someone out of their home.'

"Then she told the other woman, 'I know what you did. I know who you worked for in 2011, and all about those faked-up foreclosures they handled. And I can make sure your friends and neighbors know, too.'

"Then the other woman told Betty, 'Say whatever you want, I'm not going to force Charlotte out of her home. She has enough troubles without that.' Then Betty told her, okay, she didn't have to vote against it, she just had to abstain. She said she wanted to be sure the motion would fail, but she didn't want to vote against it herself."

"Liz," I said quietly.

Michael nodded. He was looking more and more unhappy as the sorry little tale continued.

"That's what I think. Then she threatened to tell Liz' kids about all those foreclosures, and Liz called her a monster. She actually said that, 'you're a monster, Betty,' and she said some day Betty would get what's coming to her. Then she stormed out."

I was speechless. Michael glanced at me, then continued.

"It gets worse. Betty came around into the kitchen, and we argued. I asked who she was talking to and she told me it was none of my business. I told her since it concerned the community and an issue before the board, it was absolutely my business. I asked her why she didn't just vote against it herself, and she tried to put on her sweetness and light act, but I wasn't buying it.

"Then I told her I thought she was a nasty person. That's when she lost it. She stamped her foot, and her face got red, and I half expected her to throw herself on the floor and start kicking her feet like a two-year old.

"She told me it's people like me who push her into doing things she doesn't want to do. 'One day you'll push me too far,' she said, and I snapped back with, 'Or one day you will, and you'll be sorry.'

"That's when Jeff came in. Betty ran out the door. Jeff just looked at me, with one bushy eyebrow raised like he does. I told him we had a difference of opinion. He asked if I was okay, and I said I was just going to finish up with the sink and he left."

"So you think it was Liz, the person Betty was arguing with?" I was having a hard time taking it in.

"That's my guess." Michael crossed his arms. "I couldn't hear her voice well enough to tell, but obviously it was a woman, one who's on the board. And Liz was a paralegal for years, so she might have been in a position to deal with foreclosures.

Then tonight, she abstained from voting." He relaxed a little, and sipped his tea.

"Makes sense." I shook my head as though that would help me understand. "I mean, it makes sense it was Liz, but the whole thing makes no sense to me."

Michael continued thoughtfully as if I hadn't spoken, "And then, after the vote failed, Liz hustled right over to Dave to make sure we knew we could make a new motion and buy ourselves time for another vote on it. Maybe that was her way of doing an end run around Betty."

"Betty sure is turning out to be a different person than I thought she was until a few days ago." I thought for a moment. "I hadn't planned on telling you about this, but she paid me a visit this morning, too."

"Oh?"

Quickly I described how Betty had shown up on the porch and our brief exchange. "It was all very civilized on the surface, but it left me feeling like I'd just come face to face with a rattlesnake."

"She must have learned about your canvassing and decided to counterattack. That would be just like her. She probably went straight from talking to you to putting pressure on Liz."

I sipped my tea, then set the cup down with a clatter. "It was bad enough when I just thought she hated Charlotte, but if she threatened me, and blackmailed Liz, I'll bet you anything she did something similar to Linda."

"I'm wondering about that, too," Michael said. "I've never seen Linda like that before, she seemed really stressed."

"I agree. Normally she seems so sure of herself, but her voice was shaking at the meeting. And she kept twisting that bracelet like she always does when she's upset."

"And did you notice the look on her husband's face?"

"No, I couldn't see him."

"He looked totally shocked. Like he couldn't believe what he was hearing."

"Well, he was right there when she promised me she'd vote in favor of the stairlift. And he warned me about Betty." I thought for a moment. "How soon do you think you'll be able to hold another meeting?"

"It depends on how quickly we hear back from the lawyer and the insurance company, I suppose. Why?" He drew his eyebrows together. "What are you thinking, Lil?"

"I'm wondering if Linda would tell me what Betty's holding over her. Do you think it's worth talking to her? Maybe she'd be willing to vote for Lottie's waiver at the next meeting."

Michael's scowl deepened. "This has turned pretty ugly, Lil. I'm not sure I want you involved any more. I don't think there's much Betty can do to me, but I don't want her going after you."

"I know it's turned ugly, I was there tonight too, remember?" Now I was getting annoyed. "And I'll bet you anything that Betty stirred that up, because when I was talking with our neighbors, even the people who didn't want the stairlift weren't nasty about it like they were tonight. And what about Lottie?" I felt indignant on her behalf. "She shouldn't be railroaded out of her home like this! Although," I paused for a minute, head tilted to the side, "after seeing all this she might decide she doesn't want to come back, and I wouldn't blame her. In fact she's already thinking about maybe having to find a new place to live. How would you feel about that?"

"That a decision like that would be very premature." He stood up. "I'm going to jump in the shower and then go to bed."

"You go on, I'm going to check on Pru. She wasn't her usual energetic self at the meeting tonight, and I'm not sure I buy the headache. Something must have happened."

"You're right, with all the hubbub I didn't notice."

"I'll be in in a minute." I pulled out my phone and hit speed dial.

After a long talk with Pru, I looked into the bedroom. Michael was already asleep, curled peacefully on his side.

A few minutes later I stood in the shower, warm water running over my back, trying to relax. It had been an upsetting evening, first with all the ugliness at the meeting, the disappointing vote, and then trying to calm Pru down. Turns out that just before the meeting she'd gotten another call from her daughter. How would I feel if I got a call from Shannon or Briana that their marriage was falling apart? Not good, for sure.

Now both my friends were suffering. I couldn't do anything for Pru except provide a sympathetic ear, but there had to be more I could do for Lottie.

No matter how much I wracked my brains, though, I couldn't think what. I thought the board would have to vote in favor if the community was supportive, but Liz' abstention and Linda's vote tonight showed how naive I was. Betty had certainly out-maneuvered us.

Could I do anything to change Betty's mind before the next vote? Did I even want to try? I thought about this morning's encounter and shivered. If Michael didn't want me talking to Linda, he certainly wouldn't want me talking to Betty.

There had to be something, but I was too tired to think any more. I'd pretend to be Scarlet O'Hara and think about it tomorrow.

Quickly I finished my shower and got into my night things.

In bed next to my peacefully sleeping husband, I tossed and turned. I was jealous of his ability to fall asleep so easily, but after an evening like this one I just couldn't shut my mind down. A long time later I fell into an uneasy doze.

A patient was flatlining. The high-pitched sound was unmistakable, and one no medical professional ever wanted to hear. I raced from one bed to another but couldn't find the dying patient. The ward was eerily quiet. Where were all the other nurses? The faster I tried to run, the slower I moved, as if I was slogging through a pool of molasses.

My heart raced and my breath came, ragged and uneven, as I tried to call for help. No sound came out of my mouth.

I knew if I didn't find the patient within the next few seconds, it would be too late for sure.

I gasped and sat up, heart racing, drenched in sweat, in my own bed next to my still-sleeping husband. I almost cried with relief. It was only a nightmare — one I'd had many times before.

Michael's sleepy voice next to me said quietly, "Nightmare again, sweetheart?"

"Yes." His hand reached out and began rubbing my shoulder. With a sigh I lay back down, willing myself to relax as his arms came around and pulled me close.

***

Hushed voices broke the quiet. "This is the last you're getting from me. You've gone too far this time."

"Not hardly, sugar, this is just the latest installment of many to come."

"You've destroyed too many lives, and now you're going after a lady who, by all accounts, is one of the nicest people you could meet. It has to stop. ***You*** *have to stop."*

"Who's going to stop me? You?" She laughed, an irritating sound as brittle as breaking glass and more painful to the ears than rubbing a balloon or fingernails on a chalkboard. "You want me to stop? You'd have to be willing to come clean, admit what you did. And you'll never have the guts to do that. You've always taken the easy road, your whole life."

She started walking away, a dark shape in the shadows, the light-colored envelope in her hand catching the light.

"Does your husband know what you're doing?"

She turned and took two steps back, saying quietly, "You won't be telling him, sugar. You'd have to admit who you really are, and we both know you're not about to do that." She laughed again and the listener cringed momentarily.

The eyes focused, unblinking and angry, on the dark figure walking away. In seconds it disappeared from view, melting into the shadowy outlines of the shrubbery surrounding the pool. Ears listened, but heard nothing except the soft whoosh, whoosh, of the pool pump.

The eyes were furious. And scared. After all these years, to see that hated face again. Hear that grating voice. Was she going to destroy them all over again? Not if they could help it! The rage, long suppressed, took over. It was surprisingly easy.

The only sound was the quiet whoosh, whoosh, whoosh of the pool pump.

Six

So far, the only sounds were the chirps of a few waking birds. That, and the quiet whoosh, whoosh, of the pool pump. Then there was a small creak as the gate to the pool area opened, a tiny snick as it closed again. Almost silent footsteps padded quietly, and then stopped.

A few minutes later, the early morning silence was decisively shattered.

It was starting.

***

From the depths of a sound sleep, I slowly became aware of a thin, high-pitched sound. For one groggy moment I thought I was back in my flatlining patient nightmare, then I realized it was real.

Someone was screaming.

"Michael, wake up!" I jabbed his sleeping form with my elbow, then glanced at my watch.

Five forty-seven AM. Ugh. I might as well be back at work.

I fumbled for my glasses and eased out of bed, struggling to fully awaken.

Who was screaming? And why? Hastily I opened the drapes a little to look outside.

Through the sliding glass doors, the sky was showing the merest hints of light at that early hour and on the far side of the pool stood a woman.

I snatched my robe off the chair and slipped my feet into the sneakers sitting on the floor by the door.

Michael, always slow to rouse, began to stir.

"Michael, you've got to wake up." I was almost yelling. "Something's happening out by the pool. Hurry!"

He groaned.

I raced out the front door, pulling on my robe as I hurried down the stairs as fast as my painful right knee would allow, and speed walked as quickly as I could to the pool.

The screaming sounded louder now.

As I got closer I realized who it was. "Pru, what's the matter?" I shouted.

The screaming continued unabated, even when I was standing right in front of her.

I shook my friend by the shoulder and Pru's hands came down from her face, but the screaming continued.

Gripping Pru's upper arms I said, as calmly as I could, "It's okay. I'm here now. You can relax." When the screaming didn't stop, I wrapped my arms around her in a tight hug. "It's okay, honey," I said softly. "You'll be okay. I'm here. It's okay."

After a minute, the screams turned to whimpers, and then, gradually, thankfully, to silence.

In the newfound quiet, I became aware of muttering as other residents also converged on the pool area, but I kept my focus on Pru. "That's better. Now, take a deep breath. In. Then out. That's good. And another."

Gradually her ragged breathing evened out.

"Now, what's the matter?"

Pru's eyes were wide and teary, her cheeks were wet, and a little ball of mucus clung to the end of her nose. She didn't speak, just turned and pointed to the pool.

I followed the pointing finger and noticed a sodden bundle of clothing in the middle of the pool where the water was deepest. The pool pump whirred quietly, stirring up the water and causing the bundle to bob gently up and down.

Realization was slow, but it hit suddenly — it wasn't a bundle of clothing at all, it was a body. A body with long, dark hair. Before I could do more than gasp, I caught motion out of the corner of my eye.

It was my downstairs neighbor Keith, moving fast. He took a running jump into the pool and propelled himself downward, then came up under the floating body and started pushing it toward the shallow end.

"Somebody call an ambulance!" I shouted over my shoulder. Carefully I helped Pru over to the nearest chair and helped her sit. "Will you be okay by yourself for a minute? I'll be right back."

Pru nodded.

I jogged toward the steps at the shallow end, ignoring the pain in my knee, hoping we weren't too late.

Trying to remember what I knew about drowning victims, I called to Keith, "We need to get her out of the water, can you do that?"

He drew closer to the steps.

I reached far enough out into the pool to find an arm. No pulse.

Quickly I calculated the time. It was 5:47 when I glanced at my watch as I got out of bed, and it was now 5:55. Eight minutes, plus however long Pru was screaming before I'd woken up and looked at my watch the first time. I was sure it was way too late for CPR, but I had to try.

"Can you lift her out?"

"Give me a second." He was breathing hard and looked pale.

I was dimly aware of other people around me as shapes in the pre-dawn light, and I heard them talking, but I was so focused on the body that I jumped when I felt a hand on my back.

Michael gave my shoulder a comforting squeeze. "I've called nine-one-one, they're on the line."

"Tell them we're pulling her out and I'm about to administer CPR," I said as Keith stood and started to gather the body in his arms.

Michael spoke into his phone, then he announced loudly, "Okay, the ambulance is on its way."

Who was the victim? The lanky build and the black hair looked familiar, but not the clothing, which seemed to be black leggings and a black, long-sleeved tee. One foot wore a dark sneaker, but the other was bare.

Keith was just lifting the body when Greg Harris exploded onto the scene. "Oh my god," Greg screamed, "it's my wife! What did you do to her?"

He jumped into the pool and knocked his shoulder into Keith, forcing him to drop the body. "We have to get her out. Someone help me!" He lifted Betty's body part way out of the water, but when he saw her face, he shrieked and let go.

One quick glance at the staring, bulging red eyes, even in the dim light, made it clear to me there was no hope. Not that I'd had much doubt.

Betty Louise Harris was dead.

"Noooo!" Greg moaned as his wife's dead body sank back into the water, "Betty!" He stumbled and thrashed around, causing his wife's body to sway and move as if it were still alive.

With a look of irritation on his face, Keith elbowed Greg aside and took another grip on the body. He had just laid it on the pool deck when, with a final wail of its siren, the emergency vehicle rolled into the parking lot.

The first responder jumped out of the ambulance and rushed over to the small crowd that had gathered. "Okay, who called nine-one-one?"

Michael waved his hand, still clutching his phone. Hurriedly he told the nine-one-one operator, "The EMTs just arrived.

The woman from the ambulance hollered over to him, "Where's the patient?"

Michael pointed, but the group of onlookers screened the body from her view.

Greg, standing in the water and looking almost as pale as his dead wife, held onto the side of the pool a few steps away. I wondered if he was going to be sick. "Over there," Michael yelled.

"Okay," announced the woman loudly. "My name's Brianna, and I'm a paramedic. Everyone stand back!"

Silently the huddled group of neighbors shuffled a few steps back, allowing Brianna to see the sodden mass. "Who took her out of the water?" Before anyone could answer she turned her head and spoke into the radio mounted on her shoulder. "Nate, I need you over here. It looks like a drowning." She knelt and put her hands on Betty's chest.

Keith stood a few feet away, drying off with an oversized beach towel. When he didn't respond to Brianna, I spoke up. "She was in the middle of the pool when I got here. Keith Johnson — the guy with the towel— got her out of the middle and over to the side. As soon as I could reach an arm I checked for a pulse, and didn't find one. Then Keith lifted her out and put her where she is now. I was just going to try CPR when you got here." I didn't figure it was worthwhile to say anything about Greg's leap into the pool which had slowed down the effort.

"Okay," Brianna nodded.

"Aren't you going to help her?" Greg shouted.

Brianna looked at him pityingly, but her only response was a loud, “Now, all of you just step back and give us room to work.”

“Can you take this?” Michael handed his phone to me. “The nine-one-one operator is still on the line. You’ll know what to tell him better than me.”

Brianna’s partner rushed toward the now-silent group, pulling a gurney loaded with equipment.

The phone squawked, and I lifted it to my ear. “What’s going on now?”

“I’m pretty sure she’s dead.”

“Who is this?” the operator demanded. “Where’s Mr. Gallagher?”

“I’m his wife, Lily. I’m a retired nurse and he just handed me the phone. I found no pulse when I checked just before the EMTs got here. They’re trying CPR now.”

“Alright, I’m dispatching deputies, it’s standard procedure. You can hang up, but tell everyone present to stay put until they arrive to take statements.”

I nodded, then realized the operator couldn’t see me. “Okay,” I said. “Thanks for your help.”

I clicked off the phone and looked at the assembled group of neighbors.

“Everyone, I have an announcement.” I sputtered and mouthed “help me” to Michael. As the residents tore their eyes away from the grim activity by the pool and focused on me, I whispered to him.

Michael shouted, “Deputies have been dispatched, and we’re all supposed to stay here until they arrive. The nine-one-one operator says it’s standard procedure.”

I could see the shock on my neighbors’ faces, and all around me I heard a low grumble.

I felt my eyes filling with tears. I hadn’t liked Betty very much — in fact, in the past few days I’d come to dislike her quite a lot — but nobody should die face down in a swimming pool.

Raised voices caught my attention briefly. Patrick and Tim were arguing, then Tim stomped off. What was that about?

I watched as the first responders attempted to revive Betty, unsuccessfully. A few minutes later a patrol car pulled in next to the ambulance.

The officer made a beeline for the group. Striding toward us, he announced loudly, "I'm Deputy Levy. Who called nine-one-one?"

Michael stepped forward, holding my hand.

"Okay, tell me what happened," Deputy Levy was young, and his lip was curled in a sneer. Looking at him, I had no desire to be cooperative, but I took a deep breath and forced myself to respond calmly, telling him about Pru and seeing the body in the pool.

He was brusque. "So this screaming woman was the first on the scene?"

"Yes."

"Do you know her name?"

"Pru MacLeod. Prudence."

"And your name and address?"

"I'm Lily Gallagher. My husband Michael and I live in unit E4," I turned and pointed to it. "It's an upstairs condo, and our bedroom windows overlook the pool here."

"Point MacLeod out to me."

Arrogant and rude, I thought. Silently I nodded toward Pru, sitting on a deck chair rocking back and forth. "I think she's in shock. The EMTs should probably check her over."

The deputy ignored my concern. "Stick around," he ordered curtly as he headed toward the paramedics. I followed.

"Brianna, Nate, what have we got?"

"Victim is deceased," Brianna responded. "Female, lived in one of the condos here."

"Married?"

"Her husband's over there," I volunteered, pointing at Greg, still standing in the pool.

The deputy glared at me then turned back to the EMTs. "Anything unusual?"

Nate shook his head. Brianna pursed her lips and inhaled, but before she could say anything, the deputy marched off, speaking into his shoulder radio.

Brianna and Nate spoke together for a few minutes. Nate seemed unhappy with their discussion, but eventually he nodded his head and walked over to the ambulance while Brianna joined Deputy Levy. Their conversation lasted a good two minutes, then he spoke into his radio again before marching over to Greg, who was now sitting on the edge of the pool, dripping.

With others now firmly in charge, reaction was setting in and I was feeling a bit shaky. I squeezed Michael's hand gently, forcing myself to take calming breaths. After a moment I said, "I need to go back to Pru."

"I know." He patted my shoulder. "I'll come with you."

Pru sat off to the side, still rocking slightly in her chair. "How are you feeling? Any better?" I leaned over and put a hand on her shoulder.

She stared at me blankly while her entire body shook. "Oh, sweetie, let me see if I can find you a blanket." I hurried over to Brianna and Nate.

"I'm sorry, I know you're busy, but my friend found the body and she's shivering over there. She may be in shock. Can you get her a blanket or something? And then we should move her inside and out of the sun."

Brianna nodded. "On it."

I returned to Pru, glad Michael had stayed with her. "What a way to start the day," he said to Pru with a smile, but she didn't respond.

Suddenly Greg jumped to his feet and started shouting at the officer. "That's a damn lie!" he hollered. "You take that back!"

Through the shouting, I became aware of a siren approaching, and a minute later another car pulled into the now-crowded parking area by the pool. Both occupants got out and strode toward Deputy Levy where he stood glaring up at Greg.

The newcomers pulled the deputy aside and spoke with him, then called the first responders over. After three or four minutes of intense conversation, Deputy Levy marched back to the cluster of residents.

"The detectives will have some questions for you. You all need to stay right where you are."

After the morning I'd already had, I was in no mood to be pushed around, especially by the arrogant deputy. I got right in his face.

"Look, officer," I said, "we can't stay out here in the sun."

His lip curled, but I continued without giving him a chance to interrupt. "Most of us were woken up when Pru started screaming. We haven't dressed, we haven't brushed our teeth, we haven't even had any coffee. And Pru needs medical attention."

Deputy Levy glared at me. "Really," he sneered.

I put my hands on my hips. "In case it escaped your notice, this is an over-fifty-five community and some of the residents here right now are well into their late seventies, like Helen over there." I pointed to Helen Martino.

"Look," I turned and pointed, "*there's* the clubhouse, right there. It has bathrooms, which some of us need to use. We can make coffee in the kitchen, and we can sit down. Some of us can't be on our feet for long periods of time. You can keep us all corralled in there, and it would be a whole lot more comfortable than standing around out here. We're tired, the sun is going to get hot, and I don't think you want someone passing out and needing medical attention while you take your sweet time doing whatever it is you're doing."

"Wait here," Deputy Levy barked.

He marched back over to the newcomers and spoke with them. After a moment the taller of the two ambled over to where I stood, fuming and staring at the ground.

"I'm Detective Jason Henderson," he introduced himself. "And you are" — I raised my head — "Nurse Gallagher?" He started to smile.

I found my lips curving up in an answering smile. "Deputy Jason!"

"It's Detective Henderson now," he said. "It's nice to see you again, though I'm sorry about the circumstances."

"Same. And I've just retired, so I guess I'm just plain Lily Gallagher now. This is my husband, Michael."

The detective nodded at Michael. "Good to meet you." Turning back to me, he said, "We need to check out a few things here, but I see your point about standing around in the sun. Deputy Levy will escort all of you into the clubhouse so you can be more comfortable. I'll look forward to catching up with you later." This time he did smile, and put two fingers to his forehead in a mock salute.

A moment later, the detective raised his voice to get everyone's attention. "People, we need you all to file into the clubhouse. Now. Deputy Levy will escort you. We'll talk with each one of you for a few minutes, and after we speak with you, you'll be free to leave."

Silently I led the way, tapped in the access code, and opened the door.

Seven

The restrooms were located at the back of the clubhouse, and I hustled straight to them. I desperately needed to pee, since I hadn't stopped to do that before I rushed out of the apartment.

I wasn't the only one. Jennifer and Deb followed me in, talking quietly. The words "who does that cop think he is, anyway?" came through clearly. I totally agreed.

The other women left, but I stayed in the stall. It was the only place I was going to have any privacy for a while and I needed a few minutes. My chest felt tight, and my brain was on overdrive, one thought chasing another. I had to slow it down before I went out to face my friends and neighbors so I forced myself to take deep, calming breaths. I'd be no help to Pru, or Greg, or anyone else, if I couldn't settle myself.

I took another deep breath, then left the stall and stepped up to the sink. My face looked pale in the mirror, and I flashed back to Betty's face when Greg tried to lift her out of the water. Those red eyes. . . I squeezed my own eyes shut, but the image was burned onto my retinas.

I turned on the water, dripped some soap onto my hand, and started scrubbing. Red eyes. . . So, petechial hemorrhage. . . not drowning then. . .

Looking down I realized I was scouring my hands furiously, as though somehow that would wash off all of the morning's hideous events. If Betty didn't drown, that meant only one thing and I definitely wasn't ready to go there. Keeping busy and focusing on other people would help to calm my tumbling thoughts.

As I stepped into the main room, I settled my glasses more firmly on my nose and looked around.

At first glance it looked like a pajama party, with small groups of residents sitting around wearing an assortment of sleepwear and footwear. Why did the the seating groups always make me think of toadstools? Perhaps it was the unappealing gray, brown, and beige color scheme of the furniture and the chintzy indoor/outdoor carpet.

Which made me think of Betty. Oh, right, Betty was responsible for the ugly decor. One of her first acts as president of the condo association board had been to replace the pleasant and inoffensive Berber carpet with something that inconsiderate residents — Betty's words — who wandered in from the pool with wet feet wouldn't damage. Betty had also insisted on the hideous abstract design of bland beiges, claiming it wouldn't show the dirt. Well, maybe it didn't show the dirt, but it sure looked awful. At least she hadn't ripped out the tile that surrounded the carpeted area.

At second glance, it didn't seem like a pajama party at all. The residents spoke in hushed voices so the room was way too quiet, and people weren't milling around the way they would if this were an actual party. Several people were darting little glances at the front doors as though waiting for something bad to happen.

In contrast to the main room, the small kitchen buzzed with activity. Helen Martino bustled around — no surprise, as she usually took over in the kitchen during community gatherings — and Patrick and Linda were helping. At the pool, I was so focused, first on Pru, and then on the body in the pool, that I'd paid no attention to my other neighbors. Now I noticed how rumpled Helen looked, an oversized shirt pulled on over her pajamas and flip flops on her feet. Her gray hair was mussed and hanging down, her face bare of its usual makeup. Oh, well, I looked a mess myself.

Unlike most of the others in the room, the Barrys were both fully dressed. Patrick wore workout gear, and Linda had on shorts, a tee shirt, and casual sandals. Her long dark hair was pulled into a messy bun wrapped in a scrunchie.

Someone had already plugged in the twenty-five-cup urn, and a tray of coffee cups sat on the counter.

"Morning. What can I do?" I asked. Linda glanced up at me, then looked away quickly.

"Nothing really. It's already crowded in here with the three of us," Helen said. "The coffee will be ready in a few minutes. It's too bad we don't have any cream on hand, but we weren't exactly planning an event. We've got dried creamer and sugar, and those will have to do."

"Do we have anything for the tea drinkers?"

"I'll find some tea bags and put the kettle on for hot water."

"Sounds perfect. I'll go around and tell the others."

I rolled my shoulders to relax them, then began moving from one group to another, exchanging greetings and telling my neighbors coffee and tea would be available shortly.

I spotted Keith in the corner next to the entertainment center, sitting near Jennifer. Keith looked a bit bedraggled and he'd wrapped his big towel around himself.

I made my way over to them. "Hi neighbors. Keith, if you need warming up, Helen will have coffee ready at the kitchen pass-through counter in a couple of minutes, or tea, if you prefer."

"Good. I need it."

Jennifer just nodded.

"I'm glad you kept your wits about you this morning," I said to him.

"You've probably never seen a drowning victim still in the water," he said, "but unfortunately I have. A friend of mine in high school drowned. It happened almost in front of me. So when I saw this... her... well, I had to do something." He looked away.

"Oh, I'm so sorry to hear that, and you're right. I've seen them afterwards, in the hospital, but never in the water." I didn't want to admit that it took me a minute to figure out it was more than a bundle of clothes, and I felt a little ashamed that all my professional training flew right out of my head for a second. "Dealing with it in the hospital, with supplies and equipment and support staff, well, it's a lot different from what I saw this morning."

"Sure."

Jennifer was watching us silently. I looked back and forth between the two of them. "You two do know each other, right?"

Jennifer finally spoke. "We do. We are neighbors after all. I introduced myself when he was moving in."

Even in her nightclothes Jennifer appeared elegant, as always. Her light cotton robe worn over silky floral-print pajamas stood out against her dark complexion and curly black hair. In her early sixties, Jennifer — not Jenny, as she'd been careful to point out after I'd used the nickname once — was one of the people I wanted to get to know better now that I was retired and had more time.

"How did you happen to have a towel with you?" she asked Keith. I'd been wondering that myself.

"Habit, I guess. During the summer I like to swim early, before it gets hot, so around six is usually when I head over to do my laps. I already had my trunks on and my towel was laid out by the door, so I guess I grabbed it out of habit when I rushed out to see what the noise was about. Just as well, as it turned out."

I turned away, because I suddenly wanted my husband. I looked around and spotted him sitting with Greg and Dave next to the French doors in the opposite corner. His white hair was easy to spot, among all the bald and semi-bald men in the room. He'd thrown on the shorts he'd worn the day before, along with one of his Red Sox tee shirts. On his feet were the navy Sketchers slip-ons I'd seen by the front door when I was shoving my own feet into shoes.

Greg held a kitchen towel around his shoulders, and another one, very wet, sat discarded on the coffee table in front of him. He'd dried his face and hands, but the rest of him was still soaked. A bit of belly flab showed through a rip in the front of his tee shirt, and his pajama bottoms featured a traditional red and blue plaid design. The fuzzy slippers he'd been wearing when he jumped into the pool lay at his feet like two drowned kittens. Oops, totally inappropriate analogy.

I'd always thought Greg and Betty were a good example of opposites attracting. Where Betty could be bossy, overbearing, and worse, Greg seemed to be a thoroughly nice man. He was quick to volunteer to help his neighbors, and he donated his time to an organization that worked with underprivileged kids.

I grabbed a throw off the back of a nearby couch and draped it over his shoulders, then plopped down into the chair next to Michael. I knew better than to sit on the sofa — it was comfortable enough, but it was too low and too soft. I'd learned the hard way that once you'd sunk into its soft embrace, it was a struggle to stand up again.

"Greg, I'm so sorry about Betty," I said. "This is awful."

"I just can't believe it," he choked. Dave patted his shoulder awkwardly.

While Michael and Dave spoke soothingly to Greg, I thought about Betty. I actually felt relieved that I'd never have to face those cold eyes again. Eyes. . . those red eyes. . . that's not something that happens to a friendly, likable person.

I gave myself a mental shake and tuned back into the conversation in time to hear Greg mumble, "Oh, God, Flossie. . . What's Flossie going to do with her mommy gone?"

"I'm sure you and your pup will cope," I said, trying to sound reassuring. "I'm curious about something, though. I heard you shouting at that deputy outside. What did he say that got you so riled up?"

Greg stared at me blankly. He seemed unaware of the tears leaking down his cheeks.

"Something about a damned lie," I reminded him.

He looked away. "He said it was very suspicious, me being wet. He practically accused me of drowning my wife."

I snorted. "Seriously? That's ridiculous. Everyone knows how devoted you were to each other." Hearing the rattle of cups, I glanced toward the kitchen. "It looks like the coffee's ready, can I get anyone a cup?"

Dave looked toward the kitchen. "I see Deb heading this way with two cups, so I guess I'm set."

Greg shook his head while Michael smiled at me and said, "Sure, honey, thanks."

"Greg, you should have something warm. You don't want to make yourself sick on top of everything else. If coffee doesn't appeal, how about a cup of hot tea?"

"She's a nurse, remember," Michael said. "Best do as she says."

"Alright, I guess. Tea. Anyway, I think coffee would just make me sick."

I fixed coffee for Michael and tea for Greg, adding a couple of sugars to it. When I handed Michael his coffee, he said, "You're not having any?"

"Not yet. Pru must still be outside. I'm going to check on her first."

Officer Levy stood just outside the front door. I started to push it open but he held up a beefy hand. "I just want to check on Pru," I said, "she was in shock and she's still sitting by the pool."

"I'm sure she's fine. You wanted to be inside, so now you need to stay inside until the detective says you can go." He didn't even try to hide the sneer this time.

I stomped back over to the coffee urn and fixed myself a cup, fuming. What an officious ass.

***

How did I get here? Of all the condos in Central Florida, I had to choose this one. I should have stayed away. As it is I nearly lost my head... and I'd better be careful not to do it again. God, I could use a drink. I can't get that terrible face out of my mind. I'll probably have nightmares about it, like I don't have enough already. Why does everyone keep talking? I need some peace and quiet. Got to hold it together.

***

I plopped down next to Michael, spilling a few drops of coffee in the process. Well, at least it wouldn't even be noticeable on the ugly beige-on-beige chair. "I wanted to check on Pru, but that officious jerk Levy wouldn't let me out the door."

"The EMTs are out there, and you asked them to check her for shock." As if I needed reminding. "I'm sure they're keeping an eye on her."

"I hope you're right. But that deputy's a piece of work."

I took a deep breath, then sipped my coffee.

While we waited, Michael and I talked quietly with Dave and Deb about the world outside of Happy Oaks, while Greg sat, dumb with misery, his tea untouched and his wet clothes soaking into the upholstery, refusing to be drawn into conversation. Around the room, other residents were still speaking in hushed voices, shooting uncomfortable looks at Greg.

After what felt like a long time, but was only about ten minutes, Deputy Levy opened the clubhouse door to admit Detective Henderson. Everyone quieted down as he walked to the middle of the room.

He looked very well pulled together for someone who'd probably been roused from sleep at an early hour. His khakis were pressed, and his navy blazer fit his trim form well. I'm sure he had a holstered weapon under it somewhere, but I didn't notice any bulges. I knew he was in his late forties, and although he sported a full head of well trimmed dark hair, he was starting to show a little distinguished gray at the temples.

His blue eyes roamed the room, studying its occupants intently. Was he composing mental descriptions of each of us? Some of the deputies he worked with back in the day referred to him as "laser eyes," and watching him now I could see why.

He waited until he had everyone's attention. "Listen up people, I'll try to make this as painless as possible for you. As you're all aware, one of your residents was found lifeless in your pool this morning. With an unexplained death, we always have to ask a few questions. Once I have some basic information from each of you, you'll be free to go about your business."

I scanned the room, wondering who the detective would talk to first, then realized Pru was still not inside.

"Detective Henderson," I called to get his attention. "Where's Pru MacLeod? She didn't come in here with us from the pool, is she okay? She seemed to be in shock. I tried to check on her but your deputy wouldn't let me leave."

He took a few steps and joined me. "You're right, Mrs. Gallagher. The EMTs are looking after her. Last I saw her, she was still wrapped in a blanket. Now, I need to get things moving here. I'll be back with you shortly."

He turned and strode across the room. I watched as a deputy set two chairs at the table at the front of the room where the condo board had sat during last night's meeting. Was it only last night?

While my attention wandered, Michael and Dave talked about condo business. I was glad Michael had found a way to contribute to our little community, but I had no interest in joining in all those discussions so I tuned them out.

It was impossible not to think about Betty. Betty lavishing affection on Flossie and Greg. . . being charming even while she was bossing people around. . . boasting about her time as Mardi Gras queen in Mobile. . . getting herself elected to the condo board and insisting on having so many things her own way. . . confronting me. . .

Some of the things Betty insisted on were unpleasant but harmless, like the ugly carpet in the clubhouse, but some weren't harmless at all.

A picture of Betty's dead face swam across my mind, and I saw again what I'd noticed in the brief moment when Greg tried to lift Betty's body out of the water. I thought about the whispered confab between Brianna and Nate. I didn't want to be right about this, but why would detectives show up if it was a clear-cut accident? And if it wasn't an accident. . . I still wasn't ready to go there.

I realized Deb was speaking to me. "Oh, sorry, Deb, I was miles away."

"I was just making small talk. This is not exactly the way I planned to start my day." Deb didn't look very pixie-like this morning.

"Tell me about it. Were you asleep?"

"No, I was on my treadmill when I noticed people making for the pool. I had no idea what was going on, but I woke Dave and told him something was happening and we hightailed it out the door. I didn't even give him time to dress! Now I wish I'd stayed home and finished my workout."

"Well, that explains the serious-looking running shoes." I smiled as I took in her feet, tee shirt and jogging pants. "You're lucky you were already up. I got woken out of a very sound sleep by Pru's screaming. Of course, I didn't know that's what it was at the time."

"We never heard her, not from our apartment. But I could see something was going on. How on earth do you suppose Betty drowned in the pool during the night?" Deb lowered her voice so Greg, still sitting numbly next to her, wouldn't hear.

"It's very strange, isn't it?" But I'm not sure it was an accident." The words were out before I knew it.

"What?" Michael and Dave both looked up.

I waited. Did I really want to open this can of worms? Once our husbands went back to their own conversation I said, "It may be just my imagination and the fact that I read too many murder mysteries, but I don't think we'd have a police detective here asking questions if it was a routine drowning. This probably isn't the best time to talk about it." I tipped my head toward Greg, and Deb nodded. Michael must have overheard what I said, though, because he had that what-the-dickens look on his face.

Now that I'd voiced my suspicion for the first time, it seemed to develop a life of its own. I pictured again what I'd seen so briefly as Greg had lifted his wife's body out of the water. If I was right, it meant that someone, probably one of my friends or neighbors, someone I knew and liked, had ended Betty's life, brutally, and then tried to cover it up. It was hard to wrap my head around the idea, and it felt more than a little scary. Did I even want to know? I shivered, wishing I was somewhere else, away from all these people I thought I knew.

I noticed Detective Henderson pull a small notebook out of his shirt pocket and head for the kitchen where Patrick, Linda, and Helen were chatting as they tidied up. He led Patrick over to the table and waved him into the seat with its back to the room. The detective sat across from him, with his back to the wall.

Linda stood in the kitchen doorway watching them and twisting that chunky gold bracelet around and around. There was no sign of her usual friendliness and self assurance.

Of course I couldn't hear what the detective and Patrick were saying, but I watched the detective jot down a few notes, and then shake Patrick's hand. Deputy Levy led him out the clubhouse door.

The detective repeated the process with Linda, and then Helen. I watched as he gestured Helen toward the front door. They spoke briefly, then Helen marched back to the kitchen.

After dismissing Helen, the detective looked around the room again, this time singling out Jennifer. She spent about five minutes with him before he sent her on her way.

The detective looked over at the remaining residents — Michael and me, Dave and Deb, Keith, and of course, Greg Harris. He walked over to our corner and tapped Deb on the shoulder.

"Come with me, please."

He'd only been questioning Deb for about thirty seconds when Dave started fidgeting. "What's he saying to her?"

"Probably the same thing he's saying to everyone." I tried to sound reassuring. "What's your name, what's your address, why were you out at the pool this morning, what did you see?"

"Oh, I guess." A few seconds later he said, "I wish he'd hurry up, I'm hungry."

"I suspect we all are," Michael said. "It'll probably just be a few more minutes."

The little group was silent.

In a few minutes Detective Henderson was back, gesturing to Dave to follow as Deb walked out the front door.

Keith was next in the hot seat. Until the past couple of days, I hadn't paid a lot of attention to him. He'd always seemed distant and unapproachable, so I barely knew him at all even though he'd lived downstairs from us for six months. Apparently he was one of those who liked to work out early in the morning and kept himself in very good shape, unlike some of the other men in the community.

After Keith left, it was Michael's turn. Finally the detective gestured me over. Only Greg was left, sitting by himself.

As soon as I sat down, I said, "Jason, I know Greg is the victim's husband and I imagine you'll need more time with him than with the rest of us, but he's still soaking wet and I'm concerned about him. And Pru, how's she doing?"

"Don't worry, Mrs. Gallagher, we're aware. We'll be as quick as we can with Mr. Harris, and you'll be free to check on your friend in a few minutes, as soon as we're done here."

Settling into his chair, he picked up his pen.

"Okay, for the record, state your full name and your unit number."

"Lily Gallagher, unit E4."

"And why were you at the pool this morning?"

I explained how the screaming had woken me, and that from my bedroom window I'd seen Pru standing by the pool.

"I didn't know what was wrong," I told him, "but I figured she needed help."

"What did you see when you arrived at the pool area?"

I described the scene, and my shock when Pru pointed to the pool. "It was confusing. I just barely registered that it was a body, not just a bundle of clothes, when Keith jumped into the pool. As soon as he'd moved her close enough to the side I checked for a pulse, but didn't find one. Michael already had nine-one-one on the phone. Then Greg came running and yelling and he jumped into the pool, too."

I swallowed hard, recalling the swollen face.

"And what happened next?" Henderson prompted.

"Um, Greg shoved Keith aside and tried to lift her out of the pool. It was a pretty nasty sight. I've seen some awful things in the ER, but when it's someone you know. . ." My voice trailed off.

The detective gave me a moment to collect myself. "And then?"

"Well, he must have been shocked because he took one look at that face and dropped her back in the pool. Poor guy, he'll probably have nightmares. It was obvious to me she was past help, but then Keith took over again and finally got her out of the water. I was just about to try CPR anyway when the EMTs arrived and took charge."

"Okay, you're free to go, but I may be around with more questions later."

"Has she . . . have they taken the body away?"

"Not yet, we're still waiting for the Medical Examiner to sign off. And the pool area is to be considered a crime scene, and off limits until further notice."

"Can I at least check on Pru?"

"Of course, just don't touch anything if you can help it."

I nodded my understanding and stood. "By the way, what should I call you now? Since we'll probably be seeing a bit of each other here?"

He raised an eyebrow. "Discipline must be maintained and all that, so you should address me as Detective." He gave a mock bow and I chuckled. I'd always enjoyed his offbeat sense of humor on the rare occasions he displayed it. I dropped a small curtsey, then turned and hurried out the front door, hoping he wouldn't keep Greg shivering in his wet clothes for much longer.

Pru was still by the pool, slumped on one of the chairs with a blanket wrapped around her. On the opposite side of the pool, the EMTs and another man were gathered around something on the ground. The new guy must be the medical examiner.

"Pru, are you feeling any better?" I called out when I got close, but before I reached the gate, one of the men marched toward me. I recognized him as the detective who'd accompanied Henderson. His badge said *Lopez*.

"Ma'am, step back, this is a crime scene."

"Detective Henderson said it was okay for me to check on her. I'm a nurse and she's my friend."

"You've spoken with him?"

"I've just left him. He told me I could check on Pru when we were done."

"I guess that would be alright."

He opened the gate and I rushed over to Pru. "Oh, you poor thing." I pulled up a chair next to her.

"I'm sorry I made such a fool of myself."

"You didn't. You had a perfectly normal reaction to something awful. Don't beat yourself up about it." Pru nodded mutely.

"Do you mind?" I reached for her wrist, "I'd like to check your pulse."

"Okay."

After a moment I said, "It's still a little fast but nothing to be concerned about. Do you think you could swallow some coffee or eat something?"

Pru nodded again.

"Is she free to go?" I asked Detective Lopez. "I'd like to get some food into both of us."

"We've got her address, and Detective Henderson already spoke to both of you, right?" We both nodded. "Okay, then. We'll be around later if we need anything else."

I helped Pru out of her chair. "Do you still need the blanket?"

"Not really. I warmed up okay already, but it was just too much trouble to move it."

I folded it and placed it on the chair. Someone would retrieve it later. Slowly we made our way over to Building E and started climbing the stairs to Michael's and my condo. I glanced over my shoulder, and watched Brianna and Nate strapping Betty's lifeless body onto the gurney while the medical examiner looked on.

As I opened the front door, I called out, "Michael, I've brought Pru home with me for breakfast."

Michael poked his head out of the kitchen. He looked a lot more chipper than I felt, and had obviously taken the time to shower, shave, and put on clean clothes. He'd gone for comfort, sporting well worn denim shorts topped by his favorite tee shirt, the one that featured Wall-E and Eve flying around in space leaving purple trails behind them, and flip flops.

"Hi Pru," he said. "I was just starting to scramble some eggs. I'll throw a couple more in the bowl."

"Do I smell coffee?" I asked.

"A full pot. I figured we'd need it."

"Great. Pru, will you be okay with Michael while I take a quick shower and get myself dressed?"

"Sure, especially if I can have a cup of that coffee!"

"Coming right up." Michael gave me a quick hug, then ushered Pru into the kitchen while I made a beeline for the bedroom. Finally! I pulled off my slightly sweaty pajamas and robe and turned on the shower.

Eight

After the events of the morning, I felt grimy and I couldn't wait to feel clean. But even though the shower was warm and soothing, I hurried. Besides, I was hungry, and I was worried about Pru. She'd had that big shock from her daughter yesterday, and now she'd just found a dead body. I didn't know which one she was more upset about.

My stomach rumbled as I threw on some clothes appropriate for the early June weather. Even though it was only a few minutes after eight in the morning, the temperature was over eighty with matching humidity, so I put on shorts and sandals. Hoping the bright colors would cheer me up, I chose a shirt that was all pinks, blues, and violets. I didn't bother with makeup or jewelry.

When I walked into the kitchen, Pru was staring at the plate of scrambled eggs and English muffins in front of her.

I grabbed a clean cup and sniffed appreciatively as I filled it. Our coffee certainly smelled — and tasted — better than what I'd just had at the clubhouse. As I set my cup on the table, Michael slid a filled plate onto the table for me, and started plating up a serving for himself.

I plopped into my chair, surprised at how hungry I felt. The food looked and smelled delicious. It had been an exciting morning so far, although horrifying, and I'd developed a surprising appetite. I drenched my English muffin in butter, deciding for once not to worry about all those grams of fat that liked to cling to my hips.

Pru took a reviving sip of coffee. She picked up her fork, but then put it down again.

"Michael, this looks great," she said, "but I don't know if I can eat a bite."

"It's okay," I reached over and squeezed her hand. "You've had a big shock. But you should try. You'll feel better when you've got something inside you."

She nodded and lifted a dainty forkful of eggs to her mouth, then took a big gulp of her coffee.

Then her fork clattered on the dish. "It was just so horrible," she blurted out. "The worst thing is, I was sitting by the pool for about five minutes before I even noticed her. It. Maybe if I'd seen her right away I could have done something to help her." Her face puckered as if she was about to cry.

"I doubt it," I said. "Based on the little I saw, it looked to me like she'd been gone for a while. I don't think there's anything you could have done."

"Do you really think so?" She blinked a few times.

"I do."

"The thing was, I was already upset to begin with, you know, Lily. That's why I was up so early, I couldn't sleep, worrying about my daughter and that whole mess."

I nodded encouragingly. Michael had quietly taken his own plate of food over to the counter and eased himself onto a stool.

"So I wasn't paying a lot of attention to anything around me," Pru continued. "But then, after a few minutes I noticed this kind of dark shadow in the water. I thought it was odd, so I got up to see if maybe a branch or something had fallen in. When I got closer I saw movement and I thought maybe someone had dropped a towel in the water, but then I saw hair. . ." She gulped convulsively.

"All of a sudden I couldn't look any more, and it got really noisy. It wasn't until you had hold of me that I realized the noise was coming from me."

"Well, I was certainly glad when you stopped screaming," I said. "For both our sakes."

Pru took another sip of coffee. "This feels really good going down. I'm just starting to realize how sore my throat is."

"Not surprising, you should probably see a doctor and make sure you haven't done any actual damage. You were screaming for a long time."

"Sure, I'll call when I get home. I'll also try some tea with honey and lemon later. Maybe that will help."

"Do you want tea with honey now?"

"Thanks, but right now I need the coffee more."

"How about some honey on your English muffin?"

"Sure"

I stepped to the pantry and came back with a jar of organic Tupelo. "This is my favorite kind. I always think of that old Van Morrison song when I eat it. You know, 'she's as sweet as Tupelo honey.'" I was off key, but it made Pru smile for the first time.

She added a thin layer of honey to her muffin. Then she stopped, knife poised in mid-air. "Oh, I'm an awful person."

I felt my eyes opening wider. "What are you talking about?"

"When I was sitting there like a useless lump watching you all try to help, I didn't even realize who it was until Greg started yelling." She gulped again and her hand went to her throat, "And I thought, oh thank goodness, now Lottie will be able to move home, and then I realized what a terrible person I am. How could I think that?" She hid her face in her hands.

I went around the table and drew Pru into a hug. "We all have ugly thoughts sometimes. That doesn't make you a terrible person, it just makes you human. You need to cut yourself some slack."

She lifted her head. "You're right, I know you're right, it's just," she sniffled, reached for a napkin, and blew her nose. "It's hard."

"I know."

We were silent for a couple minutes. Then, as Pru took her last bite of muffin, there was a thunderous knocking at the front door.

"I'll go," Michael said. A moment later he ushered Detective Henderson into the kitchen, which felt a little crowded now.

The detective nodded at us, then zeroed in on Pru. "Ms. MacLeod, are you feeling better? You seemed pretty shaken up earlier."

Pru nodded. "A little, thank you." She sounded like she had a cold and her eyes were still wet.

"I'm afraid I have some additional questions for you. Would you come with me, please?" It didn't sound like a request.

"Can't you just ask me here?" Pru asked.

"It would be better to speak in private."

Pru stiffened. "Well, I want Lily to stay with me. I don't have anything to tell you that I can't say in front of her."

"If that's what you want," he agreed after a moment's hesitation.

"Why don't we move to the living room," I suggested. "Detective, we've finished the scrambled eggs, but you're welcome to a cup of coffee if you'd like."

"That would be much appreciated."

"How do you take it?"

"Just a little milk or cream, please, no sugar."

I took another coffee mug off the shelf, added half and half, and then poured in the last of the coffee. After handing it to him, I led the way to the living room and indicated a chair with a side table next to it. I set down a coaster and he carefully placed his mug on it, sat down, and took his small notebook and pen from his pocket.

Pru and I sat next to each other on the couch opposite the detective, and Michael followed and took a chair.

"So, Ms. MacLeod," Detective Henderson tapped his notebook with his pen, "You were apparently the first person at the pool this morning, and you raised the alarm. Can you walk me through what brought you to the pool in the first place?"

"I couldn't sleep," Pru began. The detective interrupted.

"Did something wake you? Did you hear something?"

"I don't think so. It was just one of those times. I have them pretty often where I wake up and just can't go back to sleep. You'll find out when you get to be my age."

I nodded in agreement.

"Okay, so walk me through your morning, from the time you got up," the detective said. "Start with the time, please."

Pru drew a deep breath, her forehead furrowed in concentration. "I'm not sure of the exact time," she said. "I try not to look at the clock when I have nights like that, because it's just frustrating."

"Approximately, then."

"If I had to guess, I'd say around five, maybe quarter after."

"What did you do then?"

"Well, I used the bathroom and brushed my teeth, then I threw on some clothes. I don't like lounging around in my pajamas. Then I went to the kitchen for a glass of water. I thought about making some coffee, but I decided I wasn't ready to do that. So I went out on my porch. I was going to sit there for a while, but then I realized how nice it was outside, and I decided to go sit by the pool. I find that being near water helps me think."

"And what was it you had to think about?"

"Oh, just some family stuff." Pru glanced over at me. The detective jotted something in his notebook, then looked at her expectantly. “So I went over to the pool, and sat in one of the chairs.”

“Which chair?”

She stared at him. “I don’t remember. Is it important?”

“If it is, we’ll come back to it. Moving on, in order to get to the pool, you just have to go down your front steps and in front of Mrs. Harris’ unit and then directly to one of the gates, is that correct?”

“Yes, that’s right.”

“Did you notice any lights on in their apartment? Did you hear anything?”

“No, nothing. It was all dark and quiet.” He nodded for her to continue.

“So I went and sat down,” Pru repeated.

“Hang on,” Henderson interrupted. “Which gate did you use to enter the pool area?”

“Well, I usually use the one in front of the clubhouse doors, but I can’t be positive.”

“Okay.”

“I was there for several minutes before I noticed something — oh!” she exclaimed.

“What is it?”

“I remember where I was sitting. After I went through the gate, I grabbed the first chair to the left, next to the four-person table in the corner. I put my keys on the table.” Pru started patting her pockets, a look of consternation on her face. “I think I left them there.”

“Yes we did find a set of keys,” the detective confirmed. “I’ll get them back to you when we’re done processing the scene. Now, please continue.”

Pru thought for a moment. “I was sitting there for a few minutes before I noticed something about the pool looked odd. It was still pretty dark out.” Her breath coming a little faster, she continued, “There was a darker spot in the pool in the deep end.

At first I thought maybe a branch had fallen in, so I walked over and realized that couldn't be it, because it was moving too much. Kind of wavy, you know? So then I figured someone had left a towel out overnight and it had blown into the water. The pool pump was running, so the water wasn't completely still."

Her eyes grew wide, and I put my hand on her shoulder. "Then I saw. . . I saw. . . hair. . . floating. . . "

I glared at the detective, who ignored me. "And then?" he prompted.

Pru swallowed convulsively. "Then I couldn't look any more. The next thing I knew Lily was holding me. That's when I realized I'd been screaming my throat raw."

"Okay, thank you. I appreciate you walking me through it."

He looked at me. "I'm trying to establish a timeline here. Any idea what time it was when you reached Ms. MacLeod?"

I thought. "Well, I did check my watch when I woke up and it said 5:47. I was coming out of a sound sleep, so I was a little groggy. It was probably a minute or more before I was out of bed and at the window. Another minute to grab my robe and throw on my shoes. I don't know how long it took me to get down my stairs and around to the far side of the pool where Pru was standing, I don't move as fast as I used to. Maybe another two minutes? So it was likely 5:51 or 5:52, maybe a minute later, when I got to her."

"You went down your front steps and through the gate directly in front of your unit?"

"That's right."

"Was anyone else there besides you and Ms. MacLeod?"

"Maybe? I'm not sure." At his quizzical look — how did he raise just one eyebrow so elegantly? — I continued. "When I first got there I didn't see anyone but Pru. After she stopped screaming I could hear other people moving around, but I didn't specifically notice anyone, or when they arrived, or if anyone else was there before I was. I wasn't paying attention to anyone but Pru."

"I didn't see anyone before... before..." Pru swallowed again, then continued. "I didn't see or hear anyone when I was sitting there thinking."

"When you noticed other people arriving, who all did you see?"

Pru just shrugged, and he looked at me.

"Well, obviously my downstairs neighbor, Keith Johnson. He seemed to figure out what was in the pool pretty fast."

"Who else?"

I tried to recreate the scene in my mind. "I heard people, more than saw them. At first I was only aware of Pru. After she stopped screaming, I heard people moving but by then I was focused on what Keith was doing, and trying to find a pulse. Of course Michael was there, because he handed me the phone. After that I noticed Deborah and David Wheelock, Jennifer Nelson, Patrick and Linda Barry."

"And Greg," Pru added. "Greg Harris. He was one of the last to show up."

"Tim and Helen Martino, too," I said. "I have the impression they were late arrivals, but I'm not sure. It was pretty chaotic. But that's most everyone from the two buildings closest to the pool."

"Tim Martino?" the detective frowned. "I've got a Helen Martino on my list, but no Tim."

Michael cleared his throat. "He and Helen showed up after Greg did. He left after I announced that the police were on their way."

"And why would he do that?" the detective asked.

"I have no idea," Michael said.

The detective made another note. Then he looked at each of us, and again I felt as though I was a specimen on a microscope slide. I was beginning to understand why some of his coworkers called him 'laser eyes.' Back when he was a deputy and in and out of my ER frequently with patients and suspects, we got along well, but I was starting to feel uncomfortable with him. Well, I reminded myself, being able to separate the personal from the professional makes people better at their jobs. As a nurse, I often had to do it myself.

"How do you explain a death by drowning in your community's pool?" he asked me.

"I thought that was your job." Then I couldn't stop myself. "Death by drowning," I repeated. "Was it really?"

"What do you mean?" This time his tone was sharp.

I took a breath. "Well, I only caught a glimpse, but it didn't look like drowning to me. I've seen drowning victims a few times in the ER."

"If not drowning, then what?" Those laser eyes were focused on me again.

I thought for a moment, then said carefully, "I didn't examine her, but what I saw looked more like suffocation than drowning. The paramedic, Brianna, saw it, too, I'm sure, because she took Nate aside and it was obvious they were talking about something pretty serious. It was only after that when Deputy Levy called for detectives."

Pru gasped, and Michael's mouth was open slightly.

The detective's blue eyes bored into me for another few seconds before he relaxed his gaze. "Very observant, Mrs. Gallagher. That'll be for the medical examiner to decide, but at this point we're investigating it as such. I'd appreciate it if that goes no farther than this room," he said firmly, fixing those laser eyes on each of us in turn.

He drained his cup and stood. "Thanks for the coffee, I'll be in touch. And you call me if you think of anything else." He handed a business card to me and another one to Pru.

"What about my keys?" Pru asked.

"I'll check with the crime scene guys and let you know. Do any of your neighbors have a spare apartment key you can use in the meantime?"

"Actually, we do," Michael said. "We look after Pru's place when she's away, and she does the same for us."

The detective gave a brief nod.

As Michael walked him to the door, Pru shivered. "I've lived here for over ten years, and I never felt unsafe until now. I hope Henderson catches this maniac fast."

"Me too. But I'm pretty sure we're not looking for a maniac."

"What do you mean?" Pru stared at me.

I shook my head, as if that would straighten out my flyaway thoughts. "I need more coffee." I headed for the kitchen.

Pru was right. Happy Oaks didn't feel happy or safe right now. Should I share what I'd been thinking since I saw those red eyes? Well, I'd already blurted it out to Deb, and just now the detective confirmed they were treating the death as suspicious.

I returned to the living room with fresh coffee in time to hear Pru say, "Poor Greg. I can't imagine what it's like to lose your husband or wife that way. How could it have happened? And especially after they had that big fight last night."

"They had a fight?" I asked, surprised.

"Oh, it was a doozy. I'm amazed you didn't hear them shouting all the way over here. As it was, after I got off the phone with you I was on my back porch watering the plants, and their porch door must have been open. Greg was yelling something about she promised she wouldn't do it any more, and she yelled back that if he gave a damn about her he would have taken care of it and not left it up to her as usual. Then she flounced out of the house and took off."

"That must have been something. I don't think I've ever heard her raise her voice in the whole time they've lived here. What's it been, about four years now?"

"That sounds about right," Pru agreed. "She's been on the condo board for at least two years, and I think they were here a couple years before that."

Michael started pacing. "Well, she certainly raised her voice to me yesterday morning"

"What do you mean?" Pru asked.

"We had an argument and she had a temper tantrum like a two-year-old. Complete with screaming."

"That's weird, she always struck me as an easygoing person," Pru said. "But two screaming fights in two days? That's a lot."

"If you'd asked me a few days ago, I would have agreed," I said. "I guess I was so busy running around talking to everyone about Lottie's waiver these last few days that you and I haven't talked. She's turned out to be quite different than I thought."

"Well, over the time I was on the board I noticed she had a way of forcing people to do what she wanted. In the nicest possible way, of course." Michael started pacing. "It got worse after she became president."

"Seriously? You never said anything about that before," I said. "What do you mean?"

He shrugged. "Sometimes during a meeting one of the other board members would start to say something and she'd give them this look, like they'd better stop if they knew what was good for them. And usually they did. And then," he finally stopped pacing and sat down again, "last night, the vote for Charlotte's waiver failed because Liz and Linda did a complete turnaround from what they told Lily they planned to do."

"Well, I guess I'm surprised but not surprised," Pru said. "I thought I was the only one, that everyone else liked her. I mean, she seemed so friendly all the time, but there was one time, a few months after they'd moved in, when Betty kind of creeped me out."

"You too?" I asked. "Why didn't you ever say something about it?"

"It was nothing I could ever put my finger on. She was being super friendly with me and in the course of conversation I let slip about something I'd done in the past that I was ashamed of. She was saying things that sounded sympathetic, but she had this look." She hunched her shoulders. "I can't describe it."

"The weird thing was, I tried to change the subject, but she kept coming back to it." Pru picked up her coffee cup, then put it down again. "She kept saying things like, 'don't worry, your secret's safe with me' and that sort of thing. I finally told her it wasn't a secret, and it wasn't a big deal, it was just something I didn't enjoy talking about. For a minute I thought she actually looked disappointed."

Michael frowned and crossed his arms. "I think she liked knowing things about people. Secrets."

"I wonder if she learned too much about the wrong person," I said, choosing my words carefully. "If she liked knowing secrets about people. . ." I took a deep breath, finally putting into words what I'd been mulling over since the detectives had arrived on the scene.

My words came out in a rush. "I don't think Betty Louise Harris drowned. I think she was suffocated, and placed in the pool to make it look like she drowned, and the detective kind of confirmed it just now. And if you two are right and she liked to know things about people that they didn't want others to find out about, then I bet she found out too much about the wrong person and they made sure she couldn't tell their secret to anyone, ever."

Michael's mouth drooped a little, and his shoulders sagged. "I'm afraid it wouldn't surprise me."

"Because suffocation is pretty personal," I added.

Pru shivered again. "Michael, if you wouldn't mind getting my key, I think I'd like to go home and shower and change out of these clothes. After what I've seen and heard this morning, I feel dirty."

"Exactly, I felt that way, too," I said. "The shower helped. Do you want me to come with you?"

Pru considered for a moment. "No, I'll be alright. I'm too wrung out for any more screaming episodes. After I shower I'll curl up on my sofa with Cocoa and a book."

"Are you sure you'll be okay with just you and the kitty? And what about your throat, are you going to call your doctor?"

"Of course," Pru said, hoisting herself to her feet with an obvious effort. "See you later."

Michael met her in the living room doorway with her spare key and walked her to the front door. He stood watching her for a minute.

Returning to the living room he sat down heavily next to me and sighed. "What a morning. I have a feeling this little community is going to be turned inside out."

"I have a feeling you're right." The thought made me sad.

"So how is it you know the handsome detective?"

"It was a few years back, when he was still just a deputy."

"Sure."

"It was when I did that six-month stint in the ER, before I decided I was definitely better suited for OB. He used to be in and out of there a lot, sometimes escorting injured suspects, or interviewing patients or whatever. He was a nice young man. I dealt with a fair number of police officers in one way and another, and he always struck me as one who got into policing for the right reasons."

"What do you mean?"

"Well, some guys turn to police work because they want to throw their weight around, have an excuse to carry a gun, that sort of thing. A few get involved because they honestly want to make the community a better place. He was one of those."

"Maybe knowing him will give you an inside track."

"Inside track? What are you talking about?" I asked.

"I can already tell you're wondering who killed Betty."

"And you're not? I'd be surprised if there's a single person in this place who wouldn't be wondering about that if they knew her death wasn't an accident. So now I've got my very own personal murder mystery to investigate." I shivered. "Except when I'm reading it in a book, I don't feel scared or nervous."

Michael reached for my hand and pulled me into a hug. "Don't let that curiosity pull you into a situation you can't get out of," he said seriously. "I know you want answers, and so do I, but you should really stay out of it and let the detective do his job."

"Yes, dear," I sing-songed, only half mockingly.

***

Watchful eyes tracked Pru as she walked from Lily and Michael's condo, around the pool enclosure, and back to her own unit. What had she seen? What did they tell the detective? Why the devil was she out at the pool in the dark anyway? Was she going to spoil everything?

Nine

After Pru left, Michael headed into the bedroom for a nap. I was exhausted, but too wound up to sleep, so I kicked off my sandals and put my feet up on the couch, trying to read. An hour later I set the book aside as a lost cause. I just couldn't concentrate.

My stomach grumbled audibly and I realized I was hungry. I shouldn't have been surprised, since it was nearly noon. What a morning! I stretched and swung my feet down, thinking about what we had in the refrigerator for lunch just as Michael came out of the bedroom.

"I need to grab something to eat quickly and then go meet with Dave and Jeff. We have some condo board business we need to take care of, now that the board president is dead."

"Oh? What's going to happen to the board?"

"I'm not sure." He rummaged in the refrigerator. "I can heat up that leftover chili from the other night, if you want. Was there any cornbread left?"

"I think so. That sounds fine to me." I joined him in the kitchen and pulled out a saucepan. "Dump the chili in here and I'll put the cornbread in the microwave to warm it up."

Once we were seated with fragrant bowls of chili steaming in front of us, I asked, "Any thoughts about who will take over as president of the board?"

"Probably Jeff. He's the logical choice since he's the vice president already. That's if he even wants the job."

"Makes sense." I took a bite of cornbread and listened to him explain the upcoming changes.

"Do you think you'll stay on the board now that Betty's gone?" I asked.

He took a bite of cornbread and chewed before responding. "That's another question I can't answer. I guess I'll need to see how it shakes out. I'll finish out the year, anyway." He thought for a moment. "I like contributing to the community, but the board has been a lot of work. Maybe more than I bargained for. The thing is, I don't know how much of that was Betty and her shenanigans and how much is just the nature of the beast. I don't have a lot to compare it to."

"But you were on the board before Betty, was it less work then?"

"I was learning the ropes when Betty sailed in and took over. Remember, I'd just been appointed to fill Fred's unexpired term after he moved into assisted living." He stood up and carried his dishes over to the sink. "Anyway, I need to get going. We'll be over at the clubhouse if you need me."

He rinsed his bowl and put his dishes and silverware in the dishwasher and then stepped out the sliding glass door. After he left, I puttered around the kitchen, absently putting things away and tidying.

I wondered how Greg was doing, and if he had any ideas about who might have hated Betty enough to kill her. Maybe I should bring him some food. That was an appropriate excuse for a visit at a time like this. What could I pull together quickly?

A few minutes later I had a pot of water coming to a boil on the stove, and the ingredients for a tuna noodle casserole on the counter. Not elegant, but quick, and I seemed to recall that Greg had gone back for seconds when I'd brought one to a potluck at the clubhouse.

While the pasta was boiling I found the casserole dish that I always used for potluck suppers, the one marked with my name so I'd be sure of getting it back.

I assembled the casserole, taped a small card with heating instructions to the side of the dish, then placed it inside an insulated bag with handles for easy carrying.

Quickly I ran a comb through my hair and swiped on a dab of lipstick. Then I picked up the casserole and left the apartment.

From the top of my steps, I could see yellow crime scene tape festooned around the pool area. Normally on a warm, sunny day like this one the pool would be a busy place, with bodies sprawled out on the loungers, or sitting around the tables that occupied the larger areas at each of the corners of the pool enclosure. Today it was deserted.

Greg would have the ground-level view of the pool from the opposite side. What a terrible thing for him to have to look at whenever he glanced out his windows.

I made my way around the pool and over to Building D, where I walked up to Greg's front door and rat-tatted with the knocker. After a moment Helen Martino opened the door. She'd obviously been home since I last saw her in the clubhouse, because she was fully dressed now, and her hair was tidied back into its usual chignon.

"Helen! I should have known I'd find you here, always helping everyone. I brought a casserole for Greg."

"Sure, come on in." Helen waved an arm in a welcoming gesture. "Let's check if there's room in the fridge." I followed Helen into the kitchen, where she bustled over to the refrigerator and started rearranging its contents.

This was the first time I'd seen the Harris' kitchen since they updated it last year. I hadn't missed much. Cold and bland, I thought with distaste, just like that ugly clubhouse carpet, just like Betty. The walls were a fashionable gray, the countertops a gray granite, and the cupboards and appliances were white. I was glad I didn't have to spend any time here.

"This was nice of you," Helen said. "I haven't made anything yet myself, but I'm sure others will be coming by with various dishes soon enough. You're the first."

"How's Greg doing?"

"Not too well, as you'd expect. Tim's with him in the living room. Dave was here earlier, and he told me he had to help Greg shower and dress. Come on through." Helen deposited the casserole into the refrigerator.

In the living room, Tim was glaring at Greg, who slumped over in his chair, sniffling occasionally. Even though he'd showered earlier, he looked rumpled, as if he'd pulled the nearest clothes out of the hamper. Flossie was curled up in her little doggie bed next to an empty chair, probably the one Betty usually sat in, and the air around them felt heavy with grief.

This room was all Betty, with bland colors and abstract designs, but, surprisingly, ruffles everywhere a ruffle could be attached. On one wall was a decorative plate showing an airbrushed image of Flossie dressed in a little pink tutu with a matching pink bow around her neck. In a competition for the trashiest pet images, Betty could have given Dolores Umbridge a run for her money, I thought sourly, her airbrushed Flossie in a tutu against Umbridge's foul kittens. How did Greg stand it?

I crossed the room quickly. "Greg, let me say again how sorry I am about Betty."

Greg looked up. "Why?" he snarled. "Did you kill her?"

I stepped back, stunned.

"Oh, God, I'm such a mess." He hid his face in his hands. Then he shook his head. "I'm sorry, I shouldn't have said that. I just. . . Anyway, I've just lost my wife, and the police were acting like I killed her or something."

He dropped his face into his hands again, and his voice was muffled. "I don't know what to do, what to think, and somehow I have to do it all without Betty. So I'm saying things I don't mean. Anyway. . ." his voice trailed off.

I nodded. "That's totally understandable. Is there anything I can do? Someone I can call for you? Do you want someone to come stay with you?"

Greg looked at me blankly. "Call? For what?"

Wow, he really was a mess. I didn't think he'd be telling me anything helpful. Aloud, I said, "Do you need to notify anyone about her death? Any family members?"

Helen spoke up. "Greg, didn't Betty keep an address book somewhere?"

"Address book?"

Helen looked helplessly at me and nervously patted her chignon. "I think it's too soon."

Tim chose that moment to join the conversation. "Pull yourself together, Greg, you're acting like a little baby." He wasn't talking so much as barking, like a drill sergeant commanding a bunch of unruly troops.

"Tim, that's not helpful," his wife said. "Can't you be nice for a change?" Tim glowered at her, then abruptly stood up and announced, "I'm leaving." He stomped out of the apartment.

"Greg, have you had anything to eat today?" I asked gently.

He didn't respond, so Helen answered for him. "I got him to drink some coffee, and I toasted him a bagel. He only swallowed a couple bites."

"We need to find something that will slip down easily. Is there any yogurt or anything like that in the fridge?"

"I'm not sure, I'll look." She bustled into the kitchen.

"Greg, you know I was a nurse for a long time, right?" I asked. Greg nodded. "So I'm telling you as a medical professional that you need to eat something. You'll feel better and be able to think more clearly once you have some food inside you. You need to eat."

Helen came back waving a cup of blueberry yogurt and a spoon. I took them from her, placed them on the end table next to Greg's chair, and pulled a footstool over. Sitting down, I opened the yogurt, stuck in the spoon, and held it up to Greg's mouth.

"Eat!" Obediently, Greg opened his mouth. A few minutes later, the yogurt was gone.

"Helen, would you get Greg a glass of water?" A minute later Helen handed me the glass and I held it up in front of Greg. "Can you drink this yourself or do I need to help you?"

Greg reached for the glass and gulped down about half of it.

"That's better," I said approvingly. "Now, how do you feel?"

Greg looked surprised. "A little better, actually."

I smiled. "I understand this is hard, maybe the hardest thing you've ever been through, but it will be a lot easier if you remember to eat and drink regularly. Your car can't run on empty, and neither can you."

He nodded.

"Good. Now, let me ask you again. Is there anyone who needs to be notified?"

"Hang on a second." He walked over to the roll top desk in the corner and came back with a book.

"Here's Betty's address book." He held it up. "Anyway, she still has a sister in Mobile, and some friends who would want to know. And I suppose I'll have to break it to my mother and some of my family. We lost our son a few years back, so at least he's spared this."

I'm sure my surprise showed. "Betty told me you didn't have any kids and all your folks are gone."

Greg groaned. "She and Mom didn't get along, so, anyway, after we moved here she just refused to talk about her. She'd tell people our parents were gone, but it's not true. And she hated to talk about our son Jimmy, so it was easier to just tell people we never had children."

"I'm so sorry." I couldn't think what to say. "That must have been hard for you."

Greg nodded.

"Do you want to call your mother, or would you like someone to help you with that?"

"I can call my mom and Betty's sister, and they can tell other family members and closest friends."

"Sounds like a plan. Now, you don't have to do this today, but you need to start thinking about making arrangements."

"Arrangements?" He looked at me blankly.

"For a funeral or memorial service, and everything that goes with it."

Greg buried his face in his hands. "Betty always took care of everything. I wouldn't know where to start."

"There are people who can help with that," Helen said, "but you'll still have some decisions to make. Can you do that?"

Before he could answer there was a knock on the front door, and Flossie's head lifted expectantly. Deb Wheelock's voice floated in. "Greg? Can I come in?" Flossie put her head down again, and whined softly.

"Sure, in the living room," Greg hollered.

A moment later Deb entered the room, carrying a casserole dish in a carrier. "Great minds think alike." I smiled at her. "I just brought one a few minutes ago."

"I told Dave I'd meet him here after the guys are done with their board business," Deb said. "Let me put this in the fridge," and she headed toward the kitchen.

A moment later she was back. "Greg, what can I say? I'm so sorry for your loss. I can't imagine what you're going through."

“Thank you,” Greg mumbled.

“I think I’ll get out of the way,” Helen announced. “Greg, you’re in good hands. Let me know if there’s anything I can do. And remember to make those calls.”

“Okay, Helen, thanks for coming by. Sorry I’m being such a drip.”

“Oh, you’re fine,” Helen said. “If you ever needed an excuse for bad behavior, this is it. Bye Lily, Deb, I’ll see you all later.”

***

From a shadowed vantage point, watchful eyes noted the activity coming and going from the Harris’ apartment. Did those fools know they were being watched?

***

Greg watched Helen’s retreating figure, then sighed heavily. “Anyway, I guess I need to make some phone calls. Calls I surely never wanted to make.”

“Do you want us to leave?” I asked.

“No, please stay. I feel better not being alone right now. I’ll just go in the other room.” He lumbered toward the guest bedroom, which doubled as an office. The door shut behind him, and a moment later his voice rumbled.

“How do you think he’s handling it?” Deb asked quietly.

I shrugged. “Okay, I guess. He was kind of a mess when I got here, but Helen and I got some yogurt and a glass of water into him, and that helped. I’m going to try to have him eat some real food after he’s made his calls. What kind of casserole did you bring?”

"It's my baked ziti with sausage. I had one in the freezer so I just pulled it out."

"We'll give him a choice, then, since I brought tuna noodle."

"This is a terrible situation," Deb said after a moment's thought. "He and Dave are such good friends that I put up with Betty for Greg's sake. I'm not all that sorry she's gone, but nobody should die like that."

I shivered as I remembered those red eyes. Earlier, when I was still all stoked up on adrenaline, it didn't seem real. Now I was starting to realize we most likely had an actual murderer in our midst. We were going to have to be careful.

In the next room, Greg suddenly raised his voice. "Damn it, how can you say that?" he shouted. "If that's what you think, then stay home. Or go to hell. I don't care."

A moment later he stomped back into the living room, angrier than I'd ever seen him before. Actually, I don't think I'd ever seen him angry before. He looked surprised for a moment, as if he'd forgotten we were there, and made a visible effort to pull himself together. Flossie trotted over to him and rubbed her head against his legs. Absently he reached down, scooped her up, and held her against his chest. She licked his chin.

"Sorry," he said, "you heard that?"

We nodded.

"Betty's sister, Mary. When I told her Betty had died she asked who she should send the thank-you card to. She's glad that Betty's gone. Anyway, I guess she won't be coming for the funeral."

"Will she let Betty's friends back in Mobile know?" I asked.

"I have no idea. How could she be happy?" He sounded like a bewildered child. "God, what a mess." He subsided onto a chair.

"Did you reach your mother?"

"Mom? Oh, yeah. Anyway, she was pretty shocked, but she'll spread the word to the family."

"Where does your mother live?"

"She's back in Mobile in an independent living place. She's ninety-six, but she's still pretty feisty."

"Will she be coming here for the service?" Deb asked.

"I doubt it. Her mind is still sharp as a tack, but I don't think she's up for any traveling, or staying in a strange place."

"Well," I said briskly in my best nurse voice, "can we tempt you to eat something a little more substantial than that yogurt you had earlier? We both brought casseroles. Deb's is baked ziti with sausage, and mine's tuna noodle. Which would you like?"

"I don't want," he began. His stomach growled audibly and Deb and I both grinned. "Maybe I do after all. How about some of the tuna noodle?"

"Sure, I'll go heat it up for you. What would you like to drink with it?"

"We usually have some sweet tea already made up in the fridge. I'll have some of that."

Spooning out a serving of casserole to warm in the microwave, I tuned out Deb and Greg's conversation in the living room while I thought furiously.

Should I tell Greg and Deb that Betty had likely been murdered? The urge was almost irresistible, but Detective Henderson had made it very clear I wasn't to share the information with anyone else. Actually, I'd already said something to Deb about my suspicions. Oh well, it would come out sooner or later.

The microwave dinged. "Greg, do you want to come in here, or shall I bring it to you on a tray?" I called out. A moment later he appeared in the kitchen doorway, Flossie trotting at his heels. She went over to her own dish and lapped up some water.

"I'll sit here if you'll both keep me company," he said. I nodded and set the plate down at the kitchen table, along with silverware. Next to the casserole was a small serving of salad I'd put together from what I'd found in the fridge. I took a glass from the cupboard and poured the tea, then placed it on the table in front of him.

"There you go. Deb, would you like some tea?"

Deb nodded, and I poured a glass for her as well. With a glass of water for myself, I joined them at the table — I like iced tea, but what southerners like Betty and Greg called sweet tea set my teeth on edge.

Greg ate silently. "Thanks," he said to me when he finished. "That hits the spot." He emptied his glass, then looked up, eyebrows furrowed. "How could this have happened? What was my wife doing in the pool in the dark?"

"Do you know what time she left the apartment last night?" I asked. He looked at me blankly. Again.

"I have no idea. Anyway, sometimes if I'm snoring real bad she'll go sleep in the guest room, so anyway, when I realized she wasn't beside me in bed I just assumed she was in the other room. Then all that noise and commotion outside woke me up. I can't believe. . ." his voice trailed off.

Hearing voices outside, Flossie and Greg both raised their heads. There was a knock on the door. "Come in," he shouted, and Dave and Michael stepped into the apartment.

"That was a fast meeting," Deb said to her husband. "Usually they go on for hours and hours."

"Well, we only had one order of business, and technically it wasn't a meeting. It was only the three of us, and we were just trying to figure out what the board needs to do now."

"Damn condo board," Greg muttered. "Since Betty got elected, she spent way too much time with it. I'll be glad not to have to hear about the condo board all the time."

"Well, then we won't subject you to it now," Michael announced gravely. "How are you doing?"

"Not so good, but better since your wife forced me to eat," Greg said.

Michael smiled. "She can't help herself. It's all those years of nursing. But speaking of eating, I could force down a snack. Lily, are you ready to go home?

"It's okay, we'll stay with him a while," Deb said. Dave nodded.

"You're a good neighbor," Greg said gruffly to me. "I'm sorry I said. . . you know."

I patted him on the shoulder, mildly amused that sitting down, his shoulders were almost at the level of my own while I stood next to him. "It's okay, Greg. Let us know if you need anything, or if you just want some company."

As soon as we were away from Greg's front door walking toward our apartment, I said to Michael, "I can see you're bursting to tell me what happened at the meeting, so spill."

"As I expected," Michael said, "Jeff agreed to step up as President for now. Liz Steinbach called Jeff to find out what was going on and he asked if she'd like to take over as vice president. She agreed."

"What about the vacant position?"

"Technically, the board could appoint someone to fill it for now, but we think the residents should have a say. When we have the official meeting, we'll open up nominations from the floor. If there's only one candidate, we'll just appoint them. If we have more than one we'll have to hold an election."

I asked when the special meeting would happen. "Today's Friday, and we need a minimum of three days warning for the meeting to be official, but we don't want to rush. We'll announce it tomorrow, for next Thursday evening. And," he paused dramatically, "we'll vote on Charlotte's waiver then. Assuming we get the answers we need from our insurance and legal people, of course."

"Really? Oh, Michael, that's great. I can't wait to tell her."

"Not yet. That's not public information, so you need to keep it to yourself."

"Can't I at least tell Lottie?"

"Jeff's planning to. It's better coming from him."

"Oh, alright. And maybe by then we'll find out more about what happened to Betty, and who's responsible."

I took a few more steps before I realized he wasn't with me. I turned, and Michael was standing stock still in the middle of the path staring at me. "We?" he asked. "You mean the detectives, right?"

***

Those eyes still watched. From the shadows there was a good view of the Harris' apartment. Lots of people coming and going. Would there ever be a moment to slip in there and look for the proof the bitch said she'd hidden?

Ten

It was mid-afternoon when Henderson's phone rang as he was reviewing information with his team in the clubhouse.

He picked up and said, "Henderson." He listened, nodded a few times, said, "I'll be there in a few minutes," then hung up. He turned to his deputies. "Okay, I have some people to talk with. You know what you need to do." He replaced his notebook in his pocket and walked away.

He was surprised. He hadn't expected his first call in this investigation to be from Michael Gallagher. It was too early to expect a breakthrough in the case, but you never knew.

When he came up the stairs, Lily was sitting on the porch with a book.

"Mrs. Gallagher," he nodded, "your husband around?"

"Sure, come on in." She led the way into the apartment calling, "Michael, Detective Henderson is here."

"Would you like something cool to drink?"

"Sure, a glass of cold water would be fine."

She gestured him toward the kitchen table and set the glass in front of him as Michael entered the room. Silently she filled a glass with iced tea for her husband and handed it to him, along with a spoon and the sugar bowl.

"So, Mr. Gallagher, what is it you have to tell me?"

"Well, I don't know how important this is, but Lily persuaded me to call you. She said you'd probably hear this from someone else anyway, so I might as well tell you myself."

"Go on." He pulled out his notebook.

Mr. Gallagher took a breath. "I had a very unpleasant encounter with Betty Harris recently. It's sad, but I think as you talk with different residents here you'll find that a lot of them also had unpleasant conversations with her. She was not a nice person."

"Tell me about it, Mr. Gallagher."

"Oh, Michael, please."

"Alright, Michael. Can you tell me when this unpleasant encounter took place?"

"Yesterday morning."

"Go on. Yesterday morning. Walk me through it."

Michael sipped his tea and looked Henderson in the eye. "I overheard Betty making what sounded like threats toward someone, and after that person left she and I had words. Loud words."

After Michael finished explaining, Henderson tapped his pencil on the table a few times. "Any idea who Mrs. Harris was arguing with?"

"I don't want to say for sure. It was a woman, and she was obviously on the condo board, so that narrows it down to either Linda Barry or Liz Steinbach. Liz used to be a paralegal, so you can draw your own conclusions. Also, at the meeting, Liz abstained from voting."

"Got a list of board members?"

"I'll get it." Michael headed toward the office.

"I'm afraid this is going to expose some ugly stuff in this community," Lily said. "It's always been such a friendly place, but I'm not liking what I've been seeing and hearing today."

"Sudden death will do that," the detective said. Then he asked, "What do you know about your downstairs neighbor?"

"Who, Keith? Or the snowbirds directly below us who left in April?"

"Mr. Johnson."

"Not a lot, considering he's already been here about six months." She thought for a moment. "He seems pleasant enough, but distant. Mostly keeps to himself, although he did come to our community St. Patrick's Day corned beef supper. He told me yesterday he swims every morning, but I've never seen him hanging out on the loungers getting a tan and socializing like some of the others."

"How about your other neighbor, Ms. Nelson?"

"Jennifer seems sweet. She's one of our younger residents, and she's still working so I don't see a lot of her."

"How long has she lived here?"

"I'm not sure. Three or four years?"

Michael came back into the kitchen with a piece of paper in his hand. "I couldn't find anything printed with all the board members, so I just wrote it out for you. Names, units, and phone numbers." He handed it to Henderson, who placed it in his notebook.

"Thank you, Mr. Gallagher. Michael. I'll be in touch."

As Henderson reached the bottom of the stairs, he saw Keith Johnson sitting on his porch. "Mr. Johnson, I'd like to ask you a few more routine questions."

Mr. Johnson didn't speak, just opened the door and ushered Henderson into the kitchen. This one was a mirror image of the Gallaghers', with the kitchen to the right of the entrance instead of the left. Although the room was very similar, it didn't have the warm, friendly vibe of the kitchen Henderson had just left.

It was scrupulously clean, with nothing sitting out on the counters and not a bit of clutter. Minimalist, that was the word. Nothing stuck to the front of the refrigerator. Even the colors were cold. Where the Gallaghers had painted their kitchen a bold red, the walls here were dead white, and where their cabinets were a warm oak, these were stark white as well. It felt sterile and impersonal, where the other kitchen vibrated with the personality of the owners.

Henderson didn't think Mr. Johnson would have much to offer, but these second interviews sometimes provided useful information, once the initial shock or excitement wore off.

Mr. Johnson motioned the detective to a chair at the table, but didn't offer any refreshment. Henderson pulled out his notebook and phone, silently assessing the other man. He had obviously cleaned up and changed into fresh clothes since he'd left the clubhouse that morning. He now sported a navy polo shirt, neatly ironed khaki shorts, and tan Skechers slip-on sneakers with no socks. His only jewelry was a basic Timex watch on his left wrist. He was a couple inches shorter than Henderson's six-foot-two.

After a few seconds of this scrutiny, Mr. Johnson moved uneasily in his seat and cleared his throat.

Henderson allowed the silence to grow. Finally he tapped his notebook and began. "Right. You told me earlier that you were already up when Ms. MacLeod started screaming, is that right?"

"Yes."

"What time was that?"

"No idea. Early."

"Okay, take me through your actions starting when you woke up."

"Well, most days I swim first thing in the morning. My alarm goes off at five thirty, and I try to be in the pool by six. So I already had my swim trunks on when the screaming started. I threw on a shirt and shoes, and grabbed my towel that I put by the front door last night, then I hightailed it over to the pool to find out what was going on."

"Did you see Ms. MacLeod out there, screaming?"

"Yeah, I noticed someone when I walked out the door, and while I was jogging over another woman came up to her. I guess that was Mrs. Gallagher."

"Could you tell who it was right away?

"Not at first. Not until I got closer."

"Where was she standing?"

"Near the other end of the pool from here."

"Can you point it out for me?"

Mr. Johnson stood and marched over to the sliding glass door at the front of the kitchen. "There!" He pointed toward the far end of the pool. "She had her back to the pool and she was screaming her head off."

"So you went out," Henderson prompted.

"I went out and headed toward her. Then when I got close I saw the body in the pool so I jumped in to try to help."

The detective nodded. "Go on."

Keith swallowed and took a breath. "So I got her nearly to the side when Greg Harris came barreling along shouting and jumped in, too. He shoved me out of the way."

"Was Ms. MacLeod still screaming?"

He considered for a moment. "No, I think she stopped by that time."

"Who else was there?"

"Not sure. When I came out I was zeroed in on the screaming, and then on the body in the pool. I was aware of other people around at first, but I couldn't tell you who specifically, except for Pru McLeod and Greg Harris. And my neighbor upstairs, Lily Gallagher, of course. She was the one who came over and reached out for an arm to check for a pulse once I was close to the side."

"So did Mr. Harris lift his wife's body out of the pool?"

"No way. He took one look at her and screamed like a little girl and dropped her. I had to move him aside to lift her out."

"What about after you got the body out of the pool, did you notice who else was there then?"

"Let's see. Pru, Greg, Lily, I think she called nine-one-one. And I think her husband. Um, Dave Wheelock and his wife, the Barrys, Martinos, I'm not sure."

"And what was your relationship with the deceased?"

"Relationship? With the deceased, you mean Mrs. Harris, right?" Henderson nodded. "Nothing. I mean, it's a small community, and she waltzed around like she owned the place, but I didn't have anything to do with the condo board or her."

"You didn't socialize with the Harrises?"

"I don't socialize with anyone."

"How long have you lived here?"

"Just over six months. I bought the place the week before last Christmas."

"And where did you move from?"

"Atlanta."

"Why did you choose to move here? Did you know someone in the complex?"

"Nope. I'd just retired and I was ready to settle down, I wanted to be someplace warm and sunny year round, so I started looking in the Orlando area. I'm not much of a beach person, so inland is fine with me. Cheaper real estate, too."

"Settle down?" Henderson raised a quizzical eyebrow.

"My job had me on the go all the time."

"What kind of work did you do?"

Mr. Johnson smiled for the first time. "You know that George Clooney film where he flies all over the country firing people? That was pretty much me, except my job wasn't to fire people, it was to examine their books. I was based in Atlanta, but if I was home one or two days a month that was about it. I was on the road all the time."

"Any family?"

"Nope." Henderson waited for him to elaborate, but he didn't. Oh well, he thought, if he needed to dig around for more details later, he would.

Henderson stood. "Thank you for your time. If I have any further questions for you I'll be back in touch. For now, please don't leave the area without informing me."

Mr. Johnson opened his mouth, but before he could say anything, Henderson said, "I'm sorry, it's routine. Because you interfered with the body, you have to keep yourself available."

"Interfered? Is that what you call it when somebody tries to help?" Mr. Johnson said loudly. Then, more quietly, "I knew I should have just stayed here and minded my own damn business."

"We'll be in touch."

Henderson let himself out while Mr. Johnson stood unmoving in the kitchen.

Henderson wondered if he'd learned anything useful from either of the interviews. He'd definitely gotten some insight into the victim, but would it move the investigation along? Probably not, but you never knew.

It was interesting, the job Mr. Johnson had. Man was definitely a loner, not very sociable. Look at the way he chose to swim at six in the morning, before other residents were likely to be at the pool. The question was, did the job make him a loner, or did he choose it because it fit his inclinations?

As he walked toward his car, he tucked his notebook away and hit a speed dial number on his phone. There was one thing that would be easy to check.

Eleven

The next morning, wearing yoga pants and a tee shirt, I stood in front of the bedroom sliding glass doors doing my morning stretching routine. I'd needed a good night's sleep after all the excitement yesterday, and thankfully, I'd gotten it, my dreams only slightly punctuated with images of floating bodies.

As I stretched, I thought about my conversation with Pru yesterday. She'd texted me just as the detective was leaving, and I'd popped over to her apartment where she'd unloaded about her daughter Heather's impending divorce. She finally admitted what had her worked up the most — the thought that they'd have to end their annual family vacation on the Jersey shore. Turns out, the cottage they all stayed in every year was owned by Heather's soon-to-be-ex-husband's family.

I'd suggested she invite Heather and the kids down here instead, and her response came fast.

"Maybe, but I can't exactly envision them coming here when someone was just killed and thrown into our community pool."

Ouch.

Then she got this thoughtful look and said, "Of course, it's only the beginning of June. In this market, I'd be able to sell this place and move into somewhere safer by the middle of August."

She was quite serious, and I had a hard time believing what I was hearing. So now, if I wanted my two best friends nearby, I had to help Lottie move back, and stop Pru from moving away? Obviously we had to catch the guy who'd killed Betty before either of those could happen.

Noting some activity in the pool area, I reached for my glasses. A uniformed police officer was removing the crime scene tape. I wondered if anyone would actually use the pool after what happened — I knew I wasn't ready to go back there yet. Probably not for a long time.

Finishing my last stretch, I followed my nose to the kitchen where Michael was pouring himself a mug of freshly brewed coffee.

"I see the police are done with the pool area." I reached for a mug. "Is there anything special we need to do to clean the pool before people use it — if they even want to?"

"Good morning to you, too," Michael smiled. "I hadn't thought about it. I guess someone should talk with the pool service. I'll mention it to Jeff."

"I hope today's a little more normal," I said as I fixed my coffee. "I don't want all this excitement and drama. It's certainly not how I expected to be spending my time as a new retiree."

Michael nodded. "I wonder how Greg's holding up. Maybe I'll stop over after breakfast."

"I'm sure he'd appreciate that. Maybe you can find out about funeral arrangements and such."

I was just stacking the breakfast dishes in the dishwasher when my phone buzzed. I looked at the caller ID. "Oh! It's Helen. I wonder what it's about. She never calls me."

Michael stopped working his Sudoko puzzle and watched as I accepted the call.

"Hello, Helen, how are you?"

"Lily, can I stop over for a few minutes? There's something I'd like to talk with you about."

"That's fine, we've just finished breakfast. When did you want to come by?"

"Would fifteen minutes be okay?"

"Sure, I'll see you then. I'll put on a fresh pot of coffee."

I disconnected. "That's weird. Helen wants to come over. I can't remember the last time she stopped by, if she ever did. What could she want?"

"Well, you'll find out soon enough. I'll get ready to go on over to Greg's." He left the kitchen while I refilled the coffee maker.

A few minutes later I saw Helen trudging slowly up the stairs. She was wearing one of her usual outfits, a colorful blouse over black leggings, but her hair was falling out of its chignon and she'd overdone the makeup.

Before she could knock, I opened the kitchen slider. "Helen, come on in. I just put the coffee on, it'll be ready in a minute."

As I settled her at the kitchen table, I noted deep circles under her eyes that concealer couldn't cover. I was setting a mug, sugar, and half and half in front of her when Michael came in.

"Hi Helen, good to see you. How are you holding up after all the excitement yesterday?"

"Okay, Michael, how about y'all?"

"Good. Busy. Turns out there's a lot of condo board business to deal with when the board president passes away. Anyway, I just wanted to say hi before I take off to check on Greg and then go meet Jeff to go over some of that business."

"Take care, Michael," Helen said while I gave him a little kiss on the cheek.

Michael went out the kitchen door into the hall, and a moment later we saw him heading down the steps carrying a file folder.

"Wasn't yesterday terrible?" I poured coffee into both our cups. "I felt like the day went on forever, but fortunately I was able to sleep pretty well last night. How about you?"

"No, not so well." Helen added a little cream to her coffee, stirred, and sipped. "Is it true what everyone is saying?"

"What is everyone saying? I haven't talked to anyone this morning except for Michael."

"That Betty was killed?"

I plopped into my chair. "Who did you hear that from?" I couldn't hide the surprise in my voice. Pru and Michael wouldn't have spread it around, not after the detective told us to keep it to ourselves, and the police certainly wouldn't.

"Tim told me. He said everyone was talking about it in the exercise room at the clubhouse this morning. Of course, this morning that's all they were talking about, Betty's death."

"That's understandable. But where did they get the idea she was murdered?"

Helen wrung her hands. "Oh, Lily, don't use that word, please. It's just so awful. I can't bring myself to say it."

"I agree, it is awful, but if it's true the sooner we face it and find out who did it, the sooner we'll be able to get back to normal."

Helen sat silently for a minute, then burst out. "Lily, I'm a terrible person!"

"What do you mean?"

"I'm not sorry she's dead." She was looking at her lap and I could barely hear her.

"Well, if that makes you a terrible person you're in good company with almost everyone here, from what I'm learning," I said. "As far as I can tell, the only person who's truly sorry is her husband."

Helen stared at me for a minute. "Really?"

I nodded.

"She had a real mean streak, you know?" Helen said. "She always seemed so friendly and all, but she had a way of twisting you around."

"I'm hearing that from quite a few people. Did she do it to you, twist you around?"

"She did, more than once," Helen admitted. "Well, there were a couple times before, but then just the day before yesterday..." She paused. I waited.

She took another sip of coffee, then put her cup down and said, "I don't know why I'm telling you this, but I have to tell someone and you always seem so understanding."

She was wringing her hands again. "I was in the clubhouse on the phone. I thought I had the place to myself, but when I finished, Betty suddenly stepped out of that shadowy alcove over by the restrooms. She threatened to tell Tim about my call."

"You don't want Tim to know about it?"

Helen slouched down in her chair, frowning. "Oh, I'll tell him about it, but in my own sweet time. It's not something he'll be happy about. Betty made like she was going to march right out and spill it to him right away, and it's something he's going to be real mad about. Real mad." Her hands started shaking.

"And have you told him yourself yet?"

"Not yet, but with Betty passing on and it being, you know, well," she paused and looked down, "would that detective think I did it, to keep her from telling Tim?"

"I doubt it, but I suppose that would depend on exactly what it was you were keeping to yourself." The thought of Helen, with her shaking, nervous hands, killing someone was laughable and it was hard not to smile. Still, her distress was real.

When she didn't respond, I said, trying to sound calm and matter of fact, "Michael also had a run-in with Betty recently, and he was worried about it, too. So I'll tell you the same thing I told him. If you didn't kill Betty, it's better if you tell the detective about it yourself before he finds out some other way."

"Of course I didn't kill her!" Helen exclaimed indignantly.

"If you're asking for my advice — "

"Yes, I guess I am."

"Tell Tim, and then once it's in the open with him, call the detective. Because I don't know where the guys got the idea Betty's death wasn't an accident, but I think they're right. And if that's the case, everyone here will be under suspicion."

Helen's face went so white that the blush on her cheeks looked like clown makeup, and I was afraid she was going to faint. I jumped up and pulled her chair away from the table. "Bend over. Put your head down for a minute."

I took her wrist in a practiced grasp and found her pulse. When it was steadier, I asked, "Feeling a little less wobbly? You can sit up now."

The worry lines on her forehead stood out sharply. "Oh, Tim's going to be so mad." She seemed to be more worried about telling her husband than talking to the detective. Curiouser and curiouser.

Helen wasn't a patient, and I had no legal obligations here, but I plunged ahead anyway. "Okay, I'm going to ask you something that I occasionally had to ask patients. Please don't take this the wrong way, but I need to ask, has Tim ever been violent towards you? Are you afraid he'll hurt you?"

Helen gulped. "No." She didn't sound very sure.

"Because if you're worried about your personal safety, maybe you should tell Tim and the detective at the same time."

"Oh, that would make him even madder, but he wouldn't be able to yell at me as easily if the detective is sitting right there, would he?" Helen's eyes brightened. "I think that's a good idea." After a moment's thought she asked, "Would it be too much to ask you to stay with me while I do that? I think I'd feel better, having another woman with me."

"I'd be happy to. Your husband doesn't scare me." I was not looking forward to what was likely to be a loud and obscenity-strewn conversation with Tim Martino, but curiosity won out. "Now, who do you want to call first, Tim or the detective?"

"Detective Henderson."

I plucked the detective's card off the front of the refrigerator where I'd stuck it on with a magnet that read *If I'm ever on life support, unplug me and then plug me back in. See if that works.* Then I picked up my phone.

"Detective, it's Lily Gallagher," I said when he answered. "I'm with Helen Martino and I've got you on speaker. She has something to tell you about a recent situation with Betty Harris, and she'd like her husband to hear it as well."

"Can you tell me what it's about?"

"No, I don't know, just that it happened the day before Betty's death, and Helen is worried it might make you look at her harder, and it'll also make her husband very angry."

"Where's Mr. Martino right now?"

"He was at home when I left to come over here to Lily's," Helen said.

"I'll stop by in about ten minutes. What's the apartment number?"

"It's D3, right next to the Harrises."

"Alright, I'll see you shortly then."

"Thank you," Helen and I both said at once.

Helen tilted her head to one side and considered. "I think we should watch from here until we see the detective near my apartment. Then we can all go in together."

I thought about changing out of my yoga pants and decided not to take the time. I was beginning to understand where the phrase "burning curiosity" came from, because I felt as if I would burst into flames if I didn't find out what Helen was talking about. It was hard work carrying on a normal conversation, and a relief when I spied the detective's car pulling up.

I grabbed my phone and reached for the slider, then stopped. Normally during the day we didn't lock the apartment if we were nearby, but these weren't normal times. Instead of opening the sliding glass door, I locked it, retrieved my keys from the blue and white bowl on the hall table, and locked the front door behind me. Michael's keys weren't in the bowl, and I just hoped they were in his pocket and not sitting on his dresser. Oh, well, I'd be close by if he was locked out.

The detective must have seen us coming down the stairs, because he was waiting on the sidewalk in front of Building D.

"Mrs. Martino, Mrs. Gallagher, how are you today?" he asked politely.

"Alright," I said. Helen merely nodded as she led the way to her front door.

***

Watchful eyes noted the detective standing in front of Building D. What was he up to now? What was he going to find out? The eyes tracked the women joining him, and then blinked in relief as they went into the Martino woman's apartment. If only Harris would leave for a while...

***

As soon as the door opened, Tim barreled in from the living room, roaring, "Where the hell have you been, woman?"

"Tim, we have guests." Helen's voice shook slightly. "Lily Gallagher and Detective Henderson are here."

"What the hell do they want? What do you want?" he growled.

The detective stepped forward. "Mr. Martino," he said, "I'm here because your wife has something to tell us. And she asked Mrs. Gallagher to be here."

"Fine. I'll be in my study."

Tim turned away, but the detective said loudly, "Hold up, Mr. Martino. You need to hear this, too."

Tim's eyes were bulging slightly, and his face was turning red. The detective took the opportunity to lead the group of us into the kitchen and directed us to sit around the table, probably so he could watch everyone easily with those laser eyes. He placed Tim directly across from him.

I took a quick peek around the kitchen. Even with the identical floor plan, it was completely different from my own. This one had dark counters, black appliances, and the cabinets were also dark, maybe cherry. It would have been unbearably somber if not for the brightly colored accessories and knick knacks on the counters. I spotted an old-fashioned cookie jar like one I remembered seeing as a child in one of my friend's houses, with colorful raised images of different kinds of cookies on its ceramic surface.

Tim glared at Helen, and she shifted her chair a little farther away from him. She took a deep breath, but the detective jumped in before she could speak.

"Mr. Martino," he began, "I understand you were at the scene yesterday morning and you left before you were interviewed."

"Did she tell you that?" Tim glared at Helen.

"As a matter of fact, no. We heard it from several people, though, so I'd like you to tell me why you ducked out like that."

"Because I don't like to waste my time."

"Well, we're going to waste a little time here now, or if you'd prefer we can waste some time down at the station."

Tim deflated. One second he was rigid and puffed up, and the next he was slumped over and small. It wasn't right to be so amused at someone else's discomfort, I told myself sternly.

The detective asked Tim pretty much the same questions he'd asked me in the clubhouse yesterday morning. When he asked what had brought Tim out to the pool so early, Tim glared again at his wife. “Her. She’s so damned nosey. She wanted to know what the screaming was about. As if I cared.”

“You didn’t have to come, Tim,” Helen interrupted.

The detective shook his head at her, and she subsided.

“And what was it about?” the detective asked Tim, “the screaming.”

“That damned Betty Louise Harris got killed in the pool. Our *community* pool.“ Tim sounded indignant, as if the fact that it was the community pool somehow made it worse.

“Describe the scene, please.”

Henderson walked Tim through a description of what he saw and who was there, then asked, “And why did you leave after you were asked to stay and wait for law enforcement?”

“I told you, I didn’t want to waste my time.”

“Or maybe you were trying to hide something?”

“What could I possibly have to hide?” Tim was incredulous. “I hardly knew the bi- woman.”

Henderson leveled those laser-like blue eyes at him.

“How is it you know she was killed since we only got the preliminary results earlier this morning? Everyone else assumed she drowned, so why didn’t you?” The laser stare was still focused on Tim.

“All the guys were saying it down at the clubhouse.”

“Their names?”

“David Wheelock, Jeff Ericson, Sam Hoffman. That new guy, Keith.”

The detective made a note, then looked at Tim. “As it happens, they’re right. Mrs. Harris did not drown. She was placed in the pool after being manually strangled to death. And I’d like to know how they knew.”

Helen gave a small cry. “Oh dear, oh dear,” she moaned, wringing her hands.

“Because of the timing and because this is a gated community, we’re starting with the assumption that someone who lived here was responsible. Until we find out who that person is, you are to make yourselves available for questioning on short notice. So stay close to home."

I didn't think it was possible, but Tim deflated further.

"Now," the detective said smoothly, turning to Helen, "I believe you have something you wanted to tell me, Mrs. Martino?"

Inside I was cheering. *Bravo! Way to bring Tim down a peg before Helen shares her secret.*

Helen cleared her throat nervously. "Betty and I had words the day before she died." She was looking down at her hands.

She explained how she had made a flight reservation, then called her son. When she mentioned Timothy Jr., Tim leapt to his feet, roaring. "I told you never to say his name in this house!"

Tears trickled down Helen's cheeks as the detective stood to his full height. "Sit back down. Now!" After Tim sat, he added, "You are not to interrupt again. If I want to hear what you have to say, I'll ask you."

Tim glared at him. Still standing, the detective said, "Mr. Martino, explain to me why you refuse to have your son's name mentioned."

"He's a disgrace," Tim sputtered. "He's a damn fairy. A fag. He's an abomination."

"You mean he's homosexual?"

"Isn't that what I just said?"

"Not exactly." He sat again and turned toward Helen, who'd gotten her tears under control. "Please continue, Mrs. Martino."

"So I told Timothy I was coming to his wedding no matter what his father said," she said, "and then Betty showed up. There's an area near the restrooms," she explained to the detective, "that's almost impossible to see from the main room. It's like an alcove, and I didn't realize anyone else was in the clubhouse. All of a sudden Betty came strutting out like she owned the place. She was saying things like she thought I shouldn't have secrets from my husband and maybe she should tell him herself.

Of course I planned to tell Tim, but I wanted to choose the right moment."

She paused. "You know, it wasn't so much the words she said but the way she said them, if you know what I mean. She scared me."

"That's not hard," Tim muttered.

The detective glared at him then turned to Helen. "And why did you think you needed to tell me about this?"

"Well, Tim told me everyone was already saying she'd been killed and I was afraid you'd find out and think I did it. You know, to keep her from telling Tim before I had a chance to."

The corner of the detective's mouth quirked slightly, but he quickly restored his face to its usual impassivity. "I see. Well, thank you for coming forward."

"You don't think I did it, do you?" Helen asked plaintively.

"Ma'am, I need to ask this. Did you strangle Betty Harris and place her body in the pool?"

"Of course I didn't!"

"Do you know who did?"

"Of course not."

"Thank you for your statement." He stood to leave.

"Oh, and Mr. Martino?" He waited until Tim looked up as he stood towering over the older man. "I advise you to keep that temper in check. We'll be keeping an eye on things here for a while. Don't get up, I'll see myself out."

The kitchen was silent until after the detective closed the door behind him and walked off the porch. Tim started to open his mouth, but before he said a word Helen stood.

"There's no point in yelling at me, Tim, it's done. I'm going to Timothy's wedding whether you like it or not. In the meantime, I'm going to sleep in the guest room. Lily, would you help me gather a few things I'll need tonight?"

Tim's mouth gaped open, but no sounds came out. *Good for you, Helen, it's about time!* I thought as I followed her into the master bedroom.

***

After leaving the Martinos' apartment, Henderson contemplated the pool for a few moments, then walked along the sidewalk to Building A. He quickened his pace when he saw a small Asian woman carrying a tote bag emblazoned with the Whole Foods logo.

He intercepted her. "Mrs. Nguyen?" She nodded. "I'm Detective Jason Henderson."

"Hello," she said quietly. "I suppose you're here about the accident yesterday?"

"That's right, ma'am."

"We didn't know nothing until after police came," she said, a little defensively.

"Did you or your husband hear anything unusual early yesterday morning?"

She shook her head. "Only sirens."

"Did you hear anyone screaming?"

"You mean Pru? My neighbor tell me she was at the pool screaming and screaming." Henderson nodded. "No, we don't hear. Too many buildings in between." She gestured in the direction of the pool.

"Okay, thanks, my sergeant may be around to ask you a few more questions later."

She scurried up the stairs to her apartment, A2, while Henderson walked to the front door of A1 and rang the bell.

Linda Barry opened the door. "Oh, it's you. I suppose you want to come in and give us the third degree." She was dressed much as he'd seen her the day before, but today her shorts were white and her tee displayed the outline of the Seattle Space Needle. Her feet were bare.

He smiled. "The third degree, Mrs. Barry? I don't think so. That's not exactly my style. I do have some questions for you and your husband, though."

"Patrick's in the living room."

As Henderson followed Linda, he suddenly stopped dead. One entire wall in their dining room showed an image of Niagara Falls from above. It was so detailed he could almost see the movement of the water roaring down. "Wow! That's really something."

Linda turned around. "Oh, yes," she said, smiling. "That's the part of the country we come from, and we love the Falls. We used to take our kids there all the time."

"I thought maybe you were from Seattle, judging by your shirt."

"No," she laughed, "but our son lives there and I enjoy visiting."

"Is that wallpaper?"

"Nope. It's a thin sheet of something with glue on the back. You stick it to the wall like wallpaper. You can find all kinds of scenes, and you can even special order them if you have a picture you want to use. We had that made when we moved down here, to remind us of home. That's the view of all three falls from the American side," she continued. "The only place to get a picture like that is from a helicopter or the Observation Tower at Prospect Point. It sticks way out over the gorge. It's kind of scary, actually."

"Did you take the original photo?"

"Oh, no," Linda laughed. "That's a professional shot. We have been up there ourselves, though, up at the Observation Tower."

"It's very dramatic." Arriving in the living room, Henderson greeted Patrick, who was sitting in a recliner with a magazine in his lap.

"What can we do for you, detective?" Patrick asked.

Noticing Patrick's bare feet, and realizing how pristinely white the tile floor was, he asked Linda. "Would you like me to take my shoes off?"

"Thanks, but that's not necessary." She seemed very relaxed, and she'd lost that deer-in-the-headlights look she'd worn yesterday morning when he interviewed her at the clubhouse.

He turned to Patrick. "I'm just trying to get a better sense of what happened yesterday. We're talking again to everyone who lives here." He sat opposite Patrick.

"What's to investigate? She drowned."

"Unfortunately, it's not that simple. In fact, I'm surprised you haven't heard since the rest of the community seems to be buzzing with the news."

"What's that?" Linda asked. "We haven't talked to anyone today."

"Mrs. Harris did not drown, Mrs. Barry. The evidence shows she was strangled, and then placed in the pool afterward. And since both of you were there, fully dressed, when you couldn't possibly have heard Ms. McLeod's screams, I'm afraid that makes me more than a little bit interested."

Linda gasped, her hand going to her mouth. "Oh, god," Patrick moaned. "Not again."

"What was that, Mr. Barry?"

Patrick stiffened. "I'm not saying another word. Not unless I have someone here I can trust."

"You have the right to have an attorney present, but it's really not necessary."

Patrick looked at his wife, then drew a deep breath. "I want Lily Gallagher here."

"Lily! Why?" Linda asked, wide eyes staring at her husband.

"Because she deserves to understand what you did, and I don't want to go through it twice."

"Oh."

Henderson looked from one to the other. "You want Mrs. Gallagher to be here?"

"Yes. Or else I'll get a lawyer, and since I don't have one on speed dial that will take a while before you can ask your questions."

Henderson shrugged. "Let me see if she's willing," he said. "I'll be right back." He went out to the porch, phone in hand. What was it with all these people wanting Lily Gallagher around when they talked to him?

Twelve

After Detective Henderson left, Tim marched out of the apartment, his back even more rigid than usual. I finished helping Helen move her toiletries and a few days' worth of clothing from the master bedroom to the guest bedroom and bath.

"I'm such a fool," Helen said bitterly, "letting him bully me for all these years. Wasn't it amazing the way the detective got him to back down? I never thought I'd see the day."

"Like the Duke of Plaza Toro," I grinned. Helen looked at me blankly. "From Gilbert & Sullivan's *The Gondoliers*?"

"Not familiar with it."

"Well, in the early years of their marriage, the Duke used to bully the Duchess. She was completely miserable. Then one day she stood up to him, and he stopped the bullying. They ended up with a strong marriage."

"Lily, you know the strangest things."

"I do." I smiled. "But the best thing is, now Tim knows the detective will be watching him if he gets out of hand. I have no idea how you've put up with it."

"I won't be putting up with it in future. I've had it."

"Good for you! Maybe Tim will mellow a bit with everyone."

"I wouldn't count on it, but wouldn't that be nice." She didn't sound like she believed that was a real possibility.

"And if he gets out of hand again, you can always call me for moral support."

"I'll do that. Thanks so much, Lily. For everything." She smiled. "I think I'll call Timothy while Tim is still out. Tell him I've finally stood up to his father. He's been telling me I should for years."

I hummed a jaunty tune from *The Gondoliers* as I walked back to my own apartment. I'd enjoyed watching Tim deflate way too much. If that made me a terrible person, well, there was a lot of that going around. And Helen's encounter with Betty was another sorry piece to the ugly puzzle that apparently made up Betty's life. How many others in our little community had Betty jerked around? How could I find out?

The thought of asking questions was tempting, but one person had been killed and I definitely didn't want to make myself a target. I'd always enjoyed puzzles, but for now I'd do better to stick to my mystery books. Now, what was Georgie up to when I'd left off reading?

Just as I arrived at my front steps, my phone rang. I was surprised to see the detective's number on the caller ID. "Hello?"

"Mrs. Gallagher, you seem to be a very popular lady this morning. I wonder if I can impose on you for a few more minutes."

"What is it?"

"Can you come over to the Barry's apartment? This is very unorthodox, but for some reason Mr. Barry insists he wants you present while I talk to them."

I was stunned. I'd known the Barrys for several years, but we'd never been close. "Um, okay. When?"

"Right now."

"Okay, I'm in front of my place, give me a couple of minutes."

I disconnected. I was puzzled as I turned and headed back down my walkway and made my way over to Building A. Georgie would have to wait.

The detective was standing out front when I arrived at the Barry's building, and he turned his laser vision on me.

"What's going on?" I asked. "I don't understand why I'm here."

"Frankly, I don't either. I came to interview Mr. Barry, and he insisted that he wouldn't answer my questions without a lawyer unless you were here. I assume you and they are close friends?"

"Not at all. That's what's so strange."

"Well, as I said, this is very unorthodox, and I would prefer it if you weren't here. Nothing personal, you understand." His lips twitched in the faintest hint of a smile. "You'll need to agree to stay quiet while I conduct the interview, unless I ask you a direct question. If you can't do that, I'll wait until Mr. Barry calls his lawyer."

"I'll do my best."

"Thank you. Shall we?" He led his way to the front door, knocked once, then stepped inside.

Patrick met us at the door. "Lily, thank you for coming." He led the way into the living room and motioned me toward a chair, then sat next to Linda on the couch. The detective took another chair where he could see all three of us, and I noticed his notepad and pen were already on the table next to it.

Linda gave me one quick glance, then looked at her lap as she twisted her bracelet around and around.

The detective picked up his notebook and aimed those laser eyes at Patrick. "Alright, Mr. Barry, I'm allowing Mrs. Gallagher to be present, at your request." Patrick nodded.

"So would you tell me, please, why you and Mrs. Barry were at the pool yesterday morning, fully dressed, when you couldn't have heard Mrs. MacLeod's screams."

Patrick took a deep breath, and looked at his wife. "We were there because I had an appointment with Betty at six AM at the clubhouse." His voice was shaking a little.

I must have looked as shocked as I felt, because the detective shook his head at me before turning back to Patrick.

"What was the purpose of the appointment?" he asked.

"Well, it's complicated."

"Explain it to me."

Patrick cleared his throat, but Linda jumped in. "There was a terrible tragedy in Buffalo a few years before we moved down here," she said. "It hit Patrick really hard, because it was his building."

"His building?"

"There was a fire. See, he had bought this downtown office building with my cousin just before the economy crashed in 2008. It needed a lot of work, but it would have turned out really nice. They had started renovations, and then they had to stop because the money dried up. Then the fire happened. That was bad enough, but the next day they found that someone had died in that fire."

"All those questions, for months, all those questions. And I felt so responsible. Someone died in my building."

"How were you responsible, Mr. Barry? Did you start the fire?"

"Of course not!" he exclaimed vehemently, "but —"

The detective interrupted. "Were you charged with anything?"

"No, but..."

"Well, then. Can we deal with the present day?" He jotted something in his notebook.

Linda grabbed Patrick's hand.

"Now, Mr. Barry, what does a fire a few years ago in Buffalo have to do with why you and your wife were at the pool, fully dressed, yesterday morning when the body of Mrs. Harris was found?"

Linda looked directly at her husband. “Patrick, this is murder, we have to tell the truth. No more secrets, remember?”

He squirmed a little in his chair.

She continued, “Detective Henderson, Betty Harris was a blackmailing bitch, pardon my French. She had arranged to meet my husband at six yesterday morning and was demanding money to keep quiet about that fire in Buffalo. I went with him because we were going to tell her together to stuff it.”

“Oh, God, not again,” Patrick moaned, his head in his hands.

“Mr. Barry, I know this is hard for you, but you need to pull yourself together to answer my questions or I’ll have to take you down to the station and ask them there.”

Linda leaned toward her husband and squeezed his shoulder. “It’s okay, honey, we got through the mess in Buffalo, we can get through this.”

After a moment Patrick raised his head. He was pale and I could see a sheen of sweat on his forehead, but he mumbled, “Alright. I’m okay, ask your questions.”

“So maybe I’m confused,” Henderson said, “but if you didn’t burn down that building in Buffalo, what was there for Mrs. Harris to blackmail you about?”

“After the fire I felt like people were always talking about me, looking at me sideways. They never figured out how the fire started, so there was always this question about what happened, and the fact that someone died, well, I couldn’t handle it.” Patrick frowned. The detective waited in silence.

“My real business was residential rental property, not commercial. And my tenants, well, I always thought I had a good relationship with most of my tenants, but after that fire it seemed like they were nervous around me. A lot of them moved out when their leases were up, people who’d been happy renting from me for years.” Patrick wiped his forehead with the back of his hand.

"I guess you could say I was traumatized. I had a few panic attacks, and I had to start taking anti-anxiety medication. Plus, we took a big hit financially, and as soon as the economy recovered, around 2014, I started selling the apartments. After I sold the last one, we left Buffalo and moved here. I just couldn't look people in the eye back home."

He swallowed a couple of times, then continued. "This was supposed to be my chance to start living a normal life again. And then she found out and started in on me. Betty. She threatened to tell my friends and neighbors that I was an arsonist. I didn't want my new neighbors to start looking at me funny." He lifted his chin and looked directly at the detective. "I didn't want to go back on the anti-anxiety pills, but when Linda and I talked last night we got some things out in the open and we decided I wasn't going to pay any blackmail."

"And," he straightened up, "I sure didn't kill her. I still have nightmares about the guy who died in my building fire, and I didn't even know him."

"Who was he?" the detective asked.

"We never found out for sure. They decided he was probably a homeless guy who found a way in and curled up out of the cold. There wasn't a lot left when they found him." Patrick swallowed hard and clenched his fists.

"It was very traumatic for my husband," Linda said, twisting her bracelet. "For both of us."

"I'm sure it was," Henderson agreed. "Any idea how Mrs. Harris found out about it?"

"Oh, yeah," Patrick said. "She bragged to me about what a great detective she would have made. See, everyone who moves in here has to be approved by the condo board, right? So they do a background check. That's pretty routine. But then she takes that background check and does some digging of her own. She looks up old property records, newspapers, all that kind of thing. She acts real friendly with new residents and tries to find out personal stuff about them, and then digs around until she finds some dirt. She even pays for a couple of those online services where you can get information about people."

The detective made another note. "How long have you lived here?"

"We moved down in September, 2015. We actually bought the condo a few months before that, what was it, honey, April? May?" he looked at Linda.

"May, 2015, that's when we bought it."

"So, she had from May of three years ago to dig around into my background," Patrick said.

"She liked knowing things about people," Linda said. "Even stupid, little things that are just embarrassing. Like with Deb."

"Deb?" the detective asked.

"Deborah Wheelock. Betty knew something Deb was embarrassed about, and this one time she tried to use it to force her husband to change his vote on the board or she'd tell the whole community about it. In fact," she looked down at the floor, "the night before last, before Patrick decided we weren't going to let her push us around, she got me to say something I didn't agree with, and vote a certain way, at a board meeting."

"Tell me about it." The detective wrote something in his notebook then looked up at her.

Linda was twisting her bracelet so fast I expected sparks to start flying off it. "There's this resident, Charlotte Delaney. She has a second-floor apartment, and a couple months back she had to have her foot amputated. She asked for an architectural waiver to put in one of those stairlift things to her apartment. Poor thing's been stuck in rehab all this time." The words were coming out in a rush, as if she'd been holding them in for too long. "So Betty didn't like Charlotte, but she always wanted to come across as this sweet little thing, so she pressured me into voting against it so she wouldn't have to vote against it herself. That was just the morning before she died, and I'll never forget the look on Charlotte's face when I voted. Or yours, Lily." Her lip curled in disgust. "That was how she operated." For the first time since I arrived, she looked at me directly.

"Oh, Linda, that's awful. She threatened me that morning, I wondered whether she got to you, too." The words just burst out, and the detective glared at me.

"Mrs. Gallagher, please don't interrupt."

Linda continued talking, as if she couldn't stop herself now that she'd started. "I didn't know it at the time, but she'd already arranged to meet Patrick at six the next morning so she could put the screws to him. Neither of us were able to sleep that night, so we talked, and we agreed we'd go to meet her together and we'd tell her no deal."

The detective jotted another note.

"Okay, to get back to yesterday," he said, "Mr. Barry, if you weren't going to give in to Mrs. Harris' blackmail and pay her any money, what were you planning to do?"

"Nothing," Patrick responded flatly. "If she started telling the residents here about the fire, I was just going to put the condo on the market and move again. In fact, if you don't find out who did this pretty quickly, we might move anyway." Linda's eyes widened and her eyebrows went up, but she didn't say anything.

"Did you agree with your husband about that course of action, ma'am?"

She nodded. "I like it here. Or I did until Betty showed what she was really like, but I'm not so attached to the place that it would kill me to move again. Oh!" she looked away. "Bad choice of words."

"In fact," Patrick said, "Linda's best friend from up north and her husband moved to Clearwater a couple years after we came down here. Her husband died recently, and she keeps telling Linda she wishes we were closer. We might go there. So I had no reason to kill Betty. Easier to move."

The detective stowed his notebook in his pocket and stood. "Thanks for your cooperation. We may have more questions later, so please keep yourselves close to home. Mrs. Gallagher, a word?"

Before I could stand, Patrick said, "Lily, thank you so much for coming. I imagine you were pretty upset with Linda's vote the other night, so it's especially nice of you to come over now."

I looked at Linda, who was still having a hard time meeting my eyes. "Lily, it means more than you know." The bracelet was whirling again. "I'm so ashamed of myself, but when she threatened me, well, you can't imagine how trapped I felt. And the worst of it is, we could have avoided all that mess at the meeting and Charlotte might have her waiver now if I wasn't so worried about upsetting Patrick by telling him about it. That's why we agreed later that night, no more secrets."

"Yes, I see that must have been hard." I understood that she hadn't wanted to upset her husband, but I was angry that Lottie seemed to be the only one paying the price for that decision.

I said my goodbyes and followed the detective out the door. Once we were on the sidewalk, he said, "If you don't mind, walk with me to my car. We can sit for a minute where we can talk in private." He was frowning a little.

He settled me into the passenger seat, then went around to the drivers side. I was extremely puzzled. What could he possibly want to say to me that required all this secrecy?

He sat for a minute, drumming his fingers on the steering wheel. "I have to say again, this is completely unorthodox, but," he turned his head to look directly at me, "I could use your help."

I gasped and opened my mouth, but he held up a hand. "You are really good with people, and they certainly seem to trust you. The fact that not one, but *two* of the residents here wanted you to be with them when they talked with me this morning, well, I'm not sure what to make of it but it might be helpful to the investigation. If you're willing."

He paused, then said firmly, "Now, I don't want you to go around asking questions, but how would you feel about doing what you do so well, and telling me if you learn anything that's pertinent to the investigation?"

I opened my mouth, then closed it again. Finally I squeaked out, "I don't know what to say."

"Just say you'll keep your eyes and ears open and stay in touch with me."

"You want me to spy on my friends and neighbors?"

"Well, that's an awkward way of putting it, but, yes, I guess so. You're smart, you know these people, and I think it could speed up the investigation."

"I guess?" I heard the question in my own voice. "Can I tell Michael?"

"Yes, of course, but it needs to go no further. Now, I have someone else to interview, and maybe I'll be able to handle this one all by myself." He grinned. "Nice to have you on board."

We got out of the car. He headed toward Building C, and I walked across to my apartment, feeling more than a little confused.

***

Watchful eyes were still keeping tabs on everyone's movements, and now they were focused on the detective. What was he doing, talking with Lily Gallagher in his car?

***

I headed home, mulling over what I'd learned this morning, and then the detective's unexpected request. I couldn't wait to tell Michael about it.

I spotted Keith Johnson sitting on his porch. "Morning, Lily."

"Morning, Keith." In the short time he'd lived in our building he'd always been perfectly polite, but he certainly wasn't warm or friendly, so I didn't stop.

As I reached the top of the stairs, Deb was turning away from my front door. We greeted each other at the same time, making us both smile. Deb flashed her usual pixie grin, and her outfit — white capris and a camp shirt printed with sailboats and lighthouses in a blue and red nautical theme — was cheerful, but her eyes were puffy, as if she hadn't slept very well.

"Deb! Were you looking for me?"

"I was. Do you have a few minutes? It's about what happened yesterday."

What was it with everyone wanting to confide in me? First Helen, then Patrick and Linda, then the detective. I thought quickly. It probably wasn't smart to be alone with any of my neighbors right now, but Keith was on his porch, and Michael would be back soon. I hoped Deb didn't notice my hesitation. "Sure, come on in."

I unlocked the door and led the way to the living room. "So what's up?" I asked when we were seated.

"I don't know what to do," Deb said hurriedly. She was sitting on the very edge of her chair. "And Dave isn't being very helpful so I thought maybe you could give me some advice."

"About Betty?" This was a switch. She was the one who'd been advising me just a couple of days ago.

"Yes." She paused, then said, 'People are saying her death wasn't a drowning, just like you thought that morning."

"The place seems to be buzzing with it."

"Is it true?" Deb's eyes were wide.

"I'm afraid so."

"Oh, no," she wailed.

"In fact, Detective Henderson confirmed it just now. He told the Barrys and me that she was strangled first, then put in the pool to make it look like she drowned."

Deb shivered. "That's awful. Do they have any idea who did it? I mean, she was a terrible person, but nobody deserves to go like that."

"If they do, they're certainly not sharing those ideas with me," I said. "But the detective did say they're talking to everyone who lives here again."

"Do you think I'm going to have to tell them the thing Betty found out about me?" She sounded anxious.

"Probably. If this is a full blown murder investigation, they'll have to turn over a lot of rocks to find out who did it."

"It's not awful by today's standards, and it was a long time ago, but it's not something I'd be happy for everyone to know about. Maybe I'm just being oversensitive."

"Want to tell me about it?"

"Not really, but if I do, maybe you can help me decide if I need to tell the detective."

"I'll do my best." I gave her an encouraging look.

"Okay, here goes." She took a deep breath and then spoke rapidly. "I was in my third year of teaching, up in Danbury, Connecticut. I was in the teachers lounge one day rooting through my pocketbook for something, and a nickel bag of pot fell out onto the table. I had no idea it was in there."

"Was it yours?"

"Oh, yes, I smoked some back in the day, but I certainly never took it to school with me. To this day I don't know how it happened. All of a sudden the principal walked in." She took a breath. "Lily, I was terrified. I thought he was going to call the police and turn me in."

"So what happened?"

"He looked at it, and looked at me, and said, 'My office! Now!' and marched out. I followed him to his office. Lily, he couldn't have been nicer, but he said he couldn't have teachers at the school who behaved so irresponsibly. He told me he personally didn't care what I did on my own time, but after seeing that bag he couldn't keep me on. I could finish out the year, but I'd have to find another job because he couldn't renew my contract. He wouldn't say any more about it, and I was lucky he didn't plan to call the cops and report it. Then he told me to stay in his office as long as I needed to pull myself together before I went back to the classroom, he'd find someone to cover for me. Then he walked out."

"So what did you do?"

"I pulled myself together, went back and finished my teaching for the day, and started looking for a new job for the next year. That happened just after the winter break, and I met Dave the next month. We ended up getting engaged and then he took a job back in Hartford, so I found a position in the high school there. As far as most people knew I left to get married."

"Well, I can't imagine what use Betty thought she could make of that. I mean, how long ago was it?"

"Around 1974. And I'm retired, so it's not like I'd be looking for another teaching job." After a moment she added, "I think she just liked making people squirm."

"What was Dave doing that brought him to Danbury?"

Deb smiled for the first time and sat back in her chair. "He'd just gotten his degree in architecture. He had to do an internship to get his license, so he was interning with one of the firms there. Once he got his license, he got hired on by a larger company in Hartford."

"Nice. I always love hearing about how people met." I pondered for a moment. "So what would you have done if Betty started telling everyone you got fired for drugs? Because that's the spin she would have put on it."

"Nothing. It was forty years ago, and honestly, I don't give a hoot. She couldn't have done me much damage."

"So no reason to knock her off?"

"Absolutely not!" Deb looked indignant until she noticed I was trying not to laugh. "Do you think I should tell the detective?"

"I don't think it's a big deal either way, but he seems like a perceptive guy. He'll probably sense you're holding out on him, and that'll raise his suspicions."

Deb sighed deeply. "Okay, I guess I'd better come clean, as they say on the TV shows."

"Well, he's around here somewhere," I said. "I've already spoken with him this morning. He certainly took Tim Martino down a few pegs! It was wonderful to see that bully put in his place."

Deb's pixie grin appeared. "Oh, I wish I'd been a fly on the wall. I don't know how Helen puts up with him."

"Well, those days just may be over for good."

"Really?"

"Watch and see. You may be surprised."

"Tim Martino not pushing everyone around? That'll be the day."

Both of us were still giggling at my description of the detective deflating Tim like a popped balloon when Michael stepped back into the apartment.

"Hey, Deb. Hi honey." He glanced back and forth between us. "What's so funny?"

I treated him to a fresh description of the detective's takedown of Tim, which sent both Deb and me into roars of laughter again.

"Wow, I'm impressed!" Michael said. "I can't remember ever seeing anyone stand up to Tim. Good for Henderson."

"Let's just hope this personality transplant lasts for a while," Deb agreed. "Well, Lily, thanks for your advice. I'm going to see if I can find the detective around somewhere. If not, I'll give him a call."

"Sure, let me know how it goes." I stood and walked Deb to the door.

When I came back to the living room, Michael was slumped in his chair. "Who knew that consoling the bereaved was so exhausting?" he asked.

"How's Greg holding up?"

"Not very well, I don't think. And that poor little dog." He sighed. "He forgot to walk her this morning, and she made a mess in the house. He didn't even have the energy to clean it up, so I did it and then the two of us took Flossie out for her walk."

"That doesn't sound good."

"No. The guy doesn't have a clue how to function without Betty. He hasn't thought about arrangements for a service at all, and if concerned neighbors weren't coming by and bringing food, he probably wouldn't have eaten anything since it happened."

"I know. I actually spoon fed him some yogurt yesterday before he could handle a meal with solid food. Does he have someone to help with all the arrangements?"

Michael looked away. "Yeah, me. I volunteered to take him over to his church to meet with the pastor. Hopefully he'll be able to provide some guidance, because I sure can't."

"That's nice of you. When are you going?"

The pastor can meet with him at four-thirty, so we'll do that and then grab a bite somewhere. I figure it'll do him some good just to get out of the apartment for a while. Can you join us for supper?"

"Sure, just call me or text me when you're done with the pastor, and tell me where to meet you."

"Okay." He started to stand, but I stopped him.

"Stay a minute. I have some news of my own," I said.

"Oh?"

I told him about my visit to the Barrys and the detective's request. He didn't say anything right away, and his eyebrows were drawn together in a deep frown.

"Well, that explains Linda's vote, then." He sighed. "We suspected it was something like that, after what Betty said to you and Liz that morning, so it's nice to know for sure. But I don't like the idea of you acting as Henderson's informant."

"To be honest, I'm not sure how I feel about it either, but if it will help him find the person who did it faster. . ."

Michael interrupted me. "Because we're talking about someone who's already killed a woman."

"I'm aware."

"But you agreed to do it?"

Was that an accusing look he was giving me? Seriously? "I did. For now at least."

"Well, I don't like it," he said again.

I didn't want to argue about it so I glanced at my watch and said, "We should probably think about lunch. I'll figure something out."

Thankfully he went along with my diversionary tactic, and went off into the office. In the kitchen I put together a couple of salads with chicken left over from a recent dinner, and pondered the detective's request. My curiosity was certainly piqued, and I wondered whether I could figure out a real murder as well as I often solved the cozy mysteries I'm so fond of. But I was also scared, and, if I was honest with myself, a little nervous around all the members of our community except for Michael and Pru.

But then I thought about Pru's statement earlier, and Patrick's, about selling up and moving if the killer wasn't caught. How many other residents were thinking the same thing?

Raised voices were coming from the pool area. I looked out the slider, but I couldn't tell who was arguing so I eased it open and stepped out onto the porch.

Michelle Hoffman was seated at the Mah Jong table, and a colorful box sat on the table in front of her. Deb stood facing her. I only caught a few words, then Deb said loudly enough for me to hear clearly, "I'm telling you, Michelle, nobody's going to want to sit by this pool after what happened and play Mah Jong. Just give it up." She turned and marched off, leaving Michelle sitting by herself.

I came back into the kitchen, feeling sad. If neighbors were already arguing and thinking about leaving, this murder had to be solved before the whole community fell apart. Would I have eavesdropped like that three days ago? Unlikely.

It was a small thing, but I reached for my phone to call the detective.

Thirteen

At long last, those watchful eyes were rewarded for their unceasing vigil. It wasn't ideal, but it would have to do. The apartment was finally empty. All the guests had left, and Greg had walked out, accompanied by Michael Gallagher, gotten into a car, and driven away. The coast was clear. Maybe sleep would come tonight.

***

The afternoon was frustrating, and Michael was no help. We discussed the detective's request some more over lunch, he argued with my decision to help, and then retreated to the clubhouse. I knew he was being protective and his anger was because he was concerned for my safety, but that didn't mean I liked it.

Feeling antsy, I called Pru and we went to visit Lottie and tell her the news.

Lottie had burst into tears — of relief, not grief. When we left, she was quite hopeful.

Shortly after five thirty, my phone buzzed with a text.

Michael: *Just finished with pastor, heading over to Olive Garden. Greg's choice. See you there.*

I scooted to the bathroom where I ran a comb through my hair and swiped on fresh lipstick. Then I grabbed my tote bag and left the apartment. I wasn't looking forward to this dinner at all, but I reminded myself I wasn't going for the food or the company, I was going to support my husband. And maybe get Greg's mind off his loss, at least for a little while.

The restaurant Greg picked wouldn't have been my first choice, or Michael's either, and the drive would take me at least fifteen minutes in the after-work traffic, even taking the back way.

I backed the Prius out of the carport and headed toward Aloma Ave. The sky was a little dark, the predicted afternoon storm moving in, and it smelled like rain. Good thing I carried an umbrella in my bag.

I turned right next to the library and did the little zigzag onto Interlachen, then followed it to Webster. A left turn, a couple of lights, and there was the Olive Garden. I looked at my watch. Sixteen minutes — not bad for this time of day.

The first drops of rain hit the windshield as I parked. Digging out my umbrella, I raised it with a practiced flick as soon as the door was open a few inches, and scurried to the restaurant entrance.

As I stepped inside, shaking a few drops off the umbrella, scents of tomato, garlic, and basil enveloped me and my stomach growled. Greg and Michael waited on the bench to the left. Michael saw me and smiled. Greg's head was drooping.

"Hi, honey. Greg, how are you doing?" I asked.

Greg glanced up. “Okay, I guess,” he said dully.

He looked gray. He was wearing gray trousers, a white shirt with a gray tie, and a navy blazer. He’d made the effort to shave, but I noted a couple of small nicks where the razor had slipped. He still wore that stunned, vacant, colorless look he’d had since yesterday morning.

Before I could sit, the hostess came over and invited us to follow her to a table. She seated us at a booth in one of the small alcoves to the left of the entrance, one of the few spots in the entire restaurant where we might expect any privacy.

“I don’t know if this was such a good idea after all,” Greg said. “Betty and I used to come here every couple of weeks. She loved their lasagna. And their garlic bread.”

“What do you like here?” I asked him.

“Oh, I usually get the chicken parmesan.”

Our server appeared, smiling and perky. “Hi, I’m Andrew, and I’ll be taking care of you this evening. Can I offer you something to drink?”

“Just a Coke for me,” Greg said.

I ordered my usual unsweet iced tea with lemon, while Michael opted for beer. I wasn’t sure how long Greg would be able to keep it together, so I told Andrew we were ready to order food, too.

Greg went with the chicken parm and minestrone soup, while Michael opted for the chicken marsala with salad. With a mental “calories be damned,” I ordered the shrimp Alfredo and salad.

Once Andrew had bustled off, I asked, “How was your meeting with the pastor?”

“Okay,” Greg said dully. “I guess we covered all the bases for a funeral service.”

“Do you have a date for it yet?”

Greg shrugged and looked at Michael, who responded, “Next Tuesday morning at ten at First Baptist.”

"Well, that's plenty of notice for anyone who wants to come from out of town. Greg, are you expecting any out-of-town visitors?"

"I don't think so. My mom's too old to travel, and Betty's sister made it pretty clear she wasn't coming."

"That's a shame."

Greg frowned and started fiddling with his napkin, folding and unfolding it. "I never understood it. Mary says Betty ruined her life, but really she did Mary a favor."

"Oh?" I said when it looked like he was done speaking.

He folded his napkin again. "Mary was dating this real thug in high school. She claimed they were in love and they were going to get married, but after he graduated he suddenly dumped her and enlisted. Anyway, back then, that meant Vietnam. He was killed over there, and Mary's life has been a wreck ever since. Anyway, I don't know how she can blame my wife for that, but she does."

"Why did Betty think he was a thug?" I asked.

"Oh, she knew him real well. Betty's eight years older — was eight years older — than Mary, and this guy was only a year ahead of Mary in school. Anyway, Betty actually used to babysit him when she was in her teens and he was a hellraiser even then."

"Why does Mary think Betty had something to do with their breakup?" Why was I asking all these questions? I didn't care about something that happened so long ago, but maybe it would give me a little more insight into Betty's character.

"I'm not sure," Greg said. "Anyway, she just always blamed her for it, said they would have been married if Betty hadn't told lies."

Michael and I looked at each other.

"Do you want Mary to come to the funeral?" I asked.

He unfolded the napkin. "I guess I hate to think of my Betty being buried while her own sister is so upset with her."

"Would you like me to call her?" I didn't particularly want to talk to the woman, but I felt I should offer, and maybe if I could change the subject he'd stop his obsessive folding and unfolding of that blasted napkin.

"I don't know if it would do any good, but, anyway, you're welcome to try."

"Okay, I'd be happy to do that for you. Is there anyone else you want to reach out to?"

"I'll have to think about it."

Andrew appeared next to our booth, lowering a tray onto a nearby stand. He placed our drinks in front of us, then unloaded the basket of warm garlic bread and warm plates. A moment later he bustled back with the soup and salad.

I left it to Michael to toss the salad. He took the pepperoncinis off the top first and added them to his bowl. Then he passed the salad to me. I served my salad, fishing all the olives out of the bowl, then handed it back to Michael. Before I took a bite, I carefully passed him a small pepperoncini that had hidden itself in my serving.

Greg watched our performance with what might have been amusement under other circumstances. Then his face fell as a thought occurred to him. "Of course, it'll have to be a closed casket."

It took a moment for his statement to register. The memory of my last view of Betty's face was hard to shake, and I didn't know how much the funeral parlor could do to make it viewable. "Is that what you want?"

"Are you kidding? I don't want any of this. If I ever get my hands on the bastard who did this, I'll make sure he knows what my Betty suffered." He pulled the napkin tight between his hands.

"Detective Henderson seems like a competent guy," Michael said. "I'm sure they'll figure it out."

"They'd better." He pushed his soup bowl away in disgust.

"Greg, you need to eat," I reminded him. "You'll feel better."

"You're right, Lily. I'm behaving badly. Again." He smoothed his napkin onto his lap — finally! — and reached for the spoon, sipping the broth tentatively.

"It's okay, Greg. You're going through a lot." I spoke quietly, trying to sound calm and soothing.

As we ate, Michael and I tried to keep the conversation off of death and loss and onto more cheerful subjects, but nothing seemed to pull Greg out of his gloom. Finally I asked how Flossie was doing.

"She misses her mommy so much," Greg said, and his eyes started to water. "She just sits all day by Betty's chair, with her head on her paws. She looks so sad. And every time someone comes to the door she perks up and runs to the door, and then comes back to the chair with her tail dragging."

"I'd love to stop by and see her after dinner, if that's okay," I said, for lack of anything better to discuss.

"Sure, she'd like that. She likes you."

Somehow we made it through the meal. Afterward, I couldn't recall what else we had talked about, I just remembered feeling desperate to find neutral topics. Under other circumstances I would have savored the shrimp and fettuccine smothered in creamy sauce, but I had to force myself to eat. Michael didn't seem to have a problem polishing off his chicken marsala, though.

I was beginning to regret my offer to stop over and visit Flossie, and debated briefly whether to just blow it off. No, that wasn't my style, but I'd make it short. I couldn't wait for this uncomfortable evening to end.

As we were leaving, I reminded Greg, "After I visit with Flossie you can give me Mary's contact details." He nodded and Michael gave me a quick kiss on the cheek before they headed toward Michael's CRV and I walked to the Prius.

It was a lovely evening. As usual in Central Florida, the earlier rainstorm came and went quickly, rolling away long before we finished our meal. It cooled things off nicely, and I guessed the temperature had dropped to the low seventies, but it still smelled damp.

Back at Happy Oaks, I parked in my carport then headed toward Building D. Michael and Greg waited for me on the sidewalk, so I hurried to join them. Greg handed me a small slip of paper. "Here, I wrote down Mary's number for you."

"Thanks." I'll just give Flossie a quick pat and head home, I thought.

Michael and Greg chatted in low voices, until suddenly the evening erupted with shrill yapping and Flossie was jumping around our feet.

"Flossie, what are you doing out here?" Greg sounded as if he expected her to answer. He rushed toward his apartment, then stopped so abruptly at the doorway that Michael, following rapidly, almost crashed into him.

"Why is the door open?" He took a few steps inside. "Ohmigod, somebody's been here. My apartment's been trashed!"

He started to take another step inside. I'd caught up with them in the doorway, which was pretty crowded by this time, and I reached around Michael and grabbed Greg's arm. "Greg, come back out here. You have to call the police. Whoever did this might still be inside."

"Greg," Michael said sharply. "Stop." He reached up and took Greg by the shoulders, turned him around, and walked him back out to the porch while I took out my phone and dialed nine-one-one.

I explained to the dispatcher and provided the address, then added, "The woman who lived here was killed yesterday, and Detective Henderson is investigating. I'm sure the two are related."

"Ma'am, we have a procedure I have to follow. Are you inside the home now?"

"No, as soon as the owner saw the damage inside, we all came back out in case the person is still inside. We're on the porch."

"Very well. You can expect the patrol car shortly."

Flossie was still barking frantically, so I picked her up and spoke to her softly. Greg paced around the porch, cursing.

"I'll be right back." I could see lights on upstairs so, carrying Flossie, I mounted the steps to Pru's apartment.

I tapped, then opened the door. Pru looked at me in surprise. "Pru, something's happened downstairs," I said. "Greg's place was ransacked. Did you hear anything earlier?"

"Ransacked?" Pru's eyebrows were raised so high they were practically lifted off her forehead.

"We were at the Olive Garden with Greg. We just got back, and Flossie was outside, the front door was open, and the living room was a mess. We pulled Greg out in case the person was still inside, and called the police."

"I didn't hear a thing. I was watching Jeopardy. Oh, I don't like this at all."

"Can you watch Flossie for a while until the police figure out what's going on? Cocoa won't mind?"

"Of course." Pru reached for the little dog. As I placed her in Pru's arms, Flossie whimpered and gazed at her sadly.

"I'm going back downstairs. I'll keep you posted."

As I maneuvered the stairs, my knee gave another sharp twinge. I had definitely been going up and down too much over the past few days. I should dig out the knee brace tomorrow. Or even tonight before bed.

Arriving back downstairs, I told Greg that Flossie was with Pru so he'd have one less thing to worry about. He nodded, but didn't say anything. At that moment, a patrol car slid to a stop along the curb in front of Building D. I was amazed they'd arrived so quickly. Maybe they were already in the neighborhood.

I watched as the two patrol officers converged on us. Happily, Deputy Levy wasn't one of them.

Deputy Melanie Sanchez introduced herself and Deputy Mario DaSilva. Despite the matching green uniforms with their heavy belts of tools and equipment, there was no question about Sanchez' feminity. Out of uniform she'd probably be a knockout, with her curly dark hair and lively brown eyes, but right now she was all business. DaSilva didn't say much, but his eyes were constantly moving, taking in everything around him.

"We're the Gallaghers, Michael and Lily," my husband said, "and this is the homeowner, Greg Harris."

"Did any of you go inside?" Sanchez asked.

When Greg didn't respond, Michael explained what happened when we arrived at the apartment.

"Is there a back entrance?"

"There's a door to the back porch."

"Probably long gone, then, but we'll check anyway. What's the quickest way to the back?"

"Just head around the building to your right," Michael said. "It's a screen door at the end of the enclosed porch."

Sanchez nodded at DaSilva, who took off at a fast walk toward the end of the building.

"Stay here," she ordered us, and stepped inside.

Greg looked around blankly. "Flossie? Where'd Flossie go?"

I knew he hadn't registered what I'd just told him. "I took her upstairs to Pru so she wouldn't be underfoot until we figure out what happened," I said.

"Oh. Good idea."

We waited tensely on the porch, nobody saying anything, for about five minutes, until Sanchez came out the door. "Nobody here."

I let out a whoosh of breath and Greg sighed

"Mr. Harris, do you want to step inside and tell us what's missing?"

Greg stumbled toward the door, and Michael and I followed.

I was appalled at the mess. Where framed photos had hung, now there were only naked picture hooks and a few holes where hooks had been. The floor was a jumble of pictures, books from the bookcase, cushions, and the contents of the coffee table. But the TV was still in place, and a tablet computer peeked out from under one of the ruffled cushions on the floor.

I glanced into the kitchen. Open drawers and cupboard doors were the only signs of the intruder. While Greg stood, seemingly frozen in the middle of the mess that had been his tidy living room, I wandered down the hall to the guest bedroom, which doubled as a study.

Here I found similar chaos. Drawers gaped open, their contents strewn about, but the laptop was still there, tossed carelessly onto a chair.

As I walked back to the living room, I heard DaSilva asking, "Mr. Harris, has anything been taken that you can tell?"

Greg looked shell shocked. "I don't understand. Why would someone break in and not take the TV?"

I took Michael aside and said, "I don't think this was a robbery. I think whoever killed Betty was here, looking for something."

"Would you check the other rooms, please, Mr. Harris?" Sanchez requested. "I'll go with you, and you tell me if you spot anything missing that should be here." She led him toward the master bedroom.

"I looked in the study," I told my husband. "It's a mess, like in here, with stuff all over the floor and books off the shelves, but they didn't take the laptop."

At that moment, Detective Henderson appeared in the hallway. "I just got the call," he announced. "What happened here?"

DaSilva stepped forward. "We're trying to figure that out, Detective, The homeowner doesn't think anything is missing." He gestured toward the TV and the tablet. "He's with Sanchez checking out the other rooms now."

The detective looked at Michael and me. "How did you two happen to be here?"

I left it to Michael to explain. I was furiously wondering how to figure out what the intruder had been searching for, and whether that would help identify him or her. I came out of my reverie when Sanchez and Greg came back into the living room.

"Detective," Sanchez said. She put a hand on her hip and looked up at him with a smile, "nice to see you." Wait, was she flirting with him? If so, he ignored it completely.

"Anything missing?" he asked, all business.

"Well, it's a mess in the bedrooms, just like in here, but Mr. Harris doesn't think anything was taken."

"In that case," the detective announced, "I think there's no question but that this is part of a murder investigation. We're going to need to process the apartment as part of a major crime, not a simple B and E."

Sanchez nodded. "What do you need?"

The detective turned to Michael and me. "Have you been anywhere in this apartment tonight besides this room?"

Michael shook his head. "I looked at the kitchen and the guest bedroom," I said. "But I only walked around and looked. I didn't touch anything."

"Good. Because we're going to need your fingerprints, for elimination purposes. Have you ever been in either of the bedrooms before tonight?"

"I helped them with a plumbing problem in their master bathroom a while back," Michael said.

"How long ago?"

"Three, maybe four months?" Henderson nodded and looked at me.

"No."

"Okay, stay here, I've got some calls to make." He walked outside, and a moment later a car door slammed.

Fifteen minutes later the place was buzzing with deputies. One of them immediately approached Michael and me with his fingerprint kit, then went to find Greg.

A few minutes later, the detective came over to us. "Mr. Harris won't be able to stay here tonight," he said. "Do you know if he has someone he can call? He seems pretty out of it."

I glanced at Greg, who had subsided onto a chair and was staring blankly into space. "I'm not surprised," I said. "First his wife is killed, and now this," I gestured at the room. "His best friend here is Dave Wheelock, maybe they can put him up for a night or two."

"Would you call him?"

"Sure." I pulled my phone out of my pocket. I was just hanging up when the detective spoke again.

"Mr. Gallagher, I understand Mrs. Harris was the president of your condo board, is that correct?"

"Yes it is."

"So who would be second in command?"

"That would be Jeff. Jeff Ericson. He was VP, and he'll likely be appointed president at an emergency meeting within the next few days."

The detective made a note on his pad. "Okay, I should ask him, but you're here and he's not. Who would I talk to about getting a look at the video camera footage from your front gate?

"Um, nobody, I'm afraid."

"What do you mean?"

"After Betty was elected president, the camera, well, she couldn't figure out how to use the software. She refused to ask any of the previous board members for help, or delegate to someone else, so it hasn't been used in a long time."

"So you're telling me there is no security footage?"

"I don't think so."

The detective's nostrils flared as he turned away.

I watched his retreat. "Well, I got hold of Dave. He's on his way over."

"Good. I hope he'll be able to put Greg up for a couple nights. Honestly, I wish we could get away from this mess for a while." Michael wasn't just referring to the state of the room we stood in although it was a hubbub of activity with deputies, camera flashes, fingerprint powder, and who knew what else..

I approached Deputy Sanchez. "Deputy, we've been fingerprinted. Are we free to go?"

"I'll have to check with the detective."

"Well, can we wait on the porch? This is all a bit much."

"Fine with me, but don't go any farther than that."

"Michael, come on, Sanchez says we can sit on the porch." I took his arm and we left through the open front door. We sat quietly, not speaking for several minutes. A few unhappy yips came from upstairs.

About five minutes later, Dave bustled up. "Lily, Michael, what's happened now?" he asked, looking at all the police cars spread along the driveway.

"We took Greg out to dinner, and came back to find his place had been trashed while he was gone," I said. "The detective's here with about a gazillion deputies. He said it's being treated as a major crime scene, and Greg has to stay somewhere else for a couple of days."

"Oh, poor guy, first Betty, and now this. It's so awful."

I nodded. "I took Flossie upstairs to Pru to keep her out of the way, but I don't think she's prepared to keep her overnight."

Dave nodded. "No problem, we can take both of them. Can I go in there?"

"I'll go with you." I stood up with a sigh, and Michael and I stepped inside with Dave. It took a moment for anyone to notice us. One of the deputies I hadn't been introduced to looked up and called out, "Stay where you are. This is a crime scene, you can't come in."

"Would you please tell Detective Henderson that Dave Wheelock is here," I said.

We waited in the doorway until the detective arrived, with Greg.

"Oh, buddy," Dave said, eyeing Greg's ashen face and bowed shoulders. "Detective, I understand he needs a place to stay for a couple days. He's welcome to stay with us for as long as he needs to."

The detective nodded. "That's very kind of you, Mr. Wheelock. Mr. Harris, you can take what you need for overnight. A deputy will accompany you while you pack." He gestured to the deputy who'd stopped us at the door and issued some low-voiced instructions, then the deputy led Greg toward the master bedroom.

"I'll need to collect Flossie's food and water bowls, and some dog food," Dave told him. "She's coming, too."

"Where is the little dog, anyway?"

"Lily said she took her upstairs to Pru's before the police arrived."

The detective nodded toward the kitchen where Flossie's dishes sat on a mat next to the refrigerator. He pulled a pair of gloves from his pocket and held them out. "Put these on, then gather what you need from here, Mr. Wheelock. Please don't touch anything you don't have to."

Once he was gloved, Dave moved into the kitchen and started collecting Flossie's supplies. By the time he was done, Greg was back with a small overnight case.

"Mr. Harris, there are no signs of forced entry. I'll need a list of everyone who has keys to your apartment."

Greg looked confused. "I don't know. I never gave out any, and it doesn't sound like something Betty would do. Maybe I just forgot to lock up when I left."

"Was anyone with you?"

Greg nodded at Michael, who said, "I was. I picked him up to meet with his pastor."

"Do you remember whether he locked the door?"

Michael thought for a moment. "Sorry, I don't. We were talking, and I wasn't paying attention."

"Do you have a spare key you can leave with me so we can lock up after we're done for the night?" Henderson asked. Greg nodded toward the kitchen.

"Top drawer next to the refrigerator."

The detective strode across the room and looked into the drawer, which was hanging open. "I don't see a key here."

"What?" Greg joined him and peered into the drawer. He pulled out a few takeout menus, a handful of advertising circulars, a couple of refrigerator magnets, but no keys.

"Damn!" The detective stepped into the living room and raised his voice. "Listen up! Our burglar may have taken the spare door key."

He ushered us all outside, and turned to Michael and me. "You can go. I know where to find you if I need you." He turned and strode back inside.

Dave grabbed Flossie's stroller on his way out. He set down the sack of her supplies on its seat. "I'm going upstairs to get Flossie. I'll be right back."

Michael and I stayed with Greg until Dave returned with Flossie in his arms. Wordlessly, Greg reached out for the little dog and nuzzled his face in her fur. They set off toward Building C, a sad procession. We went in the opposite direction, hand in hand, toward home.

As we approached our building, Keith Johnson stood up from the porch chair where he'd been smoking a cigar, and came to meet us.

"Hello, Gallaghers, I saw you come out of the Harris place. What's going on?" he asked.

"Hi, Keith. It's pretty awful," I said. "Someone broke into their apartment and really trashed the place. Now it's swarming with police."

"How were you involved?"

"We had taken him to dinner," Michael said. "We thought it would do him good to get out for a while and away from here after what happened."

As we spoke, Jennifer appeared around the corner of the staircase. "I thought I heard voices. Oh, Michael and Lily, it's you. What's going on?" She joined us at the bottom of the steps.

I sighed. "I'm exhausted," I announced. "I really don't want to talk about it, sorry, I'm not trying to be rude." A huge yawn overtook me and I couldn't hide it behind my hand. "Sorry."

"That's okay," Jennifer said. "I'm just being nosy."

"It's alright," Michael said. "Everyone will know soon enough. Someone broke into Greg's place while he was out to dinner with us."

"Oh, my," Jennifer said. "You hear sometimes about people breaking in and robbing houses during a funeral, but this is weird."

"I agree," I said as Keith shifted from foot to foot. "I'm sure every resident here will be hearing from the detective over the next couple days. So think about whether you saw anything, or heard anything, from over there between 4:30 this afternoon until about 7:30 this evening."

"In broad daylight?" Jennifer asked. "That's nuts."

"I was over there myself," Keith said. "I stopped by around five. Nobody answered the door so I just went for a walk. Do you think the guy was inside already?"

"How would we know?" Michael asked.

Another yawn split my face. "I'm going home. I'll be better company tomorrow after I've had a good night's sleep." I couldn't believe how tired I was. It must have been the strain from that uncomfortable dinner, followed by the shock of finding my peaceful evening shattered by the break-in at Greg's. As exhausted as I felt, there was no question of doing anything except falling into bed. I was too tired to even think about what that break-in might mean.

I started up the stairs to our apartment, Michael a step or two behind. Behind us, Jennifer said, "So you didn't see anything? You sit out here a lot."

Keith's voice rumbled, but I couldn't make out what he said, and for once I was too exhausted to care.

***

Of all the condos in the state of Florida, why'd I have to buy into this one?

It's all been her damn fault. Everything that's gone wrong in my life, all down to her. How could I have been so stupid? But I never, ever thought she would leave Mobile. Never occurred to me.

If only she hadn't interfered all those years ago.

Instead, I've done one terrible thing after another. Even if they don't catch me, how can I live with myself?

Well, at least the world is rid of that monster. She deserved everything she got. I'd do it again. The look on her nasty old face, I'll never forget it. I finally shut her up, but good.

I don't like that the detective was talking with Lily Gallagher privately in his car like that. What does that mean? Is she his snitch? I need to be careful around her.

This was the most fun I've had in years, trashing her place. Can't believe he didn't even lock the damn door. Too easy.

Of course, it was hard to throw that much stuff around without making a lot of noise, and I can't believe nobody heard anything. And that stupid little yappy dog. Well, the neighbors are probably used to that, and the yapping covered up whatever sounds I was making.

I can't believe I didn't find it, though. She swore she had evidence, and I was so sure it was in the apartment. What was it? Will someone find it? Will they know what it means? I need to find it before someone else does.

I hid the bag of folders from the file cabinet, but I kept that one with all the news clippings. I don't know why. I should look through it, see if there's anything about me in there. But I have to keep it out of sight. I should probably go back for the rest of them, but where would I put them? I'm sure that detective will be around sooner or later. Thank God he didn't ask me very much that first morning, I was barely keeping it together.

Where can I hide this file? I can't look at it now. Too tired. Need to sleep. Haven't slept in two days. A drink would help, but I can't risk it now. Have to keep my wits about me. Need to sleep.

FOURTEEN

A roaring sound outside the bedroom window woke me with a start. What was that awful noise? I stiffened when I remembered the shock of coming back to Greg's trashed apartment last night. I couldn't believe how tired I'd been, more like I'd worked two double shifts back to back than just gossiped with neighbors and gone out to dinner.

I rolled onto my side and curled up, thinking hard. The noise outside was getting louder, making it harder to hear my own thoughts. The mess in Greg's apartment had been overwhelming, and oddly, this was starting to feel personal to me, in a way that finding Betty's body hadn't. It felt like a slap in the face that someone had been making a mess of Greg's apartment while Michael and I had been laboring hard to cheer up the grieving widower. If it felt like a slap in the face to me, imagine how Greg must feel! Plus, after seeing the mess at Greg's, I felt scared in a way I hadn't before.

Maybe Michael was right and I should stay out of it. No. No way would I just ignore it while our community was destroyed, even if I was scared.

All I was doing was talking with people, right? How could talking with my neighbors be a problem?

That was it. I'd start with Greg, see if he had any new ideas since last night about who might have done it. It would be perfectly natural to check on him, right?

I was stretching again and thinking about getting up when Michael came into the bedroom. He had to raise his voice for me to hear him over the racket outside. "Honey, I'm sorry, but you need to get up."

I opened my eyes wide. "What's that horrible noise?"

Michael cocked his head. "Landscaping crew, they're here every week. Usually on Friday, but after finding Betty the police wouldn't let them come until they removed the crime scene tape. We're paying extra for them to work on a Sunday. Sounds like they're running the weed whacker along the bushes under the window.

"This happens every week? How long does it go on?" I'd made it as far as sitting on the side of the bed.

"All day, although they're only doing the minimum today. Seriously, you didn't know?"

"I'm brand new at being home on weekdays, so, yes. I didn't know."

"Well, Jeff just called and we need to activate the phone tree."

"Oh?"

"Apparently Detective Henderson is ramping up the investigation since the break-in. He's in the clubhouse with a couple of deputies, and they want fingerprints of all the residents for purposes of elimination. We need to let people know."

"Wow, can they do that? Fingerprint an entire community?"

"Apparently."

"No rest for the weary." I stood, ignoring my twinging right knee. My chat with Greg would have to wait. I sniffed, and then frowned. "Is there coffee?"

"I'll have it ready by the time you get out to the kitchen." Michael smiled at me.

"Wonderful. I'm going to need it," I muttered, heading for the bathroom.

A few minutes later, after brushing my teeth and splashing some water on my face, I ambled into the kitchen. I'd make my calls and have my coffee before showering and dressing for the day.

I had volunteered for the phone tree when the Board set it up a few years back because I enjoyed talking with my neighbors, but I suspected today's calls would be a lot less fun. With the residents directory and my coffee on the table in front of me, I looked up at Michael. "Okay, what am I telling them?"

"Tell them about the break-in at Greg's, and then explain that the police need all residents' fingerprints for elimination purposes. Warn them if they haven't shown up at the clubhouse by noon to have their fingerprints taken, the police will be knocking on their door."

"Oh, I'm sure everyone's going to love that. Can you imagine what Tim Martino's going to say? I'm glad he's not on my call list!"

Michael grinned. "Yup. I'm sure Jeff got an earful when he was calling around to all the board members. I'll be in the other room if you need me."

I sipped my coffee, checked the list, then dialed the first call.

I was halfway through and had just hung up from talking with Leroy Jones when my phone rang. Linda was talking before I even said hello.

"Oh, Lily, I really need your help. Can I stop over?" Her voice was shaking and she sounded upset.

"What's the problem?" I still wasn't sure I'd forgiven Linda for voting against Lottie's stairlift, and I was surprised she would ask me for a favor.

"I can't talk about it on the phone, I need to see you. Please?"

I thought for a moment. "Well, I have more phone tree calls to make and I'm not dressed yet. How about in half an hour? I'll make coffee."

"Thank you, I'll be there. Half an hour." I heard sniffling, and then, "Okay, Bye for now."

"Bye." That was odd. What could Linda possibly want to talk with me about that she couldn't discuss on the phone?

I completed my calls and checked the time. I had a few minutes before Linda was due, so I decided to call Betty's sister and check that off the list. Where had I put her number? I scrabbled around in my tote bag and found the slip of paper in my change purse.

Just when I thought the call would go to voicemail, a sleepy voice answered. "Hello, is this Mary?" I asked. "My name is Lily, Lily Gallagher, and I'm one of Greg Harris' neighbors."

I heard a yawn.

"Oh, dear, did I wake you?"

"It's not even eight in the morning, lady, just tell me what you want."

I looked at the clock. "Oh, no! You're in a different time zone, aren't you. I'm so sorry, I didn't realize."

"I work nights, so, yeah, you woke me up. Whaddya want?"

I took a deep breath. "Greg told me you're not exactly broken up about what happened to your sister, but he's hoping you'll come for the funeral anyway. You'd be very welcome."

"Why's that?"

Oh, dear, the woman was prickly. "Well, you're her only family, right?"

"That's right." Sounds of a match and a moment later a deep inhale.

"All of Greg and Betty's friends would like to meet you, and it might do you good. Get some closure, you know? I understand you and your sister weren't close."

Mary laughed. "That's one way of putting it. Okay, since you asked so nicely, I'll think about it. It might do me good after all."

"Well, I hope we'll meet," I said. "If you decide to come, text me or Greg your travel plans and we can have someone pick you up at the airport. Do you want to write down my number?"

"I've got caller ID."

"Alright, well, it was nice talking with you. Have a good day."

"Back atcha, Lily."

I put the phone down. Out of all the calls I'd made that morning, that was certainly the strangest. I had no sense of whether Mary would make the effort to come for the funeral, but I'd told Greg I'd talk with her, and I had. I sighed.

Linda would be here soon, so my shower would have to be quick. As I stood, my knee reminded me to find that darned brace. Even though it provided a good amount of relief, I hated having it on. Oh, well. After searching for several minutes, I found it and placed it on the bed.

In the shower, I thought about my conversation with Leroy, who apparently had a way with words. "Big words for a dirty deed" indeed. Well, at least the residents I called seemed to be willing to help. I couldn't imagine what Linda wanted, but I'd find out soon enough. I turned off the water and reached for a towel.

Showered, dressed, and knee brace in place, I sighed as I put water in the coffeemaker. My curiosity was working overtime again. I'd already gotten her explanation for why she scuttled Lottie's waiver, so what did Linda want?

I didn't have to wait long. A minute later Keith's voice rumbled from his porch, and a woman's voice responded. Then my doorbell rang.

Linda looked upset, no bubbly personality in evidence this morning.

I gestured toward the kitchen table and served coffee for both of us, then sat down and waited. I wasn't inclined to make this easy for her "It's Patrick," Linda finally said. "I think he's in real trouble. That detective has asked him to come to the station and answer more questions. They're going to take him down there after they finish fingerprinting everyone."

"You think the detective suspects him of Betty's murder? Why?" Surprise made my voice sound squeaky.

"He might. Oh, I'm scared." She was twisting that gold bracelet around so fast I was surprised it didn't leave scorch marks on her wrist.

"Well you already know about the arson in Buffalo. But there's something you don't know and, well, it gives my husband a big motive. It's something he kept from me for ten years. Ten years," Linda wailed.

"Something worse?"

"Yes. Much worse." She fished a tissue out of her pocket. "He knew about it, he planned it with my cousin," she said and burst into tears.

"Wait a minute, are you telling me he actually set fire to his own building?" I stared at the tears rolling down Linda's cheeks.

"No, that was my no-good cousin Frankie." She dabbed at her cheeks with the tissue.

"Your cousin Frankie?" I still wasn't feeling particularly sympathetic, but I was intrigued.

"Oh, it was a terrible time," Linda said. "It was back when the whole economy was melting down. Patrick was desperate. I never knew how desperate he was, until now. I never should have encouraged him to get involved with Frankie, I knew he was no good but I hoped maybe Patrick could be a — what do you call it — a stabilizing influence."

"It doesn't sound like it worked out that way."

"It sure didn't. And I had no idea, all this time, until the night before Betty died. I don't know how he kept it to himself." The tissue in her hand was completely soaked. I pulled another out of the box on the counter and handed it to her.

"So will you help?"

"What on earth do you think I can do?"

"Figure out who really killed Betty, of course. Please, Lily, you're smart, you seem to be friends with that detective, and everyone talks to you. My Patrick couldn't have done it. It's been eating him alive, that someone died in that fire."

I stirred the spoon around in my coffee mug while I thought. "Does he know you're here?"

"He does."

"Well, I have no idea what you think I can do, but I seem to be talking to people already, so, I guess."

"Oh, Lily, you're the best!" She flung her arms around me in a big hug.

After Linda left, I limped over to the refrigerator and grabbed the pad we used for grocery lists. Maybe making a list would clear my mind, because right now I didn't have a clue. What did I think I was doing?

At the top of the page, I printed neatly, *Enemies List*. There, that had a nice dramatic ring to it.

1. Betty's sister Mary. What caused their estrangement? Why did the sister keep calling her? Why would Betty get so annoyed when someone suggested healing the breach? Where was she when Betty died?

2. Deb Wheelock. Embarrassing, but according to Deb, not a big deal.

3. Helen Martino. Why would Betty want to insinuate herself into the Martinos' marriage? And how angry would Tim have been — with Betty — if she had?

4. Patrick Barry. That Buffalo fire was a pretty big secret he was carrying.

5. Charlotte Delaney. Betty was blocking Lottie's request for the architectural waiver that would allow her to move

back into her apartment. Why? The business with Betty's sister seemed pretty flimsy. And how could Lottie possibly have killed Betty, given her physical limitations?

6. Liz Steinbach. Betty pressured her to vote against Charlotte's waiver, using her actions in a previous job against her.

7. X. The unknown.

Writing it down wasn't helping. Annoyed with myself, I crossed Lottie's name off the list. It was ridiculous to think she'd be capable of such a thing, even if she had two working feet. Besides, how many others in our friendly little community had a beef with Betty that I wasn't aware of?

Maybe it had nothing to do with Betty's manipulative behavior. Maybe it was something more basic, like money. If that was the case, I didn't have a chance at figuring it out. I threw down my pen in disgust.

Why did it look so easy in books?

Just then, my phone rang again. "You decent? Can I come up?" Pru asked. "I'm just leaving the clubhouse."

"Sure."

She arrived a couple minutes later. She reached for the slider when she saw me in the kitchen, but it was locked. I hurried over and opened it.

Pru looked at me curiously. "You're keeping it locked now?"

"Well, with everything that's been going on. . ."

She nodded. "Yeah, me too. Anyhow, I've done my civic duty for today." She waggled her slightly ink-stained fingers in the air. "They tried to clean off their fingerprinting gunk, but they didn't do a very good job." She loped toward the sink.

"How was it over there?"

"Not bad. They had it set up like an assembly line. A deputy sat at the door taking names and filling out a little card for each person to take with them up to the table where the guy with the fingerprint kit was sitting, and then afterwards we each had to go answer some questions. Detective Henderson was there for a while, but he left and that Detective Lopez talked to me.

"And to think I'm missing all that fun," I smiled. "Michael and I had ours taken last night."

"Yeah, last night. Dish, girlfriend," she commanded, joining me at the table. "I've been dying of curiosity. You never came back after you parked Flossie with me, and when I asked Dave he just said he couldn't stay."

I filled Pru in on the scene in the Harris' apartment. "I'm sorry I didn't come back up to see you afterwards," I said. "I was exhausted and my knee was killing me. I almost didn't make it home. Keith was outside with Jennifer and they wanted to talk, but I had to excuse myself. I just fell into bed."

"It's been a busy couple of days, for sure."

"What kinds of questions did the detective ask you this morning?"

"Pretty much what you'd expect, I guess. Was I home between four and eight PM, did I hear anything or see anything unusual."

"Did you?"

"No, someone came and knocked on Greg's door around five, but then they went away again. I didn't notice anything else."

"Keith said he tried to visit around then and nobody was home."

"Keith?" Pru sounded surprised. "He doesn't socialize. And I never saw him with either of the Harrises before."

"I suspect a lot of people have knocked on Greg's door in the past two days who aren't close to him."

"Oh, sure, you're probably right."

At the sound of footsteps I looked up.

"I just got off the phone with Dave," Michael said. "They'll be done with Greg's apartment shortly and he can go back. Dave and Deb have volunteered to help him clean up the mess, and they're wondering if we can help, too."

"Since I'm wearing my knee brace, yes. But preferably a task where I don't have to do a lot of bending down. Pru, do you want to join the fun?"

"Somehow I doubt it will be a lot of fun, but sure."

Michael smiled. "Okay, I'll have Dave text me when they're ready for us." He left the kitchen, fingers already tapping on the phone.

"Knee brace?" Pru asked, raising her eyebrows.

"Yeah. The usual, but it's worse because I've been going up and down a lot of stairs since Monday."

Before Pru could respond, my phone rang again. "It's Lottie," I said. I hit the button to accept the call.

"Hey, Lottie, what's up?"

"Oh, Lily," Lottie sounded upset. "I just received a visit from that Detective Henderson and a helper with a fingerprint kit."

I interrupted her. "Pru's right here, is it okay if I put you on speaker?"

"Sure." I hit the button.

"Okay, let's start again," I said. "The detective got your fingerprints?"

"That's right. He took my prints and he wanted details about my relationship with Betty."

Even over the phone, I sensed the air quotes around *relationship* when Lottie said it.

"What did you tell him?"

"The truth. That I didn't like her at all, and I thought she was purposely obstructing my architectural waiver because she was angry that I spoke up about her issues with her sister."

"Wow, you go, girl!" Pru said.

"Then he asked where I was between midnight and six AM two days ago."

"You're kidding me."

"I wouldn't dream of it. And I got the impression he was going to check with the staff here and verify it."

"Wow, they must be really stymied if they're looking at you. And don't worry about the fingerprints, they're getting everyone's. They took Michael's and mine last night, and Pru's sitting here right now with grimy hands."

"I know, he told me. Anyway, if you can keep me in the loop with what's going on over there, I'd appreciate it."

"Of course we will. I'm going to be busy this afternoon, but maybe I can come over again tomorrow." I looked at Pru.

"Me too," she said.

"Would you? That would be super."

After disconnecting, I said thoughtfully, "The detective must be desperate for clues. Honestly, what is the man thinking, asking Lottie for an alibi?"

Pru shook her head. "Well, if we're going to be drafted into service cleaning up Greg's place, I've got a few things I need to do first. I'll see you over there."

After Pru left, I cleared away the coffee things. I should eat something, but I wasn't very hungry. Just frustrated. The more I learned, the less I understood. Obviously I was missing some important pieces of the puzzle.

And now, besides agreeing to share information with the detective, I'd told Linda I'd help her and Patrick as well. What was I getting myself into? Especially since Michael didn't want me involved. I picked up the list again, the one Pru's visit had interrupted. There was something she'd said, what was it? Oh, yes, that Betty and Greg had a fight the night before she died. She'd mentioned it the other morning, just after the detective had questioned her. What was that about? Maybe I could get Greg to tell me this afternoon.

***

Watchful, worried eyes watched as residents streamed into the clubhouse and came out with grimy fingertips. They would have to join them shortly, or have deputies coming to the apartment. They'd felt so sure the problem was solved, but what if they'd just made it worse? No, nothing could be worse than that hateful witch. She'd been begging for it for years, and she'd gotten it.

Fifteen

After lunch, I limped down the stairs to meet Michael and the others at Greg's apartment. I hated the knee brace. On the plus side, it definitely eased the discomfort, but I disliked the artificially springy feeling in that knee when I moved. And it certainly didn't add anything to my outfit of denim shorts and a bright pink tee shirt and pink and blue earrings. I wondered briefly if they made them in colors instead of just plain black, then decided a color-coordinated brace would be even worse.

Walking around the pool, I wondered if I'd ever look out at it again with pleasure, or enjoy a refreshing dip on a hot day. It looked so strange with nobody out there. Each of the gates to the pool area still sported an off-limits sign. This time the signs weren't from the police, but because the pool required a special treatment before it could be reopened..

At least the noise had died down. The landscapers must be working at the other end of the complex.

When I arrived at D-1, Flossie rushed up to me, sniffed, licked my offered hand in a perfunctory way, then trudged back into the living room, tail drooping.

I greeted Greg and the Wheelocks. Greg didn't look great, though he seemed more alert than he'd been the previous couple of days. His khaki shorts didn't look entirely clean, and his blue polo was a bit threadbare. I'd always had the impression before that he was a snappy dresser, but perhaps Betty had chosen his outfits for him every morning.

Glancing around the great room, I took stock of what needed doing. In the daylight it looked even worse than I remembered. Where to start? The actual cleaning would be horrendous. "Greg, do you have a plan for how you want to tackle this?" I asked.

Greg gave a start. "Sorry, no. Do you?"

Deb and I shared an exasperated look. Men. . .

"Between the mess the intruder left and the fingerprint dust all over everything, I suspect you're going to have to hire a cleaning service. I think the best we can do is put it back in order."

Deb agreed. "I'm happy to help, Greg, but I don't have it in me to do a deep clean of your entire apartment."

They all looked at me expectantly, like I was in charge. How did that happen? I walked around the room, surveying the mess. "How about somebody starts with replacing all the couch cushions and putting all the chairs back in place. And someone else should pick up all the stuff that's been tossed onto the floor and collect it in one place. That can't be me, my knee's acting up again. And someone will need a broom for that," I said, pointing to the smashed remains of that creepy decorative plate featuring Flossie in her tutu. I couldn't blame the intruder for breaking that particular item.

Dave volunteered for the chairs, and Deb said she'd do the cushions.

"Okay, Greg," I said, "if you'll pick up the other stuff from the floor and bring it over to the dining room table, I'll sort through it, see what's damaged, and what can be put back where it was before this happened."

"Even the books?"

"Let's start with everything that's not a book, and then do the books all together. Oh, and we'll need a garbage bag for anything that can't be salvaged."

"Okay." I followed him to the kitchen and and he handed me a trash bag, and I also grabbed a handful of paper towels. I brought them all into the dining room and cleaned off a chair and the table top. The fingerprint dust was everywhere.

I sat down at the table, dropping my tote bag next to me.

Greg started picking up pictures and knickknacks from the floor. When he came over with his first armful, I was just about to ask him about his fight with Betty when someone knocked at the front door, and he went to answer. A moment later Pru and Michael came in. Flossie wagged her tail half-heartedly, then curled up again on her bed in the corner.

"Hi, hon," I smiled at my husband, who came over and kissed my cheek.

"So what should I do?" he asked.

"Want to pick up some books?"

"Sure." He looked at the books strewn across the floor. "Pru, you're the librarian, want to give me a hand with this?"

She nodded and walked over to the bookcase. "If you'll hand them to me, I'll shelve. It is my area of expertise, after all."

"Okay."

"Hey, Greg, do these books go in any particular order?" Pru asked.

Greg shrugged. "Doesn't matter to me."

"Alright, I'll use my judgment."

While we worked, we tried to find things to talk about other than the events of the past three days. "What do you think about the Stanley Cup win the other day?" Dave asked. "I mean, the Washington Capitals?"

"I can't remember the last time the Bruins won the cup," Deb said.

"Two thousand eleven. They haven't been doing well these past few years." Dave's response was fast.

Michael looked amused. "I didn't realize you two were Bruins fans."

"Well, we did both grow up in New England," Dave reminded him.

"Oh, right, I'd forgotten. I went to a few Bruins games when I was growing up," Michael said. "Bobby Orr really turned that team around. In fact," he grinned, "I remember the parade after they won the cup in 1970. I was in my apprenticeship in Boston then, and they let everyone off for the afternoon to go cheer the team on. Afterwards, I went up to my dad's office and he was fuming."

Dave looked surprised. "Why?"

Michael smiled again. "The parade route went right by his office building, and all the cars that had been parked along the road were damaged because fans climbed on them and caved in the roofs with all their jumping around and cheering. I thought it was kind of funny, but he was outraged."

"I never heard this story before," I said. "Was his car one of the damaged ones?"

"No. But he'd been issued a company car for a trip the next day, and it was. I never knew my dad knew those words before then." He chuckled.

Greg dropped several framed photos on the table in front of me. One of the frames was bent at the corner and the glass was cracked. I glanced at the photo, a smarmy shot with Betty and Greg on either side of Flossie, all of them wearing matching Christmas sweaters. Ugh.

Carefully, so as not to cut myself on the jagged glass sticking up, I turned it over and slid up the little doohickeys holding the cardboard backing in place. Idly, I wondered if there was an actual word for the doohickeys. It didn't matter, I wasn't going to spend any time looking it up. I removed the cardboard, and pulled out the photos. Photos, plural. What?

Behind the smarmy Christmas portrait was another picture, a professional shot of ten young men in Army uniform, standing at attention and staring seriously into the camera. Puzzled, I called over to Greg.

"Hey, Greg, can you come here for a minute?"

Greg ambled over and I held it up. "I just found this behind another picture in one of the damaged frames. What do you want me to do with it?"

"I've never seen this before. What picture was it behind?" I held up the glossy photo. "Weird. I don't know anything about it."

"So what do you want me to do with it?"

"I don't care. Throw it away, it means nothing to me." He turned to walk away but I stopped him.

"Hey, Greg, I had another question." He looked at me inquiringly, but before I could ask him about his fight with Betty, Pru called him over to show him a damaged book.

A few minutes later I had finished sorting through the pictures. One other frame was damaged, so I had two unframed pictures laid out on clean paper towels on the table, and the remains of the frames were in the trash bag next to my chair.

I called across the room to him, "Greg, most of these pictures can all go back where they belong. I found another damaged one, so you'll need to get two new frames."

"Okay."

"We're about done with the books here," Michael said. "Where do you want us to go next?

"Bedroom," Greg decided.

The bedroom looked as bad as the living room. More framed photos, as well as pillows and bedclothes, were on the floor, and all the dresser drawers had been turned over, their contents dumped in heaps. Nightstand drawers gaped open, and most of the clothes had been pulled from the closet and dumped on the floor. This was going to take a while, but the room wasn't big enough for all of us.

Michael said, "It looks like practically everything in here needs to be picked up off the floor. Honey, maybe you should check out what needs doing in the other bedroom that would let you stay off your feet and not have to do all this bending down."

I was relieved that someone else had suggested it. Pru volunteered to go with me. From the doorway, we surveyed the room, which didn't look nearly as bad as the living room and master bedroom. Perhaps the intruder had run out of steam, or been interrupted before finishing his or her destruction.

The top of the desk had been swept clean, all its contents on the floor, and the drawers were open but not emptied. A few of the books from the bookcase were scattered on the floor, but most were still on the shelves. One lonely file folder sat off to the side. The closet gaped open, but held only a few items and those were still hanging on the rod. The shelf above it looked untouched. Only one pillow had been swept off the bed onto the floor, and Pru picked it up and restored it to its place.

I put the paper towels to good use while Pru sat on the floor in front of the bookcase picking up the few volumes that were on the floor.

After I wiped down the top of the desk, I started pushing drawers into place. The bottom drawer was built to hold file folders, and was empty except for a couple scraps of paper and a blank label on the bottom.

"This is odd, Pru, no files in the file drawer. I wonder if the police took them away."

"Why would they want Betty's files?"

"Maybe they thought they'd find a clue in them?" I shrugged. "Anything interesting in the bookcase?"

"Not really. Somebody likes cheap thrillers, and there are quite a few old yearbooks and a couple of photo albums."

"I wonder what kinds of photos Betty deemed worthy of putting into albums? The living room was mostly family photos."

As we talked, Flossie wandered in, looking at us curiously. "I wish you could tell us who came in and made this mess," I said as I picked up the little dog and held her close. My knee twinged. Must remember not to bend down again, I thought.

Pru stood up, two photo albums in hand, and placed them on the desk. "Here, Miss Nosy, sit down and take a look." I gratefully slid onto the desk chair.

The photos in the first album were old and faded. Most of them seemed to be pictures of Betty as a child, and then as a teenager, sometimes with other people. It was easy to identify her parents. There was a picture of Betty in a graduation cap and gown, and I remembered seeing its duplicate in a frame in the living room. Another showed a smiling Betty surrounded by what I assumed were proud family members, including a younger girl who looked a lot like her.

"Oh, I bet this is the sister who hates her!" I held it out to Pru. "Take a look."

She studied it briefly. "Could be, I know someone said Betty was a few years older. This girl looks to be about ten years old, was there that big an age difference?"

"No idea. There don't seem to be any other siblings, and that's a pretty big gap. What do you think, about seven or eight years?"

Pru nodded.

"Oh, wait." I thought for a moment. "I think Greg said something about it when we were eating dinner last night. That's right, eight years."

I quickly flipped through the second album, while Pru looked over my shoulder. We spotted a younger Greg, a few wedding photos, and then some shots of Betty, pregnant. She didn't look very happy in any of them. After that there were a handful of baby pictures, and photos of a little boy. The album ended with a picture showing a grinning child labeled *first day of kindergarten*.

"Odd. You'd think there'd be more pictures of him growing up. Greg told me he died about ten years ago, so he would have been an adult by then."

I handed the albums back to Pru, who replaced them in the bookshelf. We looked around. "Guess we're done here," Pru said, "let's see how the others are doing."

In the master bedroom, order was mostly restored, but everything was still grimy with fingerprint dust. "Greg, you really should hire a cleaning service to come through the whole apartment before you spend much time here," I said. "It can't be healthy to be breathing all this, and it's gotten into your bedding, and all the upholstery, probably the carpets, too."

"You're welcome to stay with us as long as you need to," Deb said.

"I wonder if the detective can recommend a cleaning crew that specializes in this kind of thing? Want me to ask him?"

Greg shrugged. "Okay I guess. I don't really like the idea of staying here after that break-in anyway."

"Oh, Greg, I noticed when Pru and I were cleaning up the study that the file drawer is empty. Did the police take all your files away?"

"I have no idea. That was all Betty's anyway." He wrinkled his forehead. "Seems like it was pretty full last time I noticed."

I wandered back across the hall to the guest bedroom and placed a call to the detective. I got his voicemail, so I left a quick message asking about cleaning services.

Curious about the photo albums, which ended so abruptly years before, I went to the bookcase. Wow, when Pru said there were a few yearbooks, she wasn't kidding. I stopped counting at a dozen. Who keeps that many high school yearbooks?

Oddly, they seemed to be from several different schools, and spanned the years from 1962 to 1971, my own graduation year. Idly, I pulled out the newest one and started thumbing through it. My goodness, those kids looked so young. Was that really how we wore our hair back then?

In another one, I spotted Betty's sister beaming into the camera as the senior class vice president. Angela Mary Parker was the name printed under the photo. She'd been a pretty girl.

My phone vibrated. Glancing at the caller ID, I answered. "Hello, Detective, thanks for calling me back so promptly."

"Mrs. Gallagher, what can I do for you?"

I explained about Greg's need for a specialized cleaning service.

"The department has a few companies we recommend, but I don't have that information at my fingertips. If you'll call the regular non-emergency number, they'll be able to help you."

"Okay, I'll do that. I also have a question for you."

"Shoot."

"Pru and I were tidying the guest bedroom, and we noticed the file drawer was empty. Did the police take the files, or did the intruder make off with them?"

"Mrs. Gallagher, are you trying to do my job?"

"Not at all, Detective." I crossed my fingers. "But if the police didn't take them, it's curious that they're missing, don't you think? I asked Greg, and he didn't know anything about them, said that was all Betty's stuff, but he thought the drawer was full last time he noticed it."

The detective was silent. "Well, thanks for calling back," I finally said and disconnected.

A few minutes later I found the others, now all congregated in the kitchen. "Greg, the Sheriff's Department recommended some cleaners and I've asked them to come tomorrow morning. They'll be here at ten thirty. Can you be here to let them in?"

When Greg hesitated, Dave said, "One of us will be. No problem."

I walked over to Michael. "I'm ready to hit the shower and put my feet up. How about you?"

Amid general agreement, Greg called to Flossie, and we all left the apartment.

"Pru, want to come up for a drink?" I asked.

"Sounds good. Get some of that fingerprint dust out of our throats." We started walking toward Building E. Not wanting to upset Michael, I didn't say anything, but I was disappointed I hadn't been able to talk to Greg about the fight with Betty. How was I going to figure out who'd killed her?

Sixteen

After his brief phone call with Lily, Henderson sat lost in thought for a few minutes, then picked up the phone. When it was answered, he said, "Lopez, do you recall any mention of files or file folders in the report from yesterday's break-in at the Harris apartment?"

"File folders? No."

"Okay, then," Henderson said. "Organize a couple of patrol officers. I want every Dumpster in the neighborhood searched for a drawerful of missing files." Before Lopez could object he sighed and said, "I know it's a Sunday afternoon, but we have a murder to solve."

"Okay, boss."

"Once you've done that, tell Sanchez and DaSilva to be ready for a meeting to go over the case, five-thirty sharp."

He put the phone down, making an effort not to slam it. He hated this part of an investigation, where they had so many threads to sift through and didn't know yet what was important.

His stomach growled audibly. When was the last time he ate? He couldn't remember. Realizing he'd think more clearly once he had some food in him, he grabbed his jacket off the back of his chair and strode from the room.

By five-twenty he was back in his office, somewhat restored. A fast food burger and fries wasn't the breakfast of champions, but it would tide him over for now. He'd also swung through the drive-through line at Starbucks and brought back an iced Americano to sip during the meeting. Draping his jacket over the back of his chair, he picked up his coffee and headed down the hall to the war room.

War closet was more like it. At one end of the room was a large whiteboard. A couple of card tables, folding chairs, and a computer terminal completed the setup. There was barely room for the four of them, but it would have to do.

There wasn't much on the whiteboard yet. A picture of the victim, Betty Harris, was centered at the top. Just below was a picture of the husband. Residents of Happy Oaks were listed, starting with Prudence MacLeod, the woman who'd raised the alarm, and Michael Gallagher, the man who'd called nine-one-one, then the rest. He was pretty confident they'd find their murderer already on that board, but he needed evidence which was in short supply so far.

"Sir!" Detective Matthew Lopez said loudly as he walked into the room. Lopez was a decent assistant, Henderson thought, but he wasn't sure the man was cut out for detective work. He was good at following orders, but never seemed to take initiative or think independently.

Lopez affected a more casual look than his boss, generally wearing khakis and a polo shirt instead of a suit or at least good slacks with a sports jacket. This was the first time Henderson had seen him today, and he noted without comment the brown slip-on sneakers on his feet. Lopez followed his glance.

"Sorry, sir, I don't wear these out on the street, I just keep them in my car to wear in the office when my feet are killing me." Henderson nodded his understanding. At least Lopez was perceptive, that was something.

Lopez studied the whiteboard. A minute later, Deputies Melanie Sanchez and Mario DaSilva entered. They were the patrol officers who'd been dispatched to the Harris apartment following the break-in. Henderson had worked with them before, so he'd requested them for his team. They made a good partnership, Sanchez with her quick intuition and quirky sense of humor and DaSilva more serious and analytical.

Henderson greeted them and motioned them to the folding chairs.

As soon as they were seated, he began. "It's been a busy couple of days, and we need to nail this guy before he commits any more crimes. So we're going to review the evidence, again, and do some brainstorming. If you have an idea, shout it out. We're not standing on ceremony here."

"So, first things first. Let's get the timeline up here."

He turned to the whiteboard and drew a vertical line, creating a column. At the top he printed TIMELINE in large block capitals.

"What do we know? Let's start with the facts we're certain about, then we'll add information from interview statements."

Painstakingly they reviewed the events of the morning of June 7, beginning with the nine-one-one call from Michael Gallagher.

"Do we have a time of death yet?" Henderson asked.

Lopez flipped through his notes. "Yes, I checked with the coroner just before I came down here. Between midnight and five. He said the estimate was complicated by not knowing how long the body was in the pool, or how long after death it was placed in the pool.

Henderson noted the times next to the victim's picture, then added, "cause of death, strangulation."

"Okay, what else do we know for sure?"

"Did the coroner have any more information about the way she was killed?" asked Sanchez.

"Manual strangulation. If there were any fibers, they washed off in the pool. The victim was tall, but it could have been done by a strong woman if the victim was seated at the time. More likely a man, though." He added that information to the board.

"What else?"

"Yesterday at 7:27 PM we received a nine-one-one call reporting a break-in at Mr. Harris' apartment. The call came from Lily Gallagher. DaSilva and Sanchez arrived at 7:41."

"Sanchez, what did you find?"

Henderson wrote busily as Sanchez described the scene, then asked, "What do we know about the murder victim?"

Lopez looked at his notes. "Okay, she was a busybody. She manipulated people. She was president of their condo board, which gave her access to all the residents' background checks and by all accounts she enjoyed finding out people's secrets and using those secrets against them for her own purposes. And she was good at it."

"Do we know what those purposes were? Any actual blackmail?" Sanchez asked.

"Monetary blackmail? Possibly. No evidence of it."

Next to Betty's picture on the board, Henderson wrote "blackmailer" followed by a question mark. "Alright, let's go through the witness statements. We'll start with the people at the pool on Thursday morning."

Lopez shuffled through a stack of papers, then began listing residents.

"That's it," Lopez said, "for those who were at the pool."

"Not quite," Henderson said. "We need to add Timothy Martino to the list. Apparently he was at the pool, then left before we arrived. It's in my report."

Lopez shuffled more papers. "Okay, got it. Timothy Martino, unit D3, married to Helen. Claims he only went to the pool because his wife wanted to know what the screaming was about and left before we arrived because he didn't want to waste his time."

DaSilva gave a low whistle.

Henderson put down the marker. "I had a very interesting interview with Mr. Martino. He's a classic bully, and he's used to getting his own way. He's obviously been browbeating his wife for years, and most people probably take care not to cross him. He's disowned his only son for being homosexual, only he uses other descriptive names for it, and the secret his wife was terrified to tell him is that she had booked a flight to attend their son's upcoming wedding."

He paused for breath. "Fortunately, like most bullies, he can dish it out but he can't take it. While I believe it's important to treat members of the public with respect, the polite approach won't work with this guy. If you have any dealings with him, you have my permission to be as harsh as you please."

After a moment's thought he added, "I don't know whether the victim ever tried to cross him, certainly nothing he's admitted to, but he has a violent temper. I don't have any problem imagining him putting his hands around a woman's neck and squeezing in a fit of rage. But placing the body in the pool afterwards? I think that would be very uncharacteristic."

He added Tim's name to the list, with the notation "violent, homophobic bully."

"Now," looking at Lopez, "what about the residents who were not at the pool Thursday morning?"

Lopez reviewed the list. "There are a few snowbirds who aren't living here at the moment, do you want me to include them?"

"Let's set them aside for now."

"Okay," Lopez said, "in Building A we have Kim and Minnie Nguyen in A2, and Jeff and Martha Ericson in A4. Building B, Clara and Leroy Jones in B2 and Sandra Laroux in B3. Building

C, we have Elizabeth Steinbach in C1 and Steven Collins in C3. Everyone in Building D and E is already accounted for since those are the two buildings that look out over the pool. Samuel and Michelle Hoffman are in F1, and Richard Brophy in F2. Oh, and Charlotte Delaney in F4, only she's not here."

"It might be helpful if we have a map, or at least a diagram, of the community layout," DaSilva said.

"Good idea. Now, let me clarify about Ms. Delaney," Henderson said. "She's not a snowbird, but she's currently living in a rehab center, and she's been the center of some controversy in Happy Oaks."

"What's this controversy?" Sanchez asked.

"It's the type of thing that can sound silly to an outsider, but can be extremely divisive for the residents," Henderson said. He sat down at the table and explained Ms. Delaney's situation, including her belief that Mrs. Harris was acting out of personal animosity.

"Why was that?" Lopez asked.

"She's not sure, but Ms. Delaney thinks the victim was angry because she tried to encourage her to patch things up with her estranged sister."

"That doesn't make any sense," DaSilva said.

"I agree, not a lot," Henderson said, "but I don't think our victim was a very sensible woman. I'd be curious what a psych profile would show. I suspect a healthy dose of narcissism at the very least. Maybe borderline personality disorder."

"Lopez, when are we going to get results from all the fingerprints we took from residents?" Henderson asked.

"I'll find out."

Henderson tapped his pen on the table in front of him while he thought for a minute. He reached for a manila envelope and pulled out a stack of photos, selecting several that showed the victim's neck.

"What type of crime do we think this is?" he asked, fanning them out to give Lopez, Sanchez, and DaSilva a better look.

He was met with three blank stares. "Is it a crime of passion? Is it premeditated? What's the motivation?"

"Manual strangulation would indicate it was personal, and likely not premeditated," Lopez said. "But moving the body to the pool afterwards? I don't know if that fits."

"Is it possible the victim was just in the wrong place at the wrong time?" Sanchez asked.

"I don't see how," Lopez said. "I mean, she was killed at or very close to her own home, in the middle of the night."

Sanchez tapped her fingers on the table in front of her. "If she had an appointment to meet with Mr. Barry at six in the morning, maybe she had an appointment to meet with her killer at midnight or whatever."

"Are we ruling out the husband?" Henderson asked.

"If the break-in's connected to the murder, he couldn't have done that," Lopez said. "So, maybe? The spouse is always the first suspect, but I don't see it."

"The person who broke into Harris' place was a Happy Oaks resident, right?" DaSilva asked.

"That's the assumption, for now at least."

"So we need to find out which residents were present at Happy Oaks while Harris and the Gallaghers were having dinner," Sanchez said.

"Did we get that information when we took fingerprints?" Henderson looked at Lopez. Lopez shuffled through his notes, then nodded. "We asked them where they were between four and eight PM."

"Okay, let's have the list of the residents who were on the property during that time. Start with Building A and work your way up."

"It might be simpler to tell you who wasn't on the property."

Henderson grimaced. "Go ahead."

"Kim Nguyen, A2, was at work, got home around six-thirty. Clara and Leroy Jones were attending a social at their church starting at five PM, then went to another couple's house, arrived back home just before eleven. Richard Brophy in F2 was out with a friend from five-thirty until quite late, and Samuel and Michelle Hoffman were at temple. They had dinner with another couple at the other couple's house at five, then went to temple together. They got home around nine o'clock."

"And everyone else was here?"

"Well, except for Mr. Harris and the Gallaghers, of course."

Henderson stood and placed a large 'XB' next to each of the names, indicating they were unlikely suspects for the break-in.

"That doesn't narrow it down a lot, does it? Any questions? Additions?" After a moment, he said, "Well, it's getting late. DaSilva, get a map of the community for us as soon as you can. Sanchez, stay on top of the fingerprints. Lopez, let me know immediately if your guys find those missing files. Also, I think we need to look at the money. See what financial information you can dig up, and find out if she left a will. Everyone, get a good night's sleep, and we'll come back at this tomorrow."

***

We strolled around the pool toward Building E. I was favoring my right leg while trying not to limp. "Once I'm upstairs, I'm not coming down again today," I warned my husband. "I need to put my feet up."

"That's okay. I don't think we need to go anywhere, but I'll take care of it if we do."

Keith was on his porch again, accompanied by Jennifer. They looked very cozy. "Hey, neighbors, want a beer?" Keith offered, waving with the can in his hand. "It's a new IPA I'm trying. I'd love to know what you think of it."

"I wouldn't turn it down." Michael said.

I guess I wasn't going to put my feet up just yet. Michael liked beer, but I didn't. "Well, I'll pass on the beer, I've never developed a taste for it."

"I'd love one," Pru said.

"Can I get you something else, Lily? Sweet tea?"

"No thanks, Keith. A glass of cold water would be great, though."

He waved us to seats as he stepped through the sliding glass door into the kitchen. As I sank into a well cushioned rattan porch chair, I sighed. "You may never get me out of this chair and up the stairs," I warned Michael.

"Is something wrong?" Jennifer asked me.

"Oh, my knee. It flares up from time to time, and I've been doing too much the past couple of days."

"That's a shame. My mother had to have knee replacement a few years ago, and I remember how much pain she was in before they did the surgery. Is that what you're facing?"

"I hope not, but I'm sure you don't want all the gory details. How are you? I understand you may be the new member on our condo board."

Jennifer grinned happily. "I'd like to. This is such a nice community. Or, it has been until now anyway. I'd like to contribute something."

"Being on the board isn't for sissies," Michael said. "It's probably a bigger commitment than you expect. You're still working, right? Not retired yet?"

"I'm sure it'll be fine. I'll be working for a few more years, but it's not like I have anything else to occupy my time. Single, no kids, so I can do what I want with my nights and weekends."

"What is it you do?" Pru asked.

Before Jennifer could answer, Keith bustled back through the slider. He brought me my water first, then handed cans to Michael and Pru.

Michael popped the tab and gulped down a few swallows. "That hits the spot." He held up the can and read the label. "Oh, I've never seen this one before."

I wasn't interested in listening to the men talk about beer, so I turned to Jennifer. We chatted for a couple minutes, then Keith interrupted us. "What's going on across the way?" He waved in the general direction of Building D. "I saw a whole bunch of you coming out just now."

"Just helping Greg clean up the mess from that break-in last night," I said.

"Someone told me his place was totally trashed. Is that true?"

"Not totally," Pru said, "but it was pretty bad."

"Did they take a lot of stuff?"

"That's the strange thing," Michael said. "Greg doesn't think anything was taken. I mean, the obvious things are still there, TV, computers, even Betty's jewelry apparently. But it sure was a mess."

"The detective told us they'll be around asking more questions over the next few days," I said. "They're assuming it's tied into Betty's death."

"What a terrible thing. How's Greg doing?" Jennifer asked.

"Not great," I said. "Dave and Deb are looking after him. He and Flossie are staying with them, at least until after the cleaners finish. Hopefully they'll be able to get it all done tomorrow."

"This isn't exactly what I expected when I moved in here," Keith said. "It's not the quiet life I wanted."

Maybe because I was tired, but his comment irritated me a little. "I don't think it's what anyone wanted. It's certainly showing some rough edges in our little community."

"And speaking of community," I said, turning to Jennifer, "if you're appointed to the board, I'm curious what your thoughts are about the architectural waiver that Charlotte Delaney's requesting."

"Oh, that poor woman," Jennifer said. "Of course she should be able to move back home. That's if she still wants to after this."

"Good to know," Michael said. "At least it looks like Charlotte will be one person who'll be better off because of Betty's death. I probably shouldn't say that," he looked around a little defensively, "but it's true."

"I haven't been here as long as you," Jennifer looked at each of us, "and I don't wish to speak ill of the dead, but I don't believe Betty was a very nice person."

"Why do you say that?" I asked.

"Nothing specific, but when your skin's the color of mine, you learn pretty quickly the difference between a white person's thoughtless remark and an intentional slight."

"Well, until recently I never saw her as anything worse than bossy," I replied, "but over the past couple days I've learned that she said and did awful things to a lot of people."

Jennifer nodded. "It wouldn't surprise me. I got a lot of snide digs and innuendos from her when I ran for the board unsuccessfully."

"How about you, Keith?" I asked. "You ever have any run-ins with her?"

"I've only been here a few months."

It wasn't really an answer. I had several questions I wanted to ask Keith, but it probably wasn't appropriate to do so in front of Jennifer. Besides, I knew if I didn't climb those stairs now, I never would. I drank the last of my water and put my glass on the table. "Thanks for the drink, Keith, I needed it." I turned to Jennifer. "I do hope you're our next board member, and I'm glad you won't have to put up with Betty."

Then, to my husband, "Honey, I'm afraid if I don't get out of this chair right now, I never will. Can you give me a hand?"

He looked surprised but helped me to my feet.

"Stay and finish your beer, I'll be okay once I make it up those stairs," I said. "Keith, thanks for the hospitality. Sorry to rush off like this." I smiled and turned toward the stairs.

Pru swallowed the last of her IPA and waggled the can at her host. "Thanks, Keith, it was very good. Nice and hoppy, just what I like." She put the can on the coffee table. "I think I'll make sure Lily makes it up the stairs okay. See you later, everyone."

Hauling on the banister with my arms to take some of the weight off my right leg, I made slow progress. As I limped into the kitchen I asked, "Iced tea? Or would you prefer a glass of wine?"

"I'll save the wine until after I've showered," Pru said. "Tea's good for now. Even after that beer I'm still thirsty."

"It's nice to see Keith coming out of his shell a little bit," Pru said once we had our drinks and were settled in the living room.

I slung my right foot up onto a hassock. Relief!

"It's strange, because he's been such a loner since he got here. I can hardly remember seeing him talk with anyone."

"True," I said. "I guess there's nothing like a little neighborhood murder to bring people out of their shells. Or maybe it's just Jennifer."

"You think so?"

"Well, she does seem rather smitten, don't you think? And I've noticed them together a few times now."

"It would be nice if something good came out of this mess," Pru said.

I took a sip of tea, then said, "Speaking of murder, Pru, I think you need to tell the detective about the fight between Betty and Greg the night before she died. It might be important."

"You think Greg killed her?" she asked, wide eyed.

"Oh, I don't know. Right now, I suspect everyone. You and Michael are the only people in the place I'm comfortable being alone with."

"Wow." She swirled the tea around in her glass, considering. "I think that's a big stretch. From everything I've seen, he worshiped that woman, and he seems completely broken up."

"True, but I still think you need to tell the detective what you overheard. I don't want to have to sic him on you."

"Okay, okay, but not tonight."

Then, changing the subject to what was uppermost on my mind, I asked, "Got any dinner plans?"

"Not at all. I haven't even thought about it. Definitely not until after I've showered, though."

"Unless Michael has something he's planning to whip up, we'll order some takeout. Want to join us?"

Just then Michael came through the front door. "What was that hurried exit all about?"

I made a face. "I wanted to ask Keith some questions about his dealings with Betty, but I'm too tired to be diplomatic so I decided I'd better leave."

He frowned. "Well, in that case, I'm glad you did. I don't like you in the role of Lily the Investigator. You should leave the pointed questions to Henderson."

"Well, I don't like not feeling safe in my own home, so the sooner we find out who killed Betty, the sooner I can stop feeling like I have to watch my back all the time. Besides, I sort of promised Linda I would. It's that more than anything." I sighed.

"You what?" His hands were on his hips and he was frowning.

Oops, I hadn't told him about Linda's visit that morning. I filled him in, and his frown deepened.

"So let me make sure I understand this. First you told Henderson you'd share information with him, and now you've told Linda you'll help get to the bottom of it. What part of 'there's a killer in the community and you need to stay safe' don't you understand?"

Pru was watching us, wide eyed, head turning like she was watching a tennis match.

I started to stand up, then fell back into my chair. Immediately Michael's irritation morphed into concern. "Are you okay? I mean, besides your knee?" he asked.

"I'm fine, Michael. Just tired. I think it's more mental than physical."

"Well," Pru said, "I don't think you've done anything that would incite someone to murder. You're not like Betty at all."

"Up until a few days ago I didn't think Betty was like Betty," I said. "I can't believe she had me fooled all this time."

"You're lucky."

"The good news is, I'll bet Lottie will get her waiver now, if Jennifer's in favor," I said. "Let's see, who voted for it the first time?"

"Only me and Dave," Michael said.

"So if you two as well as Jennifer and Linda vote in favor, she'll have it. And with Betty gone, I imagine Liz will vote for it, too. When's the meeting?"

"It'll be the fourteenth, next Thursday. "

"That gives us a few days to do some lobbying," Pru said.

"I'll talk with Liz," Michael said, "see where she stands now."

My stomach rumbled audibly. "Oh, dear. Pru and I were just talking about dinner before you came in. Did you have something planned?"

"Nope. You?"

"Not at all. If we order takeout, can you go pick it up?"

"Sure. Let me grab the menus."

He came back with the stack of takeout menus we kept in the kitchen for times like these. I pulled one out. "I need some comfort food. How about Steak 'n Shake?"

"Sounds fine to me. Pru, does that work for you?"

"Yes, but I need to zip home and shower before I eat."

"Same. But Michael, if you're going to pick up the food you should go first. I'll phone in the order once you're out of the shower, then I'll get cleaned up while you run over to pick it up."

"Sounds like a plan, honey. Pru, I'll see you shortly." He headed toward the master bedroom. "Oh, I almost forgot," he said, stopping in the doorway. "When we were cleaning Greg buttonholed me and Dave into agreeing to be pallbearers at the funeral."

"Really? I thought that was usually reserved for close friends and family." I don't think I hid my surprise.

"Well, since Betty didn't have any family she was still speaking to, Greg has to call on his friends, even if they're not that close."

"That's terrible. And sad." I thought for a moment. "Are you up for it?"

"No, but I'll manage. I just feel bad for the guy."

"Does that mean you'll be stuck going to the graveside service as well as the church part of it?"

"I'll find out." He turned back toward the shower.

***

I guess now's as good a time as any. My head is pounding like hell.

Now, let's see what's in that damn folder. Not sure why I grabbed this one out of the whole drawer full. Old news clippings. Must be something in there.

Can't see very well, maybe a flashlight would help. I don't want to turn the lights on. If they're off maybe all my nosy neighbors will think I'm not here. Yes, that's better.

Watchful eyes flicked over old newspaper clippings, brittle and yellowed, dating back to the 1960s. Small-town gossip, sporting events, several lists of local boys killed in the war. Lot of garbage. High school prom queen beaming from the page, almost makes me smile. She looked so happy. A few marriages, births, small-town stuff. Not what I'm looking for.

Nothing. No sign of anything that looks like the evidence the bitch threatened me with. Maybe she didn't have anything after all, maybe I'm finally free. Maybe now the nightmares will stop and I won't have to see that other face, the one I executed all those years ago. But he deserved it, trying to get us all killed. All those bastards over there. I got rid of him so he couldn't destroy my life, and now I've gotten rid of her. It doesn't seem to have helped my life much, police everywhere, nosy neighbors, still no sign of the evidence. If there was anything in those other folders, it's too late now. I should have moved them when I had the chance.

Need to sleep. Maybe if I just take a little nap. Maybe then my head will stop pounding.

Seventeen

My knee was still stiff and sore the next morning, so after breakfast I decided to loosen it up with a gentle walk around the Happy Oaks complex. After adjusting the knee brace, I carefully made my way down the front steps.

I swung to the left and walked alongside the pool. It was a lovely, sunny day, but still nobody occupied any of the pool chairs. I sighed. What a thing to happen.

As I approached Building D, I saw Deb heading toward me with Flossie on her leash. "Hi Deb. Hi Flossie, where are you off to?"

"Morning, Lily." Deb smiled her pixie smile at me. "We're just out for a stroll. Greg's feeling a bit sorry for himself, so I used Flossie as an excuse to leave him to Dave while I got out of the way. How about you?"

"Just walking off the stiffness in my knee. I'm not going anywhere particular. Want some company?"

"Sure."

"How's Greg holding up?"

She shrugged. "Some moments he's fine, and others not so much. What you'd expect, I guess. Right now, he's not the easiest of house guests." She shrugged, then asked, "And how about you?"

"Pretty good," I said. "No, if I'm honest, I'm pretty stressed. I'll be glad when they find who's responsible. I feel like I have to look over my shoulder all the time."

"I know what you mean."

Flossie started whining and pulling on her lead, and I realized we were approaching the back door to the Harris' apartment. Deb's normally cheerful mouth turned down. "Poor thing, I think she wants to go home."

The little dog didn't seem to be focused on the door, but on something nearby. "Ouch. I didn't think a dog this small could pull this hard," Deb said as Flossie yanked her off the path.

I looked at where the dog was heading, pushed my glasses firmly up on my nose, then touched Deb's arm. "Deb, do you see something in the azalea bushes?"

"There's something in the bushes?" With a frantic jerk, Flossie ripped the leash out of Deb's hand and took off, barking and whining. She crawled under a bush and stood there, barking so hard her little body was shaking.

"It's a garbage bag," Deb said. "What's a garbage bag doing in the bushes, and what's in it to get Flossie so worked up?" She darted toward the bushes. "Let's get that thing in the Dumpster."

"No, Deb, stop!"

She looked at me over her shoulder as I hobbled to keep up with her. "Why?" Flossie was practically shaking herself apart with her barking.

"I have a hunch about what it might be, and if I'm right we need to leave it alone. Can you pick Flossie up?"

Once Deb had a firm grip on the dog, and was watching me as if I'd lost my mind, I crouched down, ignoring the pain in my knee, and carefully eased my arm through the bush. "If it's what I think it is we shouldn't move it, we'll leave that for the detectives." I started prodding the bag. "I think we've just found Betty's missing files."

"What missing files? What's going on?"

"Oh, that's right, you were in the other room." I said. She frowned, so I explained. "When Pru and I were straightening Greg's guest bedroom yesterday, we discovered the file drawer was completely empty so I called the detective. He wouldn't tell me, but I got the impression they'd missed the missing files. So to speak."

"Maybe that's what the break-in was about, finding something in one of Betty's files?"

"Maybe. If that's what's in this bag, it would certainly lead you to think that."

"So what are we supposed to do?" Flossie was squirming like crazy, trying to get back down on the ground.

"Call the cavalry," I said cheerfully as I backed out and stood. My knee wasn't at all happy. Flossie was still whining as I pulled my phone out of my pocket. Looking through the recent call history, I found the detective's name and pushed the call button. At this rate, I should put him on speed dial.

"Detective, I think we've found the missing files," I said when he picked up.

"Oh? Mrs. Gallagher?" His tone was guarded. "And who is 'we?'"

"Actually, Flossie was the one who found them."

"Flossie? What's her last name? Is she a resident there?"

I tried to keep my voice even as I said, "Sure, she lives in D1."

"Oh, the dog." Now he sounded annoyed. I could tell he was working to keep the exasperation out of his voice when, after a moment of silence, he said, "Tell me about it."

I decided further teasing wouldn't be well received. "Deb Wheelock and I were walking with Flossie, and she led us to them. She started whining and barking and pulling on the leash. We're near the back door to the Harris' apartment."

"Stay where you are." The call disconnected..

I turned to Deb. "The detective said to stay put. I guess that means someone will be showing up here to take charge of this bag."

"Well, I'm not going to just stand here. I'm supposed to pick up more dog food for Flossie, so since I've got Greg's keys, let's at least sit on the back porch."

"Good idea."

After Deb unlocked the back door, Flossie was ecstatic and immediately began scratching on the inside door to the apartment. Deb picked her up and sat down with her while I sank onto the matching chair. A few minutes later a uniformed deputy rushed over, looking around.

"Officer," I called out, stepping out the porch door, "are you looking for us?"

"Your name?"

"Lily Gallagher, and this is Deb Wheelock. Did Detective Henderson send you?"

"Yes, I'm Deputy Brent Walker," he introduced himself. "Show me what you've found."

I led him over to the bush where the garbage bag was hiding.

"Did you touch it? Move it?"

"I touched it, yes. I did my best not to move it," I said. "I only ran my hand over it to try to figure out what was in it, and it feels like paper to me."

"Okay, Detective Henderson will be here shortly. He'll want to talk to you."

"I'm sure he will."

The deputy walked away a few paces and spoke into his radio. I went back inside the porch and sat down.

About fifteen minutes later the detective strode toward us. He spoke with the deputy briefly, then looked at me and sighed.

"I've got a team coming to examine the bag, so I sure hope you're right and not wasting police time on someone's trash." His tone was brusque. "Tell me again how you came across it."

I pointed to Flossie. "It wasn't me, it was Flossie," I reminded him, and explained how Flossie had led us to the spot.

"Mrs. Wheelock, do you have anything to add?"

"No. It was just like Lily said. We were having a quiet stroll when Flossie started going nuts. Lily spotted the bag and pointed it out to me, I guess her eyes are better than mine."

As we were talking, Pru approached around the end of the building. "Lily, I saw the deputy from my window, what's going on now?" she asked, catching sight of me in the doorway. Then, recognizing Henderson, "Oh, hello, Detective."

"Ms. MacLeod," he said, "please don't come any closer."

"What, is this another crime scene?" Her voice was a little higher than normal.

"Possibly. We're treating it as such for now."

"Damn," Pru said. Behind Henderson's back, I was gesturing to her, pointing in the other direction and miming walking with my fingers. "Okay, I'm leaving."

I whispered to Deb, "Go let her in the front door. She can join us here without messing up their crime scene."

"Oh, so that's what all that hand motion was about." Deb's pixie grin was back as she handed Flossie over to me. She unlocked the back door and went into the apartment. A minute later she was back with Pru, both of them giggling.

"This reminds me of being snuck into the dorm after curfew by my friends so the dragon lady in charge wouldn't catch me," Pru chortled.

A moment later a roar sounded from the other end of the building, then the detective shouted. "Mr. Martino, stay right there!"

"What the hell is going on here now?" Tim growled, stomping toward him. "Why are the police tramping across my back yard?"

"We have another crime scene here, now step back. Go back inside your apartment. Now!" When Tim didn't move, the detective took a few steps toward him, and Tim finally turned away and went in his back door. I stuck my head out the screen door and saw several more neighbors standing on the sidewalk, gawking in our direction.

"So what is it?" Pru asked. "What did you find now, Lily?"

"Not me," I protested. "Blame Flossie. I think she found Betty's missing files."

"No way."

I just smiled. "I suspect we'll know in a few minutes."

Twenty minutes later the area in back of the Harris' apartment was awash in spruce green uniforms. A photographer shot dozens of pictures of the bag, the bushes, and the surrounding area. After that was done, a pair of deputies wearing gloves gently eased the bag out from behind the bushes and laid it carefully on a large sheet of plastic they'd spread on the ground, where they took more photos.

The detective approached and, with gloved hands, untied the bag and slid back the top of it. A couple of file folders peeked out.

Pru and I grinned at each other.

He was scowling. "Alright, take it back to the lab and dust everything for prints. Bag, folders, paper, every damn thing." He stood up and removed his gloves. Walking away, he pulled out his phone and spoke briefly. Then he marched over to the porch, eyes widening slightly when he noticed that Pru had joined Deb and me.

"She's not contaminating your crime scene," I pointed out.

"Thank you for your call," Henderson said. I thought it sounded a bit grudging. "You've saved a few deputies some unpleasant Dumpster diving."

"So what's your hypothesis, Detective? Did the thief stash it there for later retrieval?"

"That's what we'll attempt to figure out." He started to walk away, then turned back. "Mrs. Gallagher, ladies, please don't tell anyone what you found, and leave the investigating to the professionals. This man has already killed once, and if those files are part of the same crime, likely it was to hide something the victim had uncovered about him. I would hate for you to become his next victim."

"So it was a man, then?" I asked innocently, trying to hide the fact that I was getting goose bumps as the import of his words sank in.

"It's likely. We don't know for sure. Ladies, take care," he said, and rejoined the other officers.

We left the porch and went into the apartment. Flossie ran around excitedly, sniffing at everything for a minute, then her little tail drooped again and she sat down, watching suspiciously while Deb gathered more supplies for her. As Deb clipped the leash back onto her collar, the front doorbell rang.

"Would you?" she asked, and I went to see who was at the door.

It was the cleaners. Deb looked at her watch.

"Ten thirty. Right on time. I'll tell Greg they're here." She sent a quick text.

Turning to the woman who was obviously in charge of the crew, I asked, "Does one of us need to stay here?"

"That's up to you," the woman said, "but it's not necessary. We're fully licensed and bonded, and very experienced." She nodded to one of her assistants, who started hauling in cleaning supplies and equipment.

"It's okay," I reminded Deb, "this company was recommended by the Sheriff's Department."

"Alright," Deb said to the cleaner. "I guess you should call the owner when you're ready to leave so someone can come lock up. Any idea what time that will be?"

"Job like this? It's mostly fingerprint dust, right?" Deb nodded and she said, "Probably between four and five o'clock."

"Alright then, we'll leave you to it."

Deb picked up Flossie's leash, Pru grabbed the bag she'd put Flossie's food into, and the three of us left the apartment as another helper brought more cleaning supplies from the van parked at the curb. He had to make his way through the crowd that had gathered.

"Too bad nobody here has any curiosity," I murmured. "If our residents ever bothered poking their heads out, they might have caught this guy already."

Pru laughed, a bit nervously.

I tried to identify everyone milling around on the sidewalk. My neighbors Jennifer and Keith were there, standing close together. Helen Martino was there, but not Tim. I guessed he was watching from his back porch. Liz Steinbach, Michelle Hoffman, and, surprisingly, Clara and Leroy Jones were in the crowd as well. Was the murderer one of them? Impossible to know. People were hurling questions at us.

"What's going on?" "What are the cops doing here again?" "Did someone else get killed?" "No, there was no ambulance."

"Pru, can you do this?" I asked quietly. "It's too many people for me."

Pru nodded.

She held up a hand, and they gradually quieted. "Good morning, all. There's not much to tell you. No, there wasn't another murder. Yes, something was found, and the police have taken it away. No, we don't know what it was. There are cleaners at Greg's apartment, he hired them to clean up the mess left after the break-in. They don't know anything about it either, they're just here to do their job and the timing is pure coincidence."

Behind me, my neighbors were chattering away. "Pru, Deb, do you want to come up?" I asked. "I could do with a cup of coffee, how about you?"

"I think I should take Flossie back to Greg," Deb said. "Pru, why did you tell them we didn't know what was found?"

"Henderson asked us to keep it quiet, remember?"

"Oh, that's right. Should I tell Greg?"

Pru just shrugged, but I answered. "Good question," I said. "You'll need to tell him why the cops are back, so I guess if he asks you should tell him to ask the detective. In the state he's in, he may not even want to know."

"True. Okay, well, I'll see you later, then. Sorry our walk was cut short."

"Give me a shout if there's anything Michael and I can do," I said, and Deb nodded and she and Flossie turned to the right, and Pru and I turned left.

"Have you told the detective about Greg and Betty's fight yet?" I asked.

Pru frowned. "I should have told him just now, but honestly, I forgot all about it. I'll call him later."

"Today?"

"Yes, today. Promise."

***

Watchful eyes saw the arrival of Sheriff's Department vehicles, and noted the activity behind building D. Too bad there'd been no opportunity to retrieve that damn bag, what with all the police presence constantly around and residents on the alert. If her evidence was in those files after all. . . I feel sick. It's getting harder and harder to act normal. Can't let my guard down. . .

***

After lunch, Henderson and the team gathered in the war room again. A black plastic garbage bag covered in fingerprint powder, about fifty file folders, and a stack of paper sat on the tables in front of them.

"Alright, team, we need to sort through and log all of this." He pointed to the folders and paper spread out on the table. "They were found this morning hidden in the bushes behind the victim's apartment. We don't know how long the bag was there, although it was probably stashed after the break-in on Friday evening."

He rolled his shoulders a few times to relieve the tension in his back. "Let's do a rough triage to start. Put all the financial files in one of these banker boxes," he said, pointing, "legal in another, personal and family in a third. If a file doesn't fall into one of those categories, leave it on the table. Once we have them sorted into categories we'll examine them more closely. We're looking for any evidence the victim had on the murderer."

"Sir, can I ask a question?"

"What is it, Sanchez?"

"Do we have a warrant for this?"

"Good question, Deputy. No, and we don't need one. It was found discarded in a common area of the condominium association. So even though Mr. Harris views it as his back yard, it's not his private property. Think of it like something we find in a dumpster, or set out at the curb with the trash for pickup."

"Thank you, sir."

She grabbed a marker and wrote *Finance* on the end of the first banker box and placed it on a chair. Then she did the same with *Legal* and *Personal*.

"Okay, gloves on," Henderso ordered. Once they were all gloved, Henderson picked up a folder that was sitting by itself with a sticky note on it. "This one wasn't in the bag, it was left in the Harris' apartment. No idea if that's significant." He flipped through it quickly, and handed it to DaSilva. "Legal," he announced. DaSilva put it in the Legal box. He plucked another folder off the stack, and glanced through it. "Personal" went to Lopez and "Financial" to Sanchez. In a few minutes they'd established a rhythm, and the boxes were beginning to fill up.

Suddenly Henderson stopped in mid-flip. He looked at the front of the folder, and checked the tab, which was labeled *Vacation*. "Everybody stop!" he shouted.

Lopez looked up, the folder in his hand suspended over the *Personal* box. Sanchez and DaSilva looked surprised.

"I have something strange here. Someone, clear a space on the table and get me a chair."

Once that was done, he sat and carefully placed the folder on the table. The others crowded around. One by one Henderson lifted various travel brochures, shook them, then placed them face down. One was a thick brochure from Princess Cruises, almost big enough to qualify as a magazine, for a luxury around-the-world cruise. Beneath about a dozen smaller brochures was a fat manila envelope. Its flap was tucked in, not sealed, and he turned it upside down. Out came two thick stacks of bills, each with an elastic band around it.

"Lopez, I want a rough count before we turn these over to the fingerprint team." He handed Lopez one stack, and he took the other. Placing his gloved fingers carefully on the elastic band, he lifted the stack and fanned the corner. All the bills appeared to be hundreds. "Let's see, 250 bills per inch. I need a ruler."

DaSilva scurried out, and came back a minute later with someone's desk ruler. Henderson measured his stack, then handed the ruler to Lopez. "I've got about $22,000 here, you?"

"About the same."

"So, roughly $44,000 in cash." Henderson placed the two stacks of bills back into the envelope. "Lopez, log this, then take it downtown for fingerprinting. Highest priority."

Lopez took the envelope and left the room at a run.

Henderson reached for the next folder.

"Sir, can I ask another question?" Sanchez asked hesitantly. He looked up and nodded.

"Isn't that using a lot of resources, fingerprinting hundreds of bills?"

"Think about it, Deputy," he said. "Our victim is someone who enjoys manipulating people, making them jump when she snaps her fingers, and now we have all this cash. Where do you suppose it came from?"

"Um, blackmail?"

"Right. It's not likely she saved it out of her grocery money, is it? It's more likely to be blackmail money. And if she blackmailed someone and they paid her in cash, with any luck their fingerprints will be on the bills. If we can pull a usable print that matches one of the residents at the condo complex, we've likely got our killer."

Sanchez nodded.

Henderson handed her the file in his hands. "Finance," he said, and picked up the next folder.

An hour later Lopez skidded back into the room. "They say it'll take at least two or three days. Even expedited. They're really busy. Plus, there's no way they'll do each bill, just a random sampling."

Henderson looked grim, but all he said was, "Personal," as he handed the last folder to DaSilva.

With all the folders sorted into the appropriate banker boxes, the top of the table was clear.

"Okay," Henderson said, "in light of what we've already found, let's go through the financials first. We may have to involve the forensic accountants, but let's see what we can find without them now." He hefted the *Finance* box onto the table. After looking through the contents, he abstracted a folder labeled *Bank Statements*.

"Let's start with this. We're looking for anything that seems out of the ordinary. Income or expense. Lopez, you and DaSilva team up on this."

He pulled out another folder labeled *Tax Returns*. "Sanchez, you're with me on this one."

Thirty minutes later, he was tapping his pen on the table in frustration. "It all looks pretty straightforward to me. Three years' worth of returns, the income is all from social security and an IRA, a few dividends, standard deduction, nothing at all of note."

Sanchez nodded her agreement. "Lopez, DaSilva, did you find anything?"

Lopez glanced up from his papers. "Nope. They have a checking and savings account at SunTrust, deposits every month from Social Security. They get some payments from a brokerage account, probably dividends. That's it."

"What about expenditures? Anything you wouldn't expect?"

"Just normal household expenses, insurance, property taxes, homeowner association fees, utilities, car repairs, doctors, pharmacies, that sort of thing."

"What about grocery stores and restaurants?" Sanchez asked.

Lopez looked surprised. "I don't recall seeing any now that you mention it."

"I didn't notice any," DaSilva said.

"Any regular cash withdrawals? Some people still shop for groceries with cash," Henderson pointed out. "Gas stations?"

Lopez perused several pages. "Nothing."

Henderson tapped the marker on the whiteboard. "So maybe they were paying for those sorts of expenses with cash obtained from her blackmailing activities." He made a note on the white board next to Greg's name, "ask about cash expenses."

"Safety deposit box?" he asked.

"Not that I saw."

Henderson wrote "safety deposit box" with a question mark next to Greg's name on the whiteboard.

"Okay, let's move along," Henderson said, pulling the *Legal* box up onto the table. "Keep your eyes peeled for any information about a will."

There weren't many folders in this box. One was devoted to the purchase of the condo, another to ownership of their cars. Both the 2012 Ford Escape and the 2014 Mustang had been purchased and titled in Alabama before the couple moved to Florida.

There was no information about any wills.

"Let's take a quick break before we get into the personal files," Henderson said. "Be back here in ten minutes."

He found a pile of messages on his desk, and skimmed through them quickly, frowning at one. "Probably nothing," he muttered to himself as he picked up his phone and dialed.

"Ms. McLeod, Detective Henderson returning your call."

After listening for a minute he said, "I see, alright. Thanks for telling me."

Arriving back in the war room, he stood in front of the whiteboard and held up his hand to get attention. "Alright people, we need to conduct a couple more interviews. I just got a call from someone who overheard the victim and her husband having a loud argument the night before she was killed. Sanchez, you're with me. I want you to take notes. And Lopez, you need to talk to Elizabeth Steinbach and confirm whether she was the person heard arguing with the victim on June 7. DaSilva can go with you. These files will keep."

Eighteen

As Henderson approached the Wheelocks' apartment, he saw Deb through the kitchen slider, pulling food out of the refrigerator. He knocked on it, and she jumped.

She opened the slider. "What can I do for you, Detective?"

"Mrs. Wheelock, is Mr. Harris here?"

"He and Dave are in the living room watching the Braves game. This way."

Henderson marched into the living room, Sanchez trailing behind him.

"Mr. Wheelock, Mr. Harris," he nodded at each of them. "Mr. Harris, we need to talk to you. Someplace private?"

"I don't mind if Dave hears what you have to say," Greg protested.

"But I do. If we can't talk here, we can go down to the station and hold our discussion in one of the interview rooms."

Greg looked surprised, but not alarmed. "Alright, alright, let's go in here." He led the way to the study. As they were walking down the hall, the Wheelocks held a low-voiced conversation behind them.

The second bedroom was set up as a combination study and guest room. A Murphy bed took up most of one wall, but left plenty of room for seating when folded up. Flossie lay curled in her dog bed under the window. She raised her sad little face as they entered the room, but didn't get up.

Henderson pointed Sanchez toward the desk, and took a chair next to it. He waved Greg to a seat facing him.

"Mr. Harris, this is Deputy Sanchez, she'll be taking notes and I'll also be recording this interview."

Greg's mouth opened and closed, but no sound came out. Sanchez opened her notebook and took out a pen while Henderson turned on the record function on his phone and placed it on the desk. "Interview with Gregory Harris at 5:15 PM June 10, 2018," he intoned, "Detective Jason Henderson and Deputy Melanie Sanchez in attendance."

"What's going on?" Greg finally asked.

"Mr. Harris, I want you to describe to me the events of the evening of June eighth, the night before your wife was killed."

"What?"

"You heard me. I can narrow it down for you. I'm interested in everything you said and did on June 8, from eight-thirty PM on."

"I don't know, it was just a normal night. We had dinner, we went to the condo board meeting, we came home, we went to bed." Greg's voice shook.

"And what did you and your wife talk about after you came home?"

"How should I remember?"

"You don't remember one of the last conversations you had with your wife before she was killed?"

"No."

"Perhaps it would jog your memory if I tell you that one of your neighbors heard the two of you shouting at each other just before nine o'clock."

Greg's face went white. "No," he whispered. His eyes darted around the room as if he were looking for a way to escape.

"Yes," the detective said. "What were you fighting about?"

"We weren't fighting, Betty and I never fought."

"Mr. Harris, I'm sorry, but this is a murder inquiry and I've just learned that you and your wife were arguing a few hours before she was killed. If you won't tell me about it right now, I'll have to take you in."

Greg's eyes widened. "You think I might have killed Betty? Are you nuts?"

"In cases of violent death, the spouse is always the first suspect."

He slumped, defeated. "I didn't. I never would have harmed her."

"You still need to tell me about it."

"Betty and I, we loved each other." His face crumpled as he blinked rapidly. Henderson waited.

After several minutes, Greg began to speak.

"Anyway, you've got to understand about Betty, it wasn't really her fault. So anyway, her family didn't have much, growing up. She started doing odd jobs and then babysitting as soon as she was old enough, so she'd have some money for pretty clothes, or even just, you know, clothes that weren't ready for the rag bag. Or so she could get a Coke after school with her friends, that kind of thing. She always liked nice things."

He looked at Henderson, who continued to sit, saying nothing. At the desk, Sanchez' pencil was flying.

Greg swallowed. "Anyway, she worked hard all through junior high and high school. But, well, she developed this bad habit. See, she found out that some of the kids she babysat for did things they didn't want their mamma and daddy to know about and they'd give her their lunch money or their allowance if she'd agree not to tell on them. So then she started trying to find out their little secrets, and she got pretty good at it. Anyway, by the time she left school, it was a habit. She'd find out someone's little secret, and figure out a way to take advantage of it. I never liked it, and I tried to get her to stop, but it was like a sickness with her."

He paused, and Henderson said, "Go on."

"Anyway, at first after we got married I'd try to stop her, but she was too smart for me. It was like a game for her, and she enjoyed fooling me about it. She knew I didn't like it. So anyway, every once in a while she'd buy me a really nice gift or something, you know, something that was really out of our budget, and anyway I knew it was her way of showing me she was still up to her little tricks."

After a while, I just sort of gave up and tried not to know. Anyway, outside of that she was always good to me, she was a good wife, a great cook, and she was fun to be with. She was a good mother to our son when he was little, and she was good at managing our budget. She made my paycheck stretch a long ways, so I stopped bugging her about it."

He looked down at the floor. "Anyway, a few years ago, I guess she messed with the wrong person, because all of a sudden she was scared. I mean, really scared. She never did tell me what it was about, she just said, 'honey you don't want to know.' And she was right. I didn't."

He glanced at Henderson, then fixed his gaze on the floor again. "Anyway, that was when we sold our place in Mobile and moved here. That was how scared she was. I made her promise then that she wouldn't do it any more, that we'd start with a clean slate. And she agreed." He swallowed a couple of times.

"After we came here, I thought she was keeping to our agreement, but then anyway last Wednesday night she showed me this brochure for an around-the-world cruise, and she told me we were going to be able to take that cruise pretty soon. She was proud of herself."

He sat for a minute, staring at his hands. Finally he sighed and started talking again.

"I couldn't believe she was up to her tricks, after she promised and everything, and, well anyway, we had a big fight about it. I just felt sick at my stomach, and I told her I couldn't bear to look at her. I told her I was going to bed and she should sleep in the guest room and we'd talk about it in the morning."

"And then, in the morning, she. . ." he dissolved into tears and covered his face with his hands.

Henderson was unmoved. "Mr. Harris, tell me how you paid for your groceries."

Greg sniffed and wiped his eyes, looking baffled. "What do you mean?"

"Did you use a credit card? Debit card? Cash?"

"Oh, I don't know. Betty took care of all that."

"What about meals out, restaurants, movies, that kind of thing?"

"Cash, I think. I don't know. Is it important?"

Henderson didn't answer. "Mr. Harris, tell me what was in the file drawer in the desk in your guest bedroom."

Greg shrugged. "Betty took care of all our household stuff. She handled the banking, and she paid the bills, took care of insurance. That was where she kept all that stuff. I didn't pay much attention."

"Are you aware that the files were missing after the break-in?"

Greg looked blank. "I don't know."

"Well, they were gone, and the file drawer was empty. But we've recovered them."

"Oh, that's good, I guess."

"One file was labeled *Vacation*, and there was a brochure for a luxury around-the-world cruise in it. Would that be the brochure your wife showed you?"

"Probably. I'd have to see it." Greg looked down at his lap again.

"Would it surprise you that we also found an envelope in the file, with a substantial amount of cash in it?"

Greg's head came up. "No, I'm sorry to say. I mean, I don't know anything about any cash, but anyway it wouldn't surprise me."

"Did your wife tell you anything about the money?"

"No, just that we'd be able to afford the cruise soon. Anyway, to tell you the truth, detective," he said, looking him in the eye for the first time, "I just didn't want to know."

"Alright. We'll be in touch." Henderson stood, and Sanchez closed her notebook.

"You're not arresting me?"

"Not at the moment. Stay where we can reach you."

In the car on their way back to the war room, Sanchez asked, "Sir, did you believe him?"

"Actually, yes. I can imagine that being married to someone like that is a little like being married to an alcoholic or a kleptomaniac. You can search the house every day for hidden bottles or stolen goods, and keep confronting them and be miserable, or you can try to protect yourself by ignoring it and hoping for the best. He obviously chose denial."

After a beat he added, "And besides, he definitely didn't trash his own apartment. And it fits with what we found. It's a long shot, but I hope they find some useful fingerprints on that cash."

"What kind of secret would someone pay that much to protect?" she asked.

"Don't jump to conclusions, Deputy," Henderson said. "How long did it take to amass that forty-four grand? It could have been one big payment or hundreds of little ones."

Sanchez relapsed into silence.

Lopez and DaSilva were still out when they arrived back at the station, so Henderson left Sanchez in the war room while he returned to his desk. He'd been sifting through his inbox for about five minutes when Lopez called him. "We're back, sir, ready to report."

"I'll be right there."

When he entered the war room, Lopez was looking pleased. "You interviewed Ms. Steinbach?" Henderson asked. He sat, and motioned Lopez to sit across from him.

"Indeed we did, sir," Lopez smirked.

"You recorded it?"

"Yes."

"Okay, I'll listen to the recording later, but it's already been a long day. Can you summarize?"

"Steinbach was a paralegal —"

Before he finished his sentence, Henderson interrupted him. "Ms. Steinbach. It never hurts to be polite to the people we're interviewing, even in private."

Lopez shot him a surprised look. He was certainly different from any other detective Lopez had worked with, but he was the boss.

"Yes, sir." He continued, "From 2005 until she retired last year, Ms. Steinbach worked for Mullins & Hardwick downtown. In 2011 the firm was accused of being involved in fraudulent mortgage foreclosures. Her signature was on some of the documents in question. She swears she signed what they told her to sign, and she never knew about the fraud until law enforcement showed up."

"So somehow the victim got hold of that information?" Henderson asked.

"Oh, yeah. She was threatening to tell Steinbach's — Ms. Steinbach's — kids and grandkids that their mom had been responsible for a lot of people losing their homes."

"What did she want in return?"

"She didn't seem to be after money. At least, Ms. Steinbach said she'd never asked for a penny." Lopez pulled at his earlobe.

"No, what she wanted was a vote. She wanted Ms. Steinbach to vote against this architectural waiver for Ms. Delaney."

"Did Ms. Steinbach have any idea why that architectural waiver was so important to the victim?"

"I asked her that, sir, and she said she didn't know for sure. But she had the impression that Ms. Delaney had really pissed off the victim, and she wanted her out of the community."

"And did Ms. Steinbach vote against the waiver?" Henderson asked.

"No, she abstained, but it amounted to the same thing."

"Well, that ties in with what others have told us," Henderson said. "How did that sit with her?"

Lopez considered for a moment, his head tilted to the side. "She did say she felt so bad for Ms. Delaney after that meeting that she decided she'd rather have her kids learn the truth than let Ms. Harris push her around any more."

"It's easy to say that, now that Mrs. Harris is gone, so I'm not ready to rule her out entirely." Henderson stood. "Okay, DaSilva and Sanchez, type up those interview notes and leave them on my desk. Lopez, you and I will go through the rest of those personal files."

Nineteen

I was staring despondently into the refrigerator when Michael walked into the kitchen. I turned to him and asked, "Were you planning to eat breakfast in the morning?"

"Um, is that a trick question?" He shrugged. "I guess so, why?"

"Because the proverbial cupboard is bare. With everything that's been going on nobody's been to the store. We're out of milk, eggs, cereal, pretty much everything. I guess I need to make a grocery run."

"At this hour? It's after eight thirty."

"I know, but I'd rather do it tonight and not have to scramble around in the morning." I sighed. What a day. It had started quietly enough, but after Flossie found those missing files the place had been buzzing. I wasn't quite sure what I thought about them. It seemed like the person who trashed Greg's apartment was looking for something, but why bag up the files and remove them, and then not take them away? It didn't make sense.

"Want me to come with you?"

"No, it's okay. I'll just grab the essentials, but we're going to have to do a real shopping sometime tomorrow."

"If you're sure."

"I'm sure."

A moment later I came out of the bedroom with my tote bag and a couple of reusable grocery bags. "Back shortly." I unlocked the front door and stepped out onto the porch.

Keith was sitting on his porch and greeted me as I came down the stairs. "Hey, Lily, where are you off to this late?"

"Hey, yourself. It's just an emergency grocery store run. We seem to be out of everything we need for breakfast. I need to hurry, though, if I'm going to get to Publix before they close."

He nodded. "Sure, see you later."

I hurried to the Prius and checked my watch. I should be fine since the store didn't close until nine and it was only two minutes away. I'd whiz through, grab what I needed, and get back home as quickly as I could.

Twenty minutes later I pulled back into the carport. It wasn't fully dark yet, but it was getting there fast, and I was a little nervous. Until three days ago I'd always felt safe inside our little gated community, and I wasn't happy with that change at all. Maybe I should text Michael to meet me at the carport. No, I was being silly. I'd be fine.

Quickly I opened the hatchback and reached in for the grocery bags. Darn, one of them had tipped over and a couple of items were loose. As I leaned in to grab them, I heard a small scuffing sound. Before I could stand up, a hand reached in and covered my mouth. I tried to scream, but no sound came out and the grip on me tightened. I couldn't turn my head because an arm like steel held me in position.

My assailant hissed into my ear, "Stop poking around if you don't want to end up floating in the pool, too." I heard a shout, then running feet, and a violent shove sent me face-planting among the grocery bags. Swift footsteps raced away.

My shaking legs gave out, and I tried to yell, but my mouth was dry as a desert and no sound came out. If I hadn't been facedown on the floor of my car, I would have fallen. My heart was pounding and I shivered, then realized I was covered in a thin sheen of sweat. The ridges of the floormat dug into my cheek.

"Who did this to you? Are you alright?"

I recognized Patrick Barry's voice. I tried to answer, but only a faint croak came out. I swallowed and ran my tongue around my dry mouth. Finally I squeezed out a question. "Did you see what happened?"

"No, I saw you pull in so I was heading over to say hi and then I saw the guy sneak up behind you. I yelled and he took off."

I tried to stand, but my legs were still shaking so I carefully eased myself around until I was sitting in the open hatch and focused on calming my ragged breathing. "Thank you."

"What can I do?"

"Just give me a minute." It took several minutes for my breathing to return to normal. I wasn't sure my legs would support me, but I tried standing, and I wasn't wobbling too much.

I started to reach for my grocery bags, but Patrick said "No. Let me do that." He hefted them and I picked up my tote bag, then felt around for the keys which I'd dropped when I got shoved. I closed the hatch and pressed the button to lock the car with unsteady hands.

I managed to walk over to my building, but when we got to the stairs my legs started shaking again. "Stay there!" Patrick set the bags down and ran up the steps while I held onto the railing at the bottom of the staircase. He banged on our door. "Michael, Lily needs help!"

He hurried back down the steps and a few seconds later Michael rushed out. "Lily, what's going on?"

Patrick stepped aside and let Michael help me up the steps, then, as we made our way inside to the kitchen, he followed with the grocery bags.

I collapsed into a chair.

"Oh my god, Lil, you're as white as a sheet. What's wrong?"

I opened my mouth to answer, but instead I heard roaring in my ears, and then the room started to spin. The next thing I knew I was on the floor with Michael leaning over me."Are you okay? What happened? Do I need to call nine-one-one? Honey, say something."

"I. . . I. . ." I couldn't choke the words out.

Patrick told him what he'd seen at the carport, and Michael scowled. "Is this true? Lily, who did this to you?"

I drew a deep breath and sat up. "I think I just got a death threat. I don't know from who."

"What???"

When I finished telling Michael what happened he looked as grim as I'd ever seen him. He pulled out his phone. "I'm calling Henderson, and you need to stop talking to people and stirring up trouble. Leave it to the police."

I felt sick to my stomach. I knew it was an effect of the adrenaline overload I'd just experienced, but it was unpleasant. I swallowed a few times and, once again, tried to control my breathing. By the time I got it back to normal again Michael was finished with his call.

"Henderson's on his way over," he said.

Patrick sidled toward the door. "I should go."

"No, please stay, the detective will want to talk to you," Michael said.

I knew that telling Henderson was the right thing to do for the investigation, but I was afraid my carport assailant would see him and think I was a much bigger threat than I was. What did I know, anyway? Not a lot.

Up until now I'd been a little nervous, but now I was down deep terrified. At this moment I wanted nothing more than to crawl into my soft, safe bed and pull the covers over my head until the man was caught. Man? I couldn't be sure, but I'd had the impression of height, and the person who'd grabbed me was very strong. So probably male.

"Patrick, was it a man or a woman, could you tell?"

"I'm sure it was a man. He looked to be around six feet tall, although it all happened pretty fast and of course it was nearly dark, so I can't be sure."

Michael was quietly putting away the groceries. When he finished, he sat next to me and took my hand. "You're freezing!" he said with concern.

"Adrenaline rush. It'll pass."

"How about some tea?"

"That sounds good. Something soothing. Chamomile?"

"You've got it."

He started the kettle, then left the room and came back with the throw from the back of the couch, which he wrapped gently around me.

I was cradling the warm mug in my hands and Patrick was sniffing experimentally at his when someone knocked on the door. Michael went to answer, carefully turning on the porch light and checking who it was through the window before admitting Detective Henderson.

After walking me through the attack at the carport and listening to Patrick's account, the detective asked, "Could it have been Mr. Harris?"

"No way," Patrick said. "He wasn't nearly tall enough."

The detective nodded. "Why you? Why would he go after you? Why not Mr. Harris, or somebody else here?"

"I don't know."

He waited in silence.

"I don't feel like I know anything. I didn't know Betty very well, so it's certainly not like she would have confided in me. I've tried to be a good neighbor and help Greg, but so did lots of other people. And I found that stash of file folders, but so did Deb. I don't know why he targeted me."

"Well," the detective stood, "I suggest you keep your head down. I know you've been talking to people — "

"Which you asked me to do," I pointed out. "I thought you liked that people tell me things. Am I supposed to just shut up and hide out here at home now? I don't think so!"

"If that's what it takes to stay safe."

"Well, I can't. The funeral is the day after tomorrow."

Michael opened his mouth, but I jumped in before he could speak. "And don't tell me to stay home, Michael. I can just picture myself, home alone, while everyone else, except maybe the guy who attacked me tonight, is at the church. I'd be a sitting duck."

"But," Michael began.

The detective interrupted. "She's right. She'll be safer in full view. But," and he turned to look me in the eye, "you should stop asking questions. We'll get this guy."

"And what do I tell people about the bruising on my face that will show up tomorrow?"

"As little as possible." He left hurriedly.

Patrick stood. "I should go, too, and leave you to recover in peace."

"Thanks for rescuing me." As he moved toward the door I said, "Hang on, you said you saw the Prius and were coming over before the other guy showed up. What's on your mind?"

"I have something I want to chat about, but it'll keep until you're feeling better."

Michael walked him to the front door and came back looking worried. "Are you sure you're alright?"

"No, but I will be. A good night's sleep will help, if I can manage that."

***

Watchful eyes saw Lily and Patrick — so that's who it was — go up the steps, then watched as Henderson arrived a short while later. What was she telling him? What if she didn't back off and stop talking to everyone? Need to sleep, but not until after the detective leaves. Then sleep for a while. Or try to.

Twenty

Needless to say, I didn't sleep well. In the morning, I was pushing food around on my plate, wishing I could just go back to bed and never talk to anyone again, when my phone rang. "Hey, Deb," I answered, trying to sound cheerful when I felt anything but. "What's up?"

I listened for a moment, then interrupted her. "Oh, dear, let me put you on speaker, Michael's right here."

Deb's voice sounded strained. "Hi Michael, I was just telling Lily I'm calling to see if you're planning on going to the visitation tonight."

"This is the first I'm hearing about any visitation." I turned to my husband. "Michael, did Greg and the pastor discuss a visitation at that meeting?"

"Nope."

"Well, then, this is news to both of us, when did he decide to do it?"

"I don't know, he just told us this morning, too," Deb said. "I don't know why he thinks a visitation would be a good idea, but it's just starting to sink in with him that Betty wasn't exactly popular. He seemed to be doing a little better, but since the detective talked to him yesterday he's falling apart again, so please tell me you're coming tonight. If people from Happy Oaks don't show up, he'll be there all by himself."

Michael and I looked at each other. "I don't want to, but I suppose we should," I said after a long hesitation, "just to support Greg."

"Okay, we'll come," Michael agreed.

"Oh, thank you," Deb said gratefully. "Do you think you could talk Pru into coming too?"

"I can try. What time and where is it?"

"Seven o'clock, at Baldwin-Fairchild on Aloma."

"Alright, I guess we'll see you there."

"Thanks Lily. Thanks Michael. I'll see you tonight if not before."

After hanging up, I turned to Michael. "I'm a little surprised. You really didn't know about the visitation?"

"Nope. When I took Greg to meet with his pastor, there was no mention of it."

I shrugged. "I'd better call Pru."

"Okay. I'm supposed to meet Jeff over at the clubhouse in a few minutes. It looks like we'll be able to just appoint Jennifer at the beginning of our meeting on Thursday since nobody else has volunteered for the opening. Then we can go straight to Charlotte's waiver."

"Oh! Maybe we should bring Lottie tonight as well."

"Do you think she'll want to go?"

"Oh, honey, I don't think any of us wants to go. That's not the point." I gave a small shiver. "At least it'll be closed casket. I don't ever want to see that face again."

Michael poured the rest of the coffee into his insulated to-go cup and I loaded the dishwasher. Then I picked up my phone.

Pru agreed to come, but she wasn't happy about it.

When I called Lottie, she sounded very chipper. "Lily! Hi, I have PT in about five minutes."

"I'll be quick," I promised. "Greg has arranged for a visitation this evening since the funeral is tomorrow morning. We're trying to round up some support for him, any chance you'd be willing to come?"

"Oh, dear," was Lottie's response. "I suppose it will look awful if I don't."

"We feel the same way, with far less reason than you."

She sighed. "Can you pick me up?"

"Of course! Pru's coming with us too, so we'll pick you up at quarter to seven."

"Alright, see you then. Gotta go."

I needed to get ready for the day, and also find something to wear to the visitation tonight, so I headed for my closet. I was standing in front of it, staring blankly at my clothes, when Michael came out of the bathroom, patting his face with a towel. He tossed the towel onto the bed and put his arms around me from behind. "I know you hate this, Lil, but we won't have to stay long. Just put in an appearance so Greg knows we're supporting him."

"You're right," I sighed. "But I'll be glad when it's over."

"Me, too. And in the good news department, the pool people tell us we'll be able to reopen it tomorrow, so maybe this place will get back to normal."

"If anyone wants to swim in it after what's happened. I can't imagine any residents wanting to swim and sunbathe after the funeral."

"True."

"But, Michael, will we really be able to get back to normal?" I hated hearing the desperation in my own voice. "There's still a murderer running loose, most likely right here in Happy Oaks. I don't understand someone hating another person enough to do that to them. And if the detectives have a clue who did it, they're not letting on."

"That's true too, but I can understand it better than I can understand that guy who's holed up in his apartment with four kids, shooting at cops in Orlando right now." Michael had been upset when we heard that news earlier.

"You have a point, I guess. That's such a terrible situation I can't even think about it. Their poor mother!" I turned around and rested my head against my husband's shoulder, tightening my arms around him. "I feel so helpless, and I have no idea what to do."

"You let the detectives do all the doing, what you need to do is keep out of it!" He looked at me intently.

I stepped back and stared at him with narrowed eyes. "You'd better go and meet Jeff."

"Will you be okay here on your own? I don't have to go."

"No, I'm not okay. I'm scared, and I don't know who to trust, but I'm a big girl. I can do this." Maybe if I said it often enough I'd be able to convince myself.

"I don't want you poking around and getting hurt again."

"You think I do?" I put my hands on my hips. "I also don't want a murderer running loose around here."

"Henderson's a competent guy. He won't thank you for getting in his way."

"Then I won't. You're going to be late."

"Okay, okay. I shouldn't be long." He picked up his keys and wallet off the dresser and left the room. A moment later I heard the front door close and lock. I frowned. A week ago he would never have thought to lock the door behind him when I was in the apartment. Would we ever feel safe in our home or our little community again?

I wish Michael hadn't asked if I'd be okay on my own. I hadn't thought about it until that moment, but now that the seed was planted I started to worry. Was I? I certainly hadn't been okay last night, getting shoved around, threatened, and then fainting in my own kitchen. Right now, I was better by myself than trying to go out and face people. And when I had to be with people, who would I feel safe with? Michael, of course. Patrick, since he'd rescued me from the attacker. Pru, Lottie, it was a short list. I didn't want to suspect people I knew and liked, but I needed to be on my guard from now on, for sure.

I turned to the closet again. I pulled out a black dress and a pair of black, low-heeled pumps to wear to tomorrow's service, but what about something for the visitation? Could I get away with the same outfit for both? Probably not. With my preference for bright colors, my wardrobe didn't include much that was appropriate for somber events.

Then someone knocked on the front door.

Immediately my heart started pounding, and the shoes I was holding hit the floor. I tiptoed to the slider and peeked out. Patrick was standing on the porch. With a big whoosh I let out the breath I didn't realize I'd been holding and went to answer it, wrapping my robe around me.

"Patrick, hi."

"Good morning. Sorry to pop by so early, but I met Michael outside, and he said it would be alright. I just wanted to check on you after what happened last night."

"Sure, come on in." I looked down at my robe. "As you can see, I'm not ready for company."

"That's okay, I won't stay long."

I led the way into the kitchen. "Coffee?"

"No, thanks. So how are you?" He stared at me intently. "You have a bruise starting." He gestured toward his cheek.

"I haven't looked in a mirror yet this morning, but I'm not surprised. It's very sore," I said. "But I'm okay, I guess."

"Really?"

I sat down heavily. "I'm terrified, if you want the truth. When you knocked on the door just now I about jumped out of my skin. And I'm angry, too. Angry that someone would do this to me, and angry that someone is doing this to our community."

"Sounds like a pretty normal reaction to me. Linda complained that I kept her awake all night with my tossing and turning, but I kept replaying it in my head, trying to figure out who it was."

"Any luck with that?"

"Nope. I can tell you it wasn't Greg — not tall enough — and he wasn't short enough to be Tim. Beyond that, it could have been any man here. It just happened too fast."

"Well," I said, "part of me wants to hide out here until this is all over, but I'm not going to be allowed that luxury. Are you and Linda going tonight?"

He raised an eyebrow. "Going where?"

"Oh, haven't you heard? Greg decided to hold a visitation this evening."

"Nope, didn't hear about it. Maybe he'll forget to invite us, if we're lucky."

I glared at him. "If we have to go, then you should, too. It's what neighbors do."

"You're probably right. Linda will insist on it."

"Your wife is a wise woman."

"Don't I know it. He was silent for a moment, then he said quietly, "Look, tell me if I'm out of line here, but I just wondered if the detective had said anything to you after he took me in to the station the other day. I got the feeling I'm his best suspect."

"Well, if you were before, I doubt you are now. Not after last night. Unless. . ." a terrible thought had occurred to me and my heart started to beat faster again.

"What is it? You've gone chalk white." The look of concern on Patrick's face was real, not fake, wasn't it?

Suddenly I wasn't comfortable being alone with him any more. Keeping quiet about that arson in Buffalo, and his role in it, were excellent motives for murder no matter how often he said he was tired of keeping secrets. Talk was cheap. What if that whole scene last night had been staged?

"Do I need to call Michael? What's going on? Are you going to faint again?" Patrick asked, reaching for his phone.

I took a deep breath. Either he was an Oscar-worthy actor, or I was letting my imagination run away with me. I looked at him and said, "No more secrets, right? That's your new mantra?"

He nodded.

"Okay, I just had the terrible thought that you could have staged that scene last night purely to deflect suspicion from yourself."

He blinked and opened and closed his mouth a couple of times. Finally he sputtered, "I guess I deserved that. But just because I was a complete fool ten years ago doesn't mean I'd ever hurt someone else to protect that secret. Especially now."

I waited, but didn't say anything.

He thought for a moment. "Look," he said, "I'm younger than most of the men here. I was too young to be drafted when they finally ended it, but my older brother was, and he died in Vietnam. If they'd still had the draft when I turned eighteen I would have filed as a conscientious objector. I could never bring myself to kill another human being."

I tried to smile. "Okay, to answer your question, the detective hasn't shared any of his thoughts about you with me. You heard him last night, he warned me about getting involved any more, so he's not going to tell me anything."

He nodded unhappily. "I should go, I've disturbed your morning enough. I guess we'll see you this evening. Where's this thing being held?"

I gave him the details as I walked him to the door. I still didn't know if I could trust him, but at least he hadn't killed me.

***

Watchful eyes clocked everyone going in and out of the Gallaghers' apartment. They saw Michael leave, looking worried, and walk to the clubhouse. Then a minute later Patrick went up the stairs and knocked on the door. He was inside for about ten minutes, then he left. The eyes had a score to settle with him, damn his interference. Unlikely that Patrick could identify Lily's attacker, or the detective would have shown up to make an arrest before now.

Twenty-One

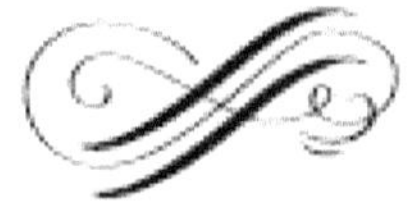

I had a hard time choking down our early dinner. Even though I didn't want to go to this visitation, it was better than staying home alone, where I'd been all day hiding behind locked doors and jumping at every little noise.

After stacking the dishwasher, I changed into the outfit I'd chosen. It wasn't exactly funereal, but for me it was subdued. A navy blouse, gray slacks, and navy shoes with a low heel, with my pearl necklace and earrings. It would have to do.

Michael wore practically a matching outfit, with gray trousers, a white shirt, and navy blazer. Both of us were much more comfortable in casual clothes, but I couldn't help thinking how handsome he was all dressed up. With his white hair, he looked very distinguished.

"You clean up good." I grinned at him. It was an effort.

"So do you," he smiled back then stared at my face intently, "I can hardly notice the bruise on your face."

"Thank goodness for makeup. Do I need to bring a purse?" I asked. "I didn't have time to clean out my tote bag and transfer stuff to an appropriate small one, but I'll have to do that before the funeral service tomorrow."

"No, we're taking my car, so you don't need keys or anything. You'll be fine."

"Okay, let me just text Pru that we're ready. She said she'd meet us by the car." Fortunately, these slacks had a pocket I could slip my phone into.

Pru was coming down her stairs as we reached the sidewalk, so we converged on Michael's silver CRV at the same time. Pru's outfit mirrored mine, in reverse. She had selected a navy skirt, a white blouse, and had a gray sweater over her shoulders. "Are you cold?" I asked, surprised. "It's about eighty-five degrees out here."

"Not at all. Just preparing myself in case the funeral home is one of those places that doesn't understand the difference between air conditioning and refrigeration."

I chuckled and Michael smiled appreciatively. "Let's get this unpleasantness over with," Pru said. "I can't stand these things in the best of circumstances."

"No argument there, we're certainly not planning on hanging around, are we, Michael?"

During the short drive to the rehab center to pick up Lottie, we discussed the big news of the day, the hostage drama taking place just a few miles away. One of the police officers at the scene had been shot and was in the ICU, and the Orlando PD was releasing hourly news bulletins about the standoff with the shooter in the apartment.

"I wonder if this is going to pull resources off our murder investigation?" Pru asked.

"Not likely, since the Sheriff's Department is in charge of ours, and Orlando PD for the shooting," Michael pointed out.

"Oh, that's right."

Arriving at the rehab center, Michael pulled up in front of the entryway.

When I stepped inside, Lottie was in her wheelchair near the front desk talking to a young woman. As I came closer, she reached into her fancy Baggalini purse and handed Lottie a business card.

"Oh, hi, Lily," Lottie said. "I'm all ready to go."

The woman turned to me and held out her hand. "Hi, I'm Lindsay Thomas, ReMax Realty."

"Lily Gallagher."

Lottie shrugged her shoulders at me."Someone told Lindsay I might be thinking of selling the condo so she stopped by. I told her I have an appointment to get to."

"Well, I'll let you ladies go," Lindsay said. "You've got my card, so call me if there's anything I can do."

As soon as the door shut behind her I asked, "You called a Realtor?" This wasn't good.

"I didn't actually, but somehow she heard about my situation and she came by. I was trying to figure out how to get rid of her when you got here." She sighed. "I know I may have to move, but I'm not making any premature decisions."

"Well, that's a relief."

Wheeling to the desk, she signed herself out with a flourish, then wheeled herself to the doors, which opened automatically. "That's about as much wheeling as I can manage by myself," she said ruefully, "but I'm getting better. My arms are a lot stronger than they were, for sure."

"You're making great progress. Now, let's get you into the car."

Once Lottie was settled in the passenger seat, I joined Pru in the back and Michael stowed the wheelchair. "Everyone ready?" he asked. "Let's do this thing."

Pru started to say something, then stopped herself. "Lily Gallagher, is that a bruise on your face?"

I gulped. "It is."

"How did that happen? Michael, you been beating your wife?"

I tried to laugh, but it came out sounding forced. “Nope, not him. Our resident killer. At least I assume that’s who it was.”

Pru and Lottie both started talking at once, asking what had happened.

“If you’ll calm down, I’ll tell you.” The rest of the short drive to the funeral home was filled with horrified questions and answers as I explained. I was proud of myself — my voice only shook a little.

We pulled up in front of the funeral home at a few minutes after seven. “We’ll have to finish this later.” I glanced around. “Look, there are only a couple of cars in the lot. Poor Greg. I still don’t know why he decided to do this. He wasn’t planning to when he met with his pastor.”

“Maybe where he comes from it’s the done thing, no matter what,” Pru said.

I helped Lottie into the wheelchair that Michael had already rolled around next to the passenger door, and we made our way inside.

Arriving at the correct room, we stopped in the doorway for a moment. The casket sat at the far end of the room directly in line with the doorway, and several rows of chairs lined both sides of a center aisle leading up to it. Greg stood by the casket, with Dave and Deb next to him where normally other family members would have been.

He was beaming.

“What the. . .” Michael said.

Then I gasped. “Oh my goodness, it’s an open casket.”

Greg caught sight of us and rushed over. “Isn’t it great?” he said happily, taking my hand and pulling me toward the casket. “The embalmers did such a fantastic job with her they told me I could do an open casket after all. Anyway, now all her friends can say goodbye properly. Doesn’t she look great?”

I forced myself to look at the casket. Yes, the embalmers had done a good job, but Betty still looked dead. I was quick to look away. "Greg, I'm so sorry for your loss," I said quietly.

"Oh, yeah, thank you Lily," Greg responded before darting away to pull Pru and Michael forward. I took charge of Lottie's wheelchair.

"Do you want to look?" I asked quietly.

"Not really, but you should probably roll me over to it for form's sake. This is so weird."

"It sure is," I agreed. "Who are you, and what have you done with Greg Harris, the grieving widower?"

"Exactly."

After paying our respects, I asked Deb quietly, "What on earth has gotten into Greg?"

"I don't know. He was happy as a lark yesterday when he came back from the funeral home, but he didn't tell us anything, just that he'd decided to hold this visitation. I hardly recognize him."

"Well, everyone handles loss differently, so I suppose if he can find some comfort in this, that's a good thing," I said. "Seems pretty macabre, though. I mean, he's acting more like she's the Mardi Gras Queen again, not his murdered wife."

"I guess." Deb frowned. "I hope he's doing well enough to move back into his own apartment, though. Having him around is turning into a real roller coaster ride. He was happy yesterday morning, then after the detective came by he was withdrawn and jumpy again."

"The detective came by?"

"Yes. I don't know what they talked about, Henderson took him into the study and shut the door. He said it was that or questioning him down at the station."

"Weird." I looked around, wondering how I could find out more about that.

A few more of our neighbors had filtered into the room while Deb and I were talking. Michael had moved over to the other side of the casket, where he was speaking with Liz Steinbach and Martha Ericson while Jeff spoke with Greg. Pru had taken a seat next to Lottie's wheelchair at the far side of the room.

I joined Michael in time to hear Martha Ericson sputter, "I can't believe that Greg Harris. What was he thinking? I never would have come if I'd known it was going to turn into a circus. This is supposed to be a solemn occasion."

I bit my tongue. Martha and I didn't see eye to eye on very many things, so I didn't want to admit I agreed with her. I left it to Michael and Liz to respond while I idly watched the door, which had the advantage of putting my back to the casket.

An attractive, dark-haired woman hovered in the doorway, then stepped in confidently and sat down near the back. I recognized Deputy Melanie Sanchez in civilian clothes. So the police had a presence here. I knew they often attended the funerals of victims so it made sense they would also attend the visitation.

Another group came through the door, including the Hoffmans and the Barrys. I watched as they noted the open casket, surprise rippling across all their faces. Greg was back in his spot next to the casket, not bustling around any more, but he still beamed like a happy little boy proudly showing off a favorite item to his classmates at a show-and-tell. Next to him, Dave had such an unhappy look on his face he looked more like the grieving spouse than Greg did.

The newcomers went to Greg and paid their respects as another couple entered. Jennifer's hand was tucked under Keith's arm, and she looked radiant. "Looks like they're becoming an item."

Michael watched them for a moment. "I'm not sure he's so happy," he said. "He looks like he's here under duress."

"I think we're all here under duress, it's just that some of us cover it up better than others."

"You may have a point."

After Keith and Jennifer went up to the casket and spoke briefly with Greg and Dave, they crossed the room to us. Remembering that last glimpse I had of Betty's face in the pool, I found the open casket unsettling, so I kept maneuvering myself so I didn't have to see it.

"Hello neighbors," Jennifer said cheerfully.

"Hi there. How are you this evening?"

"Great! Oh, how inappropriate of me," Jennifer said, a bit ruefully. I smiled.

"Fine," Keith said gruffly.

"Of course," Jennifer continued, "we didn't really know her, did we Keith, but as neighbors we felt we ought to show up. I had to talk him into it." The way she looked at him I could almost see the stars in her eyes.

"That was nice of you, I hope Greg appreciates your support," I said.

"I wasn't expecting an open casket," Keith said, swallowing hard.

"I agree, none of us were," I said. "It was a big surprise, and frankly, not a pleasant one."

"You can say that again." He certainly seemed agitated, but then, lots of people are nervous around dead bodies.

Before I could respond, Patrick and Linda approached us. Linda was back to being her bubbly self, and making an obvious effort to tamp it down for the occasion. "Hey, Lily, Michael," she said, smiling broadly. "How are you this evening?"

"Yes, how are you doing," Patrick asked. He looked at me in concern.

"I'm fine," I said. I didn't want to talk about my assault here. Patrick turned to Keith and Jennifer and said something to them, while Linda reached over and patted my arm.

"I'm so sorry about, you know," she said quietly.

"Thanks. I'm just glad Patrick was there."

"What's *that* supposed to mean?" someone said. I was surprised at the angry tone, and saw Keith and Patrick eyeing each other. Keith looked belligerent and Patrick just looked surprised.

Jennifer tugged on Keith's arm. "Let's go talk to Liz."

There was a stir by the doorway, and I looked up to see a woman in a bright red, off-the-shoulder dress that would have been more appropriate on a dance floor. She was tall, and thin almost to the point of emaciation, with dishwater blond hair, and she reminded me of someone. I watched, fascinated, as the woman sashayed up to the casket. Greg was engrossed in a conversation with Helen Martino but looked up as the woman said loudly, "Hello, Greg, long time no see."

"Mary?" Greg said. I tried to edge a little closer. "Mary, is that you?"

"We should leave," Keith said to Jennifer, but she shushed him.

"In a minute. This looks interesting."

Keith pulled his arm away from her possessive hand. "Not to me."

"Well, Greg, honey, it looks like I finally got my dearest wish," the woman announced loudly. I realized who she resembled — she was a version of Betty who'd lived a much harder life. Besides, I recognized the raspy voice from our phone conversation the other day. "I get to see my rotten sister stretched out in her coffin. It's about time. Did ya finally get tired of her bullshit?"

Greg sputtered and Dave stepped forward. "So you're Betty's sister?" He reached up and put a restraining hand on Greg's shoulder. Greg snapped his mouth closed.

"Yup. Mary Parker Stone. Pleased ta meetcha." She held out her hand. "And you are?"

"Dave Wheelock, and this is my wife Deb. We're friends of Greg's." He shook her hand.

"Well, isn't this nice," she turned, surveying the room, right hand on her hip.

Finally Greg found his voice. "Mary, I'm glad you decided to come after all. Anyway, I know you and Betty had your differences, so, anyway, I appreciate that you're willing to bury the hatchet and be with your sister at the end. How did you find out about it? It was pretty last minute."

"Oh, I got skills," she said grinning. "Gimme a phone and Google and I can find most anything."

Must run in the family, I thought.

"Besides, I still want to know who to thank." She threw him a huge smile, then turned to look around the room again. All the other conversations had stopped, and everyone was focused on her. "Since I'm her only living relative, shall I stand up here with you, sugar?" she asked.

"Um, that's okay," Greg said hesitantly. "If you want."

"Before I do, won't you introduce me to all your friends?"

Deb stepped forward. "Here, I'll take you around."

Greg looked relieved. I noticed Deputy Sanchez speaking quietly into her phone in the back of the room. Deb introduced Mary to the nearest group, and then to Pru and Lottie. I stepped forward as they approached. "I'm Lily Gallagher, and this is my husband Michael," I said. "We spoke on the phone, Mary. I'm glad you decided to come after all."

"Pleased ta meetcha," Mary responded, "It was nice of ya to call. Made me think, ya know?" Then, looking over my shoulder, her face changed. "Neil?" she said in surprise, "Neil, is that you?" Her eyes seemed to take up her whole face, and the blush on her cheeks stood out harshly.

I turned around to see who she was looking at. "Sorry, you must have me confused with someone else. I'm Keith Johnson, and this is Jennifer Nelson."

"Oh, sorry," she mumbled and looked away. Deb introduced her to the others, and moved on to the next group. Mary looked back at us, frowning.

A few minutes later Mary was standing next to Greg, cheerfully greeting new arrivals.

"Well, that was certainly more excitement than I expected this evening," Pru's mouth was so close to my ear I could feel her breath. "This isn't a visitation, it's a circus."

"I agree. Are you ready to get out of here?"

"I sure am. In fact, I was ready to leave before I got here. Lottie is, too."

I tapped Michael on the shoulder. "Ready to go? I think the excitement's over."

"Sure."

Lottie was already wheeling her chair toward the door. Michael hurried to catch up with her, and took over pushing.

As we approached Michael's car, we heard a woman saying, "You didn't have to yank my arm like that."

"Sorry," a gruff voice answered. "That whole scene was creeping me out. I needed to get out of there." I recognized Keith's voice, and I agreed with him completely.

Outside, I took a deep breath of the warm evening air. "Well, that was *not* what I expected."

Lottie laughed. "That was the strangest visitation I've ever attended, but you know what? After seeing how the sister behaved, and realizing how truly rotten a person Betty must have been, I actually feel better. I'm glad you talked me into coming."

"A few more days, and I hope you'll be even better when the new board votes to grant your waiver," Michael said. "Jennifer will be the new board member, and she's on your side."

"Oh, that will be grand."

Just as I was about to open the car door, I saw Detective Henderson striding toward us. He made a beeline for Lottie.

"Ms. Delaney, a word?" he called out as he approached.

"What is it now, Detective?" When he hesitated, she added, "I'm happy to talk in front of my friends."

"Alright, this will just take a minute. You told me you thought Ms. Harris was angry at you over something to do with her sister." Lottie nodded. "I'm having a hard time understanding that. Did you know her sister?"

"No, I didn't. But I was a family therapist and I've seen how damaging it is when family members don't get along. All I did was encourage her to mend her relationship with her sister. She didn't like the idea of being held accountable and that she should take some responsibility for fixing it."

"What was the reason she and her sister fell out?"

"I have no idea. But if you want to find out more," she grinned, "you can ask the sister directly. She's right inside. We just met."

"I intend to," announced the detective, unsurprised at the news. I assumed that was the reason Deputy Sanchez had placed that phone call.

"Thanks for your help. Ladies, Mr. Gallagher," he nodded to us and turned toward the funeral home.

Twenty-Two

After returning Lottie to the rehab center, we detoured over to Jeremiah's for some Italian ice, one of my favorite treats. Goodies in hand, we found a vacant picnic table.

"Do you think they're ever going to catch the guy who killed Betty?" Pru asked. "I'm getting whiplash from looking over my shoulder so much."

"I hope so," I said. "Maybe the detective will learn something from Betty's sister Mary."

"That Mary, she's a strange one." Pru and I both nodded in agreement.

"Michael, you're dripping." I handed him a napkin from the stack I'd grabbed at the counter. Even this late in the day, it was still plenty warm and Michael's soft-serve cone wasn't holding up well. Pru and I had chosen more wisely. It was much easier to keep a gelati, a layered concoction of soft-serve ice cream and Italian ice in a cup, from dripping on you than a cone.

"More licking, less talking," I suggested.

"Yes, ma'am!" he said cheerfully.

We were silent for a few minutes. Something was eating around the edges of my brain, but I couldn't pin it down. Was it something I'd seen? Something I'd heard? Oh, well, it would come to me eventually.

Pru suddenly giggled. "If this were a Hollywood script, we'd have a dramatic scene in the middle of the funeral tomorrow, where the detectives would burst in and make an arrest. And then we'd all look at each other and say, 'Oh, I never suspected him, he seemed like such a nice man.' It's the only thing that could possibly rival this visitation tonight."

I cracked up. "And the guy would scream, 'You'll never take me alive,' run out of the church, and race away in the hearse, peeling rubber."

"Exactly."

"Oh, you two." Michael shook his head. Both of us roared with laughter.

As I wiped my eyes with a napkin a few minutes later, I said, "Wow, that was great! I've needed a good laugh for days."

"Me, too."

"Oh, you two," Michael said again, causing both of us laugh helplessly.

After I'd composed myself for the second time, I picked up my spoon. "Oh dear, my ice is more like a cold drink," I complained, frowning at the liquidy goo in my cup.

"So's mine, but it was worth it," Pru said.

"Can't take you two anywhere," Michael grinned as he ate the last bite of his cone.

I kissed his cheek. "Thanks for putting up with me."

"Oh, any time. Now, if you two hyenas are finished. . ."

"Well, almost." I paused. "There was a Realtor giving Lottie her card when I went in to pick her up. Apparently the word's getting out. She says she didn't call, the woman just showed up."

Pru drained the last of her melted ice from the cup. "Poor Lottie. I can't believe the vultures are already circling. I mean, it's not as bad as the stories you hear about someone showing up and offering to sell the house while the widow's getting dressed for the funeral, but it's close. I bet that made her feel even worse."

"She seemed almost embarrassed about it," I said. "I wish there was something I could do."

"You're doing plenty," Michael said. "In fact, too much. You know that Charlotte doesn't want to move, so unless she absolutely has to, I wouldn't worry about it."

"You're probably right, but it took me aback."

Later, back in our apartment, I looked with disfavor at the dress I'd picked out for the funeral. I really didn't like to wear black. I found the matching black pumps where I'd dropped them when Patrick knocked on the door this morning. I still needed to transfer necessities from my big tote bag to the small purse that went with the outfit, but I was tired. I'd do it in the morning. The funeral wasn't until ten, I'd have plenty of time.

***

Not far away, watchful eyes filled with tears. Seeing her face today was so unexpected and shocking. Did I keep it together? I must have, but I don't even know. I'm really losing it now. After all this time I can't believe it still hurts so much, like it happened just yesterday. I've been playing a part for so long I didn't think there was anything of me left. I was wrong. Sleep. I'll never get through this without sleep. Why can't I sleep? Maybe it would be better if I just went to sleep forever. Better for me, better for everyone. God, I can't believe I saw her face today.

An image came, out of nowhere. Betty, in the pool, wearing only one shoe. What happened to the other one?

***

After we went to bed, Michael dropped off to sleep right away, but I wasn't so lucky. I needed sleep, but my mind was racing. It was hard not to toss and turn, but I didn't want to wake my husband.

What would cause someone to commit murder, besides something obvious like an argument getting out of hand? This was cold blooded, so what could bring someone to take that awful step of depriving another of life?

Love and hate, of course, desire for gain, fear of loss. Mentally I reviewed what I knew about Betty's victims, but after a while I gave up. It was useless thinking about it, I'd never figure this out. I just hoped the detective would, and soon.

My phone buzzed and startled me. Who was texting me this late?

Patrick: *This is all your fault. You should have minded your own business.*

As I read it, my breath caught. I slipped out of bed quietly and padded to the kitchen. I tried calling the number, but it went straight to voicemail. Then my phone lit up again. "Linda, I just got a strange text from Patrick, what's going on?"

"Oh, Lily," she said, and I heard the tears in her voice. "Patrick went to get something out of the car a while ago, and he's still not back. It shouldn't have taken him more than two or three minutes. I'm too scared to go out and look for him after what happened to you last night, I don't know what to do." She sounded frantic.

"Did you call the detective?"

"Just voicemail."

"Well, given everything that's been happening here, maybe you should call nine-one-one."

"Okay."

There was no way I was going to sleep now, so I started to pace.

Why would Patrick send me a text like that? What was my fault? It didn't make any sense. Unless — I stiffened. Not unless that text message had been from the killer using Patrick's phone. Why would the murderer send me a threatening message from Patrick's phone? And, more concerning, how did he get Patrick's phone? What happened to Patrick? How was it my fault?

I was thinking furiously, but I couldn't come up with anything I'd learned in the past few days that would help me identify who did this. I still had that little niggle at the back of my mind, the one I'd felt before but couldn't pin down, but I didn't know anything. What could I have done that threatened the guy?

I'd felt confused and sorry for myself all day. Now, anger and helplessness were layered on. Not a good combination. I hated feeling unsafe, and even more I hated not trusting the people I came in contact with every day. This was no way to live. But what could I do? That was where the helpless feeling came in.

If these were normal circumstances, I would have thrown on a robe and scooted over to Linda's apartment to keep her company, but after what happened to me last night, and now with Patrick missing, I didn't dare set foot outside the apartment.

I was still pacing, my mind churning uselessly, when two dark cars approached. One of them parked in front of the clubhouse, and the other continued toward Building A. What was going on now? Nothing happened for a while, then two people got out of the car by the clubhouse. They each had a powerful flashlight, and they started walking toward Building A, obviously looking for something — or someone. Who were they? I hoped they were police.

For the second time that day I wanted to do nothing more than crawl back into bed and pull the covers over my head. I didn't, though, because I knew I couldn't keep still, so I continued pacing. Now, instead of just walking around the kitchen, I was looping through the length of the apartment. Kitchen, dining area, living room, back porch, living room, dining area, kitchen. I looked out the slider and now I saw another car and figures with flashlights around the pool area. I made another loop through the apartment, and when I came back to the kitchen, I could see the flashlights still bobbing around.

Suddenly I heard a shout and all the flashlights converged. There was a bustle of activity, but I couldn't tell what was going on. Had they found Patrick? Was he hurt? Was he dead? I watched in horrified fascination. Then, with a screech of tires, another car arrived on the scene and I recognized Detective Henderson jumping out and racing over toward the flashlights. So the people with lights must be deputies.

A moment later an ambulance pulled in and two EMTs quickly opened the back and pulled out a stretcher. They were hurrying, so that was a good sign. It meant whoever they had come for wasn't dead.

With all that police activity, I figured it was safe to go outside so I grabbed my robe and thrust my feet into whatever shoes were by the door and hustled out. As I drew near the activity, Linda rushed up from the other direction, a deputy holding her by the elbow.

She pushed her way through to where the EMTs were crouched over a figure on the ground, and I followed.

It was Patrick, and he was groaning, so still alive. What a relief.

The detective saw Linda and took a few steps toward her, then stopped dead when he noticed me hovering behind her. He stared at me, then strode forward until he was glaring down at me. "What are you doing here?"

"I was worried about Patrick. Linda called me a while ago after he went missing."

He grabbed my arm and steered me away from the group. "So you came rushing outside, by yourself, the night after you were assaulted, knowing that something had happened to Patrick. Are you crazy?" I'd never seen him angry before, but he was pretty steamed at me and not holding it in.

He turned around and hollered, "Lopez!"

"Sir?" Lopez materialized next to us.

"Escort Mrs. Gallagher back to her apartment, check that it's clear, then get back here."

Lopez nodded at him, then took my arm and started leading me back to Building E. "I can walk by myself," I snapped, pulling my arm away. "Is Patrick going to be okay?"

"We think so. He's got a big lump on his head and he's been unconscious for a while. EMTs will take him to the hospital and they'll likely keep him overnight, keep an eye on him."

"Could he say what happened to him?"

"Nope."

When we got to my front door, Lopez turned to me. "Key?"

"Um, I didn't lock it," I said. He didn't say a word, just stared at me then unsnapped his holster and put his hand on his gun. That's when I realized how stupid I'd been to leave the apartment at all, let alone to leave it unlocked.

"Anyone here?" he asked.

"Michael's asleep in the bedroom." My legs started to shake and I collapsed onto the nearest chair.

"Okay. You wait here." He eased open the door and stepped inside. I sat, shivering a little. It seemed like I waited a long time. Long enough for the EMTs to put Patrick into the ambulance and roll away, with no sirens or flashing lights. Was that good or bad?

"All clear," Lopez said as he came back out onto the porch. "I did my best not to disturb your husband. He didn't even twitch, he's sound asleep."

"Thank you." I took a deep breath. "I'm sorry to be such a bother."

He looked at me, expressionless. "All in the line of duty, ma'am. Now, you go inside and lock that door." He waited until I did, then turned and went back down the steps.

Finally I was able to climb into bed, but I still couldn't sleep, worrying about Patrick, and mostly giving myself a good kicking for rushing out of the apartment without even thinking about locking up. Just because the deputies were out by the clubhouse didn't mean my sleeping husband would have been safe inside.

My mind drifted back to who could have done it, then I gave myself a good mental shaking.

Why was I still thinking about this? I was never going to figure it out. I needed to let it go, let the detective and his team handle it, and hunker down and not make any more waves.

Sleep eluded me, but if mentally beating yourself up counts as exercise, I got the best workout of my life that night. And I had to go to the funeral in the morning.

***

The watchful eyes had found what they were looking for, and, holding it tightly, walked silently back home. Why did Patrick have to show up? How much had he seen? What would he remember? That whack with the flashlight had been pretty hard. Maybe killed him, too. Too bad. Interfering bastard, why did he have to come along?

And that Lily Gallagher. Maybe sending the text was a mistake. Oh, well, too late now, and there had already been so many mistakes. What did one more matter?

Inside, the flashlight was put away and the sneaker dropped into the trash. Better take it out to the Dumpster first thing. For now, a drink, and some sleep. Nothing more to do tonight. Everything would be better with sleep. Still have to get through tomorrow, act normal, be a good neighbor, go to the funeral in just a few hours. Skin crawling at the thought of seeing her face again. Eye mask and earplugs tonight. Sleep.

Twenty-Three

I dropped into a heavy, exhausted doze just as the sun was coming up. Shortly after eight the tantalizing odor of fresh-brewed coffee woke me as Michael came into the room, mug in hand. "I thought you might need this sooner than later," he said. "I know you had a terrible night."

"You have no idea. Honestly, if we don't figure out who killed Betty pretty soon, I'll be so sleep deprived I won't be able to function. I just want to be able to get through today without drama." Gratefully I took the mug and sucked down a big gulp of caffeine. "And you missed the latest attack."

"What?" His eyes grew wide. "You're okay, it wasn't you again, right?"

"No, it was Patrick. Linda called me around midnight because he went out to the car for something and never came back. She was frantic, so I told her to call nine-one-one."

"I should think so. Is he alright?"

"They found him more than an hour later, with a huge bump on his head. He doesn't know who hit him, but he must have been out cold all that time. EMTs came and took him to the hospital. I should check how he's doing."

As I reached for my phone, I said, "Something's been tickling around the edge of my brain for a couple of days now, and I just can't pin it down. Something I saw or heard that's important."

"You mentioned it yesterday. I'm sure it'll come to you."

"I hope so." I looked distastefully at the clothes I'd laid out for the funeral. "I think I'll wait to shower and dress until after breakfast. I'm not very hungry, but I know I'd better eat something."

"Eggs and bacon?"

"I don't think so. I need something that'll slide down easily."

"How about some oatmeal?"

"Oh, that would be perfect. You made coffee, so I'll get it started while you shower. I'll just call Linda first."

"Sounds like a deal."

Michael headed for the bathroom while I hit the call button and aimed for the kitchen.

"How's Patrick?" I asked as soon as Linda picked up.

"Better, thank goodness. We're in the hospital. They kept him overnight."

"What happened to him?"

"I'll let him tell you. I'm putting you on speaker."

A moment later Patrick said, "Lily, I think whoever attacked you the other night got me as well."

"Oh, no. What happened?"

"I was on my way out to the car, and I caught a glimpse of a light moving around over by the clubhouse. I decided to check it out, which wasn't very bright of me as it turns out."

"What kind of light?"

"I think probably a flashlight, and it was bobbing around in the bushes, like someone was looking for something."

Linda said something to him in a low voice, then he was back. "By the time I got near where I thought I saw it, the light was gone. I decided I must have imagined it, so I turned around to head back home. Next thing I knew I was waking up on the ground with one heck of a headache and people standing all around me."

"Well, I'm glad you're alright. Do you know how much longer you'll be at the hospital?"

"I'm not sure," Linda said. "They said they'd discharge him as soon as the doctor checks him one last time. We'll be at the funeral if we can, if Patrick's up to it."

"Did you stay with him overnight?"

"Of course. Besides, no way would I spend the night at home by myself after what happened."

"Well, don't feel like you have to come to the funeral. If anyone has a good excuse to miss it, you do."

"We'll just play it by ear. Talk to you later," Linda said.

The oatmeal was almost ready to dish out when Michael joined me, freshly showered and shaved and wearing a lightweight robe.

"I figured if I put on my good duds I'd just slop cereal on them," he said when I noticed. "I'll dress while you're showering. Did you get hold of Linda?"

"Yes, neither of them got much sleep, of course, but they'll be discharging him soon. Probably not in time for the funeral, though."

"That's a relief. I'm glad he's okay."

"It sure is. I wish I had a good excuse to miss this darned funeral."

"Me too, but it'll be over quickly."

"Not really, because then we have to come back here for the reception. One way or another we'll be spending most of the day on it."

"Well, at least we'll be able to duck out of the reception whenever we want."

"The sooner the better."

I must have sounded abstracted because Michael picked up on it. "What's the matter, honey?"

"Oh, this thing that I can't put my finger on. I need to stop thinking about it, but I can't seem to. It's like when your tongue keeps going back to the missing tooth or the new filling."

"Well, maybe it'll come to you in the shower. That's where I seem to get my best ideas."

"Maybe." I was doubtful.

Later, while I was reaching for my towel, I remembered that I still hadn't cleaned out my tote bag, and I didn't really have time to do it now. What a pain. Quickly I dried off, then snatched the bag and dumped all its contents onto the bed.

I picked out a few old receipts and tossed them in the trash, then set my change purse and sunglasses aside. I organized the rest of it, some to go back into the tote bag and some to be put away. I grabbed my wallet and keys from the mess, added a few tissues — it was a funeral after all, and weeping is contagious even when you're not attached to the person who died — and a lipstick, and shoved them all into the little black clutch I'd be taking to the funeral. That should do it. Oh, wait, where was my phone? I took it off the nightstand and jammed it in.

There was one piece of paper left.

I reached for it and realized it was a photograph, lying face down. What on earth?

I picked it up and flipped it over. Oh, it was that strange picture I'd found behind the family photo in the broken frame at the Harris' apartment. How had it gotten into my bag?

I replayed the moment in my mind. Maybe it was just as stupid as my bag sitting on the floor next to the trash, and I dropped it into the wrong receptacle. I looked at it curiously, and suddenly that little irritating thing that had been niggling at the back of my brain for days made sense. Yes, one person in the community had been acting out of character, but there was such an obvious explanation for it that I'd overlooked it.

"Oh. My. God," I said aloud. I'd been wrong about a lot of things since Betty was killed, but I didn't think I was wrong about this, and it explained everything.

I sat down hard, my breath coming in small gasps. It all made sense. Everything. Well, everything except what happened to Patrick. I could do this. With shaking but determined hands, I dialed the detective and left him a message. With luck, he would be on his way to the funeral anyway. Now I just needed to keep it together until he called me back. Should I say something to Michael? Better not, he had enough to deal with.

Quickly I changed into my funeral clothes. If party clothes were glad rags, I wondered, were funeral clothes sad rags? Sure, why not. I ran a comb through my hair, swiped on some makeup, added pearl stud earrings, and I was ready to go. After this was over, I was going to change into the brightest blouse I owned.

After collecting Pru and Lottie, we drove to the church, barely arriving in time. Between my lack of sleep and my discovery, I was feeling antsy and on edge. I wasn't sure I was a good enough actress to behave normally if I came face to face with the person in the photo.

The flower-covered casket was already in place at the front of the sanctuary when we entered. Quickly and quietly, we found seats in the rear pew, as far away from that ghastly open casket as we could sit. It was also the perfect vantage point for watching all my neighbors.

Just as we got settled, Keith and Jennifer slid into the pew across the aisle from us. Keith had dark circles under his eyes, but Jennifer still looked radiant.

During the service I watched everyone. A woman with dishwater blond hair and wearing dark clothes sat next to Greg in the front. It was probably Mary. I was relieved to see she'd ditched the red dress and was wearing appropriately dark colors. I spotted most of my neighbors scattered throughout the small sanctuary, with the Wheelocks just behind Greg and Mary.

Aside from Happy Oaks residents, only a few other people were present. One of them was Detective Henderson, trying to blend in near the back. I caught his eye and he held his hand to his ear in a "call me" signal. There was no sign of Patrick and Linda.

When it was time, Michael slid out of the pew to take his place by the coffin. Greg was hiding his face in his hands. I saw Dave in the front, but the other pallbearers were strangers.

Michael, Dave, and the other pallbearers marched slowly down the center aisle balancing the coffin. Greg followed with Mary. Her face was dry and composed, but his was wet with tears that he was making no attempt to wipe away. She had her arm tucked under his elbow, and, seeing him stumble a little, I had the impression it was more to guide him down the aisle than for any sort of comfort.

As they came closer, I saw Mary studying something, or someone, her eyes narrowed, but they had gone past before I could see what she'd been looking at. I could guess, though. I waited with my friends until the church was mostly empty, then slipped out and got Lottie's wheelchair. As we exited, Michael came up the steps.

"They don't need me any more," he said in a low voice. "They've got people from the funeral home handling it all from now on."

"Does that mean we can skip the graveside?"

"I think so. I doubt anyone will be there except for Greg, Mary, and the pastor, but I think we've done our duty."

"I agree," Pru said. "I think we've done more than that. I'm ready to go home and put my feet up."

"You can't," I reminded her. "Greg's having that reception in the clubhouse in an hour."

"Oh, mercy, do I have to go to that, too?"

"It's the neighborly thing to do."

"Lottie, did you want to attend the reception?" I asked.

"No, but I suppose I will if you're all going. Do you think I'd be in the way if I go straight to the clubhouse? Since I can't make it into either of your apartments?"

"I don't think it'll be a problem," Michael said. "Why don't you all wait here and I'll bring the car around once the graveside folks have left."

We agreed, and he started walking to the parking lot.

We exchanged greetings with several of our neighbors. Except for Linda, all the board members had made an appearance, including Tim Martino, who was glowering at everyone indiscriminately. He and Helen didn't appear to be speaking to anyone, or to each other, and Helen's eyes were red. I didn't think it was because of grief over Betty's death.

The hearse left with only three cars following. No surprise there. A minute later Michael pulled up.

Once we were settled in the car, I wiggled my right foot. My shoes had low heels, but they were enough to put a strain on my knee. "I'm going to hobble up to the apartment and change my shoes before the reception," I said. "These heels are making my knee flare up again. I'll change into flats and meet you over at the clubhouse. In fact, I might even put the darned knee brace back on. Too bad I don't have one in black." It would also give me a chance to call the detective.

A few minutes later we pulled into Happy Oaks. "I'll help Lottie, honey," Michael said, "you go ahead and take care of that knee. Pru, are you coming with us?"

"I guess."

"I'll just sit here a minute and nerve myself for the hobble up the stairs."

As soon as they were out of sight I hit the door lock, whipped out my phone, and called the detective. He spent several minutes berating me for coming outside last night.

Finally I interrupted him. "Look, I appreciate your concern, but that was last night and I have information for you now, remember?" I was still telling him about my discovery of the photograph when I saw him pull into the parking area by the clubhouse. "I need to get home and change my shoes, my knee is killing me. Would you be willing to walk with me while we continue our conversation? Because I don't dare go by myself anyway."

"Of course, where are you?"

"I'm in Michael's car, the silver CRV."

"Okay, I'll be right over. You can show me the picture you found."

A minute later he was knocking on my window. Carefully I eased out of the car. "You're a lifesaver. For obvious reasons I don't want to be going anywhere on my own right now."

The detective stood in the kitchen and called his deputy while I kicked off my shoes and carried them to the bedroom. With my knee brace on, I pulled a pair of comfortable black sandals out of the closet and slid my feet into them.

"So, what's the plan?" I asked when I walked back into the kitchen, photo in hand.

I handed it to the detective. He flicked his eyes over it.

"Recognize anyone?"

"Maybe," he said. Then, impatiently, "What's so important?"

"Look at the names underneath."

He glanced at them, then his eyes narrowed. He focused on me, laser eyes boring a hole in my face. "Tell me."

As I explained, his impatience turned to curiosity, and then his eyes widened when the penny dropped. "Tell me again where you found it."

"It was hidden in a frame behind a Harris family photo. I found it when I was helping Greg clean up after the break-in. It was tucked behind another picture in a broken frame, that's how I came across it. Greg didn't recognize it, in fact he told me just throw it away. I thought I had, but I must have dropped it into my tote bag instead of the trash bag."

The detective quirked an eyebrow at me and I explained, "Both bags were sitting on the floor next to my chair. I only found it this morning when I was cleaning out the tote bag before the funeral."

"Hmmm," was the detective's only response.

"I also think he was probably the young man Mary was engaged to, the one Betty considered unsuitable."

"What makes you think that?"

"The look on her face when she saw him last night." I replayed the scene in my mind. "Up until that moment she'd been trying to shock everyone, acting so happy that her sister was dead. She was all smiles and big personality. But when she saw him she looked absolutely gobsmacked. She literally turned white."

"If you say so, but I'm still skeptical."

"Well, if I'm right that would be a pretty big secret, wouldn't it?"

"It's possible, but by itself it's not enough. We need evidence. Hard evidence."

"I'm sure you can find the evidence once you start looking."

He nodded, and placed the photograph into an evidence bag which he tucked into the inside pocket of his jacket.

"Thank you."

"You're welcome," I attempted to smile. "Now, I'm expected at the clubhouse, but I'm not comfortable walking around out there by myself right now."

"I'll escort you over and then see where Lopez is at."

"What's the plan after that?"

"The plan is for you to go to this repast and act normally. We'll take care of it from here."

"Can I tell Michael about it?"

"I'd rather you didn't."

That wasn't going to be easy.

Twenty-Four

Watchful eyes blinked hard. Keep it together, keep it together. This was unexpected. What was that detective doing back here, and with Lily Gallagher? What did she know? It even looked like she'd been expecting him. Did she find out something? What could it be? She couldn't have found the evidence I've been searching for. Could she? Another voice was babbling in his ear and he tried to blank it out.

What was the detective doing there with her? He'd better leave, just make his excuses and get out. He couldn't think straight with the other voice droning on. He didn't care about the stupid reception. Wait, maybe he did. He turned to his unwelcome guest.

Keep it together.

***

Mrs. Gallagher limped out with Henderson, locking the door behind her. He stopped on the porch and scanned the area between the apartment and the clubhouse. There was nobody in sight. As they approached the clubhouse door, he asked, "Mrs. Gallagher, are you alright now? I see my deputy waiting for me and I need to have a word with him."

She nodded. "I'm fine. Michael's inside, and I plan to stick to him like glue. Thanks for walking me this far."

"My pleasure." He watched until she entered the clubhouse. Then he turned toward Lopez' car, wondering what his partner had found.

Was Mrs. Gallagher right? And what were the odds of the suspect choosing to live in the same community as a woman who'd known him years ago? He felt a faint whisper of hope that they might be able to wrap up this case.

Opening the car door, he sank into the passenger seat. "What do you have for me?"

"We got fingerprints back on those wads of cash. The results are, well, see for yourself." Lopez handed him the fingerprint analysis.

Henderson looked at it in mounting disbelief. "I've never seen anything like this before. But this is all we need to make an arrest. Here's something else." He handed the photo in its evidence bag to Lopez.

Lopez studied it for a minute before figuring out what he was seeing, then gave a low whistle.

"Have you seen him since you've been parked here?" Henderson asked.

"Yes, he went into the clubhouse about ten minutes ago."

"Okay, I'm going to try to do this without causing a lot of fuss and kerfuffle, but we'd best call for backup just in case. Tell them to come quietly. No sirens or flashing lights. I'm going inside. Text me when the backup arrives. I want two people posted at either end of the patio, unobtrusively, and two at the front door."

He glanced around. "That oak tree over by the corner of the building might be a good spot for you. You'll be in the shade and have direct line of sight to the front door and the patio in case something goes wrong. I'll give you a minute to get in position, then I'm going inside."

"Right." Lopez spoke into his radio for a minute. "Backup on its way, sir." He left the car.

Henderson watched him for a minute, then opened the door. He'd be glad to wrap up this case.

Entering the clubhouse, he first looked around for Lily. Michael's white hair stood out like a beacon and he noticed both of the Gallaghers sitting in the far corner. He noted that she'd selected a chair that let her survey the entire room. She smiled at him, looking a little pale. He saw Ms. Nelson chatting with Mr. and Mrs. Martino near the kitchen. He couldn't stand here in the doorway, but he wanted his back to the room. He felt exposed.

The door opened again behind him and he turned quickly. "Oh, Mr. Harris, so sorry again for your loss." The Wheelocks and Mary Stone accompanied Greg.

"Thanks, Detective," he said. He looked tired and drawn. Henderson didn't want to cause a scene here but he didn't think he'd be able to avoid it.

He followed them into the main room, still searching for his quarry. People stood around in small groups throughout the large space and Mary was urging Greg to go around and thank his guests for coming. Seeing him near the doorway, several people came over to speak with him and it quickly turned into an impromptu receiving line.

As he continued scanning the room, he heard Deb say, "If everyone starts lining up here in the middle of the room, it's going to be a mess. Let's move over toward the patio. That way Greg can greet people without causing a traffic jam."

"Makes sense," Mary agreed. With her hand under Greg's elbow, she moved a few steps to her right, then a few more.

Deb nodded approvingly, while Greg hardly seemed to notice. Henderson stepped behind Greg, a few paces to the side. Now he was able to scan the room, and his back was protected.

Over by the patio doors the Wheelocks positioned themselves next to Greg on his right, as they had at the visitation, while Mary stood to his left. Henderson watched as they greeted Liz Steinbach.

His stomach growled. Breakfast had been a bad cup of coffee, and that was hours ago. Someone came out of the kitchen pushing a cart and started laying out dishes on the large main table. Apparently Greg had arranged for a buffet lunch. In fact, something smelled pretty darned good.

He told his rebellious stomach to be quiet while he scanned the room again. Still no sign of his suspect, and he was starting to worry. Quietly he took out his phone and texted Lopez, who responded that nobody had left the building. Was the man even here? Maybe he was sitting back in his apartment. If that was the case, he'd see the police near the patio. Henderson's palms began to sweat. No, that couldn't be right. Lopez had seen him enter the clubhouse. Could he have left, unnoticed, by the french doors?

Another group was ambling toward the receiving line, this one including the Gallaghers, Pru McLeod, Charlotte Delaney, and Jennifer Nelson. Henderson walked toward them as Lily looked at him questioningly. He smiled at the group. "Morning, all," he said. "How's everyone?"

Then, as if noticing that Jennifer was on her own, "Ms. Nelson, are you here by yourself? Where's Mr. Johnson? Seems like I always see you two together."

Jennifer sparkled. "Oh, he's here. But I think he's got an upset tummy. He went to the men's room a few minutes ago."

Henderson chatted for another minute, then turned away. He'd intercept Mr. Johnson when he left the men's room.

***

When the detective turned toward the men's room, the breath I'd been holding came out with an audible *whoosh*. I was having a hard time keeping my cool. My hands were clenched so tightly my nails were digging into my palms. I forced myself to take a deep breath. I hated that I hadn't told Michael or my friends what I'd found and I just wanted this awful morning to be over and not to be scared.

I watched the detective as he made his way across the room. When he was about halfway there, the men's room door opened and Keith stepped out. He saw the detective heading toward him, and turned toward the front door.

At that moment, it opened and Patrick and Linda walked in. Patrick had a bandage wrapped around his head. Everyone turned to look at him and the room became quiet. Keith and Patrick's paths crossed about halfway between the restroom and the doorway.

Suddenly, Patrick shouted, "It was you, wasn't it? You're the one who hit me last night!"

It happened so fast I couldn't really tell what happened. One second Keith was walking, and the next second he was pulling Patrick backwards toward the door. The detective started moving fast.

"Don't come any closer!" Keith hollered, "I'll give him a lot more than a bump on the head if you come near me!" The detective stopped moving.

The residents were frozen in place, as if they were playing a macabre game of statues.

The room was completely quiet now, everyone staring. Someone had to do something. I took a couple of tentative steps toward Keith. "Don't move!" he yelled at me.

"What's going on, Keith?" I asked, surprised the words found their way past the enormous lump wedged in my throat.

"Be quiet."

He dragged Patrick back another step toward the door. "Keith, why are you doing this?" I asked again, taking another couple of steps. First statues, now red light, green light. Why were all these children's games popping into my mind? "What did Patrick ever do to you?"

"I said shut up." He was yelling.

I took another step. "Of course your name really isn't Keith, is it Neil?"

"I'm warning you, shut up and stop moving or I'll snap his neck!"

Patrick was shaking, white, and sweating. He looked the way I felt.

The detective's voice boomed out. "Is that why you killed Betty? Because she recognized you?"

Keith was shouting at the detective, cursing, screaming that she deserved everything she got and more. She'd ruined his entire life, starting when he was a child. She didn't deserve to live, and he had no regrets.

Frantically I tried to think of something that would distract him. While his attention was focused on the detective, I took a few more steps, and now I was standing next to the table where the caterers had placed the stacks of dishes. I just hoped Henderson would be able to do something, because if this didn't work I was out of ideas.

I grabbed a stack of dishes and threw them on the floor as hard as I could, aiming for the tile, not the carpet. The crash was horrific. I had expected the detective would take advantage of the distraction to tackle Keith, but the result was not at all what I expected.

I watched, horrified, as Keith crumpled to the floor and started to twitch.

I rushed forward, but the detective grabbed me and held me back. "Don't move," he said into my ear. Keith must have let go of Patrick as he was falling, because Patrick sat down suddenly on the floor. The detective grabbed him and pulled him away from Keith.

***

Watchful eyes were focused on a scene they'd witnessed thousands of times before. Jungle. Heat. Danger. He was huddled in a little indentation in the ground, behind a screen of vegetation, the grenade in his hand. Movement. Over there. Friend or foe? Couldn't afford to make a mistake. There it was again. He tensed, ready, as the enemy appeared. Slowly he eased out the pin and, with a practiced flick, tossed it at the approaching danger. Standing, he could throw a grenade over fifty feet, but from this position it was a lot less. He only hoped he was far enough away, and protected by the vegetation and the little hollow he lay in.

Boom!

Silence. Had he killed the bastard, or was the little devil lying in wait for him? Only one way to find out. He lifted his head a fraction, so he could see the clearing. Big splotches of stuff that hadn't been there before. Slowly he inched his way toward it, doing the low crawl he'd been taught in Basic. His head hurt like hell. The roaring in his skull made it hard to hear, and his vision blurred.

Well, no doubt the enemy was dead, there were a lot of pieces scattered around. Good. Served the bastard right. Seeing a fragment of clothing with an insignia on it he grinned, a terrible death's head grimace. Yup. He got him. The enemy. Time to be somewhere else.

But first, he had to be sure the enemy had been alone. Had someone been with him? He continued his crawl. Oops, looked like at least one other person got caught in the blast. There wasn't enough left to recognize, but he caught a glint of metal. He grabbed at it. It was still readable. Oh, no. Well, sorry buddy. I'm so sorry.

His head hurt worse than ever. It felt like it was going to explode. He had to get out of here before someone came to see what the big boom was. He crawled a few feet, then suddenly stopped, a wonderful idea blossoming in his pounding, aching head. He turned, and carefully lifted Keith Johnson's dog tags from around what was left of his head and neck, removed his own, and dropped them next to the body.

Placing the purloined dog tags around his own neck with bloody fingers, he crawled another fifty yards before he collapsed, bleeding from the small piece of shrapnel that had entered his skull above his left eye.

***

I stared in horrified fascination, watching Keith go through the motions of — I had no idea what. The detective was barking orders into his radio, and warning the residents to stay back. Patrick had made it to a chair, and Linda was holding his hand and crying.

"Let me through!" Lopez shoved his way through the crowd. He must have come in from the patio.

Keith had collapsed onto the floor again. Lopez grabbed one of his arms, then the other, and the handcuffs snicked shut.

"Neil Miller, also known as Keith Johnson, you're under arrest on suspicion of the murder of Betty Louise Harris, and for assaulting Patrick Barry," Detective Lopez announced, breathing hard.

"You have the right to remain silent," Detective Henderson said. He continued reciting the Miranda warning as Lopez pulled Keith to a kneeling position, where he swayed, his eyes unfocused as though he were looking at something a great distance away.

Suddenly Mary pushed through the stunned crowd and stood in front of him. "Oh, Neil, what have you done?" Tears streamed down her face.

He stared at her for a moment, his face still blank and eyes unfocused, then he smiled. "Angel! What's wrong, honey?" He tried to reach for her, looking puzzled when he couldn't move his arms. Lopez held him in place. He seemed to notice his neighbors and the deputies for the first time. "What the hell?" He rattled his handcuffs. "Why am I wearing these?"

"Oh, Neil," she said sadly.

"You're under arrest, do you understand?" The detective asked.

"No, I don't. What's going on?"

He repeated the charges and the Miranda warning.

Keith was still staring at Mary. "I'm sorry," he said to her.

"Sorry you killed my sister?"

He laughed bitterly. "Not really. The world's better off without her. But I'm sorry I was such a dumb kid. I should never have believed her when she told me you'd spent the night with that other boy. I mean, I knew what she was like. She started shaking me down for my allowance when I was eight years old, for gawd's sake, but when she said that about you, I was so hurt I couldn't think straight. After that it was just one stupid move after another."

"Well, I believed her, too, when she told me that you left the campfire on the beach and went off with the head cheerleader at that graduation party." Mary's tears were falling faster now.

"And I lived with her all my life, so if anyone shoulda known what she was like it was me. I shoulda talked to you, but I was so hurt and angry."

"After that it was all downhill for me," he continued. "And then, in 'Nam," his eyes got that unfocused look, and she said his name quietly.

"Neil. Don't go back there."

He shook his head. "Right. Well, I did something else stupid over there, and thought I'd make it better by swapping dog tags with Keith Johnson when I found him dead. Only it made everything worse. And then I made the worst mistake of all. I bought the condo here. The day I came face to face with your sister I nearly had a heart attack."

"I knew when I filled out the paperwork that someone named Betty Harris was on that board of directors, but I never imagined it was Betty Parker from Mobile. Then, just one day after I moved in, one lousy day, I was taking a break from unpacking. I was sitting at the pool getting some sun and I heard her voice. I almost wet myself." He gave a sharp laugh.

"And right away, she recognized me and started in on me. You know how she was. She made me so crazy I couldn't do anything. When I first moved in here, I thought I'd be able to make a few friends, be with people again after living my whole life alone traveling around, you know? But she made sure I couldn't even do that."

"But why," she demanded fiercely, "why didn't you ever let me know you were alive?"

"I thought you hated me."

"Oh, Neil."

"I was too much of a coward." After a moment's pause, "But the only reason I let Jennifer drag me here was because I hoped I'd see you. I wasn't planning on losing my shit the way I did. Anyway, I just wanted to tell you I'm sorry."

"Oh, Neil," she sobbed.

He looked at Detective Henderson and said, “I’m ready to go.”

Suddenly the room was swarming with deputies. “Get him out of here,” the detective said. Lopez nodded and, with two of the deputies, led Keith from the building while Mary covered her face with her hands.

Twenty-Five

The detective turned around and raised his voice. "Everyone! Please find yourself a seat. You're to stay here until we have a chance to talk with each and every one of you. Keep this area clear for the EMTs who'll be arriving momentarily to check on Mr. Barry."

Then, more quietly, "Ms. Stone, Mrs. Gallagher, please come with me." Mary was crying now with noisy gulps as tears coursed down her cheeks and dripped onto her clothing. He led us over to the far corner.

I was feeling pretty frazzled, but apparently I wasn't going to have a minute to myself.

With a crash the front doors flew open and the emergency medical team ran in, led by Brianna. One of the deputies pointed them toward Patrick.

The detective said, "Mrs. Gallagher, I need some answers from her. Can you give me a hand here?"

"If I can do whatever it is you need while sitting down."

"Of course, I'll move a chair over for you. See if you can calm her down,"

I took a deep breath as I sat. I wasn't very calm myself. My heart was still racing, so I didn't know what help I could be. But I was willing to try if it would get me some answers.

"Mary," I said softly, "It's Lily Gallagher. We met last night."

Mary looked up. "I'm a nurse," I said, "and I can see you're very upset. We all are. I'd like to help you if I can."

Mary's voice was soft now. "I don't think anyone can help me now." There was no sign now of the flamboyant woman in the red dress who'd been so excited at last night's viewing. Her shoulders sagged, her eyes were red, and her fingers plucked restlessly at her dark skirt. She didn't seem to notice when the detective quietly returned with a chair and sat across from her.

"Do you want to tell me about it?" It was hard for me to keep my voice calm when I felt so shaky myself, but long years of training helped.

Mary shook her head. "It won't do any good. There's nothing anyone can do now, it's over."

"What do you mean? What's over?"

"Neil. When I saw him last night I couldn't believe it. After all these years. He was dead, you see, and then, he wasn't. . ." she trailed off.

"I'm sorry, I don't understand."

"No, how could you?" Mary glanced up at me. "Oh, what the hell. It doesn't matter now."

I waited.

"Neil and I loved each other." Her tears had stopped, but a small, sad smile played across her lips. "We were engaged to be married, and then my bitch sister had to stick her nose in. She couldn't stand me being happy." Her voice grew strident.

"I didn't find out until a long time later what she did, all I knew was, one day I was happy and Neil and I were engaged, and the next day he broke our engagement and went and enlisted. Back then, it meant 'Nam, you know? A couple years later his family got the telegram saying he'd been killed in action."

She started crying again. Wordlessly I looked at Henderson and mimed wiping my eyes, then pointed. He turned around, spotted the box of tissues, and slipped out of his chair.

"What made you so sure Keith Johnson is really Neil?" I handed her a tissue.

"I just know." She wiped her streaming eyes. "At first he said he wasn't, but I just know. And just for a minute I started hoping again. You don't know how terrible my life has been. And then just now, he called me Angel."

"Why Angel?"

"It was his pet name for me. My full name's Angela Mary, but I always went by Mary. When we were dating he found out my real first name, and he started calling me Angel. He's the only one who ever did."

"But now — what did he do?" she asked fiercely, turning to the detective. "Did he really kill Betty?"

"He admitted it just now, you must have heard him. And then we all witnessed his assault on Mr. Barry and he probably assaulted Mrs. Gallagher as well. I'm guessing he killed your sister to protect the secret of his identity. How would she have recognized him?"

She just shrugged.

"Does he have any birthmarks or anything like that?"

"Oh, yeah," she smiled fondly. "We used to tease him about it. He had a dark birthmark on his lower back shaped just like the state of Alabama."

"Would Betty have known about it?"

"Sure. She used to babysit him when he was in elementary school. He would have been eight or nine when she was sixteen."

I turned to the detective. "She could have spotted it at the pool."

"Ms. Stone," he said, "I'm going to need to talk with you more later, but that's enough for now. I'll let you pull yourself together, but please don't leave this building. Mrs. Gallagher, a word?"

He stood and helped me to my feet. "Thanks for that, you've been a big help throughout this case, and I appreciate it. I need to organize my deputies now, but I won't keep you here any longer than I have to. You look exhausted."

"I am." I stumbled over to where Michael, Pru and Lottie were watching, worried looks on their faces. They had parked themselves in a group of club chairs, and I practically fell into the one next to Michael.

He knelt in front of me and put his arms around me. "Can you talk about it? What happened?"

"I'm okay, I'm okay, I'm okay," I said, as though repetition would make it true. "Give me a minute." Then, as he started to pull away, "No, don't move just yet."

Pru and Lottie exchanged worried glances but didn't speak.

Finally I spoke, my words muffled by Michael's comforting shoulder. "It was Keith, only that's not his real name. His real name is Neil Miller. He killed Betty."

Michael rocked back on his heels. "Keith? But why?"

"I don't know exactly. And I'm not sure if I'm supposed to be talking about it, but I found something in my bag, a photograph Betty had hidden behind another one. It was from one of the broken frames when we were cleaning up after Greg's break-in. Greg told me to throw it out, and I thought I had, but I guess I dropped it into my bag instead. Anyway, I found it and all the little things that had been niggling around in my brain clicked and I figured out it was Keith.

"Okay, I'm confused. You found a photo of this guy, and that's enough to conclude he killed Betty and for Henderson to arrest him?"

"I'm not explaining it very well, am I?"

"Not really, honey, no."

Pru interrupted. "Lily, you look like you need a minute to pull yourself together. Can I get you something to drink? Or some food?"

I shivered. "I don't think I can eat a thing, but some coffee would be great."

"Back in a flash."

Michael sat back in his chair and took my hand in his while Lottie watched us. I was slowly realizing that the buzzing in my ears was a low hum of conversation around me. I took a deep breath and looked around the room.

A few people were filling plates at the buffet. Greg sat with his head in his hands while Dave patted him awkwardly on the shoulder. The caterers were huddled in the kitchen, talking with each other and paying no attention to the food service. Someone had swept the broken plates into a pile against the wall. Mary still sat where I had left her, staring blankly into space. The EMTs were leaving, and Patrick and Linda were sitting on one of the loveseats, her head on his shoulder as he stroked her hair. Jennifer Nelson stood by herself in the middle of the room, motionless. Two of the deputies were setting up an interview area at the front of the room, as they had the morning Betty's body was found.

"Lottie," I said, "Jennifer looks like she needs a friend. Can you go over and invite her to come sit with us? I think she needs to hear what I have to say."

Lottie nodded and wheeled her chair in Jennifer's direction. "Are you sure you're up to this?" Michael asked.

"No, but I'll live. You know I always feel better when I have someone else to take care of."

"I know, that's one the reasons you made such a great nurse." He smiled at me and squeezed my hand.

Pru came back with the coffee just as Lottie wheeled over, Jennifer walking next to her like an automaton. Michael stood.

"Jennifer, you look like you could use a chair." She nodded and sat stiffly.

Gone were all the vestiges of the radiant woman we'd seen over the past few days. Everything about her seemed to droop. Her dark hair, which she'd twisted into an elegant chignon earlier, was escaping its pins and the impeccably arranged black and silver scarf was now a messy fall of fabric around her throat. Her eyes were wet.

"Jennifer, are you okay?" I asked, sipping the hot coffee Pru had just handed me.

She twisted her hands in her lap. "I'm such a fool, Lily, such a fool."

"I doubt that."

"I have a terrible track record with men," Jennifer said bitterly, "and now it seems I was falling for a murderer. How could I have been so stupid?"

"You're obviously not stupid. He had us all fooled. I never suspected him for a minute."

"Maybe they arrested the wrong man?"

"No, I don't think so."

At that moment, the detective strode back into the clubhouse. Standing in front of the room, he raised his arms. Slowly the buzz subsided as all the conversations came to a halt.

"People," he announced, "as you've just seen, we have arrested your neighbor Keith Johnson for his assault on Mr. Barry, and for suspicion in the murder of Betty Louise Harris. We may be coming around to ask further questions over the next few days, but for now we just want a record of what you saw and heard here this morning leading up to the arrest. Once we've spoken with you, you'll be free to leave. Thank you for your cooperation."

Deputy Sanchez stepped forward, picked Liz Steinbach out of the crowd, and led her toward the interrogation table while Henderson made a beeline toward us.

"Ms. Nelson, would you step over here with me, please?"

The contrast between this Jennifer and the vibrant woman I'd been seeing over the past few days was heartbreaking. "Anything you have to ask me, you can ask me right here, detective," she replied dully. "I may be a fool, but I've got nothing to hide."

"As you wish." He pulled out his notebook.

Silently Michael picked up a chair and placed it next to the detective, who nodded his thanks and sat.

"Ms. Nelson, you seem to have been the person Mr. Johnson spent the most time with, is that true?"

Jennifer nodded. "I guess so."

"How long have the two of you been together?"

She stared at him. "Together? Like, a couple?"

"That's right."

"Since never. It's only been in the past week that I've spent any time with him at all."

The detective looked skeptical. "Okay, let's start at the beginning. When did you meet the man you knew as Keith Johnson?"

"Well, he lives downstairs from me, so I met him when he was moving in. Just to introduce myself and say welcome, you know?"

"And how would you characterize your interactions with him since that time?"

"Friendly, but distant. Just hello, how's it going when I came down and he was on his porch, or at the pool. Until Betty died."

"What changed then?"

"Well, we started talking that morning when you were questioning everyone in the clubhouse, and it seemed like we hit it off. He started inviting me to join him on his porch in the evenings."

"What did you talk about when you were together?"

"Just. . . stuff. What did I like about Happy Oaks, my job, and of course, Betty's death. Everyone was talking about that."

"Did he ever tell you about himself?"

She frowned. "Not much. I knew he'd traveled a lot for work, never been married, but that was about it."

"Did he ever talk about Mrs. Harris? About any interactions he had with her?"

"No, just about that morning when she was found in the pool, wondering if you'd ever find out who killed her. Like I said, the same things we were all talking about."

"Whose idea was it for the two of you to go to the visitation together?"

Jennifer hesitated for a moment. "Mine," she admitted. "He didn't want to go, but I talked him into it."

"Did he say anything to you about Mary mistaking him for someone named Neil?"

"No, he just sort of shook his head and said it was weird. But then when we were leaving he got a little rough with me on the way to the car, which was odd. I should have realized something wasn't right."

"And whose idea was it that you attend the funeral together?"

"Mine again. I admit it, I have a thing for big dark eyes, and I was developing quite a crush. I should have known better, I have a lousy track record with men."

"Alright," he said. "Now, for the events of this morning. What did you do after you arrived back at Happy Oaks from the funeral service?"

"We went back to our building. He was complaining of a headache and he wanted some aspirin. He wasn't in a very good mood and he didn't want to come over here, but I talked him into it."

"Who did he speak with?"

"Nobody, really. I mean, he said hello to a couple people, but mostly he was just muttering about when they were going to bring out the food. We could see the caterers in the kitchen. He complained he hadn't slept well and he still had the headache, but none of us have been sleeping well. Then he said he needed to hit the restroom, and he was gone a long time."

"How long?"

Jennifer shrugged. "I'm not sure, exactly. I chatted with a few people. It wasn't until Lily showed up that I started to think about how long he'd been in there. He didn't look too good, so I just assumed he had some kind of tummy trouble along with the headache. I used to know someone who got sick to her stomach whenever she had a headache. And then you came in. Maybe ten minutes? I'm not sure."

"Do you remember who you chatted with after he went to the restroom?"

Jennifer thought. "Well, Liz Steinbach came over and we talked about me maybe being on the condo board, and then I said hello to the Martinos over by the buffet, and then I saw Michael come in with Charlotte and Pru so I went over to them."

"Alright, Ms. Nelson, you're free to go. We may have more questions for you later."

"Did he really do it?" she asked, tears welling and spilling down her cheeks.

"He admitted it. I'm sorry."

He looked around the little group. "Mr. Gallagher," he began, then his phone rang. "Henderson," he answered, then, "On my way."

"Sorry, I have to go. Mrs. Gallagher, are you alright now?" he asked.

"I'm fine, Detective, thanks for your concern. Oh, and Detective, about that hard evidence you said you needed?"

His lips tightened. "We found it," he said, and exited through the patio doors.

I watched the detective walk out the door. What evidence could they have found between the time I showed him the photograph and when he walked into the clubhouse? It must have been something Deputy Lopez told him about.

"Lily, are you ever going to tell us what you found?" Pru demanded.

"Oh, I guess I can. He didn't tell me not to, did he?"

All four of them were watching me intently, Michael with concern, Jennifer with worry, and Pru and Lottie with curiosity.

I looked around, making sure none of our other neighbors were within earshot. "When we were all helping Greg after the break-in, I found a picture hidden behind a family photo in one of the broken frames. It showed a group of young men in Army uniforms, so I showed it to Greg. He didn't recognize it, didn't know anything about it, and told me to throw it out."

"Then at the visitation last night, Betty's sister Mary saw Keith and called him Neil. He told her she was mistaken, that his name was Keith Johnson."

"I thought I had thrown out that picture, but this morning I found it in the mess I'd dumped onto the bed from my tote bag. And when I looked at it closely, I was even more puzzled. I recognized a young Keith Johnson, but it didn't make sense because the men's names were all listed under the photo, like they do for class pictures in high school. And the name for our Keith Johnson was Neil Miller. Keith Johnson's name was also on there, but attached to a different guy who bears a little bit of a resemblance to our Keith."

Michael gave a low whistle. "So if this Neil Miller had taken Keith Johnson's identity for some reason, and Betty found out. . ."

"Exactly," I said. "With what we've learned about Betty and how she operated, she would certainly have tried to turn a secret like that to her advantage. Big time."

"Mary said that Neil's family got a telegram telling them he was killed in action in Vietnam. Somehow, he came out alive, as Keith Johnson. So it was probably Keith Johnson who actually died over there."

Jennifer spoke for the first time. "I know Keith served in Vietnam. I don't remember how it came up. Maybe I asked him about that Ken Burns film on the war that came out recently. But 'I was there, and I don't like to talk about it,' was all he said."

I thought for a moment. "There's a lot more history between Betty and Neil. Apparently he and Mary were engaged in high school, and Betty did something to break it up. Mary told me Neil abruptly broke their engagement and enlisted, then got killed in Vietnam. She said that she only found out years later what Betty had done. That's why she hated her sister so much, and that's the hornet's nest that Lottie stepped into when she suggested Betty should try to work things out with her sister. What if Keith, or Neil, or whatever we call him, also found out and hated Betty as much as Mary did? It's a lot to think about."

"Well, that's it for me," Jennifer said glumly. "I'm officially swearing off men."

"Oh, I don't know, there are a few good ones around," I said, looking fondly at Michael. "You know what? I think I'm hungry after all, anyone else want some food? It would be a shame for it all to go to waste."

Pru stood up. "Fine with me. I've been starving since we left the church. Come on Lottie, let's take advantage of Greg's generosity." She wheeled Lottie toward the buffet.

"Are you going to be okay?" I asked Jennifer.

"Oh, I'll be fine. I was enjoying the attention from a handsome man, but it's not like we had a real relationship. Still, I can't help but feel I should have spotted something, you know? Something abnormal?"

"Don't blame yourself," Michael said kindly. "He must be a good actor to have gotten away with playing the role of Keith Johnson for all these years. Plus, he was new to the community, and stuck to himself pretty much all the time he was here, so you didn't have a lot to go on."

"Let's get some food before Lottie and Pru eat it all," I said, standing up. "Last one to the buffet has to eat two desserts."

Michael slung his arm across my shoulders. "And you think that's going to be you? Nope. I'll be a respectful step behind you, ma'am."

"Oh, you."

Jennifer watched, amusement warring with self pity. Well, at least she wasn't drooping as much as she had been.

Greg had put on quite a spread. In addition to small, crustless sandwiches, there were a couple of hearty casseroles, several salads, and even, to my surprise, another cart displaying a roast of beef with gravy. A caterer had just emerged from the kitchen, ready to slice what the guests requested.

On the kitchen pass-through counter they had laid out the desserts, including cookies, brownies, a large cake, and several pies. My mouth began watering as I reached for a plate.

Twenty-Six

After eating, I was feeling much better. I set my coffee cup down, finished the last bite of my brownie, and looked around the clubhouse. Not many people had left.

"I'm feeling a lot more sociable now. With the murderer arrested, and some food inside me, I think I might even be able to sleep tonight."

"I totally agree," Lottie said. "And I'm starting to let myself hope I'll be able to come home soon. The meeting's in two days, right?" she asked, turning to Michael.

"That's right."

"Well," I said, "let's remind people you're part of this community. Are you up for going around and chatting with folks?"

"Absolutely! We should start with Greg."

"Pru, Michael, are you coming? Jennifer, do you want to come along?"

"I suppose." Michael stood. "Charlotte, want a push?"

She nodded, and he stood behind the wheelchair. "Oh, alright," Pru grumbled. "No rest for the wicked."

"I think I'll sit here for another minute," Jennifer said.

Our little group moved across the room to where Greg sat, misery etched clearly on his ashen face. The Wheelocks were with him, but they didn't appear to be talking.

"Greg, how are you holding up?" I asked with concern. He looked up at me blankly, then pulled himself together with a visible effort.

"Lily, I'm doing okay. How are you?"

"You know, it's alright if you're not okay," I said quietly. "You've been through a lot in a very short time."

He nodded.

"Is there anything we can do?"

"I don't know. Anyway, part of me wants to go and sleep for a week, part of me wants to run out of here screaming and never come back."

"Hang in there, it'll get better," I said soothingly.

"I can't believe it was Keith. I mean, I didn't really know him, but he seemed pleasant enough."

"Did Betty ever say anything about him?"

"No. Certainly not about knowing him years ago. I guess she kept even more secrets than I thought. It's almost like I didn't know her at all." His face crumpled. "I thought I loved her, but she was a monster. Why didn't I see it?"

Lottie wheeled her chair forward. She reached out a hand to pat Greg on the arm. "Greg, I'm so sorry for everything you're going through."

"And I'm sorry for what you're going through. I know your waiver is coming up for a vote, and anyway I'm going to do whatever I can to make sure you're able to put in that stairlift. I'm sorry Betty was so against it."

"Thanks, Greg. That means a lot to me."

"Pru, Michael, thanks for coming. I can't tell you how much I appreciate all you've done for me."

"Anytime, Greg," Michael said. "Just let me know what you need help with."

We chatted for a few more minutes, and as we talked, Greg's color improved. Good. Maybe he just needed some distraction from his misery.

Patrick and Linda Barry came over and joined the circle around Greg. Patrick was still pale, and Linda was holding his arm. After chatting for a few minutes, I looked around to see who else was still in the room. I was about to walk over to say hello to Clara and Leroy Jones, looking a little uncomfortable by themselves, when I heard Patrick saying, "another one of Betty's victims."

"What was that?" I asked him.

He repeated himself. "Betty was able to do what she did because people had secrets. I've decided I'm tired of keeping mine, and I'm going to try to start a support group for her victims."

"She had her hooks into you, too?" Lottie sounded surprised.

"She was trying to." He grimaced. "In fact, Linda and I were at the pool that morning because she'd set up a meeting with us. She was trying to blackmail me, and I was prepared to tell her to stuff it. Who was it who said 'publish and be damned?' That's what I was going to do."

"Would I be welcome?" Greg asked quietly.

Patrick looked surprised. "Of course!"

"I'll help you organize it if you want," Lottie volunteered. "That sort of thing is right up my alley."

"That would be great." He smiled. "I'd love to think something good could come of all this mess."

"Me too," Greg said.

"Someone else should be a part of that group." I nodded toward Mary, who was sitting a few feet away. "Greg, you were married to Betty, but Mary actually grew up with her, so I bet she has a lot to process."

Looking at Lottie, Patrick said, "Let's go talk to her."

She nodded, and they turned toward Mary.

"Hi Mary, I'm Patrick Barry, a resident here. I'm sorry for your loss."

"The world's better off without her," she replied bitterly.

"Indeed, and that's why I'm officially inviting you to join the victims' support group I'm starting."

"Victims' support group? What do you mean?"

"I mean, there are a lot of people she took advantage of. I think it would be good for all of us to get together and support each other. It's a way to move forward."

"Move forward?" She looked puzzled. "Okay. I guess. I'm not in any rush to be back in Mobile. I'll have to see if Greg can put up with me a while longer."

"Good, we'll count on you, then," Patrick said. "Any other victims I should invite?" he asked me.

"Liz Steinbach."

"Really?" He whistled, and I nodded.

"And Helen Martino.

"I'd like to come," Pru volunteered. "She never had anything on me, but she sure tried and she got me pretty stirred up."

"Same with Deb," I said. "She might be interested."

"And me," Michael said.

"Maybe I should ask if there's anyone here she didn't victimize!" Patrick exclaimed.

"What do you think about making a general announcement at Thursday's meeting?" Michael asked.

"I'd be happy to."

"Good. I'll set it up."

While they discussed details of announcing the support group to our whole community, I walked over to where the Joneses were sitting. "Leroy, Clara, it's nice of you to come and support Greg."

Clara spoke up. "It's the neighborly thing to do, right, Leroy?"

"Sure. Of course, we didn't expect to see the scene we witnessed here a little while ago."

"It was pretty scary."

They both nodded, then Leroy said, "We should go soon, get some lunch. It doesn't seem right to sit here and eat after seeing Mr. Johnson dragged out like that."

"Well, Greg got in all this food because he wanted to thank his friends and neighbors for coming out today, so I think you should help yourselves to the buffet. You'll feel a lot better after you've eaten. I sure did."

"Oh, I don't know," Clara frowned.

"I'm sure the caterers have to throw away whatever's left over, so you may as well take advantage of it."

"You're very persuasive, Lily," Leroy said. "What do you think, Mama?"

"Might as well see what's there."

"Good. Have you talked with the deputies yet?"

"No, we were just waiting on them and then we were going to leave."

"Well, enjoy some lunch while you wait. Oh, and I wanted to ask, are you planning on coming to the special meeting on Thursday?"

"The one to talk about a stairlift for Ms. Delaney?" Leroy asked. I nodded, and he said, "Sure. Poor lady deserves to move back home."

I watched as the Joneses approached the buffet, then turned when someone said hello behind me.

It was the Hoffmans. "Hi Sam, hi Michelle, I didn't realize you were here."

"Yeah, I'm sure we'll think twice before going to another repast after a Christian funeral," Sam deadpanned.

"Oh, Sam!" Michelle jabbed him in the ribs.

"We've just finished talking to that nice Deputy Sanchez, and we were wondering whether it would be rude to eat something before we go."

"Not at all. They'll probably have to throw out whatever doesn't get finished. We visited the buffet a while ago, and I'm glad we did. I was pretty shaky after that scene earlier."

"We should pay our respects to Greg first," Michelle reminded her husband.

"Oh, right. Good to see you, Lily."

"You too. Will you be at the special meeting on Thursday?"

They looked confused. "The one to vote on the waiver for Charlotte so she can put in the stairlift and move back home," I reminded them.

They looked at each other uneasily and I remembered that they had disagreed with each other about it during the previous meeting. "Turns out Betty was trying to edge Charlotte out of Happy Oaks. You know Charlotte used to do family counseling, right?"

"Did she?" Michelle asked.

"She knew about Betty's feud with her sister Mary, and she tried to encourage Betty to mend her fences with Mary. Betty was angry about it, and I guess we've all learned in the past few days how vindictive she could be."

"That's terrible. Poor Charlotte. How's she doing anyway?"

I smiled. "You can ask her yourself, she's right over there talking with Mary."

"I see her. Sam, let's go say hi."

"Catch you later," I smiled. Michelle was a big gossip. Maybe the tide would turn in Lottie's favor now. Was there anyone else I hadn't talked with?

There was one more question niggling in the back of my mind.

Patrick and Linda were sitting with Lottie. I walked over to them. "Patrick, I have one more question for you."

"Okay."

"Just before Keith grabbed you, you shouted at him. How did you suddenly know he was the person who attacked you last night?"

Patrick's red eyebrows pulled together in a frown. "I don't know. I didn't even think about it, I just suddenly knew. Does it matter?"

"Probably not, I was just curious."

Patrick closed his eyes while Lottie and Linda watched the two of us.

Suddenly his eyes flew open. "Aftershave!"

Linda's brown eyes were wide. "Are you alright?"

He smiled. "I'm fine." Looking at me he said, "It was his aftershave. I smelled it faintly that night when he shoved you into your car. Then again just before I got hit on the head last night. I guess I recognized it when he got close to me in the clubhouse."

"You must have a really good sense of smell," I said. "I never noticed a thing."

"Oh, he does, he's famous for it." Linda smiled at him.

"Did you notice it at the funeral home the other night? Is that why you and Keith had words?" I asked.

He cocked his head to the side, considering. "Maybe? I know the sight of him made me edgy, but I didn't think anything of it. Of course, that was before he clobbered me."

"Thanks. I'll bet your subconscious picked up on it."

"Probably."

I scanned the room again. It looked like a normal Happy Oaks gathering, if you ignored the deputies still taking statements.

***

So here I am, handcuffed and shackled. How long have I been sitting here? Time doesn't seem to mean much any more. Nothing to do but think, and I've avoided doing that for years. Don't want to start now.

So tired. Been fighting too long. First it was the fighting in the jungle, then the fighting, night after night in my dreams after I left the jungle. I tried so hard to leave the fighting and the enemy behind me over there, but they followed me. Maybe I can stop fighting now, get some rest. How long have I been sitting here? I want to lie down, but these chains won't let me. When can I sleep? I just want to sleep in peace for a change.

***

Detectives Henderson and Lopez stepped into the room and sat down. Mr. Johnson? Miller? Henderson wasn't sure how to address the man, who looked up without interest. Henderson turned on the video camera, and announced the date, time, and their names.

"Please state your name for the record."

The shackled man looked at him and said, "Keith Johnson." It seemed to take him an enormous amount of effort.

Henderson smiled and said, "Oh, come now, I think we're past that, Mr. Miller."

"Well, if you think you know everything why are you asking me?"

"It's my job to ask. So, I'm asking again, would you please state your name for the record."

The shackled man across the table said nothing. Finally Henderson spoke. "Let the record show I'm interviewing the man known as Keith Johnson, current address unit E1, Happy Oaks Condominiums, 700 Balfour Drive, Winter Park, Florida. Alright, let's jump ahead. You had grabbed Patrick Barry and were threatening to snap his neck, when you collapsed. What happened?"

"I don't know."

"You don't know?"

"That's what I said."

Henderson watched him closely for more than a minute. The silence grew, and Lopez moved restlessly in his chair.

"You served in Vietnam, is that correct?"

"Yes."

"You were having a flashback, weren't you?"

He nodded. "How did you know?"

"It wasn't hard to figure out. My father was a Vietnam vet. He had them once in a while when I was growing up. So do you remember what happened with Mr. Barry?"

Mr. Johnson slumped. "No. One minute I was in the clubhouse feeling like I was going to throw up, the next minute I was in the jungle tossing a grenade, and then I was in handcuffs."

"Okay. What was your name when you enlisted?"

"Neil Miller. And I'd like to know how the hell you figured it out."

"All in good time. When did you become Keith Johnson?"

"It was near the end of my tour." He stopped speaking, and Henderson watched as his eyes focused on a long-ago scene. "I was in an action where my buddy Keith got killed and I was injured. Piece of shrapnel in my head. He was due for discharge a few months before I was, so I got the bright idea to swap dog tags with him so I could go home sooner. After that I was stuck, though, and I couldn't ever go home again. Note to self," he added wryly, "never make major life decisions while suffering from a head wound."

"So Keith Johnson was wrongly identified as Neil Miller, and your family and friends believed you dead all these years."

He hung his head.

"What about Keith Johnson's family?"

"Oh, they were a mess. His real father was dead, his stepfather beat his mom, and she was an alcoholic. When he got his draft notice, he told them not to expect to ever see him again, so that made it easy for me."

"So what do you want me to call you?"

"I've been Keith Johnson for nearly fifty years, you might as well go on calling me that."

"But Betty Harris knew you were Neil Miller, didn't she?"

"That bitch!" He shouted and banged his fist on the table. "She ruined my whole life. She ruined Angel's life. She ruined everyone she came near. She deserved to die."

He tried to stand, but the shackles held him in place. "If it weren't for her, I never would have broken up with Angel, I never would have enlisted, I never would have done the terrible things over there that I did. I could have had a life!"

"Calm down, Mr. Johnson!" After a moment, he sat back his chair.

Henderson looked at Lopez. They'd both seen it before. Sometimes, in the interview room, they couldn't seem to stop talking once they'd started. He wondered if the urge to confess was hard wired into a human's DNA.

After spending two hours in the interview room with Mr. Johnson, Detective Henderson felt slightly sick to his stomach. Abruptly he stood and announced they would take a break. He called for a deputy to take Keith back to a holding cell and get him some lunch, then left the room.

A moment later Lopez joined him in the hallway.

"You hungry?" Henderson asked him.

"Starving. You know I haven't eaten, I've been with you since just before noon," Lopez reminded him. "In fact, I'm feeling a bit light-headed."

"So you have. Let's grab a bite. Maybe I can face what he has to tell us better with some food inside me."

Lopez drove them a burger joint nearby.

When they arrived, Henderson greeted the young woman tidying up the stack of menus. "Hi Marilyn, is my favorite table free?"

She beamed at him. "Sure thing, Detective. You go on over."

Henderson headed for the table in the back corner of the room, where both he and Lopez would be able to sit with their backs to the wall. Perfect.

A moment later Marilyn appeared with two menus and two glasses of ice water. Henderson chugged half of his down within seconds. "Iced tea for me today, I think, and keep 'em coming."

She smiled. "Yes, sir. And you?"

"Dr. Pepper."

"Sure, I'll be right back with your drinks."

After they ordered, a double bacon cheeseburger with onion rings and a side of macaroni salad for Henderson, and a double burger with fries for Lopez, Henderson stared into space.

"Can I ask you something, sir?"

"What is it Lopez?"

"How does someone get that screwed up?"

"Oh, I don't know. One seriously bad choice, and then the lack of backbone to make it right I guess."

"No, I didn't mean Mr. Johnson," Lopez clarified, "I meant her. Mrs. Harris. If half of what he told us is true, she was pretty twisted."

"That's for sure." Henderson took a minute to think. "I'm no psychiatrist, but I bet they would have had a field day with her. Narcissistic, sociopathic, and that's just a start."

"I'd rather deal with your average, everyday gang banger than someone like her. After hearing about her I feel like I need to go home and take a shower."

"I know what you mean."

Marilyn bustled over with their meals, and for several minutes the only sound at the table was chewing.

After satisfying his initial hunger pangs, Henderson said, "if you were leading this interrogation, where would you go next? What questions do you want to ask him?"

Lopez considered. "Of course, there's a lot we need to know about Mrs. Harris' murder, but I'm still curious about his identity theft. I mean, it seems like a big step to take just to get out a couple months sooner."

"You think there's more to it than that?"

"Maybe."

"You don't think if you were in a situation where you were in fear for your life every minute of every day, you'd do about anything to get away from it as soon as possible?"

"Well, yes, and maybe that's it, but I just have a hunch there's more."

Henderson smiled grimly. "I happen to agree. I have an idea what it might be, but I'm not sure we'll ever know for certain. For now, let's focus on the present day. We can always loop back around to his service days if we need to."

They discussed their interview strategy in low voices while they finished their meal, pausing when Marilyn showed up at their table with drink refills. When she came back to clear away their empty plates, she asked brightly, "Pie for you today, sir? We've got the key lime you like so much."

"Not today I'm afraid. We need to get back to work." Lopez looked disappointed, but stood when Henderson did. "She knows I love their key lime pie," Henderson confided as they paid their checks at the register, "but I can't get away with eating it very often any more. In fact, I've been thinking I might need to swap the burgers for a salad once in a while."

Arriving back at the station, Lopez arranged for Mr. Johnson's return to the interview room while Henderson went to the war room to review reports. Half an hour later he texted Lopez that he was ready, and they met outside the interview room.

"Question him about Mrs. Harris' blackmail attempts that led up to the murder, then I'll take over."

"Yes, sir." Lopez opened the interview room door.

Twenty-Seven

So far the meeting was going smoothly. The board had officially selected Jeff Ericson as their new President, and Liz Steinbach as the new Vice President. Jennifer was appointed to the vacant seat. The residents in attendance — and it was nearly all of them — seemed cheerful and relaxed.

All except Lottie, who couldn't stop fidgeting. I reached over and clasped my friend's hand.

When Jeff announced the next order of business, "the architectural waiver that Charlotte Delaney requested to install a stairlift to her second-floor apartment," Charlotte clutched at my hand as if it were a lifeline. The room buzzed for a moment as residents shifted in their chairs and sat up more alertly.

"Her initial request was denied. Since then we've consulted our insurance and legal advisers about the stairlift. Before we go any farther, I'd like to thank Dave Wheelock and Michael Gallagher for their work on this, in spite of everything else that's been happening in our community." Several people started to clap, but he banged his gavel and continued.

"Dave, you consulted the lawyers?"

Dave nodded and stood up. "I have a letter here from our legal counsel. Basically what it says is, there are plenty of legal precedents for it, a lot of condo communities where these sorts of waivers have been okayed. He has no issue with it."

"And what about the insurance?" Jeff asked. "Michael, you handled that?"

Michael stood. "Yes, I've had several discussions with them, and also with the Fire Marshal. The Fire Marshal has confirmed the staircase is wide enough for emergency access, even with the stairlift in place. The insurance company confirmed that no extra insurance will be required since this particular manufacturer has an approved lock and key system. The chair cannot be operated without a key, and it locks automatically once it's completed its trip up or down and stopped."

"In other words," he looked at each of the Board members in turn, "there are no legal or insurance barriers to the stairlift." He sat down.

"Any questions?" Jeff asked the Board.

I was pleased to hear none of the angry outbursts that had accompanied the stairlift discussion a few weeks ago.

"Does the Architectural Committee have any additional information at this time?" Jeff asked Dave.

"They have two models that meet our approval." Dave held out a brochure.

"And both of them have this locking mechanism?" Dave nodded.

"If there are no further questions, I'll entertain a motion."

"I move we grant Charlotte Delaney's request for an architectural waiver to install a stairlift to her apartment in Building F, as per our previous discussion."

"Second!" Michael said loudly.

"Any discussion?"

The board members all looked at each other. I heard a few grumbles from the back of the room, but the atmosphere was very different from the anger that roiled the earlier meeting.

"All those in favor?"

Dave, Michael, Jennifer, Liz, Linda, and — huge surprise — Tim raised their hands.

"Opposed?"

No hands went up as Jeff scanned the board members up and down the table.

"The motion carries. Charlotte, work out the details with the Architectural Committee." Jeff banged the gavel as Lottie burst into tears.

Jeff said, "This was not on the agenda, and it's not official business, but as you all know our little Happy Oaks community has suffered a tragedy. Within the past week one of our residents, former Board President Betty Louise Harris, was brutally murdered and another of our residents, Keith Johnson, has been arrested for it."

Suddenly the room was so quiet I was tempted to drop a pin to see if you really could hear it in the sudden silence. Well, probably not with that ugly carpet on the floor.

"The detectives and deputies have been around quite a lot, and you've all talked with them. They may come around again, and they appreciate your ongoing cooperation. For now, Greg Harris, husband of the victim, has asked to say a few words."

From the back of the room, Greg stumbled forward with Mary. He looked haggard, but determined.

"Friends, neighbors, I want to talk about the elephant in the room. We've all been through a terrible time. Anyway, I've learned some things this past week about the woman I was married to for more than forty-five years, things that make me realize I never really knew her in all that time." He paused, swallowed hard, then continued, "Anyway, she's caused suffering for quite a few of you, and she abused her position on the board."

A few people looked surprised, and I noticed a lot of sideways glances as people sneaked peeks at their neighbors.

"For whatever role I've had in that suffering, I sincerely apologize, and I can't tell how you much I appreciate the way you've all supported me in this past week." He looked around the room and nodded to a few people.

"So anyway, Patrick Barry has come up with an idea that has my wholehearted backing." He nodded at Patrick, who started to make his way to the front of the room. "He wants to start a victim support group, with the able assistance of Charlotte Delaney, who used to be a family counselor in case you weren't aware. Anyway, if Betty tried to blackmail you, manipulate you, or demean you in any way, you're welcome to join. You can bet I'll be there."

Several people gasped when the word 'blackmail' was mentioned, and a murmur of conversation started.

Someone in the middle of the room shouted out, "Can you tell us what really happened?"

"We're all still trying to piece it together," Greg said. "Anyway, the detective said he'd try to be here, but I guess he didn't make it. Lily, can you help out here? Oh, and before we get into that, if you want to join the support group come talk to Patrick or Charlotte after the meeting."

I moved to the front of the room, and took a deep breath. I could do this. I took another deep breath, then began. "I found some things that ended up helping in the investigation," another deep breath, "but I don't have the whole picture either. Especially since the whole sorry incident seems to have started a very long time ago."

"What do you mean?" someone called out.

I turned to Jeff. "I don't want to hijack your meeting."

"It's fine, I think the community needs some closure on this, so getting the facts out will save a lot of time in the long run.

Go ahead." His bushy eyebrows weren't nearly as intimidating tonight as they were the last time we'd spoken.

I turned back to face the room. "Okay, so this is what I understand. It may not all be one hundred percent correct, but I think it covers the basics. I'll do my best to answer your questions tonight, but after this I don't want to talk about it any more."

I looked around the room. Most of the residents were nodding at me, waiting for me to continue.

"As far as I understand it, it all started a long time ago when two high school kids fell in love and got engaged. One of them was Mary, Betty Harris' sister." I gestured toward Mary. "The other was a boy named Neil. Betty knew Neil. In fact, being quite a bit older, she had been his babysitter when he was in elementary school, and she didn't have a very high opinion of him. She also didn't like her sister very much, so she went out of her way to tell some lies and break up their romance."

Mary's head was in her hands.

"Immediately after graduation, Neil joined the army and was sent to Vietnam. Somehow he came out of Vietnam with the name Keith Johnson. I don't know how that happened, but he apparently still suffers from PTSD as a result."

"So, Mary had a pretty unhappy time, Betty went on with her life and married Greg, and Keith, as we knew him, was pretty messed up. He chose a career that had him traveling constantly, and he never married."

"A few years ago, Betty and Greg left their hometown of Mobile, Alabama and moved to Happy Oaks. Then, in a very sad coincidence, a few months ago Keith Johnson retired and bought a condo here as well."

"Betty recognized him. Apparently he had a birthmark on his back that everyone teased him about when he was a kid, so if she had any doubts about who this guy Keith Johnson was, she would have seen the birthmark at the pool one day and been sure. In any case, being Betty, she tried to use that knowledge to her own advantage. That was what she always did." I looked apologetically at Greg. "Sorry."

"Go right ahead," Greg said. "Nothing you say here can possibly hurt me more than what I'm already feeling."

I nodded. "Okay, I learned that Betty liked to set up appointments to meet with her victims, so I'm guessing she had an appointment with Keith late at night on June eighth. Only it didn't end the way she expected. He strangled her and then, for whatever reason, placed her body in the pool where Pru found it in the morning."

"So is he the one who broke into Greg's apartment?" someone shouted.

"Apparently so. We think he was looking for some evidence that Betty had about his real identity. He didn't find it, but I did, quite by accident, and I gave it to the detectives."

"Why did he come to the pool that morning? I would have thought he would have stayed as far away as possible."

"I'm not sure," I began when a familiar voice interrupted me as Detective Henderson strolled up to the front of the room.

"I gather we're having a question and answer about what happened to Mrs. Harris?" he asked me quietly. I nodded. He winked at me, then turned to face the room.

"For those of you who haven't met me, and I don't think there's anyone here who hasn't at this point," he said, looking around, "I'm Jason Henderson, lead detective on this case."

Chatter broke out and he held up his hand. When it was quiet again, he said, "This was initially a very puzzling case, seeing as how it has its roots going back almost fifty years. I'm not sure we would have ever figured it out without Mrs. Gallagher here. I can't tell you everything — there are some things we need to save for the trial — but I'll try to give you the big picture. Someone was asking why Mr. Johnson, as you knew him, came to the pool that morning."

He waited again for quiet. "He had placed the body in the pool the night before, in an attempt to disguise a strangulation as a drowning. In the morning, when he heard Ms. MacLeod screaming, he had some notion that if he could only get his hands on the body, it would explain any of his DNA we might find. He was mistaken."

"So what happens next?"

"We'll continue to interview Mr. Johnson and gather evidence, and at some point the case will go to trial."

"Who else was she blackmailing?"

"I'm sorry, I can't answer that."

"Are we safe here?" Tim Martinez growled. "I never thought this was a dangerous place to live, but now I'm not so sure."

"Mr. Martinez, I'd say you're no less safe here than you are anywhere else. If you're worried about being murdered, then my advice to you is, don't keep secrets and try to get along with your family, friends, coworkers, and neighbors."

Tim scowled at him, and Helen giggled, a sound I'd never heard before.

"What's going to happen to Johnson?" someone shouted.

"I'm recommending he be remanded to a psychiatric hospital," Henderson replied. "He apparently suffers from untreated PTSD dating back to his time in Vietnam. His strange behavior, that some of you saw when we arrested him, happened because he was having a flashback. If he's found mentally competent, he'll stand trial for what he's done. After that it's up to a jury. But the bottom line for you folks," he looked around, focusing his laser gaze on someone in the back, "is to remember that this was not some random act of violence. It was very personal and very targeted. So you can rest easy."

A babble of talk broke out, and Lottie smiled happily at me.

Later, after taking a tearfully happy Lottie back to the rehab center, I stood in the kitchen making chamomile tea. "Would you like a cup?" I asked Michael.

"Is that the sleepy stuff?"

"Sure is."

"Why not. It's been one hell of a week, and I could use a good night's sleep."

"You and me both," I agreed. "I'm taking mine to the couch."

Sitting together with our tea a few minutes later, I said, "I thought I'd feel nothing but relief once we knew who killed Betty, but instead I'm just sad."

"Why?"

"Not sad that she's gone," I assured him. "Sad for Keith and Mary and all the lives she ruined. Who knows how many there have been?"

"I'm sorry for Mary." He was silent for a few seconds. "But I can't muster much sympathy for Keith."

"Well, think about it," I persisted. "You were one of the lucky ones, you had a high draft number so you never experienced the horrors of that war. How would you have felt at eighteen if your romance was blighted and you were immediately wrenched out of your home and plopped down in the middle of a messy jungle war? And then you made a dumb decision and could never go home again? And then you found out that your love affair had been killed by one person's lies? Plus you've got untreated PTSD and because of your bad decision you can't seek treatment without getting yourself into all kinds of trouble?"

"Well, when you put it that way I guess I'm a little more sympathetic," he agreed, "but don't expect me to feel sad for him."

"That's okay. I'm sad enough for both of us. But at least I'm pretty sure I'll be able to sleep soundly tonight, for the first time in a week."

"Me too. You ready for bed now?" he asked, setting down his empty cup.

"In a minute." I rested my head on his shoulder. "Let's just sit here for another minute."

"I've been thinking." I could hear some suppressed laughter in Michael's voice.

"Mmm?"

"I think this helpful thing of yours is just an act. You offer to help people and that gives you an excuse to find out everything that's going on. Shall I start calling you Miss Marple and buy you a pair of binoculars?"

I laughed. "No, I think Maud Silver is more my style. Now, where did I put my knitting?"

When he looked confused, I added, "If you're good, I'll lend you one of the books so you can meet her."

"Oh, she's another sleuth?"

"She is indeed. I think I'm ready to head for bed now." I was looking forward to a good night's rest. In the morning, nothing was going to stop me from reading about Georgie's adventures and finding how her royal spying mission worked out.

Michael picked up both teacups. "I'll just put these in the dishwasher and meet you in there."

Twenty-Eight

Lottie's welcome home party was in full swing. Pru and I had spent the morning cleaning and decorating the apartment. Friends had sent flowers, which we'd arranged in vases throughout the great room. All the residents had donated food for the occasion. Helen's contribution, a beautifully decorated, three-tier cake with "Welcome Home Charlotte" written across the top, still waited to be cut.

Lottie had been genuinely astonished when, after sailing up her new stairlift for the first time with a huge grin on her face, she rolled into the apartment in her wheelchair and was greeted with shouts of "Surprise!" from everyone.

It had taken some planning, but it was worth it. I squeezed Michael's hand. "It's great to see her looking so happy."

Just then Lottie rolled herself over to the table. "Helen, it's time to find out whether this beautiful cake of yours tastes as good as it looks! Would you do the honors?"

"Of course!" Helen bustled up and picked up the knife and cake server. "And the first slice is for you." She smiled at Lottie.

I stood back with Michael as we watched our neighbors and friends line up for cake. “This little community’s come through a lot in the past few weeks,” I said. “I hope we’re back to normal now.”

“I think so. And I think ‘normal’ will be better than it was.”

“I think it already is.” I scanned the room. Cake plates in hand, Tim was making an effort to be pleasant to Clara and Leroy Jones. Wonder of wonders! Helen had even told me a few days ago that he had spoken with his son on the phone for the first time in years.

Patrick and Linda were huddled with Greg in the corner, and they all burst out laughing. Minnie Nguyen and Jennifer Nelson had struck up a conversation, and Liz Steinbach, the Wheelocks, and the Ericsons were chatting.

“Let’s go try that cake.” As we walked toward the cake stand, my phone rang in that strange tone that only my daughter used. “It’s Shannon,” I said to Michael, “I’m going to step out on the porch.”

I had barely hit the button to accept the call when her face filled the screen. Black streaks indicated she’d been crying, and her lower lip was quivering.

“Oh, Mom,” she said, “I have some bad news.”

***

I hope you've enjoyed Lily and her first encounter with murder. Join her as she gets thrust into another investigation in *Chords of Deception*, available soon. If you thought an orchestra was all harmony and sweet notes, think again!

Read a Preview of *Chords of Deception*

Rest and relaxation. The good lord knows I needed it. That's what I thought I was signing up for when I retired nearly three months ago. Was I getting any rest? Relaxation? Ha! I desperately wanted a normal life, a normal retirement. I mean, is that too much to ask?

What is it they say? No rest for the wicked? Well, I don't know how wicked I was, but I sure wasn't getting any rest, standing here trying to watch my granddaughter as she began her first rehearsal with the Greater Orlando Youth Orchestra.

The poor kid had crept into the rehearsal room like a timid little mouse. She wasn't worried about her playing — she's well on her way to becoming an excellent oboist, and she knows it — but she was still finding her balance after the sudden move from Atlanta with her mom after her dad left them. And of course, being in a new school, in a new place. She needed some friends, and it didn't look like she was finding them at school so I hoped she'd find them here, in the orchestra, like I had when I was her age.

They moved in with us two months ago on the Fourth of July weekend. Independence Day. Not! I gave myself a mental shake. Enough of this pity party nonsense.

Once they finished tuning — was that Chloe playing the tuning note? I couldn't tell — they started warmup scales. There was no place to sit, and I wasn't about to stand in this bare hallway under fluorescent lights, peering into this little window, for two hours.

Maybe it would be okay if I snuck into the back of the auditorium where I'd at least be able to sit down. I had a new book downloaded to my tablet, and if nothing else, I should be allowed to relax a little bit while the kids were rehearsing. Relax — something else I hadn't been able to do much of since Shannon and Chloe moved in with us.

I turned and walked back the way I'd come. Now that I wasn't focused on Chloe, I had time to look around me. The first thing I noticed was the genuine terrazzo floor in scarlet, gold, and white. I assumed those were the school colors. Spaced every twenty feet or so on the walls were decent quality reproductions of famous paintings. This was a whole lot swankier than the auditoriums I remembered from my kids' schooldays. I guess that's one of the differences between public and private schools. A subtle odor of teenage hormones and privilege filled the space.

I decided to explore a little. After all, if Chloe was going to be here every Sunday afternoon for the foreseeable future, I should be familiar with the layout. I walked back to the entry. Its high ceilings and an exterior glass wall gave it the feel of an atrium, with two sets of double doors, glass of course, which let in tons of light.

It was a fairly standard high school auditorium setup, with some high-end touches. Two sets of heavy wooden doors led from the entrance into the auditorium itself. Along the hallway that wrapped around both sides of it were smaller rooms, although smaller is a relative term since the room Chloe and her Philharmonic group rehearsed in was about the size of three normal classrooms.

In one of those rooms I noticed a couple of people bustling around. I was about to follow the corridor to the right to check out what was down that way when a small Asian woman sitting behind the registration table by the entrance to the auditorium spoke up.

"Are you looking for something? Can I help you?" Standing, she was only about an inch shorter than my five feet four inches, but she gave the appearance of being tiny because she was so slender.

She was dressed casually in khaki capris and a black polo shirt with the GOYO logo on the pocket, and a big smile. I glanced down at my own khaki slacks and black tee shirt, and wished I could imbue my outfit with as much elegance as she did hers.

Of course, that's harder to do when I'm a size twelve and she's a size two.

I pushed my glasses back up to the bridge of my nose, and realized with surprise that the purple frames were the only splash of color I was wearing today. Even my earrings were bland, square abstract designs in black and brown. Whatever had possessed me when I was dressing this morning? Apparently I wasn't feeling like my usual, color-loving self.

I smiled back. "No, not really. I just delivered my granddaughter to her rehearsal space, and I was going to sneak into the back of the auditorium and read. But I wanted to understand the layout here, so I was being nosy and checking everything out."

"She plays oboe, right?"

"Yes, she's Chloe Paquette and I'm Lily Gallagher." I held out my hand and we shook.

"I'm Anna Song," she said. "My son Adam sits first chair oboe in the Symphony."

"Nice to meet you, Anna. You must have a good memory."

"No, but I make of point of knowing who the other oboe players are."

"Your son must be very talented."

Her smile took up her whole face. "Yes, he is!"

"I'm not sure where Chloe's seated," I told her. "I think they plan to shuffle the students around a bit once they've heard them play together."

She nodded her head, and her long bangs brushed across her forehead. "That's right, the Philharmonic is run a bit more loosely than the Symphony. Seating's not so important there." She handed me a pamphlet. "Here's some basic information about the orchestra."

"Thanks, I'll look at it later." I dropped it into my tote bag. "Do you have other kids besides Adam?"

"No, he's my only one. How about you?"

"Well, Shannon, Chloe's mom, is our oldest, and then there's Sean and Maureen." After we chatted for a few minutes I said, "I promised Chloe I'd stick around through the whole rehearsal, she was so nervous. Would anyone mind if I sit in the back of the auditorium? I brought a book to read." I patted the tote bag hanging over my shoulder.

"Of course, that's fine. Unless you'd like to help out?" She quirked an eyebrow at me and tipped her head to the right. I should have just said no thanks, and taken myself and my book away, but instead I agreed to step up, like I always do. You'd think by my age I'd have learned.

Two minutes later Anna and I were in the side room I'd noticed earlier, the one to the left of the entrance doors, where another parent (Christie, mother of Zoe, flute), organized dozens of cookies, brownies, bags of various chips, and other snacks. It seemed like a lot, but Anna assured me they'd all be gone by the end of the students' break, which happened at three o'clock. I glanced at my watch, surprised to see it was already two thirty.

Christie's hair was a riot of black curls, which she wore pulled back into a scrunchy that wasn't doing a good job of containing it as tendrils kept escaping. She wore a button-down shirt with a design featuring the iconic architecture of Paris, including the Eiffel Tower and the Arc de Triomphe, over skinny jeans. She was moving fast, so the running shoes made sense.

We set out the snacks on the two folding tables at the corner of the hallway, and promptly at three o'clock the music stopped and I heard chairs scraping, followed by chattering and laughter.

Fifteen minutes later, a fussy-looking middle-aged man came up to the table. He watched the milling students for a few seconds, then clapped his hands several times and yelled, "Symphony students, break time is over. Please go back in and take your seats."

"Mr. Katz," Christie said, "Before you go, I'd like you to meet Mrs. Gallagher. She and her granddaughter are new to GOYO this year."

He held out his hand and as I shook it I noticed his cufflink, in the shape of a G clef. "Leo Katz, I'm the manager for the Symphony. It's nice to meet you, but I need to get these students back." He bustled off, shooing students along.

In a few minutes, the hallway was empty and the music was starting again.

When Chloe had gone through the line and spotted me, her eyes widened, but she didn't say anything beyond, "Hi, Gramma." Now I noted what remained on the tables. It wasn't much. A couple of apples, one open bag of chips, and a few cookie crumbs.

I looked at Christie. "Is it like this every week?"

Christie pulled off the scrunchy holding her hair, shook her head, pulled it all together again and wrapped it in the scrunchy with a serious expression on her face. That done, she smiled. "Pretty much, although it's not quite as intense. Today, at the first rehearsal, we give away the refreshments, but after this they're supposed to take care of their own. Starting next week, we'll offer a bunch of snacks for sale, and some of the students will bring their own. If you hang around here for a while, you'll see that snack time is the most important part of the rehearsal."

By the time we finished tidying up, the rehearsal had only about fifteen minutes left to run. I wandered back out to the front. Anna was gone, but the registration table and chairs still sat there. I pulled a chair to the side and took my tablet out of my purse.

First, though, I glanced quickly at the pamphlet Anna had handed me. It was all pretty standard, with pictures of the board of directors and conductors, blurbs about them, and a description of each of the orchestras. One of the pictures stood out because, instead of a head shot, it showed a tight-faced woman standing in front of a wall of trophies. She didn't look like someone who'd be good around kids. Another picture looked familiar and I recognized Christie. So she was on the board. She hadn't mentioned that.

I dropped the pamphlet back into my tote, grabbed my tablet, and started reading. The book was the latest in a series I liked featuring the Honorable Daisy Dalrymple as the amateur sleuth, and was called *Superfluous Women*.

Ten minutes later I stashed my tablet away in my tote and walked to a spot where Chloe would see me when she came out of the rehearsal hall. The music stopped, the doors opened, and kids poured out, filling the hallway with chatter. Chloe and I spotted each other at the same time, and she whizzed over to me. She was bouncing almost as much as her auburn curls, and flashed an enormous smile at me. What a change from the nervous little person who'd walked through those doors earlier!

She was telling me about one of the pieces they'd played as we followed the crowd toward the front door, when I heard my name and saw Anna waving at me. “Chloe, hang on a sec, there’s someone you should meet.”

Anna was standing with a tall young man and a droopy young woman. She stepped forward, smiling. “Hello, Chloe, I'm Anna Song. This is my son, Adam, and this is Lauren Reynolds. Adam plays first oboe in the Symphony, and Lauren sits second chair.”

I would bet a lot of girls mooned over Adam, or whatever it is that girls do these days. His hair was dark, but not black, his eyes were brown and friendly, and his cheekbones were high and well defined. He wore black jeans and a blue tee shirt with a picture of a cat playing the oboe. I guessed he was just under six feet tall, and slender like his mother, but with some muscles visible under that oboe-playing cat. Lauren was only a few inches shorter, but appeared smaller because she slouched into herself and seemed to hide behind her long brown hair.

She was thin, but not in a healthy way, more like she didn't get enough to eat.

"Hello Adam, hi Lauren." I smiled at Adam. "Nice shirt."

He glanced down at his chest, then smiled at me. "Thanks. I have a lot of oboe-themed tee shirts. I bought one once, and ever since, people give them to me for birthdays and Christmas."

Lauren's face twitched a little nervously and her mouth moved silently in what I took to be a greeting.

Adam turned to my granddaughter. “Hello there, Chloe. How did you survive your first rehearsal?”

Before Chloe could answer, a booming baritone voice near the front door bellowed, “Lauren! Let’s go!”

The girl visibly cringed. “Sorry, that’s my dad.” Her voice was so soft it was almost a whisper. “I gotta go.”

She hurried away, mousy brown hair covering her drooping shoulders, her back bowed over the oboe case and folder of music she was carrying. At the door she joined a tall man wearing a cowboy hat and a frown, and slouched out with him. Adam watched her, his handsome face twisted into a scowl.

Chloe’s eyes were wide. “Well, that was rude!”

Adam smiled at her again. His smile was a little lopsided. “Yeah, it was, wasn’t it. He’s not a nice man.”

As they chatted, Anna leaned closer to me and said, “Your granddaughter is right, he’s not a nice man. He’s angry that his daughter didn’t get the first chair, and he doesn’t care who knows it.”

“Anyway,” she smiled, “I'm glad I met you, Lily, and I appreciate you helping out this afternoon. We have a lot of jobs that need doing around here, if you want to volunteer. I’m the librarian, but I wear other hats as required.”

“You, too, Anna. I’ll think about how much time I want to commit.”

As Chloe and I drove down the long driveway lined with laurel oaks, she jabbered happily about the other players she’d met, the music they'd played, and how cute the first cello was. She kept up her chatter after we turned onto the main road, all the way home. This was the most animated I'd seen her since she and her mother had moved in with us in July.

I was happy that she was happy, but also frustrated. My retirement wasn't turning out to be at all what I expected, and to tell the truth, much as I loved my daughter and granddaughter, I felt a little resentful. Maybe more than a little. And angry at myself for feeling that way.

And I had no idea what to do about it.

About the Author

Susanna Sullivan

Susanna Sullivan has been an avid reader since she was four years old. She fell in love with mysteries when she read her first Nancy Drew in the third grade, and always wanted to write one.

Unfortunately, a lifetime of writing for newspapers, magazines, and websites, not to mention raising five kids, didn't allow her to indulge in writing fiction until she retired. Now she's happy to present the first in the series of Lily Gallagher Mysteries.

She divides her time between Florida and a small town in Panama. You can sign up for email updates at https://susannasullivan.com, or follow her on Bluesky or Mastodon @SusannaAuthor.

If you enjoyed *Drowning in Deception*, please consider leaving a review on Amazon, Goodreads, or Bookbub. It helps other readers like you discover it.

Titles in the Lily Gallagher Mysteries

Drowning in Deception
Chords of Deception (coming soon)

Acknowledgements

Even though writing is a solitary occupation, books don't get written in a vacuum. I'd like to thank writing coach Dale Ivory for providing invaluable insight and feedback, and giving me a crash course in fiction writing. After a lifetime of technical and content writing, and being a lifelong reader of fiction, I thought I knew what I was getting into when I started writing *Drowning in Deception*. Dale set me straight...

Members of my local critique group have provided support and encouragement, and useful feedback.

My daughter Catherine, a better writer than I will ever be, has consistently encouraged me, and helped brainstorm with me when I didn't know which way to twist the plot.

And last but not least, my husband Mark, for putting up with me even though he doesn't have a clue what I'm talking about most of the time (because he's not a writer).